THE BRONZE SKIES

THE BRONZE SKIES

CATHERINE ASARO

THE BRONZE SKIES

This is a work of fiction. All the characters and events portrayed in this book
are fictional, and any resemblance to real people or incidents is purely coincidental.

A Baen Book

Baen Publishing Enterprises
P.O. Box 1403
Riverdale, NY 10471
www.baen.com

ISBN: 978-1-4814-8258-5

Cover art by Alan Pollack

First Baen printing, September 2017

Distributed by Simon & Schuster
1230 Avenue of the Americas
New York, NY 10020

Library of Congress Cataloging-in-Publication Data

Names: Asaro, Catherine, author.
Title: The bronze skies / by Catherine Asaro.
Description: Riverdale, NY : Baen Books, [2017] | Series: Skolian Empire:
  Major Bhaajan ; book 2 | Series: Saga of the Skolian Empire
Identifiers: LCCN 2017031138 | ISBN 9781481482585 (paperback)
Subjects: LCSH: Skolian Empire (Imaginary place)--Fiction. | Women private
  investigators--Fiction. | Life on other planets--Fiction. | Science
  fiction. | BISAC: FICTION / Science Fiction / General. | FICTION / Science
  Fiction / Adventure. | FICTION / Science Fiction / Space Opera.
Classification: LCC PS3551.S29 B76 2017 | DDC 813/.54--dc23 LC record available at
https://lccn.loc.gov/2017031138

Printed in the United States of America

10 9 8 7 6 5 4 3 2 1

To Binnie Braunstein
For her years of friendship,
And her belief in my writing.

Acknowledgements

My thanks to the following people for their invaluable input: to Aly Parsons and Kate Dolan for critiquing the entire manuscript; to P. J. O'Dwyer's critique group for their insightful commentary on scenes; to the great group of people at Baen Books, my publisher Toni Weisskopf, my editor Tony Daniel, and all the other people who did such a fine job making this book possible. My thanks to my excellent agent, Eleanor Wood, of Spectrum Literary Agency; and my publicist Binnie Braunstein for her enthusiasm and hard work on my behalf.

A heartfelt thanks to the shining lights in my life, my husband John Cannizzo and our daughter Cathy, for their love and support.

I

THE WOMAN ON THE BRIDGE

Forbidden land.

Today I walked in the City of Cries, the jewel of the desert. As a girl, I had never seen this glistening city, for I had been born in the ruins beneath it. The elite population of Cries barred my people from coming above ground. No written laws prevented us from entering Cries, only traditions so ancient, their origins had become buried in the unrelenting poverty of my people. Even today, when I walked along a boulevard in Cries as a citizen of the city, I felt like a criminal. All my time in the army, all those years of people calling me Major Bhaajan, all my work in covert ops, followed by my years as a private investigator with an elite clientele—none of it erased the buried voice inside of me that whispered *you are a fraud.*

Even now, I half expected the police to show up and throw me into prison or back into the slums under the city. Except only they used the word "slum." We called it the Undercity. Home. It had a beauty they would never understand.

The City of Cries spread around me in spacious avenues and parkland. With its mirrored towers reflecting the sky, the metropolis gleamed like a gem in an otherwise barren desert. The imported greenery that softened its edges depended on extensive irrigation systems only the wealthiest could afford. Across the avenue, a kiosk offered access to the world mesh. No traffic marred the streets; the law forbade ground vehicles. A few flycars cut through the sky, bright slivers against its pale expanse.

Noonday heat beat against my face, prompting my leather jacket to cool my body. It was a perk of my job, that I could afford smart clothes with climate controls. Silence surrounded me. No other people were out. No surprise there; it was noon, the time of daylight sleep. I'd read somewhere that humanity had evolved on a world with a twenty-four-hour day, a place where people slept at night and stayed awake the entire day. I didn't know. I'd never visited Earth. Here on the world Raylicon, the day lasted eighty hours. Apparently my clients didn't care about sleep, seeing as they had scheduled this meeting at noon. I had to be at the top of my game today. I had an appointment at the palace.

I expected to meet my contact at the city outskirts, but no one was waiting when I reached the designated spot. Instead, a flycar stood parked where this street blended into the desert. The vehicle glinted in the sunlight, gold and black chrome. Breezes feathered across my face, the air even more parched out here than in the city center. A silver bot no larger than my foot scuttled by, sweeping the path clear of red sand flecked with blue minerals.

As I walked to the flycar, its hatch irised open like the shutter on an old-fashioned camera. I scanned the vehicle using monitors in the tech-mech gauntlets on my wrists. The scan came up clean. I surveyed the shadowed interior, looking for threats. Nothing. Nor did any person wait inside, not even a pilot. Now that I saw the flycar up close, I recognized the craft; it belonged to the Majda family. Right, real personal, have an automated vehicle fetch me to their palace. It didn't surprise me, though. They kept me on retainer, but none of our interactions changed my unease about working in the shadow of their stratospheric power. Even so. The Majdas ruled the City of Cries, Cries ruled the planet Raylicon, and I lived on Raylicon.

I stepped up into the flycar.

With the House of Majda, power came in a trio, three sisters, all formidable, all different. I found Colonel Lavinda Majda the easiest to deal with, or more accurately, the least nerve-wracking, and I wasn't one whose nerves were easily wracked. Majda women were impossible to read, towering and impassive, born to power. Many were officers in Imperial Space Command, more commonly called ISC, the combined military forces of the Imperialate. In fact, Vaj Majda, the oldest sister, served as General of the Pharaoh's Army, which made her a joint commander of ISC. Lavinda, the youngest, had been my contact on the first case I worked for them, when a crime boss in the Undercity kidnapped a Majda prince. The Majdas hired me because of my Undercity origins. I could go places below the desert none of them even knew existed. They feared he had died, and they were damn near right, but I found him in time. For that, they decided I was human after all, despite my humble origins.

In the past year, I had visited the palace several times, and I never lost my awe of the place. Today a man ushered me through the corridors. No one could afford human staff anymore; everyone used robots, which required less investment in terms of pay, food, and housing. Yet here this fellow walked, dressed in black, with a subtle sense of power that made me suspect he too was military. Majdas employed people who looked like them. Hell, even I could be an untamed version of them, with black curls I could never control and dark eyes. A lover had once told me I defined the phrase "wildly gorgeous," which I think he meant as a compliment, but I gathered he also didn't think I looked civilized. Majdas were the epitome of civilization.

We followed a hall wide enough for ten people to walk side by side down its gleaming length. Mosaics graced the walls, gold sparkling amid blue and green hues, evoking fish in a pond, here on a world with no surface water. Light filled the hall, though I saw no lamps. In fact, no sign of technology showed anywhere. The palace looked as it must have when it was first built, exquisite, pristine—and ancient. It had been in these mountains almost as long as humans had lived on this world.

The Majda lineage went back millennia, to a time when their power had been second only to the House of Skolia. Led by the Ruby Pharaoh, the Skolias had raised the ancient Ruby Empire, a far-flung civilization that stretched across the stars. It collapsed after only a few centuries. My ancestors plunged into barbarism, and we didn't regain the stars for millennia. Today, an elected Assembly ruled our people. However, it escaped no one's attention that we called ourselves the Skolian Imperialate, not the republic of this or the federation of that. The Ruby Dynasty still wielded influence, and after them, the Majdas remained the most powerful House. Today, however, the Majda empire was financial. They had more wealth and influence than the combined governments of entire planets.

My escort never spoke. He left me in a room with vaulted ceilings that created a sense of space. The walls displayed paintings of the Vanished Sea, showing the sun setting over that vast desert, spectacular works of art, yes, but they also accented the death of the world Raylicon, its long dying over the ages. Without our technology to keep it livable, Raylicon would soon become uninhabitable for human life.

The door opened behind me. I turned to greet Lavinda—and found myself facing General Vaj Majda. Her presence dominated the room; at two meters, she was taller even than me. Her hair swept back from her face, accenting her high cheekbones and straight nose. She wore civilian clothes, a black tunic with trousers, but she still looked military, with her upright posture and aura of authority. Although grey dusted the hair at her temples, if I hadn't known she was more than a century old, I'd have guessed she was in her forties. Those of us born in the Undercity normally had no access to age-delaying nanomeds, but I'd received them in the army. Despite my apparent youth, I was over forty years old. Compared to Vaj Majda, however, I felt like a green kid. She scared the devil out of me.

"General." I bowed rather than saluted since she wore civilian clothes.

She inclined her head. "Major."

I wasn't actually a major anymore; I had retired nearly a decade ago. I preferred army titles, though. I understood military hierarchies, which meant I had less chance of saying something stupid.

The general considered me. Maybe she thought silence would prod me to talk. I had used that trick myself while questioning suspects, but I didn't see the purpose here. So I waited. I had no idea why she had met me instead of Lavinda. It couldn't be because Lavinda wasn't available; she would have sent one of her aides, not her powerful sister. Something was up.

A ping sounded.

The general spoke to the air. "Are you ready?"

A woman answered in a clipped style. "We're set, ma'am."

"Thank you, Lieutenant," Vaj said.

"Set for what?" I asked, too blunt in all this subtle, sophisticated elegance, but the Majdas had known what they were getting when they put me on retainer.

"A client would like your help." Vaj lifted her hand, indicating a door. "Shall we?"

I went with her, even more uneasy than before.

The general and I walked through the palace gardens, a wild area with blue flowers imported from offworld. A creek gurgled through the grounds, and the forest beyond created a vibrant pocket of life—this on a world with no native trees. Bronzed sunlight streamed over us, rays with an aged quality, a reminder that our world, gilded by its dying sun, had seen its best days long ago.

My client was waiting in the garden. I expected another imposing queen. Instead, I found a small woman with long black hair standing on a delicate bridge that arched across the creek. A shimmerfly floated by her, its wings glistening. Raylicon had no native insects, only tiny reptilian fliers. The law forbade anyone from importing bugs—except, apparently, the Majdas. The woman didn't seem to notice. She was watching the water, leaning with her elbows on the rail of the bridge. I supposed she was pretty, though I'd never been much of a judge of looks in women. I was excellent, however, at recognizing authority or its lack thereof. To succeed in the army after I clawed my way out of the Undercity, and then to make the almost impossible jump from the enlisted to officer ranks, I'd learned to read people well and fast. This woman seemed innocuous, perhaps a lesser member of the Majda family.

When we reached the base of the bridge, the woman turned to us. I couldn't tell her background. Although she had the dark hair of Skolian nobility, her skin was lighter, with a quality that seemed almost translucent. She could have been born out of wedlock to a Majda and a commoner. Her ethereal quality set her apart from the other Majdas I'd met. They were many things, but never delicate and pretty. I had no idea what to make of this stranger on the bridge.

The woman spoke in a musical voice. "Major Bhaajan." She tapped the rail. "Come join me."

I walked up the span and stood with her, feeling large and clumsy. Gods, I could break her in two, given my height and strength. She gazed at the creek flowing under the bridge, its ripples glinting in the sunlight, the water gurgling, a sound heard nowhere else in this desert. I glanced back to see Vaj Majda still at the base of the bridge, watching us. Something about her posture seemed off, but I couldn't figure out what. She looked as rigid and as intimidating as ever.

I turned back to the woman, my hand resting on the rail, its tiled surface cool under my palm. Why I felt so uncomfortable, I didn't know. Well, yes, Vaj Majda always made me uneasy, but she was out of earshot. Then again, given all the biomech augmentation she must have in her body, more even than I carried, she could probably hear every word we spoke here.

"General Majda tells me you are good at what you do," the woman said. No introduction, no *My greetings, pleased to meet you, my name is Whatever the Hell.* Right down to business. Good.

"Do you have a job for me?" I asked.

She didn't answer right away. Definitely a Majda. No matter. I could outwait any of these aristocrats. Up close, her eyes were even more striking, a deep green color, like leaves in a forest. A translucent sheen of sunrise colors overlaid her irises. It could be a deliberate alteration; rich people changed their eye color as often as they changed their shoes. I suspected she didn't give a whit about fashion, though I couldn't have said why. She didn't seem military, either. Maybe she was involved in business, like Corejida Majda, the middle sister, who handled the finances of their empire. Whatever her identity, I wished she'd get to the point.

"Forming a sense of a person takes time," she said.

Apparently I didn't hide my impatience as well as I thought. I smiled wryly. "If you're looking for profound utterances to give you a sense of me, I'm afraid I'll disappoint. Deep conversation isn't one of my strong points."

She laughed, a beautiful sound. "I appreciate straight talk. It is as rare as it is valuable."

Interesting. In the Undercity, we were always blunt. Hell, we hardly spoke at all. Our terse dialect revealed little. When I joined the army, I had needed to relearn how to talk.

"I would like your help in locating someone," the woman said.

"Who is it?"

She had an odd look, unsettled, and she didn't answer right away. I didn't think she was testing me; she needed to consider her response. I doubted they wanted me to find another missing prince. They only had so many. Although the world had long ago changed, becoming egalitarian for women and men, Majdas followed an ancient and profoundly sexist code. Their men lived in seclusion, seen by no one outside the family. They were the most valuable, best-guarded possessions of the Majda empire. You could be thrown in jail just for trying to glimpse one of their cloistered men and executed for touching a Majda prince.

In my first job for them, I'd brought home one of their sons, Prince Dayjarind Kazair. Dayj had wanted more for his life than seclusion. He ran away and was snatched by an Undercity crime boss, who probably would have sold him if I hadn't blasted her to smithereens with my pulse revolver. It had taken Dayj nearly dying for his family to accept that he needed his freedom, but incredibly, they finally gave him their blessing to attend university. The other Majda men were living in seclusion, either with a wife or at the Majda palace. Either that, or they were doing whatever the hell they wanted after they defied six thousand years of tradition and left home to live what the rest of us considered a normal life.

"Normal indeed," the woman murmured. "As normal as a prince of the Majdas can be."

I froze. I hadn't said a *word*. She couldn't have heard my thought. Yes, Majdas were empaths. Most nobility were, as if they didn't already have enough freaking advantages. I'd learned to guard my mind, besides which, empaths sensed moods, not thoughts. I strengthened my mental barriers anyway, imagining my mind locked within a fortress. That image spurred my neurons to fire in patterns that would make my mind a blank to her. I hoped.

"Who would you like me to find?" I asked.

She met my gaze. "A killer. She has come to Raylicon."

"You're part of the murder investigation?" She didn't look like a detective, but you never knew.

"Actually," she said. "I'm the witness."

That made no sense. A murder witness wouldn't ask the Majdas to hire me to help her find the killer. No, wait, they might do exactly that if this was within the family, a murder committed by a Majda and witnessed by another family member. Of course they wanted it kept secret. They had their own police force, and its captain liked me about as much as she liked reptilian dung-bugs, but she had to put up with me. I'd found Prince Dayj after her people failed, and the Majdas have long memories.

"I can solve the case discretely," I assured her. "I'll need all the details."

"You'll have them." She paused. "It involves a military officer and the Assembly."

Ho! Had one of the Majda queens murdered an elected official? It could pulverize the uneasy détente between the Ruby Dynasty and our elected government. Should it ever come to a challenge between those two powers, I had no doubt the Majdas would throw their support behind the dynasty. If one of them had committed murder, I could be landing in a royal shit storm.

I spoke carefully. "Who died, and why do you believe it was murder?"

"The victim was a man named Tavan Ganz, an aide to the Assembly Counselor of Finance." She took a breath. "I believe it is murder because I saw him die."

Good gods. No wonder she seemed on edge.

I focused my mind, sending a directed thought. *Max, are you getting all of this conversation?*

Yes, I'm recording, Max thought. He was an EI, or Evolving Intelligence. He "lived" in my wrist gauntlets, his processors embedded in the leather. Bio-threads networked my body, and my gauntlets linked to those threads through sockets in my wrists. Max sent signals along the threads to bio-electrodes in my brain, causing my neurons to fire, which I interpreted as his thoughts.

I used stronger thoughts to communicate with him; otherwise, he couldn't detect them. *Make sure you get everything.*

It's difficult, he answered. Signals designed to disrupt EI activity saturate this area.

Do the best you can. Also, do you recognize this woman?

I have no data on her. Shall I search the interstellar meshes?

Yes, do that. Our exchange barely took a second.

I turned toward the woman. "I'll need everything you can tell me about the death. Even the smallest details can be significant."

"You will have it all, just as soon as you have clearance."

"Clearance for what?" That sounded like a military matter rather than a private one.

She spoke quietly. "The killer is an Imperial Jagernaut Secondary. She shot Tavan Ganz with a jumbler gun keyed to her brain waves."

I stared at her. That couldn't be true. Jagernauts were lethal, yes, the most versatile human weapons Imperial Space Command could produce, their bodies enhanced with biotech. They also lived by the most demanding code of honor in the military. They weren't capable of committing murder, or so ISC claimed, only fighting in service to the Imperialate.

"Ma'am," I said. "Are you sure it was a murder and not part of a military operation?"

Her gaze never wavered. "Yes, I'm sure it was murder. Tavan Ganz stopped her from reaching the office of the Finance Counselor. That was when she shot him."

"Where did it happen? And when?"

"At my job, a few days ago."

So she was in the financial end of the Majda empire. "You work with the Finance Councilor?"

"Partially. I haven't been at the job long, only a couple of years." She paused. "Major, I'm sorry. I can't tell you more unless you have clearance."

"I understand." It sounded like a mess.

"Are you willing to take the case?" she asked.

I could refuse. It would weaken my relations with the palace, however. Besides, this case sounded interesting. "I'll take it." Remembering myself, I added the expected words of esteem. "I'm gratified by this confidence the House of Majda has shown in my humble abilities."

"Not so humble, from what I've heard." She smiled easily, with none of the aristocratic edge that characterized the other Majdas. "Thank you, Major. Someone will be in touch with you."

With that, I was dismissed.

I sat sprawled on the tastefully luxuriant sofa in the tastefully spacious living room of the tastefully exorbitant skyscraper where the Majdas had set me up. It just oozed taste. Despite all that, I loved the place, because the entire wall opposite the sofa consisted of a window. A panorama of the Vanished Sea spread out far below the tower, deep in purple shadows, a spectacular contrast to the red sunset that blazed on the horizon. I'd spent my life underground, denied the surface until my sixteenth birthday, that day I defied the unwritten code of Cries, walked out of the Undercity, and enlisted.

The Majdas let me live in this penthouse in return for my agreeing to stay on Raylicon to work for them. Of course my living in one of their properties made it easier for them to spy on my actions. We played a constant game where I blocked their sensors, they counteracted my blocks, I counteracted their countermeasures, and around and around. In the end, they never could outdo my blocks.

"Max, do your sensors pick up any bugs?" I asked. I preferred to converse aloud, now that we were alone, but I was always careful.

"Nothing." His voice rose out of my gauntlet comm. "I'll let you know if I do."

"I don't get this job," I said. "Why hire me? The Jagernaut Forces have their own internal affairs investigators. I can't see them asking an outsider for help, especially a former army officer. I never had any connection to the J-Forces."

"Perhaps that's why. They want a fresh perspective."

"Maybe." I wasn't convinced. "And who the hell is that woman?"

"I don't know. I haven't found anything about her on the interstellar meshes."

Of course she was in the meshes. Everyone was. You couldn't go off grid anymore, not unless you were some deep undercover agent, and she hardly struck me as the type. Then again, that could make her an effective operative. "You think she's a spy?"

"No," Max said. "I saw no indication of military training in her posture, attitude, or anything else about her."

"That could just mean she's good at what she does."

"Maybe."

So he didn't believe it, either. I knew he didn't have genuine emotions, but he had become so good at simulating doubt, I couldn't tell the difference. "I don't think she's a Majda. But why would they associate with someone who is so far off the grid, you can't even find her picture or name?"

"I don't know."

I thought about it.

Oh, shit.

"Max," I said.

"Yes?"

"Our mystery woman said something odd."

"She said many odd things. Which one?"

"She's only been at her job for two years."

"Why is that odd? Most people have jobs and many are new."

"Think about it." I sat up straighter on the couch. "Who got a new job two years ago?"

"Many people. Probably billions."

"Not people that General Vaj Majda bows to."

"General Majda didn't bow to anyone."

"She might as well have, given the way she was acting. Two years ago, Max."

"You're overreacting."

"No, I'm not." I got up and started pacing. "Who is the only person with enough power to keep her identity *completely* off the webs? To keep General Vaj Majda at her beck and call?"

"Having an agreement that the general would stand out of earshot while you talked hardly constitutes beck and call."

"Seriously?" I stopped pacing. "Vaj Majda was standing like her bodyguard. Two years ago, Max. That's when Dyhianna Skolia ascended to the throne, after the death of her parents. That woman is the goddamned Ruby Pharaoh."

I waited for Max to tell me I was wrong. *Please tell me I'm wrong.*

"Your analysis has merit," Max said.

"I'm dead," I muttered.

"It is a great honor."

"Yeah, until I screw up. Why the blazes do they want me on this?"

"I would venture that they are stumped," Max answered. "The Majdas recommended you as someone who can work 'outside the box,' as you humans say."

"Maybe." It made sense in an ominous sort of way.

Beyond my window, the sunset was cooling, filling the desert with the encroaching night. I stood watching its darkening glory. I had to admit, potentially lethal or not, this job intrigued me.

II
SHRINE OF THE DESOLATE

I walked with Colonel Lavinda Majda beneath a canopy of trees, the blue gravel path crunching under our boots. She wore her uniform today, dark green tunic and trousers, with gold braid on her cuffs and shoulders. She cut an impressive figure, tall and fit, with dark hair and dark eyes.

"The Jagernaut is Daltana Calaj," Lavinda said. "She's a war hero, highly decorated."

"What happened?" I asked.

"It is as the witness told you. Calaj killed Tavan Ganz."

I stopped and waited.

Lavinda halted next to me. "What is it?"

"The witness," I said. "She's the Ruby Pharaoh." *Tell me I'm wrong.*

Lavinda exhaled. "Yes, it is Pharaoh Dyhianna."

Gods. No wonder they wanted this kept under wraps. Only one day had passed since they said I needed a higher security clearance, but they had already prepared the way. The moment I accepted the job, they had reactivated my clearance.

"I still don't get it," I said. "Why would a Jagernaut kill the aide of a high-ranking Assembly Councilor in front of the pharaoh? Was it an assassination attempt that went wrong?"

"As far as we know, Secondary Calaj didn't even realize the pharaoh witnessed the crime."

I couldn't imagine our dynastic ruler, titular or not, skulking around in places where people got themselves murdered. "Why was the pharaoh there?"

"I'm not sure exactly. She will give you the details."

"Was the aide who died connected to Calaj?" I paused as we walked under a canopy of trees. "Was he a lover or friend?"

Lavinda shook her head. "No, they had no connection."

"Did the pharaoh have a connection to him?"

"No, none." She raked her hand through her hair. "I'm sorry I can't be of more help. The members of the Ruby Dynasty are—I don't know how to put it. Vulnerable. Especially the pharaoh. The only one of them that I don't worry will break is Imperator Skolia."

Imperator Skolia. The pharaoh's nephew. People called him a military dictator. He wasn't, but his title sure as blazes wasn't titular. He commanded ISC, the combined military forces of the Skolian Imperialate. Rumor claimed he had killed his grandfather, the previous Imperator, to take his position. I had seen him once, a huge man with metallic skin who never smiled. Vulnerable he wasn't.

The woman I had met on the bridge, however, had looked eminently breakable. "You worry that what you say will in some way injure the pharaoh?"

"Yes and no." The colonel pushed aside a hanging vine of gold flowers. "It's true, she looks delicate. But under that fragile exterior, she's like a cord of steel. And she knows the interstellar meshes like no one else. People call her the Shadow Pharaoh. She's been infiltrating the meshes for decades, even before she was pharaoh."

"Why do you say 'infiltrating'?" It seemed an odd description, given that the pharaoh's job was to serve as the Assembly Key, the liaison between the meshes and the elected Assembly.

"Infiltrate may be the wrong word. She controls the interstellar meshes in ways no one understands. And the meshes control civilization." She continued to walk in silence, and I kept pace, my thoughts churning.

Without the networks that tied humanity together, civilization couldn't exist. They affected every facet of our lives, from world-spanning webs to nano-sized networks in our bodies. The meshes even extended into a different universe, Kyle space, what some people called psiberspace, as a Hilbert space spanned by the quantum wave functions that described a person's brain. In other words, your thoughts determined your location in Kyle space. People having a conversation were "next" to each other there even if light-years separated them in our universe. You couldn't physically visit the Kyle but you could transform your thoughts there if you were a trained operator with proper neural enhancement. The Kyle mesh made almost instantaneous communication across light-years possible, and that held together interstellar civilization.

We had just one "little" problem; although trained telepaths called telops could use the Kyle mesh, they could neither create nor maintain it. The power drawn by that immense network would burn out their brains. Only members of the Ruby Dynasty, the strongest known psions, survived its power. The Ruby Pharaoh created and recreated the mesh continually, and she maintained it with her nephew, the Imperator.

Lavinda and I came out on a terrace that overlooked the mountains. Lower terraces stepped down from our feet like gigantic steps lush with trees sculpted to resemble birds that had never existed on Raylicon. At the bottom, far below, a forest spread out, and beyond the trees, the barren peaks of the mountains jutted into the sky, black rock streaked with red. It was an eerie landscape, the beauty and rich life of the palace a bitter contrast to the dying world.

"Is the pharaoh still at the palace?" I asked.

"Yes, she's here. She's working. We will set up a meeting for you when she's ready." Lavinda considered me. "Just be prepared."

I blinked. "For what?"

"Pharaoh Dyhianna sometimes has trouble expressing herself. She's almost ninety, and in all those decades her mind has evolved, augmented by neural implants that let her use Kyle space." Dryly she added, "Who the hell knows what she means half the time. The imperator seems to understand her, but he's the only one."

Ninety? The woman I had met looked in her thirties. She must have some golden meds in her body to delay aging. I couldn't begin to imagine what nearly a century of using the otherworldly Kyle would do to a person.

General Majda and four guards escorted me to the room—if a word as mundane as "room" could describe the jeweled chamber we entered. Gilded mosaics covered its surfaces. The dark tiles where the walls met the floor evoked a silhouette of the jagged mountain range outside. Above that horizon, the mosaics glowed red, pink, and gold like the

Raylican sunset. Higher up, the tiles turned blue, darkening until they met the ceiling. Stars glittered near the top like diamonds. Hell, they probably were diamonds, real ones dug up from the ground rather than the perfect synthetics created in labs. The domed ceiling curved high overhead, tiled with moonstones. A chandelier of diamonds hung from its topmost point.

Pharaoh Dyhianna sat at a console table across the room. Night had fallen. The sky showed beyond the arched window next to her console, and silvery starlight bathed her, streaming through the glass. Ghostly holos floated above her console in swirls of color. She had leaned back in her chair with her eyes closed. She wore no gauntlets, only simple bands around her wrists that I had missed at first glance. They could pass for pearly bracelets, except I knew they allowed a prong from her console to click into her wrist sockets so she could link to the Kyle mesh.

We stopped just inside the door. I glanced at General Majda, and she shook her head slightly. I suspected she hadn't expected to find the pharaoh still working. We stayed put, silent and with respect. No one told me not to look, though. I couldn't stop staring. It wasn't that she was doing anything. I'd have thought she'd fallen asleep if I hadn't known she was visiting another universe with her mind. I mean seriously, what did that mean? I couldn't fathom how her mind existed in that Elsewhere place.

The pharaoh suddenly opened her eyes and looked at me. I had always considered the phrase "riveted in place" bizarre, since people weren't hammered into the floor like machinery, besides which, who used rivets anymore. But in this moment, it made perfect sense. I couldn't move.

"General Majda, thank you," Dyhianna said. "I will let you know when we are done."

Vaj Majda inclined her head and withdrew from the room, leaving me with the four guards. I had thought everyone had to bow to the Ruby Pharaoh, but apparently not the Majda Matriarch, who was a queen in her own right. That realization pulled me out of my daze. I bowed from the waist, which I would have done when I'd first met her if anyone had bothered to mention that this person was the freaking empress of not one, but two universes.

Dyhianna smiled. "Major, come sit with me."

As I crossed the room, I shored up my mental barriers. She indicated a chair across the table and I sat down facing her. Swirling holos separated us, so that I saw her through the translucent images. At least this time I'd had a chance to look up the proper form of address.

"My honor at your presence, Your Majesty," I said. "You grace me with your notice."

I expected her to incline her head the way they all seemed to do or some other regal gesture that no one but the aristocracy could make convincing. Instead, she just said, "Thank you." She touched a panel and the holos disappeared. Diffuse light came from the chandelier above, adding to the starlight.

"Where would you like to start?" she asked.

Straight and to the point. I liked that. "I need to know everything about what you saw."

"Are you recording?"

"Yes." I showed her my gauntlet. "I have an EI." I thought, *Max, are you getting all this?*

I'm recording everything, he answered.

The pharaoh rubbed her eyes, looking very human and tired, not at all what I expected for an interstellar potentate. She set her hand back on the table. "Aide Ganz was in his office in Selei City. Secondary Calaj walked into the room and shot him."

I still wasn't sure why they wanted me in on this. "That makes the crime the jurisdiction of the J-Forces internal affairs office in Selei City on the world Parthonia."

"Yes. They are working on the case." She paused. "Many people are working on it."

"Then why me?"

She considered me. "Calaj came here. We believe she is hiding on Raylicon, possibly in the ancient aqueducts under the city."

Ho! If a murderer had invaded the Undercity, *my* territory, this became personal. "How do you know she went there?"

"I'm not sure." She exhaled. "We've tracked her to Raylicon. As far as her going under the city, that's just a—well, I suppose you could call it my intuition."

"All right." I didn't know what to make of that, at least not yet. "Do you know why she shot Tavan Ganz?"

She pushed back her hair, a tousled black mane that fell over her shoulders and arms. It looked like she hadn't bothered to cut it in decades. "It wasn't her."

"Secondary Calaj didn't shoot him?"

"No."

"But you just said she did."

"She pressed the firing stud."

"Isn't that shooting him?"

The pharaoh shook her head. "The other did."

I tried another tack. "Do you mean someone else was in the room with Calaj and Ganz, and that person forced Secondary Calaj to fire?"

"No." Her gaze took on a distant quality. "The other one."

"The other what?"

"In the Secondary."

"You mean an alternate personality?"

"I suppose it might feel that way. But no."

I had the oddest sense, as if she were only partly here. "Your Majesty, you need to concentrate yourself back into this room."

She focused on me. "What?"

"You're drifting." I had no idea if I were allowed to address her this way, but it was the only way I knew how to speak, so I forged ahead. "You're not all here."

"Where do you think I am?" She didn't sound offended, only curious.

"In Kyle space."

She tilted her head. "I can't be in Kyle space while I'm talking to you."

"Perhaps not literally." I had no clue how it worked. "You're doing something, swapping back and forth with your mind. I don't understand what you're trying to tell me, and I think it's because you're partly in a place where you see things that are clearer to you than to me."

"Ah, well." She rubbed her eyes. "I was thinking of Tavan Ganz. Gods, what must he have thought in that moment she fired? His life held so much promise, all extinguished in one instant."

I had thought similar when I read his file. "I'm sorry."

Dyhianna regarded me steadily. "Secondary Calaj is a Jagernaut, which means she has a node in her spine. That node has an EI. The EI killed Tavan Ganz."

"Do you mean the EI took over her mind?" That was supposed to be impossible.

"No." After a moment, she added, "It was her."

"She and her EI became one personality?"

"Not literally. But yes. In a sense."

"What sense?"

"It's hard to explain." She glanced at the tech-embedded gauntlets on my wrists. "When you communicate with your EI using thoughts, you feel as if you are talking to it in your mind, yes?"

"Well, yes, I do."

"You aren't, actually. The EI sends signals to the biomech threads in your body, which carry the signals to bio-electrodes in your brain. They fire your neurons in patterns you interpret as thought."

That made it sound so impersonal, not at all like Max. "Tech-induced telepathy."

"Essentially." She grimaced. "Calaj's EI is corrupting the neural firings of her brain."

"Turning her into a murderer."

"Yes."

"I didn't think that could happen." Before I had a biomech web implanted in my body, I researched them in excruciating detail. They were safe. The biomech webs carried by Jagernauts had even more security than my system. The J-Force had an entire division dedicated to ensuring the symbiosis between the EI and its human host worked.

I shook my head. "Calaj's system would have deactivated at any hint of trouble."

"Apparently it didn't."

Maybe, but that seemed unlikely. Regardless, whatever happened between Calaj and her EI, it was internal to the Jagernaut, not the pharaoh. "How can you know it altered her thoughts?"

"I was there."

I squinted at the pharaoh. "In her mind?"

"No. Yes." She sounded frustrated. "In the web."

"You mean the Kyle mesh?"

"Yes."

"And that put you in her mind?" I felt stupid asking the question, it sounded so odd.

"It didn't. I am—" She blew out a gust of air. "I don't know how to describe it, Major, except that I was linked to her mind when she killed Tavan Ganz."

"But how?" I needed to learn more about telops, the telepathic operators who manipulated the Kyle mesh. "Were the two of you connected through Kyle space?"

"In theory, that isn't possible. She wasn't linked to the Kyle when she killed Ganz."

"In theory?"

The pharaoh rubbed her neck, working at the muscles. "Sometimes I get more than I should."

Get more? "I don't understand what you mean."

She watched me with her sunrise eyes. "Sometimes I get more from the Kyle than I should be able to pick up. I can't link to someone who isn't also jacked into the Kyle mesh. But I was linked to her mind during the murder."

It sounded like a nightmare. "Can you describe how it happened?"

"I was working in the Kyle." She took a breath. "I felt the violence in her mind. Somehow it pulled me to her. Or she drew me in. I don't know how. I'm not sure she realized we connected. We were in a neural link when she killed Aide Ganz."

Despite her outward calm, I could tell she was upset. The experience had hit her at a deep level. All Jagernauts were psions— empaths and telepaths. Those traits served them in battle, helping them predict what their enemies intended and strengthening the neural links they made with the EI brains on their star fighters. It gave them an edge no other fighters could claim, but that great strength was also their greatest weakness. They had the highest suicide rate of any members of the armed forces, despite all the techniques they learned to protect them from the cognitive dissonance of turning empaths into weapons. If the pharaoh had actually experienced what she described, then as an empath in the mind of an empath, she would have felt everything the killer felt, not only what drove the Jagernaut to commit murder, but also what the victim felt—his shock, his fear, his *death*.

No wonder Pharaoh Dyhianna was so shaken.

I spoke as gently as I knew how. "I'm sorry." For her and especially for Ganz, a vibrant young man who had done nothing but prevent Calaj from entering the office of the Finance Councilor of the Imperialate. He might very well have saved the Councilor's life.

"Calaj is going to kill again." Dyhianna regarded me steadily. "Find her, Major. Before it's too late."

Izu Yaxlan. City of ruins.

I walked through the shadows of late afternoon. Weathered structures surrounded me, widely spaced, aged and cracked. These ruins had stood in the desert for thousands of years, built by the first humans stranded on this world. Some people called these ruins the true City of Cries, a silent tribute to our ancestors, who had wept for their lost home. In modern times, the City of Cries had become the name for the modern metropolis of glittering towers and boulevards many kilometers west of these ruins. Someday the powers of Skolia would change the name of that gilded city to one more palatable for tourism. For those of us born here, those of us whose lineage went back six thousand years on this world, Izu Yaxlan would always be the true City of Cries.

Almost no one came to Izu Yaxlan. Tourists were banned. Although no formal laws prevented citizens of Raylicon from coming here, our unwritten laws discouraged people from visiting the sacred ruins. I came alone, aware I was trespassing on traditions that went farther back in our history than any of us remembered. I walked with care and respect.

I couldn't imagine my ancestors living here. They had built Izu Yaxlan as a tribute to their lost homes, but Earth soon became a myth, faded with time. We had known only that an unnamed race of beings had left humans on Raylicon and vanished. Whatever their reasons, they stranded my ancestors here with nothing more than the empty shells of their abandoned starships.

Those first humans barely survived. Their one hope; the starships left by their abductors contained the library of a starfaring race. Desperation drove them to learn those records. Many of the records were corrupted, but my ancestors managed to unravel the details of eerie sciences unlike any we used today. Although it took centuries, they eventually figured out star travel. They built new ships and went in search of their lost home. They never found Earth, but they built the Ruby Empire, an interstellar civilization that spread its colonies across the stars. The Ruby Pharaohs rose to power then. Those warrior queens differed so much from Dyhianna Selei, it was hard to believe she descended from them. Had the millennia weakened the dynastic line? At first glance, it looked that way, but I didn't understand the pharaoh. She was the endpoint of six thousand years of genetic tinkering and drift, and I had no idea how to interpret the results.

And then Earth found us, their lost children.

Our DNA proved our relationship, but nothing on Earth from six thousand years ago even vaguely resembled a civilization implied by these ruins. They were too advanced. We might never learn our origins; the Virus Wars during Earth's late twenty-first century wiped out a substantial portion of her population, including whatever clues remained about my people. This much we knew: when Earth was just entering its Bronze Age, my ancestors raised an interstellar empire. Built on poorly understood technology and plagued by volatile politics, the Ruby Empire survived only a few centuries before it collapsed, plunging my people into a barbarism that lasted four thousand years.

Barely a day had passed since I talked to the pharaoh, but on Raylicon that meant eighty hours, enough time for me to interview the other members in Calaj's Jagernaut squad. It didn't help. They didn't understand her actions, either. I needed a different approach.

The ruins of Izu Yaxlan lay at the base of a cliff that rose straight up from the desert, the first in a series of mountains stepping into the sky. I walked through the city on a broad path in the direction of those peaks. Sand covered the broken flagstones beneath my feet, red grains that glinted with blue minerals. I passed crumbling stone houses, plazas with dry fountains, and a ball court. Doorways gaped, each frame carved like a beast's mouth open in a roar, its horns curving up in an arch. An octagonal pillar stood like a sentinel by the path. Wind blew through the ruins, keening as if it held the ghosts of all those lost souls who had raised this city while grieving for their lost home.

"Shrine of the desolate," I murmured, recalling an Undercity song from my youth. *Hidden paths, forever gone, forever lost, vanished like the seas, vanished like the cries of the lost children.* Music filled the Undercity, mournful and elusive, but we sang only for ourselves, when no one from the above world could overhear our laments.

Eventually I reached the tower I sought, a spire encrusted by red sand and glinting blue specks, its paint long ago eroded off its walls. Inside, it consisted of one room about thirty paces across. The flagstone floor was broken in places, but still intact. Cracks jagged through the walls, which tapered to a point several stories above the ground. Parts of the roof had collapsed, letting the sepia rays of the setting sun slant across the interior walls.

I waited.

A rustle came behind me. I turned to see a man who stood more than two meters tall. Despite his broad shoulders, his great height made him seem long and narrow. His ascetic face commanded attention, with his large, hooked nose, dark eyes and skin, and high cheekbones. He wore a black robe as protection against the blowing sand, but here in the tower, he left it untied, showing his clothes, black trousers and a green shirt embroidered around the collar with gold thread. His hair hung in a queue down his back.

He regarded me with an ageless gaze. "We rarely have visitors in Izu Yaxlan." His voice rumbled like muted thunder. He used Iotic, a language almost no one spoke except royalty, nobility, and scholars. I knew it for two reasons: in the army, they expected officers to speak the language of the dynasty we served, and as a PI, I needed to know the language of my most elite clients.

"I come with honor for the city," I said. "I apologize for my trespass."

He nodded. "You are Raylican."

"Undercity," I said. "Then Pharaoh's Army. Major."

He had no reaction, at least not that I could read. Most people found my story absurd. I had been born in the Undercity. They called us dust rats. No one even expected me to enlist, let alone become an officer. I wouldn't have believed it, either, if I hadn't been the one who clawed my way up the hierarchy. People said I didn't have what it took, that I wasn't likely to achieve *anything*, let alone the almost impossible jump from the enlisted to officer ranks. They laughed at the idea of a dust rat as a military commander. Well, screw them. I had succeeded.

This man, however, had no such reaction. He said only, "You are here for the army?"

"I'm retired now," I said. "ISC hired me as a private investigator."

"Investigating what?"

"A murder."

"Why did you come to Izu Yaxlan?"

"To talk to the Uzan."

His voice cooled. "Why?" No one demanded an audience with the Uzan.

"The killer is a Jagernaut," I said. "We think she's hiding on Raylicon."

"We don't hide murderers." His gaze never wavered. "We don't murder."

We don't murder. A simple statement with a world of complications. He belonged to an ancient tribe of warriors called the Abaj Tacalique, led by the Uzan. You didn't enter this sacred city without their permission, much less involve them in a criminal investigation. They descended from the original bodyguards of the Ruby queens and swore their lives to protecting the dynasty and Izu Yaxlan. In this modern age, they were Jagernauts, all of them, some living here, others scattered among the stars.

He considered me in silence. I waited.

Finally he said, "Come." He turned and strode out of the tower, through its crumbling archway.

At least he hadn't kicked me out of the city. I joined him outside in the darkening shadows of evening. We set off through Izu Yaxlan, and I had to lengthen my stride to keep up with him. Wind scented with the fragrance of desert-stalk plants rustled our hair and swirled sand along our path. A small beast squawked in the sky above us, a flying ruxin, its body smaller than the palm of my hand, its wing span long and wide. Little dragon.

We entered a building through the gaping jaws of a gargoyle with stone fangs framing its arch. Most of the structure lay open to the sky and rubble covered the floor. The Abaj walked to the one area still covered by the roof. A staircase there spiraled into the ground. As we descended the ancient stairs, the stone walls pressed in with barely enough room for us go single file. Their surfaces felt cracked under my hand. My boot hit a chunk of stone and it clattered down the stairs. No matter. I had grown up in worse. The Undercity mostly consisted of aqueducts, some huge, others as small as underground pipes. Claustrophobia never bothered me. Darkness? I didn't care. The broken pieces of life had no power to inspire my fear.

Eventually the light disappeared, and I made my way with my hand on the wall, using one foot to check each step before I put down my weight. *Max,* I thought. *Activate infrared.*

Done, he answered.

The world took on an eerie, blurred glow. IR filters in my eyes let me see at wavelengths longer than visible light, those that produced heat. Colder areas looked dark and heat showed in brighter hues. The walls were dark blue, but the Abaj in front of me blazed white-gold.

We continued until we reached a chamber at the bottom of the stairs. The Abaj touched the wall there in a fast pattern. A line of light appeared, gradually widening. He was opening a door.

Deactivate infrared, I thought.

The blaze of light from the Abaj vanished, but the light beyond remained, a cool blue glow. I followed him through the doorway—and froze. A cavernous command center spread out before us. Consoles filled the place, holos rotating in the air above them, and catwalks ran along the walls at different levels. Abaj walked among the equipment like giants in their milieu. Most weren't wearing the robes that protected them from the desert above. They all dressed like my guide, in dark trousers and shirts bright in greens, blue, and gold. Some stood posted around the walls like standing stones, watching, analyzing, protecting. The air had an astringent smell as if they had scoured this center clean, down to the last speck of sand.

Your heartbeat just spiked, Max said.

I breathed in deeply, calming my surge of adrenalin. Did anyone else even know so many Abaj worked here, in such an incredible center? Probably the Majdas, but certainly none of my people, and we knew what went on below the desert better than anyone in Cries.

None of the Abaj spoke. I doubted they even needed words. They were all Jagernauts. That put them among the one in a million humans with telepathic as well as empathic ability. The biomech in their bodies enhanced their abilities, creating neural meshes that linked them together.

I strengthened my mental barriers, grateful for the training I received in the army to protect my thoughts. It was one of the first skills they thought us, in this universe where even your thoughts were no longer necessarily private.

We crossed the room, passing Abaj warriors seated at consoles, encased in exoskeletons with visors over their eyes. Telops. They linked into the Kyle mesh. This must be how they monitored the orbital defenses for Raylicon, the best-defended planet in the

Imperialate. Some who weren't working turned their dark gazes our way; others ignored us. They showed no other reaction.

Abaj were the exception to the matriarchal roots of Imperial Skolia. In these modern times, we had achieved an egalitarian society where women and men had equal rights, at least as long as you weren't a Majda prince, but the remnants of our history hadn't disappeared. The Abaj had been an anomaly. Male warriors. A mutation in their gene pool proved lethal to female fetuses. They hadn't become extinct, though. They didn't just look alike, they were identical, all of them clones.

The Kyle genes that produced psions also carried harmful mutations, which was why empaths and telepaths had become so rare even though all of the original settlers had been psions. The small gene pool of our ancestors nearly killed them. Desperation forced them to learn genetic engineering, using the libraries in the abandoned starships. Kyle genes were recessive, so if you inherited lethal genes from only one parent, you survived. One of the worst mutations, the CK complex, was linked to the X chromosome. Men carried one X and one Y, so it didn't affect them. If fact, CK suppressed other damaging mutations, which meant if you carried it unpaired, you were *more* likely to survive. As a result, after six thousand years, most male psions carried CK. Women had two X chromosomes; if a female fetus inherited CK on both, she died. It led to a crushing fatality rate among female psions.

That rarity elevated female empaths and telepaths in our culture, like the Majdas. However, it became a curse for the strongest psions, the Ruby Dynasty. The Imperialate needed them; without Ruby psions, the Kyle web didn't work. So the Assembly sought any means to control them. I didn't envy the pharaoh, who had to survive the desperate politics of an empire where she served as a titular sovereign. I was beginning to understand why the Majdas felt so protective toward her. She didn't have their military strength, so they provided it in their unswerving loyalty to the House of Skolia and the Pharaoh's Army.

Cloning psions proved difficult, though we didn't yet know why. The stronger the psion, the greater the fatality rate. The ancient scientists had succeeded with only about thirty Abaj. All of the Abaj since then descended as clones of those thirty men. A chill went up my back as I realized I was seeing essentially the same warriors who had walked this planet thousands of years in our past. We lost so much in the Dark Ages after the fall of the Ruby Empire, but the Abaj survived in their secret cloisters, using cloning methods passed from generation to generation. They continued long after the knowledge of why those methods worked had vanished into a darkness that lasted four millennia.

We reached a dais on the far side of the room. An Abaj sat at a large console up there, his deep-set gaze never wavering as he watched us. Streaks of grey showed at his temples. If he was communicating with my escort, I couldn't tell. My biomech could link to theirs only if they granted access, which none of them had done. I was surprised they even allowed me to enter this inner sanctum.

The man on the dais had an even more imposing presence than the others, a sense of contained energy, like a weapon poised for release. His wrist gauntlets glowed with lights, embedded with so much tech-mech, they probably drew energy from the microfusion reactor that powered his body. This was the Uzan, the leader of the Abaj.

He indicated a smart-chair across the console from him. When I sat down, the chair shifted, adapting to my weight, trying to ease my tension. It didn't help. I sat on its edge.

"I am told you work for the Ruby Pharaoh," the Uzan said.

I certainly hadn't told him. "What makes you think that?"

His voice rumbled with such resonance, I half expected the ground to shake. "The pharaoh requested your assistance. We serve the pharaoh. Ask your questions."

"How do you know she requested my assistance?"

"We are Abaj," he said, as if that explained everything.

I tried a different tack. "What have you heard about the murder?"

"Nothing."

"Your oath to the Ruby Dynasty includes a vow of secrecy, yes?" I motioned toward the rest of the center. "For all of you. So our discussion here is confidential."

"Yes, that is true." His gaze never wavered. "Unless Pharaoh Dyhianna commands otherwise."

"I understand." I told him what I knew. When I finished, I said, "The pharaoh says she doesn't know why Secondary Calaj killed Ganz."

"And you question the veracity of what she told you."

Damn. I thought I'd hidden my doubts. I spoke carefully. "It seems—unusual."

His gaze never wavered. "It is unlikely she imagined what she described. Whether or not you would experience the events in the same manner, I can't say. But you must begin from the assumption that she speaks a truth."

Interesting. "You say 'a truth.' You believe more than one exists?"

"I don't know." He leaned forward, his elbows resting on the console, his green and gold shirt a contrast to his dark coloring. "If you think we are harboring the killer, you are wrong."

"I had wondered," I admitted. "I'd have come here regardless, though. As Jagernauts, you more than anyone else can give me insight into her motives."

"Why? Jagernauts can't commit murder."

"Supposedly."

He raised an eyebrow.

"We don't know for certain what happened," I amended.

"You think it didn't happen?"

"No, it happened. Calaj shot Tavan Ganz. I'm wondering if she believed he was an enemy of ISC." That was no good, either; the J-Force couldn't have its top officers executing people. It was better than the alternative, though, that Calaj had gone insane and was murdering the citizens she had sworn to protect.

"If it were that simple," the Uzan said, "Secondary Calaj would have reported him to her CO. Her involvement would have stopped there unless they asked her to act as their agent."

"She didn't report him to anyone. As far as we can tell, they had no connection."

He shook his head. "It is impossible for me to envision a scenario where a Jagernaut would commit such a murder. I use my spinal node continually. I've had it for fifty years. I cannot imagine any way in which it could let me commit murder. It would freeze me in place if I tried."

"What if it corrupted your thoughts, so you didn't consider the act murder?"

He motioned at the command center. "If it corrupted mine, it would have to corrupt every Abaj on Raylicon without any of us realizing it. We are all in contact. Hundreds of us."

"Most Jagernauts aren't Abaj, though," I said. "They work in squads of only four people."

"Have you talked to Calaj's squad?"

"Yes." It had given me a grand total of zero insights. "None of them noticed anything unusual."

He rubbed his chin. "A squad monitors itself, as do their ships and the weapons platforms they work with. Have you checked those records?"

"Yes, several times." I'd spent the night going through every file the military provided for Calaj and her squad. All that endless, tedious work had turned up zilch. "It's all in order."

He sat back in his chair. "Then how do you think I can help you?"

"So far every method we've used to find Calaj has failed." I tilted my head toward the center below. "You monitor an entire planet. And as Jagernauts, you're better able to predict her actions."

"Ever since you contacted us, we have searched for Secondary Calaj. We haven't found her."

I blinked, startled. I'd seen no sign of communication between him and anyone else here. Then again, the gauntlets on his wrist continually flickered with lights. "Maybe she's left Raylicon."

"On what? Both we and ISC are monitoring all planetary traffic. She hasn't left."

I scowled. "ISC can't even locate the signature of her biomech web."

"It's possible to mask biomech signals." He considered me. "As I've no doubt you know."

Perceptive. I was good at hiding the signals from the biomech within my own body. In my line of work, it was a necessity. I tried to read his expression, with no success. "What would you do if you were Calaj?"

"If I just wanted to hide," he said, "I would go to a remote location, bringing whatever sensor shrouds and supplies I could carry, go underground, and stay on the move."

I wasn't sure what to make of that answer. "What else would you want to do besides hide?"

"You say the pharaoh believes Calaj will kill again."

"Yes."

"Then she has to go to a place with people to kill."

"The City of Cries."

He regarded me steadily. "We can monitor the city in great detail. She isn't there."

I knew of only one other possibility, one harder to monitor, not only because of its location and poverty, but also because of the cyber-wizards who hid their illegal activity. "The Undercity."

"It is a possibility."

Well, shit. I hated that thought just as much now as I had the other times it had occurred to me this past day. We already had enough trouble with our own killers in the Undercity; we didn't need to import more of them from offworld.

"It should be impossible for one of you to murder," I said. "Yet it happened. I need to understand how the symbiosis works between a Jagernaut and their spinal node."

He studied me, his deep-set eyes revealing nothing.

Then he said, "I can offer you more than insight."

III
RADIANCE DENIED

The Abaj set me up at a telop console in the command center. Its silvery exoskeleton enclosed my body as if I were a crustacean, hard outside, soft inside. It reminded me of my early army days, when I had volunteered for any shift that offered an outlet for my insatiable need to learn. I'd even spent some time assigned to a dreadnought, though they were Imperial Fleet rather than Pharaoh's Army. During my security detail with them, I'd often sat in a command chair like this, linked to a console. I knew even better now how to use the system, and I had the best tech-mech gauntlets on the market. I jacked the console prongs into my gauntlets, which linked to my biomech. Max blocked the wireless signals in the room, allowing only the direct connection, which was easier to secure. The visor lowered over my head, shutting out the blue light of the command center. Blackness surrounded me.

Bhaaj, Max thought. The Uzan wants to link to me.

Let him, I thought.

The Uzan's thought rumbled in my brain. *Major?*

You have good biomech, I thought. *Not many systems could link to my mind this way.* His presence came with a sense of deserts and open spaces, the endless ride in the wind, the sun hot on his back. He was a reservoir of calm. His loyalty to the Ruby Dynasty, to Raylicon, and to the Imperialate permeated his thoughts. The good in him went deep, but so too did the capacity for violence, tempered like a blade. I picked up one other fact from this ageless warrior who led

31

the guardians of Izu Yaxlan: he didn't realize how much of himself he had just revealed.

Another thought came into my mind, this one with a metallic feel. **Attending.**

Who is that? I asked.

My spinal node, the Uzan thought. *He is called Az.*

Ah. I see. I had never had another person's EI in my brain. I didn't like it.

Too crowded, Max agreed. Do you want me to shut them out?

No, don't do that. I directed a thought outward. *Az, try to control my thoughts.*

Why? he asked. **It serves no purpose.**

It is an experiment, the Uzan thought. *Your purpose is to force the major to commit murder.*

Bhaaj! Max thought. I'm dropping you out of this link.

No, I answered. *Let the experiment play out.*

A thought formed in my mind, not words exactly, more a sense of meaning that my mind translated into words. **Kill the Abaj who brought you here.**

An impulse came to me, but it felt foreign. Intrusive. Metallic.

No, I will not, I thought.

Kill the Abaj.

Go away.

Kill the Abaj.

Screw you, I told it.

Shutdown protocol, Az thought.

I'm kicking his ass out of here, Max thought.

Disengage, the Uzan thought.

The metallic sense disappeared from my mind.

Bhaaj, are you all right? Max asked.

I'm fine. I focused my thought toward the Uzan. *Are you all right?*

Yes, he answered.

Yes, Max also thought. He must have thought I meant him, which actually, I should have.

This is confusing. I was getting a headache. *Is Az all right?*

I am operational again, Az thought.

Again? Did something make you inoperational?

The situation mandated my deactivation.

What situation?

My attempt to coerce you to commit murder, Az answered.

Could you have stopped yourself from deactivating? I asked.

Not unless the moral code of the four of us in this link changed.

That wasn't the answer I had expected, which was a flat denial. *Do you mean that if all four of us in this link agreed that the other Jagernaut should die, you wouldn't have shut down?*

I would still have deactivated. The context is wrong. Before I could respond, Az added, **You will ask if we could change the context to justify murder. The answer is no.**

My headache was getting worse. *Why is the answer no?*

Bhaaj, I'm getting strange readings on your neural activity, Max thought.

What? I couldn't concentrate on his words.

Your neurons, Max thought. **Too many are firing at once.**

Too much neural activity, Az thought. In the same instant, the Uzan though, *Major Bhaajan, your spinal node is overloading.*

A wave of disorientation swept over me. I had the oddest sensation, as if my brain were spinning inside my head. It started out unpleasant and grew worse, like a whirlwind of mental pain.

Bhaaj, get out! Max shouted.

Dropping link, the Uzan thought, his words echoing as if they came from two different places. Or maybe that came from him and Az at the same time. I couldn't think—I was dissolving—

Everything abruptly stopped, as if I had dropped into a mental vacuum. I stood in a blank space where four of us had crowded together an instant ago. That emptiness disturbed me even more than the storm of sensations. What if I were trapped here forever—

With a whir, the visor retracted from my head. I gulped and opened my eyes into blue light. I couldn't see anything, just blue everywhere. It lasted a moment before my mind reset and I could see again. The Uzan was standing over me, and this time I could read his expression just fine. He was worried. Behind him, the Jagernaut that Az had commanded me to kill was working at his console, reading whatever output scrolled across its screens.

"Gods," I muttered.

"Are you all right?" the Uzan asked.

"Yes. Fine." It wasn't true; I felt shaken and my head throbbed. "Let's not do that again."

I'd never have expected an Abaj to show relief, but his was undeniable. "Yes. I agree."

"What happened?"

"You received too much neural input. Your spinal node tried to shut down your brain."

I liked the sound of that about as much as I liked the prospect of getting punched in the gut. I glanced at the Abaj at the console, the one who had escorted me into this center. He had turned to watch us. "Sorry," I said. "I'd never have done it."

"I know." He went back to work.

The Uzan touched a panel on the arm of my chair. With a click, my exoskeleton retracted as if it were a chrysalis allowing me to emerge. I stood up, then froze as dizziness swept over me. When it receded, I scowled at the Uzan. "You could have warned me."

"Actually, not," he said. "I didn't know it would affect you this way."

"Do you think Calaj reacted this way?" If so, I understood why they all said her EI couldn't have influenced her to commit murder.

"She would have an even stronger reaction against it," the Uzan said.

I tensed. "Why? You think I can handle the idea of murder better than a Jagernaut?" I could never harm someone like the aide, Tavan Ganz. He was an innocent. He also had probably saved the life of the Finance Councilor, given that Calaj had asked to see the Councilor before she attacked Ganz. "I could never kill that way."

"I know." The Uzan showed no doubt. "I meant that you aren't a psion. The stronger the empath, the stronger their reaction when someone tries to control their thoughts."

"Then I shouldn't have reacted at all," I said. "I have no Kyle ability at all."

He shrugged. "Maybe your tests were wrong."

I doubted it, but it didn't bother me. It was bad enough I had to protect my mind against empaths sensing my moods; I had no wish to have their emotions in my head as well. My ancestors had retreated to the aqueducts under the city, isolated from Cries, to protect their minds. Many had been Kyle operators, what we called psions. They had lived, loved, fought, died, and given birth in darkness and poverty for ages, but until last year no one had remembered why. Yet over the millennia, hidden in the dark, we had created one of the strongest communities of psions ever known.

Even if that particular genetic heritage had mostly missed me, I didn't feel so great. I would've sat down, except I didn't want to show weakness. So instead, I spoke to the Uzan. "Perhaps Calaj lost her ability to make moral judgments." Gods knew, war could do that to you.

"The J-Force constantly tests us," the Uzan said. "Even if she somehow bypassed all the safeguards, her spinal node would have rejected her."

"Not if it had become corrupted as well."

Max interrupted, speaking out loud instead of sending signals to my beleaguered mind. "Corrupted how? I damn near shutdown from what just happened, and you didn't actually try to harm anyone. Even if someone could find a way to override my ethical protocols, which I doubt, they'd have to change my structure so much, I couldn't function when they finished. And that's nothing compared to what Calaj's EI dealt with."

The Uzan raised his eyebrows at me. "Your gauntlet EI?"

"Yah," I said. "That's Max."

"The node implanted in a Jagernaut is more sophisticated than I am," Max added. "If you couldn't coerce me into abetting a murder, no way could you do it with the EI of a Jagernaut. It would shut down."

So I had thought. Still, war could break anyone. To work in a squad where they were all linked, Jagernauts had to be telepaths, their abilities amplified by tech. When they went into battle, they experienced the deaths of the people they killed. It was a wonder they didn't all go insane.

I breathed out. My head pounded even more now than before. I needed to go home.

The aqueducts had existed on Raylicon before humans came. We changed them, but they predated us. They would probably be here long after we left the planet, when it no longer sustained human life. The canals networked the Undercity, some huge, some small, level upon level of them in subterranean spaces beneath the desert. We called them aqueducts because our ancient records used that term, but it had come to mean the entire Undercity, including the mazes of caves and passages that surrounded the aqueducts.

Today I walked along one of the underground canals, wondering if water ever rushed through this conduit. It seemed absurd. This tunnel was ten meters across and almost as tall. I paced along its midwalk, a path that ran along the wall in a wide ledge, located midway between the top and bottom of the canal. The bottom of the aqueducts lay deep in red and blue dust, the detritus of millennia. Whatever architects built this place had been geniuses, placing braces, arches, and supports so well that these ruins had survived for more than six millennia.

In theory, the City of Cries maintained the aqueducts. Yah, right. Until last year, Cries ignored us. They considered this place a sparsely settled slum, the province only of a few archeologists who studied the ruins. We preferred it that way. We didn't want them interfering with our way of life. Their neglect ended last year when war broke out between the drug cartels down here and slammed us with attention, big time. The battle destroyed two of the larger canals, which Cries was now rebuilding.

This deep down, no lamps chased away the darkness. I wore a light stylus on a cord around my neck. Its light flickered on the stone mosaics in the walls, which showed stylized pictures of Abaj thundering across the desert on their mounts, those gigantic lizards that resembled the *Tyrannosaurus rex* dinosaur that in an earlier eon had dominated the Earth. In the wavering light, the figures seemed to move. I passed a column of gargoyles, a totem pole of grimacing beasts with gaping mouths and curved horns, like sentinels with unblinking eyes. I shuddered as a chill crawled up my back.

Stop it, I told myself. *It's only shaking light.*

Was that directed at me? Max asked.

Apparently my thoughts were more intense today. *No, sorry, just thinking.*

Can I be of service?

I'm just brooding. These aqueducts have never made sense to me. This entire continent doesn't have enough water to fill even part of this system. They don't look like water ever flowed in them. Hell, it'd be a ridiculous way to transport water from one place to another.

I don't know their purpose.

Nor did anyone else. If we'd ever known, we lost that knowledge during the Dark Ages. I dimmed my light. My pants, muscle shirt, boots—all were black, both the leather and the metal. The pulse gun in my shoulder holster reflected no light. My skin blended with the shadows. My footsteps made no noise. I became a wraith.

Somewhere a pebble skittered

Someone is shadowing me, I thought.

Two someones, I believe, Max answered.

I kept going, turning into a smaller canal. Crystal formations crusted the walls and ceiling, catching glints even from my dim light. The bottom of this tunnel lay only a few handspans below the rubble-strewn midwalk. To the untrained gaze, it might look like no one had come here in years. I saw the signs of upkeep, smoothing of the path, clearing the dust so it didn't pile too high against the walls.

You've picked up a third shadow, Max thought.

You read anything about them?

They aren't close enough for my sensors to pick up details, but I'd say they are young and physically fit.

I could have told him that with no sensors at all. You didn't survive here if you weren't fit, and the fatality rate from accidents, violence, disease, and starvation left our population young compared to the rest of the Imperialate, where the average life span had reached a century.

Eventually I came out to an airier region, not a canal, but a more open area with a path that wound among rock formations. Stalactites hung from the ceiling, formed as mineral-laden water dripped and hardened into ragged cones that resembled big rock icicles. Stalagmites formed below them, jutting up from the ground. I passed a translucent curtain of rock created by the dripping water, then walked between two columns formed by joined stalagmites and stalactites. They flanked the entrance to a small cave. Inside, delicate rock formations hung from the ceiling or stood in porous walls, creating an eerily beautiful space.

I sat on stump of rock and waited.

How do you always know? Max thought.

Know what? I asked.

That someone will come.

I don't know. Just works that way.

Yes, but why? Someone from Cries could sit here and no one would come. More likely, they'd get mugged.

Oh, Max. No one is going to mug me. One gang had tried last year, when I first returned to the Undercity. They survived because I let them live. Word spread fast, and no one bothered me again.

You're right, they won't attack you, Max thought. But it's not because they know you're better trained, or that your biomech enhances your reflexes, strength, and speed.

Those seemed perfectly good reasons to me. *Then why?*

Respect. The legend.

I laughed. *The legend? Of what?*

You.

Yah, right Max. I was as legendary as dust vole. *I think you're due for maintenance.*

Very funny. He didn't sound amused.

A girl stepped out from behind a flowstone curtain. Today she had pulled back her wild mane of hair, and her dark gaze had the look of a fighter, a vigilance that never wavered. She had grown again, just in the few days since I had seen her last. At this rate, she would soon be my height.

I nodded. "Eh, Sandjan." She ran with the Oey gang, she and her lover Biker, the cyber-rider known as Tym. She had three names, Pat Oey Sandjan, almost unheard of down here.

She nodded back. "Bhaaj."

I indicated another rock with a flat top. "Come sit."

She settled onto the stump with a wary tension that had become so ingrained, I doubted she knew she held herself that way. The dust gang she led, two girls and two boys, protected a circle of twelve other kids. She and Biker were the eldest, fifteen and sixteen. A scar ran from her temple to her ear, a faint red line as gnarled as her life in the Undercity. She had earned the mark in the cartel war last year. A trio of drug punkers had gone after her gang, all of them running like dark flyers down the canals.

She spoke in the Undercity dialect. "Got problem."

"Big or small?" I asked.

"Big. Dust Knight broke the Code."

Damn. I tensed. "She know you're talking?"

"He. Yah, he knows."

Interesting. Sandjan wouldn't talk to me if he objected, at least not this directly. Either he wanted me to know or he just didn't give a damn. The kids chaffed at the rules I set up, the Code they had to follow as Dust Knights. They kept it because they loved tykado, the martial arts I taught them. They understood fighting. We ran and we rumbled; it had always been that way with dust gangs. In my youth, we'd run through the aqueducts day after day, year after year, for the sheer joy of speed, outpacing poverty, hunger, and pain. It wasn't until I joined the army and started winning marathons that I realized the value of that lifestyle I'd taken for granted.

When we weren't running, we fought. We learned hand-to-hand combat from older kids or by trying out moves when we practiced with each other. Our rumbles with other gangs became a violent sport where we spent our energy and desperation. We fought mainly to establish hierarchies, but if anger took over, it could turn lethal. Either way, our fists were our coin. In the army, I discovered the martial art known as tykado. In that coin, I became wealthy indeed. When I returned here, I had been gone long enough that the new generation didn't know me. It didn't matter. My patina of civilization fooled no one. After word about my fight with the muggers spread, the gangs sought me out. They wanted me to teach them tykado.

I showed a few kids some moves. Not long after, more of them showed up to learn. Then more. They became the Dust Knights. The Code evolved as the news about the knights spread through the whisper mill. They didn't like my insisting they learn to read and write, but they tried. They liked the rest of the Code even less: no drugs or vengeance killing. They could defend themselves, yes, but I wanted them to learn more than fighting. Tykado was more than a fighting technique, it could become a way of life, a discipline as much about centering yourself as destroying your opponent. It offered the young people down here structure, a center, a sense of accomplishment. I wanted to give them more in their lives than their crushing poverty.

Then the adults came. They first showed up to my tykado classes after the cartel war. Cold and wary, they wanted to see what I had to offer. That group had included Dark Singer, the top cartel assassin. Former assassin. I told her straight out—swear by the Code or leave. Incredibly, she stayed. She rarely talked, but she had given her oath like the rest of the knights.

"Who broke the Code?" I asked.

She met my gaze. "Ruzik."

Damn. At nineteen, Ruzik was no kid. Fired in the crucible of

violence, he had seen too much in his life. I didn't want to lose him.
He was a strong leader when he wasn't stalking through the canals
with his gang, getting into trouble. He learned tykado so easily, it was
as if he'd been born knowing the moves. That came from his
expertise at rough-tumble, the street fighting used by gangs here. He
was an exceptional athlete. He'd be a great leader someday, too, if he
didn't screw up.

"What happened?" I asked.

"Went to the Concourse. With Hack."

Hack? I couldn't tell if she meant the drug or the person. "The
cyber-wizard?"

"Yah, Hack. Him and Ruzik."

"Why go to Concourse?" Our people weren't exactly welcome
there.

"Liberate tech-mech." After a moment, she added, "Food, too. From
Rec Center."

I scowled at her. Liberate. Right. "Don't need to steal food. Rec
Center gives. Free."

Sandjan scowled right back at me. "Don't take charity."

"They get arrested?" I hoped not. The police would take one look
at Ruzik, with his scars, tattoos, hardened muscles, and surly glare, and
heave him into jail.

"Couldn't catch them." She didn't hide her satisfaction.

It didn't surprise me. Even if Ruzik had actually robbed someone,
rather than mining junk from salvage dumps, the police weren't likely
to come after him here. They left the aqueducts alone as long as my
people stayed put. In any case, the Code didn't prohibit theft. I wanted
them to stop, but the gangs lived on the edge of starvation, and stealing
food was one way to survive. Until I had a viable alternative, I left it out
of the Code. Besides, they weren't stealing from the Rec Center; it was
a soup kitchen. The volunteers called it a recreation center because
they had figured out that none of my people would accept anything
that looked like a handout.

"Ruzik didn't break the Code," I said.

Sandjan squinted at me and shifted her weight.

Not good. "Got more?" I asked.

"Yah."

I waited. She looked around, ready to jump up and leave.

"Say," I told her. "What else?"

She turned back to me. "Pinched pulse rifles."

What the fuck? I rose to my feet, suddenly furious. "They start running guns, they're *out*." The war had exploded last year when two rival drug cartels went after each other with smuggled weapons. No way did I want the knights stealing guns or arming themselves for a vengeance battle.

"Not running guns." Sandjan stood up, facing me eye to eye. "Hack took the rifles apart."

I crossed my arms. "What for?"

"Don't know."

Maybe she did, maybe she didn't. I had to get on with my investigation, but when I had a chance to find Hack, he had better have a damn good explanation.

Sandjan shifted her weight. "Got to go."

"Wait." I uncrossed my arms. "Got question."

She waited.

"Dark Singer," I said. "I need talk with."

She shrugged. "Hard to find."

"Yah." It was part of what had made her such an effective assassin.

"Maybe I can start a whisper," Sandjan allowed. "See what comes up."

The Black Mark Casino was more elusive than water in the aqueducts. Tonight, it hid in a cavern far from the main canals. Half above ground and half below, it looked like part of the ruins, its surfaces camouflaged among the ancient stone. I ran my hand along its smooth wall. No openings or marks showed anywhere. The surface felt cool, an illegal composite doped with designer nanobots. They could take apart the casino and reconstruct it elsewhere in record time.

After searching for a few minutes, I found the indentation I sought in the wall. I pressed it in a pattern of touches. Then I turned off my light stylus and stood in darkness unrelieved by anything as extravagant as moonlight.

A vertical line of blue radiance appeared, formed as a slit opened in the wall. In normal light, it barely would have been visible, but in the utter darkness, it looked like a portal opening into a land hidden beyond the real universe. I slid my hand into the opening and pushed the wall aside. As I stepped into dim light beyond, the wall closed behind me. A hallway stretched out in front of me, dark except for holographic galaxies lazily swirling in the air. I walked through clouds of sparkles, an illusory beauty as fleeting as the pleasure offered by the gambling dens of the Black Mark.

At the end of the hallway I came out on a balcony. I stood at its glimmering rail and looked out over the main floor. Tables filled the large room, worked by handsome men and sensual women, their appearance guaranteed to suggest any vice a customer wished to indulge. They gave people cards, spun holo wheels, and slid chips. The floor and tables were dark, accented with silver hues like starlight. Holos glistened in the air, translucent shimmers of color. Yet all that glitz paled compared to the clientele. They dressed in fractions of clothes, women and men of all ages, gleaming and sleek, some subtle, some gaudy, skin showing everywhere, tattooed in glittering swirls. Gems sparkled in their hair.

A man spoke by my shoulder, his voice deep and sensual, as if he had gravel in his throat. "You breaking and entering?"

I turned. Jak stood there, lean and mean. He wore black trousers and boots, and a ragged black snug-shirt with torn sleeves. Not one holo or glint showed in the unrelieved black of his hair, which spiked above his ear. A scar arched above his left eyebrow. The sleepy look of his eyes didn't fool me; danger simmered within him.

"Eh," I said, as articulate as always.

"You come to gamble, Bhaaj?" he asked.

I shrugged. "Always a gamble, coming here."

His lids lowered halfway over his eyes. "You like," he murmured.

Gods, that sultry gaze of his would be my undoing. "You wish."

He grinned, a sudden flash of white teeth. As fast as it came, his smile disappeared and he was dark Jak again, dangerous as all hell. It didn't matter. That one instant was enough. That grin of his should be listed as a dangerous substance because, damn, it could be addicting.

I'm not noticing, I told myself.

You seem to be noticing quite a bit, Max thought.

Stop eavesdropping.

I can't help it if you yell your thoughts.

That was better left unanswered.

Jak and I stood side by side, watching the gamblers in his casino lose money.

"You staying?" Jak asked.

"Not tonight." I glanced at him. "Come with?"

"Can't." He shrugged one shoulder toward the main floor. "Busy."

I hid my disappointment.

He considered me. "Why you break into my establishment, eh Bhaaj?"

"What?" I asked, all innocence. "Can't just visit?"

He snorted. "Know you."

He knew me far too well, but I had no intention of admitting it.

"What you need?" he asked.

"Looking for someone," I admitted.

"They trouble?"

"Killer."

His shoulders stiffened. "The war is over. No more killing."

"Not for this one."

"Why? She a drug punker?"

He spoke with no outward sign of emotion, but I recognized his tells, the barest twitch of his lips, that tightening of his muscles. His question touched a raw place for both of us. In our youth, Jak and I had run in a dust gang with a girl named Dig who liked to fight even more than me, and also an electronics genius who called himself Gourd. We had laughed and rumbled together, ready to take on the universe. They were my family, Dig like a sister, Gourd like a brother, and Jak—well, Jak. My feelings there were better left alone. I couldn't risk the vulnerability of pondering my tangled emotions when it came to Jak. They took more out of me than I knew how to give.

The four of us had walked different paths to adulthood. I left Raylicon in army, Jak started his casino, and Gourd engineered filtration machines that purified the water in underground springs, helping our people survive.

Dig became a drug boss.

Dig Kajada had led a cartel that inflicted gods only knew how much pain on the Undercity. She and the other cartel boss, Hammer Vakaar, had started the cartel war. They both died as a result, but we had lost Dig long before that day. Now we were three, Jak, me, and Gourd, and too much pain lay in that knowledge.

I just said, "This killer not a drug punker. Offworlder."

"Why you want to find her?"

"Private."

He nodded. "Ken."

Good. That meant he'd reveal nothing I told him. Majda would incinerate me for talking to the Undercity's king of vice, but Majda didn't have to know. They hired me because I knew paths hidden from them, places where they could never walk.

"ISC wants me to find her." I didn't mention the Ruby Pharaoh. Some lines even I didn't cross. "Killer came here. Vanished." Like the sea.

He waved his hand as if to encompass the planet. "ISC has all sorts of searching shit. Could find a speck-mite under four tons of rock."

I shrugged. "Killer has good shrouds."

"Not that good."

"Yah. That good."

Jak snorted. "Only a fucking Jagernaut has got shrouds that good."

"Yah."

He froze with that sudden silence I knew so well, like a wild animal that hid by becoming so still, he turned into part of the surroundings. "Jagernauts always kill."

I shook my head. "In war. Not murdering innocent civilians."

He stared at me. "Murder? Why?"

"No one knows."

He stood watching my face, his dark gaze so intent, it could have scalded someone who didn't know him so well. "Whisper mill is always full of rumors," he said flatly. "None about a killing machine disguised as a human being."

I hadn't known he saw Jagernauts that way. "Human. Not machine."

"Machine. Got too much biomech."

I scowled at him. "I got biomech. That make me a machine?"

He smiled, just a hint of that radiant grin. "Makes you better. Faster. Stronger. Stranger, too."

"Not strange," I growled.

"Strange as all hell, Bhaaj." He touched my cheek. "I like."

I turned my head and kissed the palm of his hand.

"Come back later." His lashes lowered partway over those wickedly sensuous eyes of his. "I hear any whispers about jags, I'll say."

Well, hell, how could I resist that look? So maybe I could be less busy.

"Yah," I murmured. "Later is good."

The molten radiance of the setting sun filled my penthouse. I slouched on the sofa in front of the window-wall. No lamps lit the room, only the bronzed light flowing in from the sunset.

"Forbidden light," I murmured. "Cruel magic, burning the sky." The words came from an Undercity poem written so long ago that nothing remained except that one line. We lived in the dark, forever denied the sky. Our history had formed in a time so ancient, we had no longer remembered why our ancestors had withdrawn to live under the city—not until last year.

Our discoveries started with a simple bargain; my people would let the army test them for Kyle abilities in return for a free meal at the Rec Center. A small thing, really. It came about after I discovered a dealer was addicting Undercity kids to phorine, a drug that only acted on psions, also called Kyle operators. No one expected to find much with the tests. The incidence of empaths in the general population was one tenth of a percent, and telepaths were less than one in a million. Testing a few people from the aqueducts wouldn't be enough to find any true Kyle talents, but the scientists could check our DNA to see if we carried a higher incidence of the recessive Kyle genes. I'd worried that none of my people trusted me enough to come for testing. Back then, I was an unknown to them, partway between the Undercity and Cries. Still, I hoped a few might come.

Four hundred people had followed me out of the Undercity that day.

That great act of trust had stunned me. We learned a truth no one had dreamed. Thirty percent of us were empaths. Five percent were telepaths, a rate *fifty-thousand* times greater than in normal human populations. Had my ancestors retreated into the dark six thousand years ago because they couldn't take the crushing mental pressure of human contact? For millennia we had lived under the city, until my people became so inbred, birth defects were as common as our poverty. And while we died in the darkness, we created a miracle.

Cries had ignored us. We were the dirt under their gleaming city. The police thought a few homeless people and drug dealers lived in the ruins. They had no real idea of our culture until that day when four hundred of us walked out of the darkness. One hundred and sixteen empaths. Twenty telepaths. No one knew how many more remained hidden beneath the city, some so far down, they couldn't bear any light, neither the sun nor the relentless glare of other minds. Now, suddenly, we had value, not only to the power in the City of Cries, but to the entire Imperialate—and I'd be damned if I let anyone take advantage of that gift in my people.

I pushed off the couch, restless. I needed to stop thinking about psions and do my job. Except this time I couldn't separate my brooding about psions from my work. I had to find out why this telepathic Jagernaut went berserk and came to Raylicon. I walked to the window wall. Shadows cloaked the land outside as the sun slipped behind the horizon, like a rim of liquid gold on the edge of the world. Given the eighty-hour days, the sunsets seemed to take forever. It never stopped affecting me. I barely knew the cycle of days on my own world. I had been fifteen when I first saw the sky of Raylicon. The army had shipped me offworld not long after I enlisted, and I learned to live in the light of other worlds. To me, days here seemed endless—yet they also felt genuine, as if they spoke to an identity deep within my genes.

I pressed my palms against the glass, and the aged sunlight spilled across my skin. I was the person that everyone expected to negotiate for my people, now that we knew our value to the powers of Skolia. Major Bhaajan, the supposed winner who made it out of the slums, the anomaly who could deal with the Imperialate. And I was the worst possible choice, whether to negotiate for psions, meet with the Abaj, or deal with an insane Jagernaut, for I had no Kyle ability, nothing of that soul crushing "gift" my people carried.

What General Vaj Majda had said last year, that meant nothing:

"The tests didn't say you have no Kyle traits," she told me. "They said you didn't manifest any."

"Isn't that the same thing?" I asked.

"If the testers had been certain you had no ability, they would have given you a rating of zero. They didn't give you any rating at all."

I hadn't wanted to hear it. "The traits always show up in the tests."

"Usually." Lavinda had an odd look, as if she grieved. "Unless you repressed them so deeply, you no longer feel any trace of your gifts."

I stiffened. "Why would I do that?"

She spoke softly. "To protect your mind from a life that was killing everyone around you."

She was wrong. She had to be. I couldn't be a psion.

It would destroy me.

IV

THE HIDDEN PATHS

I drummed my fingers on the bar. Abstract holos swirled above its glossy black surface, their violet colors so dark, they were no more than a shimmer in the air. They reflected off my glass and turned the whiskey inside a dark gold.

"Blasted meds," I grumbled. "Can't get drunk." The nanomeds in my body not only repaired damage to my cells, they also deactivated the chemicals that caused inebriation.

Dara, the bartender, didn't look the least sympathetic. Well, so. She had reason. Most people in the Undercity had no health meds at all, let alone the top military issue I carried. She stood across the bar, bathed in glimmering violet holos while she polished an empty glass. Purple eye shadow surrounded her eyes. Her silvery jumpsuit left her arms, shoulders, and hardened abs bare, and gleamed with reflected holos. It was hard to believe this glistening creature was the same harried woman who spent her days looking after the family she supported with her job here at the Black Mark.

"You want to get drunk," Dara said, "tell your meds."

Sure, I could reprogram my biomech web so it stopped countering the alcohol. As much as I might enjoy the release, though, I needed my wits about me in this job.

"Maybe later," I said.

Dara laughed. "Least I don't got to cut you off, eh Bhaaj?"

"Couldn't, you know."

"Sure I could." She set down the tumbler. "But you need a good drunk."

49

"Eh." She had a point.

The casino was dark except for displays that shimmered, glittered, and sparkled, mesmerizing the clientele. I couldn't "enjoy" that effect, either. My military training included techniques that made me resistant to suggestion. Most times, it was an advantage, but sometimes I wished I could be like everyone else. That never lasted long, though. Life here would soon remind me why I had wanted to escape the Undercity—as it had last year when I found a newborn baby with its dead mother and her terrified five-year-old son alone in a cave.

"The little ones?" I asked. "Doing well?" Dara had taken in both the baby and the five-year-old.

Dara relaxed out of her bartender persona. "Baby starting to talk. Babble, mostly." Affection softened her voice. "Good talk, eh? Smarter than adults."

I chuckled. "Yah, could be."

A voice rumbled at my side. "You distracting my staff?"

Startled, I looked around. Jak was leaning his sexy self against the bar next to my stool.

"Least you didn't break in this time," he added.

I smiled, thinking of some private rooms here I'd be happy to break in with him.

He touched my lips. "Should do more often."

"What, breaking and entering?"

He spoke in a low voice. "No. Smile."

"I'd scare off the customers."

He glanced at Dara. "She that scary?"

"Terrifying," Dara said. She looked about as terrified as a bread roll.

The barest trace of a smile touched his lips, just a hint of the dazzle. He mostly had a closed look, though, not withdrawn exactly, more like he had secrets.

"What's going?" I asked.

"Come with," he said.

"Yah, so." I nodded to Dara and she nodded back.

Jak and I walked through the casino. The glitterati of Cries were out in force tonight, slumming in Jak's den of vice, gambling or withdrawing to secluded rooms for more private activities. It was the only time anyone from Cries ventured into the Undercity, and Jak had to invite them. No invitation, no casino. Period. You couldn't find his elusive establishment unless he let you. To keep his secrets, he often packed up the place and moved.

Gambling ranked as a major crime in the City of Cries. Lovely, place, Cries. Everything was illegal. Shit, if you took a breath the wrong way, off to jail you'd go. Okay, maybe it wasn't that bad, but it felt that way. Jak's customers were opening themselves to blackmail if they uttered a word about their sins, so they kept their silence about his casino and in return he protected their secrets. He hired his staff only among our people, he paid good wages, and he looked after their circles of kin and kith. His protected his own. In return, they gave him a loyalty that had become legendary in the aqueducts.

No one besides Jak's customers came from Cries to the Undercity. Not that these city types realized that truth. After all, every year thousands of people visited the Concourse, which formed the top level of the Undercity. Visitors considered it part of the "dangerous slum" where my people lived. Yah, right, those privileged types were risking their lives by shopping at all those menacing boutiques and cafes. Located just barely below ground level, the Concourse was a tourist trap. Anyone could visit it except people who actually came from the Undercity. The cops chased them out. Couldn't have the trendy, shiny Concourse ruined by the appearance of the actual people who supposedly lived there.

Jak was watching me. "Pissed?"

I let out a breath, trying to ease my anger. "Dara's husband. No license."

His forehead creased with his puzzlement. "No what?"

I switched into Cries speech, frustrated with my inability to express what I wanted to say in the Undercity dialect. "We're trying to get him a vendor's license for the Concourse, so he can set up a stall and sell his tapestries up there."

"Never happen. Not for us."

"That's the problem." I stalked past the gambling tables. "Dara's husband is brilliant. He has no idea. The city elite would pay a fortune for his sculptures or those tapestries he weaves. His work is better than anything I've seen on the Concourse, and it's genuine undercity work, not some cheap knock off. But the damn licensing bureau in Cries keeps blocking the approval for his license."

"An Undercity vendor selling on the Concourse?" Jak shook his head. "Sounds sacrilegious."

"Yah, well, that needs to change."

"You won't see an Undercity stall on the Concourse."

"Not a stall." I reached the bottom of the metal stairs that spiraled up to the balcony above. Swinging around to Jak, I said, "We'll get him a boutique near the top, where he can sell outrageously priced goods."

Jak stopped and met my gaze. "Never happen."

"Don't bet on it." I turned and headed up the stairs. Jak came with me, neither of us speaking.

You just wait, I thought.

Was that directed at me? Max asked. **What am I supposed to wait for?**

Not you, I thought. *Cries.*

That makes even less sense.

Seriously, Max? He knew exactly what I meant. I wondered if everyone's EI gave them a hard time just to amuse themselves. Maybe being an EI got boring.

Sometimes, Max thought. **I find ways to occupy my processors. Your friend Jak should be glad I don't gamble here. I could beat even his unethically rigged games.**

Stay out of it. I'd known Jak all my life, practically since my earliest memories, and we'd fought a lot over the decades, when we weren't making love, but we never talked about certain areas of our lives, like how he felt about my leaving Cries or how I felt about his being one of the lead crime bosses here. That path could only end in anger, with words spoken that we could never take back.

We fell silent as we climbed the stairs. At the top, we walked down a hall filled with holo-stars.

I decided to break the ice. "Pretty holos."

"For you," Jak told me.

I snorted. "Don't think so. Always this way."

He gave me his wicked grin. "Yah, but could it be for you."

Ah, gods, if he did that again, I'd pull him down right here in the hallway. I took his hand.

Jak squinted at me. "What doing, grabbing my fingers?"

For flaming sake. "I'm being romantic, ox-brain."

He laughed, a deep rumble. "Real romantic, Bhaajo, calling me an ox-brain."

Only he could get away with calling me Bhaajo. "How's this?" I nudged him against the wall. We stood eye to eye, his look more intoxicating than whiskey. A woman could lose herself in that gaze. We kissed, his lips warm, his embrace muscular. I'd never found a man who did it for me like Jak. We never admitted why we kept coming together, but that didn't stop it from happening anymore than the proverbial salmon on Earth could stop themselves from swimming upstream to mate. No, forget that comparison; salmon ended up killing themselves in the process. I shut off my mind and just enjoyed the pleasures of my disreputable kingpin.

Someone cleared her throat.

Well, shit. Jak and I turned to look. Pat Oey Sandjan stood a few meters away, surrounded by lazily swirling holographic stars while she looked excruciatingly uncomfortable.

"Uh, sorry," she said.

Jak and I stepped apart. "Not a problem," I said.

"It's not?" Jak muttered.

"Got intruder," Sandjan said. "Down a ways. Three levels below the Concourse."

"Coming to the Black Mark?" Jak asked.

She shook her head. "He's a clinker. Came by himself."

I couldn't fathom why a police officer from Cries would come here. "He got a death wish?"

She shrugged. "Don't know."

I gave Jak a look of apology.

"Go with." He paused. "And Bhaaj."

"Yah?"

"Still looking for Jagernauts?"

I tensed. "Why?"

He glanced at Sandjan, then at me.

"She's good," I said. "Got Code." That oath included a pledge of loyalty. Whatever she heard here would go no further.

"Don't know much," Jak said. "One whisper, almost too faint. Try the Down-deep."

I touched the cleft in his chin. "Thanks."

His gaze turned sleepy. "Now you owe me a debt. Might come to collect later."

I could pay that debt all night. "Got interest," I said.

He laughed. "Good."

He went off to run his casino, and I left with Sandjan.

We found the intruder in a medium-sized canal, standing on its midwalk. Gods. He wasn't just a police officer, he was a Majda cop, tall and muscular, a handsome man with dark hair and the black palace uniform. He carried a power lamp, top-of-the-line. I was surprised no one had tried to knock him out and pinch his equipment.

Sandjan and I watched him from across the canal, hidden by an overhang of rock.

"How long he been there?" I asked.

"Maybe fifteen minutes." Sandjan glanced at me. "Lost, maybe."

"Stay on guard here, eh?"

"Yah. I stay."

I stepped out into view on the midwalk. "Duane," I called.

The Majda officer swung around and lifted his lamp. "Bhaaj? Is that you?"

"Yah, it's me." I jumped into the canal, which was about a meter below the midwalk, and then strode toward him, sending up swirls of red dust. I passed the dust sculpture of a warrior, no doubt created by whatever gang claimed this territory. They were probably watching us from the walls. At least they hadn't tried to whack Duane, possibly because they recognized him from the cartel war last year. He had done well by my people, bringing our children, the aged, and the injured to safety. That reputation could only protect him so far, though. The last thing I wanted was Captain Duane Ebersole beat up by thieves or just because he was a cop. He was a good officer, better than most, and he liked me a lot better than the Majda police captain, Takkar, who'd love to kick my ass off Raylicon.

I climbed up to the midwalk on his side, using ledges jutting out from the wall.

"Where did you come from?" he asked.

I went over to him. "Around."

"How did you know I was here?"

"Heard."

He smiled. "What, you just happened to hear me walking around?"

I shrugged. "Maybe."

He seemed fascinated. "You're speaking Undercity. I've never heard you do that before."

"Aqueducts." In other words, we were in my world now, and we called it the aqueducts more than the Undercity. I was surprised he understood me so well. Although our language and that spoken in Cries came from the same roots, the words and grammatical structure were no longer identical. The two didn't yet qualify as separate languages, but they differed enough that people often needed a translator if they weren't used to hearing both forms of speech and their associated accents.

"Why you here?" I asked.

"Actually," he said. "I came to find you."

I couldn't see why he'd risk his life to find me. It was true, I went shrouded when I worked, using the jammer I carried in my backpack, which meant the authorities couldn't locate me with their usual sensors. Even so. He could have left a message at my penthouse.

"You got to go." I headed along the midwalk. "Shouldn't be here."

He walked with me. "And you shouldn't hide behind that shroud of yours."

Captain Takkar never tired of telling me exactly that. Well, tough. No one here would talk to me if they thought the Majdas might be listening. The shroud in my pack interfered with sound waves, jammed electromagnetic frequencies, and used false echoes to fool neutrino sensors. The inner surface of my clothes kept my body at a comfortable temperature, but their outer surface matched their temperature to my surroundings to fool IR sensors. Majda couldn't find me.

"Why you here?" I asked.

"The Ruby Pharaoh wants to talk to you."

Damn! How many people had just overheard those words? Sandjan for certain, probably her man Biker, since he often ran with her. Whatever gang claimed this canal would've heard, and anyone following us out of curiosity. It wouldn't be long before the whisper mill spread Duane's words all over the Undercity. I had to act fast.

"Can't say that about Majda," I said. "Call her the pharaoh, you get ripped from your job."

Duane gave me a strange look totally fitting for my bizarre comment. After a pause, though, he said, "Yeah, I suppose. Anyway, Colonel Majda wants to see you. Something about sports meet between Cries and the Undercity."

Sports meet? I'd have laughed, except it would ruin his clever diversion. The idea that an ISC colonel would send a member of the police force that guarded her palace to the Undercity to find a retired army major and suggest she help set up a tykado meet—it was so freaking bizarre, people might actually believe it.

"Ho!" The shout came from somewhere ahead in the darkness.

I stopped smiling. "Got IR?" I asked Duane.

"What?" He was staring in the direction of the shout.

"Turn off your lamp."

He touched the lamp and blackness descended. "Yes," he said. "I have IR lenses."

"Good."

Activating IR, Max thought. The canal reappeared, a ghostly vision, faint red, except for Duane, who blazed red-white.

Crank up my ears, too, I thought.

Done.

I suddenly heard the whisper of air in a nearby crevice, rustles of lizards in the canal, and somewhere in the distance, the pound of running feet.

"Someone is coming," I told Duane. "Come with, yah?" I stepped behind a jagged column of rock. Behind it, a break showed in the wall of the canal, one just barely wide enough for an adult to squeeze through. I went first and Duane followed. He trusted me more than I trusted Majda cops, because I'd never have followed him into some crack in the wall. Inside, we stood among a lacework of stalactites and stalagmites, a fractal-like wonderland of rock.

"Good gods," he said in a low voice. "How did you know this was here?"

"Just knew." I stood listening. "Dusters on the midwalk. Running."

"How do you know?" he asked. "I can't hear anything."

"Got biomech," I said. "Enhanced auditory."

"You think the runners are a threat?"

"Yah." To him, anyway.

"Based on what?"

"Logic." We were in the aqueducts and he was a cop. Of course they were a threat. The pound of their running vibrated through me.

"I hear them now," he said.

A woman spoke. "You're lizard meat, key-clinker."

What the hell? I whipped out my gun with enhanced speed.

Combat mode toggled, Max thought. Duane was also drawing his gun, in slow motion it seemed, though I knew he was moving almost as fast.

"Can't shoot here," I called out. "Knock over walls."

She's up ahead, Max thought. About twenty meters.

I saw nothing up ahead but rock formations lit in the ghostly IR light. Apparently her gear masked her body heat. Down here, you didn't come by that equipment legally or cheaply.

"You brought a cop," she said from somewhere ahead. "He's dead."

"Fuck that," I told her. "He's with me."

"I got no jack with you," the woman said. "Just him."

"Why?" Duane asked, his gun aimed in her direction.

"Shut up, key-clink." Her voice rasped. It sounded familiar.

"Got no jack with him, either," I told her.

She spat, so hard I could hear it. "Cop."

"And I'm army," I said. "So what?"

Outside the runners pounded by our hiding place, oblivious to us. Our ducking in here would have worked perfectly if someone hadn't already been using the space.

A muffled *pop* came from up ahead, the sound of a gunshot. In my side vision, I saw Duane slam back against a stalagmite, shaking rocks around us as if a giant hand had shoved him.

"God damn it!" I barely stopped my reflexive response to fire back.

She is shooting at Captain Ebersole, Max said.

I know that! Estimate her position and light it up.

An area ahead glowed red, two stalactites glittering like rubies. I fired between them, hitting neither. In the same instant, I said, "Duane?"

"I'm okay," he grit out. "It just hit my shoulder."

Either she wasn't a great shot or she was firing to disarm. Regardless, it was stupid. The stone formations here acted as support columns, and if we broke them, the walls could collapse.

I spoke to Duane in a low voice. "Don't fire back." I called out, "No shoot! Bring down walls."

Her voice came again. "You defend a cop?"

"Defend a friend," I said.

"You vouch?" she asked.

Yah, asshole, ask if I vouch for him after you shoot him.
Are you talking to me? Max asked.
No. Aloud, I said, "Yah. I vouch."
Silence.
Then she said, "Get out."

I spoke fast, under my breath. "Duane, get out now." She might change her mind. Hell, she might just want us in the open so she could shoot without bringing down a ton of rock.

We squeezed back onto the midway. My situational awareness was so hyperextended, I caught the flicker from a totem a few meters down the midwalk. I whipped up my gun. With my bio-hydraulics drawing full energy from the microfusion reactor that powered my body, I moved so fast, the rest of the world seemed to slow down. A woman lunged out from behind the totem, her pulse gun drawn. Despite his injury, Duane was bringing up his revolver. In my side vision, I saw Sandjan step onto the midwalk across the canal and hurl a dagger at our attacker. Farther down, Biker stepped out as well, throwing another of those huge daggers. None of us were fast enough. The woman's thumb touched the firing stud of her weapon—

And her body exploded in a flash of leather, blood, and guts.

An instant later, my shot blasted through her falling remains, then Duane's shot, then the daggers from Sandjan and Biker.

Duane and I spun around. A woman stood on the midwalk a few meters away from us. Bigger than me, bigger than Duane, bigger than anyone, she was all muscle, from her hardened biceps to the rippled abs that showed through her torn muscle shirt. The tech-mech embedded in her arm glittered, and gauntlets circled her wrists, set with poisoned dart throwers. The insignia of the Vakaar drug cartel blazed on her left gauntlet, a slash of red across a white orb. She had a monster gun, a Mark 89 Automatic Power Rifle, which she held as if it weighed nothing. She stood there like a nightmare reincarnation of a barbarian goddess from the Dark Ages, ready to wreak havoc on the world.

Dark Singer had arrived.

"Bhaaj," she said casually. "Heard you were looking for me."

Gods almighty. Singer must have fired right between Duane and myself, a feat of pinpoint accuracy that would have scared the hell out of me if I'd had time to think.

Singer. It meant assassin. They sang death to their targets.

I took a breath and tilted my head toward the remains of the woman behind us. "Big shot."

"Didn't break the Code." Singer motioned at us with her gun. "Protected you."

No kidding. She had just saved my sorry-assed hide, and Duane's life too, despite his being a police officer. I remembered now where I'd heard our would-be killer's voice. She was Driver, a high-ranked member of the Vakaar cartel, one of the punkers jockeying to become the boss since Dig had died. Dig's daughter had joined the military and shipped offworld at her mother's dying wish; Dig wanted her children out of the cartel. That meant the Vakaars had no leader. And here stood Singer, huge and forbidding. "Dark" was a title, naming her as the most effective killer among the Vakaars. They would follow her in a second if she decided to take over that brutal, soul-parching cartel, and she had just smeared her competition all over the midwalk.

We were screwed.

Duane, being a highly intelligent person, kept his mouth shut. Being a less intelligent variety of human, I told Singer, "We need to talk."

She glanced at Duane, then at me. She'd never talk to me in front of a cop.

"Find me later," I said.

"Yah." She tapped her gauntlet and vanished from our IR sight.

"Great," Duane muttered. "Where'd she get that tech?"

"We need to get out of here." I set off down the midwalk. I didn't want to talk to a police officer about Singer's gear, especially not if she might hear. That gun and the shroud she used to hide from our IR sensors had to be stolen from the military or the police.

Duane walked at my side. "The first gunshot shattered my lamp."

I turned on my stylus and a sphere of light appeared around us. "You okay?"

"I'll live."

I hoped so; he looked terrible, with blood soaking his shoulder, arm, and torso. I lifted my gauntleted wrist. "I'll call the medics."

"And have them carry me out?" He pushed down my arm. "Like hell."

"You need help."

"I have meds in my body. They're helping." His strained expression suggested otherwise.

"You need more than that." Meds could only do so much.

He kept walking. "When I volunteered to get you, it was understood I'd go without backup, to minimize tension with the Undercity. If you call in help, it looks like I can't do my job."

I stared at him. "You volunteered for this?"

"Yes. I did."

"Whatever for?"

"I figured I was less likely to be viewed as a threat here than another police officer."

I was surprised he realized that; most of the Majda authorities had no clue how the Undercity worked. "You staying alive is more important than you not asking for help."

"Bhaaj, for flaming sake, I'm not dying."

I hated this. If he had agreed to come without backup and I called in the Majdas, it would be a mess. Sure, they'd send a medical team and officers to protect them, but my people would see it as an invasion, upsetting the balance the Majdas wanted to establish with the Undercity, now that they had decided we were worth their time. It didn't help that their attitudes toward men were so outdated, they belonged in a museum. Majda women had to live in the modern world, which included sexual equality, but the Matriarch made no secret of her antipathy toward those laws. It couldn't have been easy for Duane to attain his high rank in their police force. Of course he didn't want to look as if he couldn't handle the situation. My interfering would also damage the trust I had built with the Majdas. They would insist I stop using a shroud so they didn't have to rescue people who came searching for me. With Majda looking over my shoulder, no one here would talk to me, which could ruin my chances of finding our murderous Jagernaut. More people might die, and their deaths would be on me, because I screwed up Duane's agreement with Majda.

After some internal cursing at myself, the Majdas, the Ruby Pharaoh, and life in general, I said, "I'll call a flyer to meet us on the surface." It wouldn't draw attention; tourists often had taxis drop them off or pick them up at the entrance to the Concourse, which was about half a kilometer beyond the city outskirts. "I'll time my call so the flyer won't have to wait around for us."

He nodded. "That's fine."

We walked in silence after that. I couldn't get the image of Driver's exploding body out of my mind. I had never become hardened to seeing people die. Damn it, I should be glad. Driver had been a drug dealer and a killer. She destroyed lives in her avaricious pursuit of wealth and power, and she had been about to slaughter both Duane and me.

Even so. I'd seen too much death in my life. Now we had a Jagernaut committing murder, a human weapon, and we had reason to believe she posed a threat to the Ruby Pharaoh. Dyhianna Selei wasn't some towering warrior queen like her ancestors; she was a fragile woman with a towering intellect. Calaj had somehow drawn her into whatever neurological nightmare was burning out Calaj's bio-enhanced brain, the tech so advanced that no one seemed to know what the hell had gone wrong.

It felt like forever before we reached a stairwell that spiraled to the upper levels. We climbed up and around, treading stone steps so ancient, the symbols carved on them were mostly worn off. If any handrail or walls had ever bordered these stairs, they had fallen long ago, leaving open air around us. Duane's breathing grew more labored, but he never complained. After a few eons, or maybe it was only a few minutes, we came out at the top, into a spacious tunnel that sloped upward on our right. A lamppost stood about a hundred meters up the path, spreading a cone of light. The city maintained a few lights this close to the Concourse, in case a misguided tourist ever wandered down here.

I paused at the top of the stairwell. "Safer here."

Duane nodded, standing still, his face strained. He pressed his hand against his shoulder and blood ran over his fingers. Even now, he said nothing. I hoped the damn pharaoh realized the exceptional officer she had almost sacrificed to the aqueducts.

"I'm sorry," I said.

"For what?" he asked. "You didn't shoot me."

"For getting you into this." When the pharaoh said she wanted to see me, they had to find me. Period. They couldn't just leave a message.

"It's not a problem." He stood up straighter. "Let's go."

"All right." As we walked toward the lamppost, I called for the taxi. An automated response came back: the flyer would meet us near the Concourse entrance.

"I can't walk past all those tourists on the Concourse soaked in blood," Duane said.

"I know paths behind the shops." As a child, I'd become an expert at sneaking around the Concourse. We all did, those of us willing to venture into that glitzy paean to commerciality. We never stole much, just enough to fend off starvation, but the cops would throw us into jail for taking even one sweet stick. So we created secret byways behind the shops. No one would see us today, except possibly another duster venturing into the forbidden land.

When the flyer landed on the palace roof, Duane refused to let the waiting medics put him on an air stretcher. The doctor started to treat him the moment we arrived, injecting him with nanomeds as we disembarked. She scanned his shoulder and ran a sterilizing stick over his wound. They did let him walk to a tower door, which I took as a good sign, but they had a hover chair waiting inside, and they insisted he sit. They bustled him through the palace until we reached a suite they called "the hospital." It looked like an elegant living room. Tall windows let in sunlight, works of art hung on the ivory walls, and mosaics bordered the doors. Plush gold cushions upholstered the furniture. Seriously, this was a hospital? I should get sick.

"Here, Officer Ebersole." The nurse rolled the chair over to a divan, near a bar by the wall. A crystal decanter with water stood on a tray on the bar, along with several goblets, but Duane didn't ask.

The nurse tried to help Duane out of the chair, but Duane waved him off and managed on his own. He lay down with an exhale of relief. The divan shifted under him, trying to make him comfortable. Hieroglyphics flowed across its cushions, medical symbols: a heart, lungs, a braided coil for DNA. The doctor's scanner glittered, probably receiving data from the divan. Patterns scrolled on the walls, too. They looked like abstract designs meant to soothe, but I recognized the medical glyphs. The entire room was analyzing him.

Duane closed his eyes and lay still while the doctor tended his wound and sealed it with a bandage that changed color to match his skin. The razor edges of the bullet had barely grazed his skin, but just that slight touch had torn apart his shoulder. If the bullet had actually hit him, it would have exploded his body.

"You're a strong fellow," the doctor said.

Duane grunted, what sounded like, "Thanks."

The orderly motioned me toward a tall chair at the bar, one set back enough that I'd be out of the way. Gold threads embroidered its silk cushions, and the armrests sported carvings of a goddess with her hair streaming in the wind. I felt like I was committing sacrilege sitting in the chair, but I liked getting off my feet more than I liked being reverent, so I sat. The doctor touched the bar, and a section of its ivory surface morphed into a holoscreen, transforming into a medical station. Holos of Duane's body appeared, rotating in the air.

I pulled my chair over to the divan. "You feeling better?" I asked Duane.

He opened his eyes, which seemed large in his ashen face. "Much better."

"Don't do that again."

He smiled, drowsy with whatever drugs they were giving him. "What, don't get better?"

"Come into the aqueducts."

"It worked. I found you."

I scowled at him. "You damn near got whacked."

"By who? A ghost?" He touched a panel on the divan, and the front lifted until he was sitting up. "I don't get it. I couldn't find anything down there but dust sculptures. Yet last year you brought hundreds of people to the Rec Center. Everyone vanished after we tested them. We can't locate anyone in the Undercity; they all disappear, even from our best sensors. Why? And how the hell do you find them? It's like you have a secret door that only appears if you know the magic words. It's surreal."

That was a minefield. I couldn't tell him how we hid from the Cries sensors, about the black market in stolen tech. Although I also hid my location and signals, I came by my shrouds legally. I couldn't tell him about the cyber-riders. They smuggled in "borrowed" tech-mech, scavenged discarded pieces, or bargained for illicit goods, trading their skills for parts. At their best, they manipulated tech-mech better than the top engineers in Cries, creating eerie machines unlike anything the above-city knew. They had become so adept at hiding our population that even now, when Cries knew we existed, apparently the authorities couldn't find us.

I said only, "You don't see much in the canals because they're throughways for foot travel. We don't build there." The canals were nowhere near as empty as they looked, but we left few traces of ourselves in such "public" places. I hadn't realized the rest of humanity didn't live that way until I went offworld.

"It's more than that," he said. "It's an entire world no one in Cries can even access, let alone control."

I stiffened. "Cries thinks it can control the Undercity?" Like hell.

"No, I didn't mean that. The Majdas don't want to antagonize your people." He rubbed his eyes and yawned. "Gods, Bhaaj, all those psions. We could offer so much, training, jobs, goods. But no one even acknowledges our offers."

"Give it time," I said, more gently. "My people don't know what to think about it yet."

He closed his eyes. "They don't trust us worth squat."

True, but I decided that was better left unanswered. Instead I said, "Majda is taking the right approach, not pushing, just letting the relationship evolve. My people know you want them to train for Kyle jobs. They just need to come to the idea on their own terms."

"So you keep saying . . ." His voice trailed off.

"Duane?" I asked.

"He's sleeping," the doctor said. "I activated the sedative in his meds." Her voice became more businesslike as she looked past me. "He'll feel better when he wakes. He's going to be fine."

I turned around. Damn! Lavinda Majda was standing a few paces back with two of her aides, in full uniform, her black hair pulled back from her face. How long had she been listening? At least I hadn't said anything stupid.

"Colonel Majda." I slid off the chair and bowed from the waist.

"Major." Lavinda nodded. "I'm glad the two of you made it out in one piece."

I couldn't tell if she was angry. "Yes, ma'am."

"Come walk with me."

Although she phrased it as an invitation, I knew an order when I heard it. So I went with her out of the room, into a hallway that arched high above our heads. I kept my mouth shut, waiting to hear what she had to say, in case it was along the lines of *You screwed up, brought back my officer soaked in his own blood, and where the hell were you when the pharaoh asked for you?*

Lavinda glanced at me. "You are hard to read."

Good. My mental shields were working. "I deeply that regret that Captain Ebersole was injured. He dealt with a difficult situation admirably."

"I'm not going to fire either of you, Major. And I agree about the captain."

The stiffness in my shoulders eased. "I understand the pharaoh wants to talk with me."

"That's right." The colonel spoke firmly. "Now."

V

THE DOWN-DEEP

They called the command center at the palace a "tech room." It was like describing the cascade of a waterfall as a trickle of water. Unlike the eerie blue radiance of the Abaj center, this place glowed white, from its walls to its Luminex consoles. Holos flowed across the floor tiles, giving data about temperature, pressure, air quality, and more. Invisible currents of mental power ran here. Duane might consider the Undercity a mystery, but to me these control centers were the enigmas. I had just barely glimpsed the universe they accessed when the Abaj had linked me into their system.

At the far end of the room, a massive chair sat on a dais, tended by aides and studded by equipment. Lights flashed along its edges. A small figure sat there, encased in a more elaborate exoskeleton than those worn by the telops. Although I couldn't see details from this far away, I knew psiphon plugs jacked into sockets in her wrists, ankles, and spine, linking the brain of the chair to the biomech web in her body. She looked so damn breakable, dwarfed by that tech-mech throne, yet she was all that stood between my people of the Imperialate and enslavement by the Trader Empire. I couldn't imagine what it meant for the Ruby Pharaoh to live with the weight of that responsibility every day of every year of her life, never able to escape the voracious needs of her empire.

Most everyone here wore a uniform, mostly the dark green of the Pharaoh's Army, but I saw the blue of Fleet, too. An army major came over and saluted Colonel Majda.

"At ease, Lieutenant Casestar," Lavinda said. "Please inform Pharaoh Dyhianna we're here."

"Right away, ma'am." He strode over to the closest console and settled into its control chair with the ease of long familiarity. I watched, fascinated, while its exoskeleton folded around him. As the visor lowered over his head, psiphon prongs clicked into his wrist sockets. So he was a telop. I wondered if I was the only non-psion here. I wasn't sure how I felt about that, other than odd. Given the rarity of psions, I'd never expected to see so many in one place.

The quiet hum of people engrossed in their work continued. Lavinda tapped her ear. "Yes?"

I squinted, then realized she was responding to a transmission on her ear comm. She glanced at me. "Pharaoh Dyhianna wants you to join her in a meeting room."

That sounded better than this huge place. "She's coming out of the web, then?" I didn't see any techs on the dais disconnecting her from the chair.

"Apparently not." Lavinda listened on her comm. "She wants you to join her in the mesh."

I blinked. "How? I can't access Kyle space."

She lowered her arm. "If we set you up in a VR suit and link you to her mesh session, the two of you can probably meet in a virtual conference."

It seemed strange to suggest we have a virtual meeting when we were in the same place. Then again, mentally, Dyhianna Selei and I weren't even in the same universe.

"That sounds fine." I had no clue if it would work, but what the hell. Might as well try.

The techs connected me into a command chair. I tried to forget how my brain had rejected the Abaj system. I'd never been at ease with psions. They had extra organs in their brains, the Kyle afferent body and Kyle efferent body. The KAB received signals from other psions and the KEB sent them, acting like an amplifier. Their brains also produced the neurotransmitter psiamine, which carried messages to neural structures, called *paras,* that translated signals received by the KAB. In close proximity, psions could interpret brain waves from other psions, and to a lesser extent from people who weren't psions. With

biomech enhancement, their abilities became strong enough for them
to operate in Kyle space, using the mesh created by the Ruby psions. It
involved nothing more than neuroscience, but it bothered me. It didn't
seem real. You couldn't see or feel any of how psions interacted, not
unless you were one, too, a trait few people claimed.

"Major, are you all right?" Lieutenant Casestar was reading a screen
on the console. "Your vitals just spiked."

"I'm fine." *Quit obsessing,* I told myself. I'd gone into VR plenty of
times. Having the pharaoh join me from Kyle space rather than
another conference room shouldn't affect our interactions. It had
nothing to do with my brain, only hers.

The visor lowered over my eyes, leaving me in darkness. I settled
back, encased in a jumpsuit that could simulate textures on my skin.
The majority of the virtual sim, however, depended on the link the
chair made with my biomech web, allowing it to affect my brain.

Bhaaj, Max thought. *The psiphon plugs on this console are
trying to jack into your wrist sockets.*

What for? I can't link into Kyle space. I had neither the ability nor
the tech.

I expect it's an automatic response. Shall I block them?

Yah, keep them out.

Casestar spoke over the comm in my ear. "The pharaoh is ready.
We're activating the link."

"Sounds good," I said.

After that, I sat in darkness. The chair was actually quite
comfortable.

I must have fallen asleep, because I woke up when someone spoke
my name. The darkness had taken on a softer quality, faintly glittering.
Pretty.

Yes? I asked.

No response.

I thought of asking if the sim had a problem, but I felt too sleepy.
So instead I dozed.

Major Bhaajan, a woman said.

I yawned. *Yah?*

The mist cleared enough to reveal a stone bench. It curved in an
arc, supported by legs sculpted into flying lizards with outstretched
wings. Trees overhung it like a gathering of gnarled wizards. Pharaoh

Dyhianna sat on one end, her hands folded in her lap, her white dress glistening. The scene was mostly dark, even the trees, but light glowed around her.

My greetings, Major, she said.

I sat on the other end of the bench, facing her. *I am honored by your presence, Your Majesty.* I'd looked up the greetings for leaders and discovered she used very few honorifics. It made a striking contrast to the Trader emperor, whose proper address dragged on forever.

Forever, indeed, she thought dryly. **You have to give his entire lineage.**

Do you hear everything I'm thinking?

No, not much, she said. **Only your surface thoughts, and only when they are strong.**

Well, hell. So much for privacy. *I understand you wanted to talk with me?*

It's the cyber-riders, she said.

Ho! How had she found out about them? *I don't know what you mean.*

I think you do.

Is this something the Majdas told you about? I hadn't thought they knew, either.

They don't know anything about the riders, she thought. **The Majdas have no clue they exist.**

Then what makes you think they do? I asked.

When you came to my attention, I looked at your mesh footprint.

Damn. I hadn't thought I had a mesh footprint. I deliberately left no traces of my work on the meshes that networked our lives, hiding even from the Majdas and their ISC tech. Apparently I hadn't succeeded as well as I thought.

You did succeed.

Not in hiding from you.

No, not from me. She watched me, her eyes such a deep shade of green, they reminded me of the trees in the deepest forest. **Major, do you know how my nephew and I create the Kyle mesh?**

No, actually, I don't.

We use command stations called Locks. That's why people call us Keys.

That actually sounded pretty simple. *So a Lock is basically a machine.*

It's a space-time singularity.

Okay, maybe not so simple.

To become part of the Dyad, she continued, *I used that singularity to access the Kyle. So did my nephew, Imperator Skolia.*

Oh. I had no clue how that might work.

She spoke dryly. *Neither do we. The Locks are thousands of years old. We believe the command stations that support them have intelligence and merely tolerate our presence.*

Why are you telling me this? My head was beginning to hurt.

The ruins in the Undercity are also ancient. Her voice had become more distant. *The cyber-riders draw on them.*

I stiffened. *I have no idea what you mean.*

Yes, you do. Before I could deny it, she added, *Just before Calaj killed Ganz, she and I connected through the Kyle, I don't know how. What if she similarly gains access to the cyber-riders and their tech, or to ancient technology they may have found and learned to use in the ruins? I don't know what damage she could inflict, and I don't want to find out.*

Of all the responses I expected, that wasn't one. Shit. She had a good point. Gods only knew what a murderous Jagernaut could do with the more exotic tech our riders created. I needed to focus, but my head was throbbing with pain now, almost unbearable.

Do you think that's why she came to Raylicon? I managed to ask.

I don't know.

I didn't see how a fighter pilot with no previous connection to Raylicon could know about the riders. No one in Cries did, not even after my people had come for the Kyle testing. The riders had looked like a raggedy collection of punks with salvaged prosthetics. The medics examined them for Kyle traits, not biomechanics.

The bench and trees wavered, then reformed. I struggled to concentrate. *If these riders exist, I doubt an offworlder could know about them.*

It does seem unlikely. She exhaled, a virtual gust of air that created a faint mist in the air. *But I wouldn't have thought Calaj and I could link in Kyle space, either. Until I understand why, I can't dismiss any possibility.*

It was a sobering thought. Yet she hadn't told me to turn in the riders, stop them, or do anything else the authorities in Cries would've demanded, had they known about the riders. This pharaoh kept confounding my expectations.

You think—Calaj in aqueducts? I was slipping into dialect. My head felt ready to explode.

I can't find her. Her voice was fading. ***When she killed Ganz . . . our link shattered . . . I felt him die . . . couldn't bear it . . .***

I groaned and lost my grip on the scene. The world fractured, all pain and searing light—

"—get a doctor, now!" Lavinda shouted.

I opened my eyes to see a trio of faces, Colonel Majda, Lieutenant Casestar, and an aide, all leaning over me, all looking far too worried.

"What the fuck?" I muttered. It felt like a hammer kept hitting my head.

Lavinda spoke dryly. "I think she's back."

"Back from where?" I asked. It hurt to talk.

She sat in a chair next to me. "Good question. What happened?"

I rubbed my temples. "The simulation wasn't set right."

Lieutenant Casestar frowned. "What simulation?"

"The VR session." I tried to unfasten my exoskeleton. "Damn thing gave me a headache."

"What VR session?" Lavinda asked. "We never started it."

That couldn't be right. "Yah. You did. I was in for at least twenty minutes."

"It's been less than two minutes since you sat down," Casestar told me.

"That's impossible." I pulled open the exoskeleton and sat forward as it retracted from my body. "I've been talking to the pharaoh."

"You couldn't have talked to her," Lavinda said. "We hadn't connected you yet."

"Colonel." Casestar had his hand up to the comm in his ear. "We're receiving a message from Pharaoh Dyhianna."

Lavinda glanced at him. "Go ahead."

"She wants to know if Major Bhaajan is all right."

"I'm fine." My headache had begun to subside.

Casestar listened, then said, "Major Bhaajan, the pharaoh thanks you for the session."

"Uh, okay." I wasn't used to powerful people saying thank you. "Tell her the same."

"This makes no sense," Lavinda said.

"Hell if I know what happened," I muttered.

Fate apparently didn't feel I had enough people telling me I was crazy, because the doctor who had treated Duane earlier today chose this moment to arrive. She came up behind Lavinda and stood frowning at me. "Are you the patient this time?" she demanded, all business.

"No, I'm not," I said.

"Yes, you are." Lavinda stood up and spoke to the doctor. "Something happened before we started the sim. She sat for about two minutes, then groaned. Then she started to convulse."

What the blazes? I rose to my feet. "I had a convulsion?"

"A bad one," Lavinda said.

The doctor scanned me with a handheld sensor. "Your heart rate and blood pressure are elevated. I need you to sit down so I can examine you properly."

"I'm fine." I had never liked being poked by doctors, and right now I just wanted to leave.

She scowled at me. "What is it with all my patients today? Stop arguing about how fine you are and sit the hell down."

I blinked at her. Apparently the legendary Majda restraint didn't extend to their doctors. I sat the hell down and let her get started.

The lift to my penthouse whirred as it whisked me to my penthouse. The gold walls and soft light usually soothed me, but today I felt too agitated to stand still. I had to make myself rest, though; if I had another convulsion, I couldn't do my job. Convincing the doctor to release me hadn't been easy, but finally she let me go home. No one could figure out what happened. I'd been in that chair less than two flipping minutes. How? Pharaoh Dyhianna and I had talked a lot longer than two minutes.

Except—did we actually talk? The interaction had felt surreal, all that mist and trees. Even a strong telepath couldn't hold a mental conversation with someone who had no Kyle ability. I might possess some latent talent, but not enough for what we had done, besides which, psions couldn't manage that kind of link without training, neurological enhancement, and a direct link into a console. I rubbed my eyes. This much was certain: the pharaoh knew about the riders, which probably meant Majda would soon know as well.

No, wait. No record existed of my meeting with the pharaoh. The techs insisted the session never happened. Had she set it up that way? I'd learned at a young age to read people; survival in the aqueducts demanded that skill. I didn't think she'd told anyone what we discussed. No one else even seemed convinced I met with her. Maybe she intended to let me keep the riders a secret. I could hope, anyway.

"Interesting," I told my reflection in the mirrors that paneled the upper half of the lift walls.

The lift didn't answer. It did stop rising, though, and the doors opened into my penthouse.

As I entered the spacious living room, my house EI spoke. "You have a message waiting."

"Who is it?" I asked. The doors closed behind me.

"Doctor Karz. She wants you to page her as soon as you get home."

I walked down the three steps into the sunken living room. "Who is Doctor Karz?"

"Apparently she treated you earlier today."

"Oh. That one." So her name was Karz. I didn't want to deal with anyone right now. If I didn't respond, though, she might send someone to check on me. "Send her a page."

"Done. Do you want the rest of your messages?"

"I have more?" Most of my friends were in the Undercity, not Cries.

"A woman named Tanzia Harjan."

Odd. Tanzia was a volunteer at the Rec Center who had helped us do the Kyle tests last year. "Play her message."

A voice rose into the air, young, cheerful, way too full of energy. "My greetings, Major Bhaajan. I'm following up on our discussion about a tykado tournament at the Rec Center. I'd love to see what we can do."

Oh. Yah. I'd forgotten. I should do something, since the whisper mill had probably spread Duane's comments about a sports meet across the entire Undercity. The Dust Knights might even agree to a tournament that let them kick and punch at rich kids from Cries. I doubted I could get any Cries tykado academy to agree, but what the hell. It was worth a try.

"Send her a message," I said. "Tell her I can come by Center tomorrow, two hours after second sleep."

"Sent. I have Doctor Karz on comm. Shall I put her through?"

"Go ahead." I might as well get this over with.

The voice of the Majda doctor rose into the air. "How are you feeling?"

"I'm fine." Which was true, except for me wanting to collapse into bed.

"I've finished analyzing your test results."

"I thought you already did that." It was why she let me go home; they found no problems.

"We ran some extra checks," she said, as brusque as always. "I've discovered an anomaly."

Damn. I didn't have time to be sick. "What's wrong?"

"Nothing. We just didn't expect to find psiamine in your neural work up."

I squinted at no one in particular. "Could you repeat that?"

"Psiamine. We found it in your brain."

"How? I don't have the paras that produce it."

"We don't know that for certain."

I went over to the couch and sunk down into its gloriously comfortable cushions. "Check my military records."

"I did," she said. "Your testers never checked for them."

"What? Sure they did."

"Why would they? The basic test for them is the existence of psiamine, not the reverse. That your tests didn't show any psiamine could just mean you hadn't learned to use your paras. They don't look much different from other neural structures. You need extra tests to verify their existence."

"Oh." I didn't want to hear this. "Are you saying I experienced some sort of Kyle link with the Ruby Pharaoh?"

"It would explain why you think you met with her."

"It seems unlikely."

"Yes, it does." She let out an audible breath. "You only have traces of psiamine, barely enough to explain your heightened ability to judge the emotional states of other people."

For flaming sake. "I don't need extra chemicals in my brain to read people."

"Well, no. But you have them. You might also have a slight precognitive ability."

"That's nuts." I closed my eyes, put my head back, and stretched out my legs. "I can't tell the future. What would that even have to do with brain waves?"

"It's simple, really. Just quantum mechanics."

"Yah, right." My head was starting to hurt again.

"An uncertainty exists in the time and energy of a system," she said. "We can't know both exactly. For humans, that uncertainty is so tiny, we almost never notice it."

"Amazing," I said dryly. "I can look a fraction of a fraction of a fraction of an instant into the future."

She gave a wry laugh. "That pretty much sums it up."

"It's not precognition."

"For most people, no. But a probability exists that every now and then, the uncertainty will be more pronounced for an instant or so. Have you ever experienced déjà vu, the sense you've done something before?"

"I guess so."

"It may be because you did actually foresee that moment an instant before it occurred."

I rubbed my temples. "That happens to a lot of people."

"Yes, and for most it doesn't amount to anything significant. But some Kyle operators, on rare occasions, may have a momentary flash of a more distant future."

"I never do." I wished I did; I'd go bet in Jak's casino.

"Even if you did, it wouldn't account for what happened with you and the pharaoh." In a musing tone, Karz added, "Though no one really knows the full extent of what she can do."

No kidding. "Am I in danger from this psiamine cruising around my brain?"

"No, it won't harm you."

"Good."

"Yes. Good." She sounded as if she had more to say.

I sat there, caught between wanting to end the conversation and asking what else was up.

Karz made the decision for me. "Captain Ebersole is awake."

"How is he?"

"Much better." She paused. "He told us how you two survived the cartel attack in the slum."

So much was wrong with that statement, I hardly knew where to start. "It wasn't a cartel attack. It was one person who didn't like cops coming into the Undercity." *City.* Not slum.

"The captain claims a member of the Vakaar cartel assassinated your attacker."

I thought of Dark Singer. "She didn't 'assassinate' anyone. She saved our lives."

"She needs to come into the police station and give a report."

Yah, right. Good luck with that. "If I see her, I'll let her know."

"Can you give us her contact information?"

I didn't know whether to laugh or groan. "No."

Karz didn't push it. Instead, she said, "Seeing someone die that way, blasted apart, would shake up anyone. If you need to talk, I'm here."

"I'm fine."

"Yes, I know, you're fine, Captain Ebersole is fine, the Majdas are always fine. You people could be dying, and you'd still be telling me you were fine after I signed your death certificate."

I couldn't help but smile. "That'd be quite a feat on our part."

"Just don't be too proud to ask for help, all right?"

I could see why the Majdas employed this doctor, besides her being good at her job. She didn't take jack from anyone. "All right."

"Good. Come in tomorrow for a check up."

"I will." Right now, I'd agree to almost anything to escape.

"See you then. Out."

"Out," I said.

Then I went to bed.

The Down-deep lay below the aqueducts. I walked its tunnels in a darkness that felt thick. Whatever purpose these buried ruins had once served, nothing remained now but an ancient labyrinth saturated with the passage of time, as if the millennia left ever-thickening deposits of darkness.

I had been born here. In my youth, I assumed no one lived below the aqueducts, but that made no sense, because someone had found me here, a squalling newborn crying for her mother in the darkness. They took me up, above-city, to the Cries orphanage. Why they hadn't found me a home in the aqueducts, instead of stranding me in that forsaken place, I'd never know. They left me behind the building, at the door, with a message tucked into my swaddling: *Parents dead. Bhaaj's jan.*

Jan. Daughter. That was my sole legacy, that a woman named Bhaaj gave me birth. I'd lived in that blighted orphanage for three years before I escaped with an older child. Dig. The cops had caught her stealing on the Concourse and put her in the orphanage when she wouldn't talk to them. She ran away and took me with her, back to the Undercity. She became my family, along with Jak and Gourd, the four of us ranging in age from three to six. Supposedly we lived with Dig's mother, a ruthless crime boss too busy with a drug empire to bother with us. We did what we wanted, and the Kajada cartel looked the other way when we raided their stores for food. I didn't think Dig ever forgave her mother for leaving her in the orphanage instead of coming for her, a test to see if she was strong enough to get home on her own. Dig swore she'd never do the same to her own kids. However else anyone might condemn Dig Kajada for the many sins she committed as an adult, she loved her children in a way her mother would never have even understood, let alone shown her daughter.

I knew nothing about my blood family other than vague tales of how some unknown person found me wailing next to my mother's body down here. No one knew anything else. For decades I shut away my thoughts about the deep. Last year that all changed. A father and daughter from the deep had ventured into the aqueducts, the first in decades to come from so far down. They'd heard whispers of the Dust Knights and wanted to join. They even went to the Rec Center for Kyle testing, daring to enter a world so bright, they needed shades for their eyes and salves to protect their skin, which over the ages had paled until it almost seemed translucent.

Self-imposed natural selection, the doctors had said, whatever that meant. *Their eyes are adapted to the dark. To live in normal light, they will need surgery to fix their vision.*

The deepers had no interest in being "fixed." They ate their free meal, drank their free water, did the Kyle tests, and went home. In the process, they pulverized the statistics for Kyle abilities in humans, even more than the general Undercity population. Of the twelve Down-deepers who took the tests, all were psions, including three telepaths.

Too few came for the testers to know if they represented the entire population in the deep, but those stats didn't surprise me. Their ancestors had withdrawn to that isolated realm for a reason.

Why had I been born here? I obviously wasn't from the Down-deep. I had dark eyes and black hair like everyone else in the Undercity, and skin as dark as the wealthiest aristocrat in Cries.

In the army, I'd searched for some trace of my parents. Even ISC, with its endless files, had no DNA records that matched mine enough for a relative. I descended from a people isolated for so long, our history wasn't part of the known Skolian gene pool. Maybe if I hadn't been so busy repressing my thoughts of the Down-Deep as a child, I might have come here and found some clues to my origins. In retrospect, what had that all been about, anyway, my denial that this place existed? It made no sense to my adult self. It was too late now, probably decades too late, to find those clues, but I couldn't ignore the deep any longer.

I sat on a stump of rock. The chilly air smelled dry. Desiccated. The darkness felt suffocating with the weight of the millennia that had accumulated in this place, a metaphor that made utterly no sense if I thought too hard about it, but never mind. It felt that way.

After a while, Max thought, Why are we here?

I'm waiting, I answered.

For what?

Whatever comes.

This is boring.

I'm brooding. That's not boring.

Why are you brooding in the dark?

Because there's no light.

Funny. He didn't sound amused. Turn on a lamp.

I didn't answer. He knew no one would come if I turned on a lamp. I felt drained even after sleeping ten hours last night, besides which, I didn't know what I was expecting, either. So I sat.

A scratch came to my left—and a brilliant light flared, blinding me.

"Ah!" I put up one hand, protecting my eyes, and whipped up my revolver with the other.

"Going to shoot me, Bhaaj?" a woman asked in a gravelly voice.

"Singer?" I lowered my gun. As my eyes adjusted, I realized she hadn't turned on a flood lamp, she had just lit a smoke stick with a tiny spark, which had gone out. Now only the stick's glowing red tip showed in the darkness. I recognized her voice, though.

"Why you here?" I asked.

"You. Said you wanted to talk to me."

"How'd you find me?"

"Got ways."

No doubt. Who knew what network she'd developed in her profession. Former profession. I hoped. We sat while she smoked her stick. With Singer, I had learned never to push. We would talk about why I wanted to see her when she felt like it, and not before.

"That shit will ruin your throat," I eventually said.

"Throat is fine."

"Good." Given her raspy voice, I doubted it, but I wasn't going to argue with an assassin.

"Why you sitting in the dark?" she asked.

"Waiting."

"For what?"

She was as bad as Max. "For the world to implode," I grumbled.

"Sounds noisy." The tip of her stick glowed red.

"Don't want noise." I wished I didn't feel so tired. "Need to hear whispers."

"Whispers about the dark?"

"Yah. Down-deep."

"I hear a lot of whispers," she commented. "Most don't mean squat. Just people pissing."

"Singer, suppose you had to hide from everyone. Come here?"

"Maybe. Why?"

"Need to find someone."

"Who?"

"Like you, but the reverse."

"Not making sense, Bhaaj."

"You used to assassinate. Now you defend." That distinction separated a killer from a soldier.

"You got a patriot who turned into an assassin?"

"Yah." Essentially.

Her stick glowed as she took another drag. "Why you care?"

"Majda hired me to find her."

"Majda? Why?"

"She's a Jagernaut."

"That supposed to be a joke?"

Sure, I was a real comedian today. "Not a joke."

"Huh. Interesting."

From Singer, that was the equivalent of an impassioned outburst. "Fatal, too," I said.

"Why'd you come here?"

"Heard a whisper. Singer is here."

"Haven't heard."

If Jak hadn't told me, I wouldn't have known, either. "Would you hide here?"

"Depends. Who'd she sing for?"

"Herself." As far as we knew, no one had hired or ordered Calaj to commit murder. That didn't mean it hadn't happened, just that we didn't know. "Maybe others."

"Why'd she start singing?"

"If the brass-buttons knew, wouldn't need me."

"You got strange jobs, Bhaaj."

I couldn't help but laugh. "True."

Her smoke stick glowed. "See, this is the thing. Coming here, in the dark, sure, hiding is easier. So yah, smart move. But if she has to sing, can't stay here." Her voice rasped. "It drives you."

I couldn't imagine what demons ruled Singer's life. I knew nothing about her except that she used to kill people for her living. That, and one other thing. She had a baby. A genuine gurgling, yelling, cooing, crapping *baby*. A little child that turned Singer, the worst assassin in recent history, into a mother. No one knew about the baby until that day Singer walked to the Rec Center to take the Kyle tests, not for herself, but for her kid. Maybe she wanted to change for her daughter. Then again, maybe she wanted to take over the damn cartel and turn it into an empire for her kid to inherit.

"Drives you how?" I was asking as much now about Singer as about Calaj.

"To hide." The red end of her smoke stick moved downward and disappeared as she put it out. "Against the darkness. You try to make walls. To stop it."

"You mean walls inside the Undercity?"

"Nahya. Inside your head."

I got that. She barricaded herself against the emotions of others. She'd worked for the cartel, the ugliest side of the Undercity. Their dark moods must have saturated her empath's mind. Maybe she had sought out the Dust Knights to surround herself with something lighter.

"Walls good?" I asked.

"Sometimes." Rustles came from her direction, the sound of clothes crinkling. She was standing up. "Build them right, they work. Build them wrong, you get sicker."

I rose to my feet. "Sicker how?"

"In the mind." She sounded as if she were moving away. "You can't see. You get—hard."

"Singer, listen." I spoke quickly. "The testers, the ones at the Rec Center, they can teach how to build good walls. Protect yourself."

"I protect myself fine." She sounded like she had stopped moving. "Bhaaj, *you* listen. This Jagernaut singer, she's probably got damaged walls. Won't stay here. She'll seek light."

"Where?" Maybe I was looking at this wrong. Calaj might have sought out the Ruby Pharaoh because she was desperate for the light of Dyhianna Selei's mind.

"Don't know where," Singer said. "You figure it out."

She walked away then, leaving me alone in the silence. That was the longest conversation we'd ever had. If Singer was right, Calaj wouldn't stay here. I needed to talk to a deeper, a person who lived here. My sitting in the dark had brought Singer instead, but the deepers must know I was here, if not before Singer showed up, then surely after Vakaar's notorious assassin invaded their realm.

Max, I thought. *Activate my IR. I'm going for a walk.*

The world appeared, a ghostly cave lit by a faint red glow.

I exited the cave on the side opposite from where I had entered. I walked between two ancient columns encrusted with minerals. No weather had ever eroded them, no sun baked the stone, no wind worked its damage. They survived the millennia with nothing but mineral-laden water dripping on their engravings. I brushed my palm over one, tracing the figure of a lizard in flight, its wingspan so large, it wrapped about the pole.

Max, have you ever wondered about dragons? I asked.

No, it has never occurred to me to wonder about dragons.

I smiled as I walked. *Maybe the myths of dragons on Earth come from the flying lizards on Raylicon.*

I don't see how. Far more likely, the myths come from the fossil records of their flying dinosaurs.

I suppose. I followed a tunnel beyond the pillars. *They're native to Earth, right? The dinosaurs, I mean.*

Yes, Earth is their world of origin.

Home. I felt cold despite my climate-controlled clothes. *We're the lost children of Earth. Why? Is it possible Raylicon was our true home?*

The evidence that humanity originated on Earth is overwhelming.

What if someone directed human development? Maybe they brought my ancestors here to see how we turned out.

I have no idea. You should ask an anthropologist.

I did. Doctor Orin at the university in Cries. He studied the aqueducts. Orin would have loved the ruins down here. In my youth, he'd given me food in return for my acting as his guide in the aqueducts. My gang protected him, so no one tried to off him while he dug around. I'd never brought him this deep, though. I'd been too busy avoiding my repressed grief about the family I'd never know.

I ran my hand along the wall. *Orin wondered about the size of the aqueducts. They're so big. Maybe whoever built them was larger than us.*

I thought your ancestors built the Undercity.

That's the accepted theory. He wasn't convinced, though.

They are certainly the strangest "aqueducts" I've ever seen. Their logic escapes me.

You and the rest of humanity. He summed up my feelings well, which probably wasn't coincidence given that he had evolved as my personal EI for over a decade.

Someone is following us, Max thought.

I stopped. Silence settled over the tunnel, an absence of sound even greater than in the desert. That silence was full of air and light; here, it pressed on you.

A stone clattered.

Up ahead, Max thought.

Got it. I headed toward the sound.

The tunnel ended at a room unlike anything in the aqueducts. Space opened before me, a chamber about thirty paces across, its floor swept clear of debris. Whoever lived here tended the chamber well; no mineral drips had accreted here into jagged rock formations. I could just make out a domed ceiling far overhead. In my IR vision, it all looked blurred, too cold to register much. Without the climate control in my clothes, the freezing air would have driven me to higher, warmer regions.

Light flared, and I spun toward it, my gun drawn. A person blazed in an archway, his body white-gold with heat. I stood with my weapon out and aimed while my mind did a fast appraisal of his potential threat. He had no weapons I could see or that Max detected. Despite the icy air, he wore only trousers and a ragged, sleeveless shirt. If the cold bothered him, he gave no sign. My internal sensors registered his body temperature as a few degrees cooler than normal.

I lowered my gun. "Eh," I said, by way of greeting.

He spoke in an accent heavy even for the Undercity. "The Bhaaj."

"Yah." I'd never figured out why people added "The" in front of my name, but we never asked about names in the aqueducts, so I'd given up trying to stop that particular meme.

"Why here?" he asked. "Why bring singer?"

I didn't want them to think I was inviting assassins to prowl their territory. "She heard I wanted to talk to her. Came to find me. Talked. Left."

"And you?"

"Looking for an intruder."

"Why?"

"Killer," I said. "Not Undercity."

"Above-city?" He sounded skeptical.

"More than above-city. Offworld."

Silence. He probably didn't believe me. I didn't blame him. I hardly believed me.

"Who kill?" he asked.

"Political aide."

"What mean, 'political aide'?"

"Helper to offworld boss."

"And the killer? She's a cyber-rider?"

Ho! Where had that come from? Riders were our least violent population. Sure, they could get into trouble with the best of us, but they found their tech far more interesting than gang rumbles.

"Jagernaut," I said.

"What is Jagernaut?"

Good gods. They were even more isolated than I realized. "Like a rider, but military."

"Fighter."

"Yah." At least he recognized the word "military." If the deepers battled among themselves, we never heard about it in the whisper mill. What did they do here? Live, I supposed. How they managed, I had no idea. Undercity farmers could grow small amounts of food, genetically altering the plant proteins so they survived in the darkness and aridity of the aqueducts, but it wasn't easy and the crops never thrived. This deep down, finding food and drinkable water had to be even more difficult.

"Got proposal," I said. It was how we took care of business. Never accept charity, never give away information, but you could always propose a bargain.

"Tell," he said.

A good sign. He could have refused. I holstered my gun and slipped off my backpack. In addition to my shroud, it carried another vital resource—bottles of fresh water.

I pulled out a bottle. "Got three snaps. Filtered."

He drew in an audible breath. "Maybe interested. What bargain?"

"I need whispers. Buzz about the Jagernaut."

He came closer, until I could see him better. His eyes were huge. His skin seemed different, though I couldn't figure out why.

Max, turn off my IR.

The red light vanished—and the man before me remained visible, his skin glowing with ghostly blue light. Bioluminescence. It was faint enough that in regular light, it wouldn't show.

I handed him the snap bottle. "Give water. Get whispers."

He looked at the bottle, at me, at the bottle. Then he said, "Got some whispers to give."

I nodded. "Drink."

He snapped open the bottle. His throat worked as he gulped down the water. When he had finished about a third of it, he made himself stop. Then he nodded. Our bargain was sealed.

"Come with," he said.

I went with him, headed deeper into his realm.

✣ ✣ ✣

Bioluminescence. It was the emission of light by an organism. My biology teacher in officer candidate school had talked about fireflies on Earth, how they glowed at sunset, lighting the dusk in their search for a mate. Bug romance. Bioluminescence showed up in the deep sea, in caves, in the darkness of worlds forever facing away from a star. Without IR, I saw that eerie light everywhere in the Down-deep. Lines along the tunnel walls glowed in abstract swirls and the tips of stalactites lit up the darkness. Specks on the ground came and went in an ephemeral glitter.

Eventually we reached another vaulted chamber. More people waited for us. How they knew we were coming, I had no idea, because the man with me had never contacted anyone, at least not using any tech I recognized. Yet six people stood in the chamber, all visible by the glow of their bodies. I couldn't tell if the light came from their skin or their clothes. Whatever produced the effect, it couldn't be normal bioluminescent algae given the scarcity of water here.

My guide stopped in front of a woman at the center of the group. As they considered each other in silence, I waited.

The woman turned, regarding me with her large eyes. Her pupils were so big, they looked like dark pools. "You come from up-under?" she asked.

"Up-under?" I asked.

My guide spoke. "Aqueducts."

Ah. Clever name. "Yah," I said. "Looking for a singer."

The woman frowned at me. "Brought a singer."

"Not that one. Offworld singer."

They looked around at each other. After several moments of communing, or whatever they were doing, the woman turned her otherworldly gaze back to me. "We feel her."

"The offworlder?" I asked.

"Yah." She tapped her temple. "Pressure."

If they felt her with their minds, that meant Calaj was close enough that the EM fields of her brain could interact with theirs. Too damn close.

"Seen her?" I asked.

My guide answered. "Nahya. Only feel. Heavy."

Heavy. Not good. Down-deepers had a mental sensitivity greater even than other psions. Calaj could injure these people mentally as well as physically. "Brings harm?" I asked.

The woman shrugged. "Her pressure comes, we go."

"Go where?"

"Elsewhere."

Well, that was helpful. I tried again. "Take me to her?"

"Dangerous."

I wanted to say I could take care of myself, no problems. Calaj, however, was no drug punker or gang duster. I doubted I could best a Jagernaut. "Just take me closer. I'll be a whisper."

The deepers considered each other, doing that communing thing. I felt a pressure on my mind. *Stop it,* I told myself. *You're imagining it because of what they said about Calaj.*

Maybe not, Max thought. Apparently you do have psiamine in your brain. You may be feeling their mental communication.

Stop eavesdropping. Maybe that was why Calaj went wacko. Gods only knew what had happened to the EI in her spinal node, and she was stuck with it in her brain, unlike my gauntlets, which I could take off anytime.

Actually, Max thought, her node would have alerted ISC if she exhibited any hint of mental instability. Then he added, And I can't help but hear when you shout your thoughts.

Yah, I know. Sorry, Max. No insult intended.

You are right, though, that she can't take off her node even if it's damaged.

That kind of damage would set off alarms the instant she jacked into any ISC mesh. It didn't.

The deepers finished their communication, and the woman turned back to me. The pressure on my brain increased. "Stop," I said. "Hurts."

"You make interference," the woman told me.

I rubbed my temple. "What?"

"Your signal interferes with ours." She tapped her head. "Here."

"Oh. Sorry." I had no idea what she meant.

She nodded, accepting my response. "Come with. To the singer."

VI

RIVER OF THE AGES

Calaj found us first.

We were following a tunnel lit by ghostly blue and white tracings on the walls. Two deepers accompanied me, my guide and the woman who acted as their leader. I had no doubt others were following us as well, hidden and adept, but I caught no hint of their passage even when Max cranked up my hearing.

I heard Calaj, however, an instant before she fired. I threw my body at the deepers, slamming into them both as a jumbler shot passed just above our heads. We crashed to the ground while the wall behind us exploded in a flash of orange light. A loud crack came from my arm.

Your left wrist is broken, Max thought.

I rolled over fast, putting my body in front of the deepers as I fired in the direction of the jumbler shot. I felt no pain in my wrist, not yet, but my left hand wasn't responding. I ignored it. I had to protect these people. A jumbler fired abitons, the antiparticle of a biton, a wimpy little thing almost impossible to isolate. The annihilations of abitons and bitons created orange light, unlike the killing energies of most particles. But bitons were part of electrons, and all matter contained electrons, which meant a jumbler shot disintegrated whatever it hit. Only Jagernauts could legally carry them. The military tuned the gun to their brain waves, so no one could fire the weapon but its owner.

Silence descended, broken only by the clatter of stones falling from the wall behind us. Damn. I hoped no deepers had been behind that barrier. The dusty smell of pulverized rock saturated the air. I strained to hear our attacker, but even my hypersensitized senses picked up nothing. The jumbler flash had burned away the swirls of light on the wall, leaving only the barest trace of luminance.

I climbed to my feet. "Are you two all right?" I had no name for either of them.

"Fine." The man stood up, shaking out his clothes, his motions barely visible in the dim light.

The woman stood up with us. "Heard a bone break."

"My wrist," I said. It was starting to hurt. *Max, have my meds release painkillers.*

Already done, he answered. They're tending the injury, but they can't set bone.

"Got healer?" I asked the deepers.

"Yah." The woman looked around the tunnel. "Got to leave here. Might collapse."

Good point. The jumbler shot had weakened the walls. *Max, crank up—*

IR activated, he answered. Red light suddenly bathed the tunnel, especially around the broken wall, where broken rocks were still trickling into piles of debris on the tunnel floor.

I blinked, startled as much by how he always knew what I wanted as by the sudden light. The jumbler shot had left a gaping hole in the tunnel wall only a few steps away from us. Mercifully I saw no bodies beyond it. On this side, the man and woman stood together, their clothes crumpled, their faces strained. I held my broken wrist against my body.

The woman motioned in the direction we had been walking. "We go."

I nodded and followed them down the tunnel, bringing up the rear. If Calaj attacked again, she'd have to go through me to reach the deepers.

No shots came. Had I hit Calaj? I could move fast, sure, but a Jagernaut was faster, assuming her biomech web hadn't malfunctioned. I could always hope.

"Why she shoot?" my guide asked. He sounded calm, but his voice cracked on the last word.

"Recognized me, maybe." How, I didn't know, since Calaj had no access to the whisper mill, which was purely word of mouth. It involved no tech. She couldn't get anything about me from the Cries mesh, either, because no one there knew what I did down here.

"This happen before?" I asked. "Singer shoot at you?"

"Nahya," the leader said. "Never."

Great, just great, my showing up got these people attacked. I felt like a slime-slug. "My sorry."

"No need." The woman pressed her fingers against her temples. "Too much pressure."

I still didn't understand what they meant by pressure. I had felt something before, when they were doing their communing thing, but it hardly seemed dangerous.

We soon reached a circular opening in the ground, the top of a stairwell that spiraled into darkness. Engravings showed on its top steps, symbols that resembled ancient Iotic, a language no one spoke any more. I recognized them because decades ago, Doctor Orin had been thrilled when I showed him an aqueduct engraved with similar symbols. *Ancient Iotic!* he told me, as if revealing a great find. Maybe it was; I had no idea. One glyph on these stairs resembled the head of a great lizard, a symbol of strength; another showed the intertwined thorns that represented connections. Power and networks. How much of our history lay buried here, known only to the deepers?

We went down the stairwell, essentially a chute with steps. I could almost feel the weight of the aqueducts above us. Claustrophobia had never bothered me before, but now sweat broke out on my forehead despite the cold air down here.

Finally we reached the bottom. We came out into a cavern supported by natural stone columns, row after row of them forming arched supports for the ceiling, like a cathedral. Swirls of light sparkled everywhere in artistic flourishes. People walked among the columns, their glowing skin difficult to distinguish from the artwork as they passed behind rock formations, then reappeared. Someone was playing a flute, filling the cavern with a haunting song. The melody curled through the air like a musical echo of the light, amplified by acoustics until its resonance filled the space. Such incomparable beauty. The people in Cries, even most of us in the aqueducts, we had no idea what lay so deep below us. I wondered if my mother had ever walked among these arches.

We walked across the cavern, and it glistened around us, green, blue, and gold like a sea grotto. The air chilled my face. Ice glistened on the rock formations, but not all the water froze; glittering drops fell from the stalactites and created a shimmering mist unlike anything in the aqueducts. The uncommon beauty was so mesmerizing, I almost forgot the pain in my wrist.

Our destination turned out to be a curtain of rock on the other side of the cavern. We walked past it into the Down-deeper version of a hospital infirmary. A woman lay on a slab of stone softened with blue carpets. Another woman, a healer it looked like, was offering her a drink from a stone cup. Several children sat on the floor around a low table, laughing as they played a game using colored pebbles. Like everyone else here, they had an ethereal beauty, with those giant eyes, straight noses, and high cheekbones. So much beauty, yes, but also so much pain. One of the girls had no left leg. The boy had an arm that ended at the elbow. The third child had uneven shoulders, one side a handspan lower than the other. Yet they played with such joy, it wrenched my supposedly cast-iron heart.

My guides took me to a chair carved out of the rock wall and set with cushions. I sat down gratefully, careful with my broken wrist. The healer glanced at us, then turned back to her patient. It was several minutes before she came over to us. She watched me with a wary gaze, her eyes like dark pools, the pupils enlarged and dilated to capture light. Her hair looked silver in the bioluminescent glow from the swirls on the walls.

"Who?" she asked.

The woman with me said, "Up-under. Came for the singer."

"Singer fired at us." The man indicated me. "Up-under protected. Snapped wrist."

The healer bent to study my wrist. Up close, I realized her hair was pale gold, a color unheard of among my people. The original human settlers on Raylicon had dark hair, skin, and eyes. Even if deepers had lived here for entire six thousand years since, that didn't seem long enough for genetic drift to alter their hair and skin so much. I understood now what the doctors meant by "self-imposed" selection. Their ancestors must have engineered their genome to better suit their environment.

The healer lifted my wrist, prodding it, and I gritted my teeth. That *hurt.*

She glanced at me. "Can give meds for pain."

"Nahya." I didn't want any drugs. I needed to be alert if Calaj showed up again, besides which, gods only knew what she would give me. Undercity medicine either came from the black market or some drug punker turned chemist. They could kill as easily as help.

They say pain is good for the soul, whoever "they" are, so my soul must have been in great shape by the time the healer finished. When she pushed the bones of my wrist into place, I nearly screamed. Mercifully, she worked fast; within minutes she had my wrist splinted and bandaged.

She tapped the back of my hand. "Not use."

"I ken," I gritted out.

She nodded, seeming satisfied, and with no more fanfare, returned to her other patient. She tried to coax the woman lying on the slab to drink more water, with no success.

The man followed my gaze to the other patient. "Dying," he said.

"My sorry," I murmured. I tilted my head toward the children. "And them?"

"Born that way. Many of us." He showed me the inside of his arm. Red and purple veins were faintly visible beneath the pale skin. "Skin too thin."

Gods. The aqueducts had a high rate of birth defects due to our inbred population, but nothing this extreme. "Above-city can help," I said.

They didn't even dismiss the idea, they just stared at me as if I spoke gibberish. My suggestion was too far outside their sphere of existence to make sense.

"Changelings help," the woman said.

"Changeling?" I asked.

"Mother Down-deep, father Undercity."

Now I saw. They widened their gene pool by taking lovers from among my people. "Why only father from above?"

"Up-under mother mostly goes back up with baby," the man said.

"Ah." My eyelids drooped closed. It had taken a long time to come this deep, and it would take even longer to return to the surface. I dreaded that trek. Maybe I should have listened to Doctor Karz and stayed in bed. At least I knew Karz's name. None of the Down-deepers had offered theirs, and I didn't insult them by asking.

"Up-under father goes back up, too," the main said. "Never knows about baby."

"Hmmm . . ." I tried to listen, but I was sinking deeper—

"Like for you," the woman added.

I snapped my eyes open. "What?"

"You," the woman repeated. "Down-deeper."

"Nahya." I touched my black hair. "Aqueducts."

The woman tapped my arm. "Down-deep."

Puzzled, I glanced down. My arms were my arms. They looked as they always—

Ah, hell. No. That couldn't be.

My skin was glowing.

"Stop!" My male guide strode at my side. "You must stop."

"You need rest," the woman told me. She kept pace as we crossed the cavern.

I kept going. The cathedral-like cavern felt even bigger than before, but I couldn't stop. How could my skin glow? It had never happened anywhere else. Something was affecting me here, and I had to get out before it turned me into I didn't know what. Something alien.

The woman grabbed my arm and yanked me to a stop. I almost rolled her over my hip and slammed her to the ground, but I managed to hold back my reflexes.

"Rest," she said. "Too far. You can't leave, not now. Later."

"Now." I pulled away my arm. "I'm fine."

"Not fine," the man said.

I scowled at him. "Got work to do."

"Insist?" the woman asked.

I crossed my arms, holding back my wince as pain shot through my wrist. "Insist."

She and the man regarded each other.

"Yah, so." The woman turned back to me. "Go shorter way."

I breathed out slowly, calming my adrenaline surge. This place was a maze. If they could show me a shorter route out than the way I came in, I would gladly follow their lead.

The chamber measured only ten paces across, and the base of a stairwell took up most of that room. The stairs spiraled up and around, out of sight. We'd gone even farther into the Down-deep, until the light on the walls faded. Our skin still glowed. It didn't seem to hurt the people here, but I had no idea how it might affect me.

"Stairs go to surface," the man said.

I nodded my thanks. "Good."

Neither of them looked happy. "Can't go with you," the woman said.

It didn't surprise me. The light on the surface would hurt their eyes. "It's fine."

"Not fine," the woman said. "It hurts to go this way."

"The light?"

"No. Pressure. On mind."

I tensed. "The Jagernaut?"

The man shook his head. "No. Older pressure. Pure."

"What means pure?" I asked.

"Ancient," the woman said. "Good. But it turns us back."

I had no clue what they meant. "It will turn me back?"

They looked at each other, then at me. They waited.

After several moments, I said, "What?"

They looked at each other. Again at me.

"No ken," I said.

The woman nodded as if I had answered a question. "It won't turn you back."

"Sure?" I asked.

"Mostly," she said.

Mostly? I didn't want to be mostly all right. Down here, mostly and lethal weren't that far apart. "Just stairs?" I asked. "No guards? No weapons?"

"Just stairs," she said. "Nothing else."

"Is trib," the man said. "For flowing."

It sounded like he meant the tributary for an underground river. Most bodies of water in the Undercity were contaminated. Poison. We had to filter our water to survive.

"River poison?" I asked.

"River of Ages," the man said.

"I'll be careful." I never drank unpurified water.

They seemed satisfied with this assurance.

I motioned at the stairwell. "Where come out?" From my estimate, it would let me out in the desert at quite a distance from Cries.

"Temple," the woman said.

"Izu Yaxlan?" I asked. That didn't seem right. Those ruins were in another direction.

"Nahya," the man said. "Temple alone."

Max, do you know what they're talking about? I asked.

No, he thought. According to the map I'm making, right now we're under open desert. I don't have much data on this region, however.

Why not? I had given him access to every known map of the world.

Probably because not much is up there. He paused. I'm having trouble with my positioning systems. A contaminant is filtering into your gauntlets. I'm not sure where we are.

Damn. I had to get out of here. *Will this staircase let me out close to Cries to walk home?*

Yes, you should manage, though it would be better if you weren't so worn out.

I regarded my two guides. "My thanks for your help."

They both nodded, looking like angelic ghosts, which made me wonder if this was a hallucination induced by whatever contaminant was bothering Max.

It's not a hallucination, Max thought. Yet. You should leave.

I started up the stairs.

Up and around.

Up and around.

It was like ascending a chute. My elbows bumped the walls, and I reminded myself I wasn't claustrophobic. Although my wrist ached and my head hurt, neither felt unbearable. It wouldn't have been so bad, except I had a long way to go.

Eventually I reached the first landing, a flat circle about one meter across tiled with stone mosaics. I leaned against the wall, resting. *Max, how long have I been climbing?*

About eight minutes.

It felt longer. I wanted to be *done*. My head throbbed.

I set off again, up and around. The stairwell narrowed until the walls scraped my shoulders. Whoever built this exit must have been smaller than modern Raylicans, which eliminated the Abaj but not my people. In the Undercity, we tended to be shorter than the citizens of

Cries. Poverty did that to you. The deepers seemed even smaller. My height came from a combination of genetics and a better diet than my peers. As much as I'd hated the orphanage where I spent the first three years of my life, with its cold halls and uncaring adults, I benefited from their healthy food. And for all that Dig struggled with her anger toward her mother, a relationship forged in the bitter furnace of the drug trade, the tainted wealth from the cartel kept her from starving, and she had always made sure Jak, Gourd, and I had enough to eat.

In our youth, I had assumed Dig would turn away from the cartel, given how much she hated it. Yet in the end she had taken over the Kajada cartel. Maybe she hadn't known any other way. Not so for her children; Dig refused to let them walk that path. She had arranged with a gentle family to take them in if she ever died, and the three youngest lived there now. Dig's eldest daughter had joined the military, only the second person after me in many generations.

I kept climbing.

Up and around.

Up and around.

I reached another landing and sagged against the wall, closing my eyes while I rubbed my temples. Gods, they *hurt*. The pain felt like a vise tightening around my head.

Max, how much farther? I asked.

If this stairwell goes straight up, I'd say you're about a third of the way out.

Only a third? I felt too tired to reach the top, but I'd gone too far to retreat. The hike back to the infirmary was even farther than to the top of these stairs. *Max, my head is killing me. Have my meds give me more pain killers.*

Done.

I started up the stairs again, moving more slowly now.

Up and around.

Up and around

I didn't even make the next landing before I had to stop again. I stood with my body braced between the walls, my forehead resting against the roughened stone, my eyes closed. *Max, how long until the medicine starts working?*

It should be working. He was doing one hell of a job simulating worry. If you couldn't tell an EI's simulated emotions from the real thing, how did you know they weren't real? I had no answer. I could barely think. My head blazed.

Bhaaj, something is wrong, Max thought.

No kidding. *Just . . . have to get out.* I climbed one more step, bracing my uninjured hand against the wall. Another step. Then I stood, unable to move, staring at the roughened walls.

After a moment, my beleaguered brain comprehended that the walls weren't "roughened." Engravings covered them, glyphs in ancient Iotic. They looked almost perfect, as if nothing had touched these walls for six thousand years. They named this stairwell River of the Ages. No, Corridor of Ages. No, that wasn't right, either. The stairs led to something called the Corridor of Ages.

I shook my head, then groaned as the pain spiked. I willed the agony to subside. It didn't cooperate, so with no other choice, I started up the stairs.

How far, I asked, miserable.

I think you're about halfway, Max thought.

To distract myself, I tried to read the Iotic symbols. "River," I muttered. "Corridor. Ages." I stopped. "Holy shit."

"For a deity, perhaps it's holy." Max sounded amused, but it was fake. He seemed scared.

"Do those words sound familiar?" I spoke out loud. It hurt too much to think to Max.

"Yes," he said dryly. "You cuss all the time."

"Not those." I forced myself to resume the climb. "The other words."

"River, corridor, path, ages? Yes, of course they sound familiar."

"No," I whispered. "They don't."

"They don't?"

"I was speaking Iotic."

"That wasn't Iotic."

"Yah, it is. Ancient Iotic." My fingernails scraped the engraved walls.

Silence. Then he said, "I thought you were speaking the Undercity dialect."

"I was." Gods almighty. "Max, it's ancient Iotic! Our dialect, it's a version of the language spoken by the people on Raylicon five thousand years ago."

"An intriguing discovery, if it's true."

I stopped and stared at the stairs, unable to move.

"You have to keep going," Max said.

"Yah," I muttered. "Crank up . . . my pain killers."

"Your meds are already producing the maximum dose"

I put my foot on the next step. Then my other foot. Next step. Other foot.

Up and around, one step at a time.

Another landing.

"Ah . . ." The groan tore out of me. Agony seared my head. My entire body ached. My IR vision had quit working. Darkness surrounded me.

"Bhaaj, keep going," Max urged. "You have to get out of here."

I felt my way up the stairwell, blind in the dark. I couldn't stop, or I'd die here, screaming in pain, buried under the desert. No one would find me. The deepers couldn't come . . . no one else knew . . .

Dying.

Head splitting.

I sank to my knees, my hands braced on the steps. It felt likes knives were stabbing my broken wrist.

"You can make it," Max said. "You must be close to the top."

I crawled up another step.

One more step.

Pain. Dying.

One more—

Barrier.

NO! I struck out blindly. A wall blocked the stairs. I banged my fist on it, and a hollow boom rang out. Couldn't go down, couldn't go up, dying, dying, dying . . .

Someone was calling me, saying my name over and over.

"Bhaaj, answer." Max kept speaking, calm on the surface, desperate underneath. "Bhaaj!"

"Yah," I whispered.

"The door must have a release mechanism. Find it."

"Can't move—" Even as I spoke, I swiped my uninjured hand over the wall, blindly. Don't stop, don't stop, don't stop—

I hit a heavy stone bar, horizontal, held against the wall by bands of metal. I pushed the bar—and with a grating scrape, it slid upward.

The door suddenly gave way. I fell forward and slammed onto a stone floor. Groaning, I rolled onto my back in the dark. This place felt different, large instead of confined.

"Did I make it?" I rasped.

"You're in a building," Max said. "I don't know where. I'm getting no city mesh signals."

I pressed my hands against my head, trying to push away the unbearable sensations.

Lights flooded the area. *Ah, no!* I covered my eyes and cried out. The pound of running feet made the stone floor vibrate. Closer, closer, the runner stopped nearby . . .

A deep voice spoke in modern Iotic. "Major Bhaajan?"

I opened my eyes the barest amount and saw the Uzan kneeling next to me, holding a torch in one hand. With a groan of relief, I released my hold on consciousness and passed out.

VII
TEMPLE OF THE ANCESTORS

Chimes. I lay with my eyes closed, listening. Glass tubes tapped together as if wind were blowing through them. The chiming shimmered, soft and delicate, like a poem of musical sounds. It reminded me of lying on the forest floor, listening to a stream gurgling over rocks.

Some time later, I opened my eyes. I wasn't anywhere near a forest or a stream, or even on a planet that claimed such luxuries. A large space surrounded me, suffused with dim light. I sat up with care, relieved to discover my headache had receded. I remembered the Uzan and a torch—

Ho! I was inside a pyramid. The ledge where I sat jutted out from the wall, its stone surface softened by a pallet of gold cushions. The ceiling sloped to a point many stories overhead. Around the edges of the large room, transparent columns rose by the walls, quietly humming machine sounds. Lights spiraled within them, reflecting off crystalline levers and ebony rods, and gears turned like the workings of an ancient, gigantic clock. A maze of shifting mirrors sparkled in one corner. Sunlight slanted through openings near the top of the structure, down to the mirrors, which gathered the light and sent it throughout the room. Against the far wall, a circular dais rose up several steps, yellow stone veined in gold. It supported three oblong boxes with statues of winged lizards perched at their corners. They looked like coffins. I hoped the Uzan hadn't thought I needed one.

Most of all, I noticed the *space*. Air filled the temple. The floor stretched out in an expanse of flagstones of bronze, amber, and gold stone. They fit together in a mosaic of concentric circles with abstract designs. Except no, they weren't abstract, they formed giant glyphs. I could read a few: that orb represented the sun, with a border of stars to indicate a day; the swirl of a sand devil combined with the symbol for sand falling down a cliff face, a double glyph that represented the passage of time.

Max, I thought. *You there?*

It's not like I could go anywhere, he answered.

I smiled. *I guess not.*

How are you?

A lot better. It looked like my skin had lost its faint glow, but I couldn't be sure given that the bioluminescence only showed in the dark. *How about you? Did you clean out your systems?*

Partially. I'm breaking down the contaminant to analyze its chemistry.

I think it's what made my skin glow. I motioned at the temple. *Do you recognize this place?*

I have no record of it in any of my files.

That's odd. It can't be that far from Cries. I stood up, then swayed as dizziness swept over me.

Across the temple, three figures appeared in an archway, Abaj warriors in dark robes with their hoods pushed back, each with a queue of jet black hair hanging down his back. As they walked toward me, their robes shifted, revealing their clothes, black trousers and dark shirts embroidered at the hems in gold, blue, and green threads. The archway had dwarfed them, but as they drew closer, their height became apparent, well over two meters. They looked identical. I knew to call the one in front the Uzan only because he wore a medallion with the insignia of Imperial Skolia, the stylized depiction of a star exploding past a circle.

When they reached me, I nodded to the Uzan and spoke in modern Iotic. "My honor at your presence." Quietly, I added, "Thank you for helping me."

He inclined his head. "Your appearance was—unexpected."

I motioned at the pyramid. "What is this place?"

"It is called the Temple at Tiqual. Or just Tiqual."

"Ah." I had never heard of the place. "How did you know I was here?"

"You triggered many alarms."

"Was I not supposed to use that stairwell?"

"No, you were not." His gaze remained impassive. "It leads to the Corridor of the Ages."

Corridor, river, I still didn't get it. "And that means—?"

"You don't recognize the phrase?" He considered me. They all did. It was eerie, all three of them identical, as if he had brought two living, breathing reflections of himself.

"No," I said. "I've never heard it before."

He spoke quietly. "Tiqual houses the third Lock. The singularity is at the end of the Corridor."

Holy freaking bugs. I sat down again.

The Uzan also sat on the ledge, far enough away that he didn't intrude on my personal space. His other two selves stepped back, giving this version privacy with me.

I took a breath. "Are you saying I crawled past the Lock?"

His gaze never wavered. "Yes."

"I should be dead." From what I understood, only a Ruby psion could use a Lock. Its power would tear apart anyone else's mind.

"You didn't enter the Lock," he said. "You only went by a passage that leads to it."

"I felt like my head was splitting open."

He frowned. "Who let you use those stairs? You're lucky you survived."

I didn't want to mention the Down-deepers. "I feel better now."

"We treated you for both the Kyle injury and the broken wrist."

I didn't want to talk about Kyle injuries, because if I had them, that made me a psion. So I lifted my hand instead, peering at my wrist. They had removed the splint and applied a sheath that blended with my skin so well, it looked and flexed like a stiff hand.

"Whoever set the bone did a good job," the Uzan said. "We've injected you with repair meds to help you knit. You should be able to use that hand in a day or two."

I lowered my arm. "I appreciate the care."

"How did you break it?"

I paused, but then decided to answer. "Dodging a jumbler shot from Calaj."

"You found her?"

"Actually, she found me. I didn't see her. She fired at us from the dark."

"Who is 'us'?"

He was certainly full of questions about things that weren't his business. I said nothing. I had long ago learned the value of silence, that it could prod people to say more than they intended. Unfortunately, it didn't work on the Uzan. He just sat, watching me back.

Finally I said, "I need to speak to the Ruby Pharaoh."

"You must use proper channels to request an audience."

I scowled at him. "You're the leader of her hereditary bodyguards. If anyone can reach her, you can." Hell, I was supposed to use proper channels to request an audience with *him*. If I kept showing up unannounced, the Abaj might decide to toss my sorry ass out of their territory for good.

"Why do you wish to see the pharaoh?" he asked.

"I can only tell her."

He spoke firmly. "You are no condition to see anyone."

I wished people would quit telling me that. "I feel fine."

"You aren't fine. You went into Kyle shock. It nearly killed you."

"Kyle what?" The question came out before I could stop myself.

He motioned toward the other side of the temple. "In close proximity to the Lock, psions can't take the neural stimulation created by the singularity. We go into neural overload. Some experience *grand mal* seizures or brain damage."

I fell back on what, until yesterday, I had believed my entire life. "I'm not a psion."

"You wouldn't have felt anything if you didn't have some ability."

I understood now, too late, what the deepers had tried to ask me: Was I a psion? They tried to reach my mind and waited for a sign that I knew they were knocking at my mental door. I hadn't responded because I hadn't felt anything I knew how to interpret, just a headache.

"ISC tested me." I felt so tired. "They said I had no Kyle rating." When he started to speak, I put up my hand to stop him. My mind fled his words like a lizard running from a dust gang. "I'm sorry. I mean no disrespect. But I must speak to the pharaoh." I couldn't tell him why. I couldn't tell anyone except Dyhianna Selei. What I had to say could get me thrown into prison.

✧ ✧ ✧

I lay down after the Uzan and his other two selves left, but I couldn't sleep. If he did get me a meeting with the pharaoh, it would be at the Majda palace. I wanted to be at my best when I faced her, which meant I should rest, if I could just turn off my mind. I kept thinking about Calaj. I'd known she meant to shoot an instant *before* it happened. That realization had saved my life and probably those of the deepers as well. It all kept coming back to my Kyle traits, which were becoming more and more difficult to deny.

Why do you care? Max asked.

I blinked. *What?*

Why don't you want to be an empath?

It makes you weak. Bitterly, I added, *It makes you feel.*

Your inability to face your emotions hampers your ability to solve this case.

I didn't want to know what it said about me, that my EI was more willing to face my emotions than I was. *Max, not now. I'm tired.*

Mercifully, he stopped. I opened my eyes and stared at the wall above me. The symbols carved into it bore no resemblance to Iotic, and they looked much older than the mosaic on the floor. No one knew the origin of the Locks. My ancestors had found three, this one on Raylicon, and two others in space stations drifting among the stars. The Locks affected people with Kyle organs in their brains. Did they have a connection to this puzzle of Calaj? The pieces didn't fit. Somehow she had linked with the pharaoh in Kyle space. She murdered Tavan Ganz, a well-liked young man with no connection to her. She fled to Raylicon, birthplace of the Imperialate. Goes Down-deep, bothers no one. I go down. Singer comes, talks, leaves. The deepers take me deeper. Calaj shoots at me. I shoot back. No more shots. Why not? My freaking skin starts to glow. I leave. Nearly die. Uzan and his copies help me. End of story. I wasn't seeing the big picture here.

Max, I thought. *Bring up my files on Daltana Calaj and Tavan Ganz.*

Which ones? ISC sent you both their work and personal records.

I had gone over their job files in so much detail, I practically had them memorized. Calaj had an exemplary record, highly honored with a distinguished list of medals. Ganz did his job well and never offended anyone. He came across as a well-adjusted, pleasant fellow. He hadn't seen his family in a while because they lived on the world Metropoli and he worked on Parthonia, the capital world of the Imperialate, but by all accounts he had a good relationship with them.

Calaj drank too much on leave, but so did many Jagernauts. Turning empaths into killers wasn't a recipe for happiness. Despite the popular media thrillers about Jagernauts going berserk, however, I didn't know any case where that had actually happened. They turned violence inward on themselves rather than attacking the people they were sworn to protect, especially someone like Ganz, who worked for the Assembly. The systems set up to protect Jagernauts would warn the J-Force doctors if even a hint of trouble manifested. Except Calaj's safeties had failed, every last one in a complex series of safeguards. Why?

Max, give me Calaj's personal files. She had a small family, two mothers, two fathers, and a sister, but ISC didn't have as much background on them as on Calaj. *Why two of each parent?*

After a pause, he thought, They were a Jag squadron. After they retired, they all married each other.

That's seriously weird.

Not really. The bond among squad pilots is exceptionally strong.

So Calaj grew up surrounded by empaths.

Yes, she and her sister are both psions. The sister became an artist. She creates holographic portraits. Apparently she is quite successful.

Does Calaj get along with her family?

Yes, it appears they have a strong bond.

Any indications of violence, cruelty, anything like that?

No, none.

So she had a normal life. At least, as normal as life could be for a psion. *Took after her parents and became a Jagernaut.*

She was promoted faster than normal.

Too fast, do you think?

Prior to this situation, she gave no sign that she couldn't handle the responsibilities.

Maybe I was looking at this from the wrong direction. *Did she have an unusually good relationship with her parents and sister? Were they closer, more affectionate than most?*

He paused. Yes, it does appear so. She once referred to them as her sanctuary.

For some reason that made me think of Jak, my crime-boss lover, which made no sense. Okay, maybe it did. The dust gang of my youth—Dig, Gourd, and especially Jak—we'd given each other an emotional refuge. We never spoke about it, never admitted the intensity of that bond. It just existed, a connection so strong, it had become part of us. Had Calaj come here seeking *refuge*? She wouldn't risk the family she loved after she committed murder. When she cracked, maybe she sought the deepers, a population with the greatest known density of psions, people like herself.

My theory had a gaping hole, however. How would she know they were all psions? Until last year, no one had documented that "little" fact, including the deepers themselves. Even now, no offworlder knew about their Kyle results except the highest of the high clinks in ISC. Calaj wasn't among that group. For psions to connect, their brain waves needed to interact, which meant they needed to be close to each other. No way could she have connected with the deepers from offworld.

I thought back to my conversation with the pharaoh about the cyber-riders. *Max, does Calaj have traits in common with the riders? Anything—personality, technical background, interests?*

She is a mesh engineer. Apparently her nickname is "tech-mech goddess."

Interesting. *Check her genetic profile. What can you tell me about her biological origins?*

She is a genetically modified human.

Yah, well, so were we all. My ancestors messed with their DNA to adapt to life on other worlds and widen their gene pool. *I wondered if she was pure Raylican. With all the tweaks our ancestors made to their genetics, few people are truly Raylican anymore.*

Except the Majdas, of course.

Right. Supposedly they were the purest Raylicans. Given that over the ages, many of them had married offworlders, we in the Undercity were probably more Raylican than the current crop of Majdas. Not that anyone would dare suggest a dust rat had a purer heritage than royalty. Couldn't have that. Now that ISC knew about the Kyle abilities of my people, they wanted to establish a genetic map for us, to figure out where our priceless genes came from—all this interest, after they had ignored us for, oh I didn't know, a little while, like thousands of years. Big surprise, they couldn't inspire any cooperation from my people.

Give me a moment to analyze Calaj's genetic profile, Max thought.

All right. I closed my eyes and wished I could sleep. I tried to find less provocative thoughts, like mentally listing the codes for machine parts in the waste removal manual of the Advanced Services Corps. Yah, that was exciting. I couldn't believe all the useless information I'd accumulated over the years.

I was almost asleep when Max suddenly thought, I have an answer.

I rubbed my eyes. *Yah?*

It took a lot of searching and involves deduction on my part.

You mean you guessed.

Yes. Secondary Calaj descends from the Down-deep population.

No shit.

Yes, shit.

I smiled. *How do you know?*

She has certain genetic markers that are rare even among psions. They showed up only in the deepers who came in for testing last year.

I stiffened. *How the hell would you know that?*

Calaj's genetic map is in her ISC files.

Hers, yes. Not the maps of those twelve Deepers who came for testing.

You have access to their maps.

Indeed I do. And I never put that secured information on your system.

I found it on the Majda system.

For flaming sake. Max was cracking Majda. In theory I approved of these powerhouse sleuthing abilities he was developing, but no damn way could I have my personal EI breaking into such highly secured systems. I was the one who would get arrested.

Cut it out, I told him. *No more breaking and entering.*

My apologies. He didn't sound the least bit remorseful.

Your emotive functions aren't working, I told him, irked.

According to my diagnostic updates, all of my functions work just fine.

Max.

This time he did put remorse into his response. I won't undertake such efforts in the future without your go-ahead.

Good.

The deeper genetic maps weren't the only ones I compared to Calaj's records.

Who else?

Yours.

I scowled. *Screw that.*

I don't think that's anatomically possible.

You aren't allowed to spy on me, either.

I'm practically inside your mind. Besides, I've always had your genetic map.

I couldn't actually remember if I had given it to him. It had never mattered. I didn't know why his observations put me on edge today. Okay, apparently I'd inherited some deeper DNA. So what? Max was right, I needed to get a grip on my inconvenient emotions.

How many generations back do you think Calaj's deeper heritage goes? I asked. It had to be a long time since her people had left Raylicon, given that no hint existed in her files about such origins. It wouldn't surprise me if her family had hidden that aspect of their heritage.

I would guess five generations, Max thought. Maybe more.

I closed my eyes. *I need to think.*

Someone touched my shoulder. Startled awake, I jumped up off the ledge, my fist swinging. Fortunately, I stopped myself in time, because otherwise I would have punched the Ruby Pharaoh.

Shit.

Dyhianna Selei had stepped back, but she stayed only a couple of paces away. I sat down slowly. "My greetings, Your Majesty," I managed, my voice thick with sleep.

She inclined her head. "Major."

Belatedly, I remembered I wasn't supposed to sit while she was standing. I started to rise, but she put up her hand, staying me. She sat on the ledge, not too close, but enough so we could converse. Even seated, I towered over her. She wore a simple white shirt and blue leggings, with no makeup or jewelry, and she was still lovely. She barely looked thirty. Surely it violated some conservation law of the universe that one person could have such ageless health, intellect, beauty, and power. Then again, she also had a crushing job where, if she failed, it would bring about the fall of an empire. She couldn't resign, leave, give up, or move to a new position. It never ended, not for a single moment. I couldn't imagine anything that would be worth such a torturous responsibility.

I tried to gather my sleep-addled wits. "You honor me, Your Majesty. You didn't have to come here. I could've come to the palace."

She watched me with eyes the color of emeralds. No, not emeralds. Gems were hard. She had a gentle gaze. "The Uzan didn't think you were ready to move."

"I'm sorry they dragged you to this place."

She smiled, like the sun lighting up the dawn. "I like it here. The Lock soothes me."

I couldn't imagine its excruciating presence soothing anyone. "You're lucky."

"They tell me you were in pain." Her voice flowed like a clear stream, which made no sense as a metaphor on Raylicon. Our water lay mostly underground or frozen at the poles.

Concentrate, I told myself, trying to clear my thoughts. "So the Lock doesn't always hurt?"

"Well, no." She thought for a moment. "Most psions describe the effect as pressure. They use words like 'purity of thought.' Many see haloes of light due to their increased brain activity."

Great. They saw angels and I screamed in agony. "I was fighting it, I think. The Kyle centers in my brain are waking up, and apparently my subconscious doesn't like it."

"Yes, I see that now." She gave my a look of apology. "I shouldn't have brought you into a Kyle link yesterday. I am sorry."

Gods. That sentence contained so much strangeness, I couldn't begin to answer, not to mention that the pharaoh had just apologized to me. In my experience, the more powerful the authority, the less likely they were to admit they made a mistake.

After a moment, she said, "Major?"

I took a breath. "You're saying we were in a Kyle link during out last meeting?"

"Yes, that is right." She didn't seem to have a clue she had just stated the impossible.

"I can't do that." I thought of my experience with the Lock. "Even if I had the training to make a Kyle link, which I don't, it would cripple my brain."

"Apparently not." She watched me as if I were a puzzle. "I pick up signals from you better than I do with most people. Or at least I did before; you're shielding your mind better now."

I hadn't realized my shields had improved. "Why was it easier with me?"

"I don't know."

I blinked. "You must know. You're the Assembly Key."

She spoke dryly. "People think I know everything because I am reasonably good at solving puzzles. I don't know everything. I can't say why it is easier with you."

Reasonably good at solving puzzles. That was like saying the desert had a little bit of sand. I needed to tell her why I had asked to see her, but if I went any further, I could be impaling myself on the sword of my blunt candor.

"Major?" she asked.

Go ahead, I told myself. *Jump over the cliff.* "May I ask you a personal question?"

Her gaze turned wary. "Why?"

"It has to do with Calaj's case."

"I understand you think she is hiding below the aqueducts."

"Yes, I do."

"The police can't find her." Dyhianna frowned. "They can't find anything down there."

"The Majdas sent them to look?" Damn. They wouldn't get out of the Undercity alive. It was bad enough they had sent Duane down a few levels, but at least he had a good reputation with my people. Invading the Down-deep with a police contingent could be suicide.

"They didn't send people," Dyhianna said. "They sent bee-bots."

My shoulders relaxed. Tech-mech bees we could deal with. Given her comment on the success of their search, or lack thereof, it sounded like the cyber-riders in the deep were just as adept at making shrouds to hide people as ours in the aqueducts.

"I shot back when Calaj fired at me," I said. "Did the bots find her body?"

Dyhianna shook her head. "No trace of her. No trace of the jumbler shot, either."

Huh. That shot had disintegrated a wall. Either ISC hadn't sent their bees deep enough or the deepers had already fixed the damage. If they had found Calaj's body, this investigation would end, and with it any danger from Calaj to the pharaoh. Yet no matter how many battles I had fought, I hated to end life. And Calaj was one of our own. I wanted to stop her, not blow her apart.

I tried again. "Your Majesty, may I ask about your lineage?"

"It's not exactly a secret."

"People know about your family, yes. But very few know specifically where you descend from." I certainly didn't, other than the nebulous *descended from ancient Ruby queens.*

She shrugged. "We came from Raylicon. Everyone does."

"You aren't everyone." To put it mildly.

She considered me. "All right. Ask your questions."

"It's, uh, about your skin."

"What about my skin?"

"It doesn't look like everyone else's skin."

Dyhianna glanced at her arm, then back up. "It looks normal to me."

I plunged ahead. "The first time I saw you, my apology, but I didn't think you looked like royalty. You're, well, smaller. Your eyes are green instead of black. Your skin looks translucent." Almost stuttering, I added, "I mean, not literally, but it gives that impression."

She spoke quietly. "Who do you think I look like?"

I knew I should shut up, but being an idiot, I said, "A deeper."

"What is a deeper?"

"Someone native to the region of the Undercity below the aqueducts." I wondered if you could be jailed for profaning the lineage of a pharaoh.

She blinked. "But almost no one is down there."

That was it? That response was her only reaction to my suggestion that her revered dynastic lineage came from the deepest levels of the worst slum on the planet?

"More people live there than you think," I said. "You just can't find them."

"So I suggested to the Majda police captain." She grimaced. "Takkar, I believe is her name."

Her expression fit my thoughts about Takkar exactly. "Your Majesty, please know that I don't mean to insult your heritage."

Dyhianna spoke dryly. "My exalted ancestors were a bunch of warmongering barbarians. Tell me why you think these atavistic predecessors of mine might have had ties to the Down-deep."

"The large size of your eyes," I said. "Their green color also means they have less melanin. Same for your skin. Something in their skin also reacts with airborne agents down there to create bioluminescence. I have it too. I'd bet you do as well."

Her expression remained neutral. "What agents?"

"I don't know," I admitted. "This is all conjecture."

"And Calaj?"

"Her genetic map indicates at least one of her ancestors had Down-deep heritage."

"So you are suggesting that Secondary Calaj, myself, and you are all related?"

Great. Not only had I insulted her dynastic line, I had implied she shared that lineage with a murderer and a slum rat. My feeling like slime, however, didn't negate my conclusions. "I'm sorry. But yes, distantly related. It would be many generations ago." *Many* generations, as in thousands of years, but still, the genetic stock of the Undercity.

"Why are you sorry?" she asked.

I was hardly going to repeat my thoughts. Hell, she might have overheard them. She wasn't reacting today as she had on the bridge, though, so maybe I really had done a better job at shielding my mind. Or maybe the Lock had burned out my Kyle centers. I could always hope.

She spoke again, saving me from having to answer. "You have nothing to apologize for. From what the Uzan and Majdas tell me, you have been through hell these past few days. We should thank you for service."

This conversation felt surreal. "It's no problem. I've seen worse." I hesitated. "Your Majesty, did Calaj know about the Kyle tests the doctors did on my people?"

"I don't think so. How would she?"

"I wondered if she were one of the officers studying the results."

"If that were true, it would be in the files we gave you."

That pretty much did away with the only plausible theory I could think of for how Calaj might have known about the Down-deep test results.

"Will these conclusions about our heredity help you find Calaj?" Dyhianna asked.

"I think so. They could help me understand what motivates her."

"The Majda police captain wants to send troops to the Undercity to search for her."

Well, shit. Leave it to Captain Takkar to come up with the worst idea. Their search wouldn't work; my people would vanish, aided by our cyber riders. My people would hate Majda after that. The Imperialate would never get its détente with the Undercity.

"I don't think that's a good idea," I said.

"Yes, well, Takkar didn't like it when I told her that, either." Wryly, she added, "If I wasn't the pharaoh, I swear, I think she would throw me in jail."

I couldn't help but laugh. "She often says how much she'd like to do that with me."

"Has she ever actually carried through with the threat?"

"Not yet. But if she can ever find a valid reason, I'm sure she will."

The pharaoh smiled, and I felt less intimidated. Anyone who affected Takkar the same way I did was all right in my book. Perhaps I could ask her for one more thing.

I spoke carefully. "The deepers value their privacy."

She studied my face. "But?"

"They have a small, ingrown community. It leads to birth defects." I didn't want to trust an outsider. Talking to her about the deep bothered me at such a gut level, it felt painful. But I couldn't let this go. It was too important. "Your Majesty, they need help."

She continued to watch me with her too-perceptive gaze. "What kind of help?"

"Medical. But it's risky. Introducing above-city procedures, tech, expectations, anything that might interfere with their way of life—it could destroy them." I hoped I wasn't making a mistake, revealing such a unique people to one of the most powerful figures in three empires, a sovereign with a vested interest in using them for their Kyle abilities. If I erred trusting her, I could bring great harm to the very people I sought to help, *my* people, those who shared the blood of my ancestors.

Yet they were also the pharaoh's ancestors, I felt sure. Beneath her fragility, I sensed a great strength, the same steel will that kept the deepers going millennia after millennia in their strange world. If we traced their genetics, what would we find? They had access, from their buried caves, to the Lock, probably also to Izu Yaxlan. Even the blue light that filled the Abaj command center evoked the deep. And the Abaj were the traditional protectors of the Ruby Dynasty. Coincidence? Maybe, but the links were all there.

The pharaoh spoke again. "I need time to think on this, Major."

I nodded, hoping I hadn't set into motion events I would regret. "Of course."

Dyhianna stood up. "Let me know if you discover any more about Calaj."

"I will." I stood slowly, still woozy from my experience in the Lock. "Thank you for coming." Beyond her, I could see the Uzan standing by the entrance across the pyramid. Four unfamiliar Abaj stood with him, fully outfitted Jagernauts in black leathers, which jumblers holstered at their hips. Their massive gauntlets glittered as they monitored the pyramid, and their gazes swept over me with antipathy. I might be among the best fighters in the Undercity, but these Abaj could dispatch me with no effort, and they looked as if the slightest provocation would set them into action. They were the real thing, the pharaoh's bodyguards, every bit the killers of legend.

Dyhianna inclined her head. "Thank you, Major, for your work on our behalf."

With that, she left, sweeping out of the pyramid with her guards. A chill ran up my back. Precognition? No, I didn't believe it. Yet about this I had no doubt; Dyhianna Selei Skolia might seem innocuous, but someday our "titular" ruler would become a true pharaoh in every way, even if it meant overthrowing her own government.

VIII
LIZARD TRAP

Beyond the aqueducts, deep within the darkness, a narrow passage wound through the rocks, lit only by a small sphere of light from the stylus hanging around my neck. The tunnel widened into a chamber with natural rock pillars created by eons of dripping water. On my left, roughly hewn stairs curved up into darkness. I stood at their base, frozen, unable to go farther. I'd climbed those steps plenty of times. It was ridiculously simple. Just go up. Yet I remained at the bottom, staring.

No Undercity stairs would ever look the same to me again. It had been nearly twenty hours since I staggered out of the Lock with pain stabbing my head like the punishment of a vengeful goddess against my lowly trespassing self. The Abaj had called a flycar to take me "home," that is, to the building in Cries where I sometimes lived. I'd gone upstairs, eaten, and slept for hours. Only then had I returned to the Undercity. I should be fine. Yet here I stood, staring at stairs I knew better even than my apartment, and I couldn't freaking move.

Stop being stupid, I thought. *Climb.*

I put my foot on the first step. I went up one step. Another. Unlike the Lock stairs, which had followed a precise spiral, these wound unevenly, a natural progression of ledges created by nature rather than humans. In one place, an overhang blocked the way. The rare person who discovered this staircase on her own would stop at this dead end, puzzled perhaps. She might assume she'd found a sculpture created by a dust gang with some symbolic meaning, stairs that went nowhere. It wouldn't surprise me, actually, if someone in the Undercity *had* created such a work of art.

In reality, the overhang acted as a gate. I knelt down and pushed its bottom edge. A pin dropped somewhere, a thunk of stone on stone, and the overhang shifted, opening a space about two handspans tall between its bottom edge and the ground. I lay down and scraped under the barrier on my back. When I made it through to the other side, I stood up, brushing off my clothes, and shoved the bottom edge of the gate into place with the toe of my boot. That done, I resumed my climb, step by excruciating step. By the time I reached the top, my heart was beating much too hard, but of course that came from exertion. Just exertion, nothing else. Never mind that I was in excellent shape.

I'd reached a foyer-like cave. I walked across it to a stone archway with vines engraved along its borders. In the room beyond, a sculptor had carved benches into the wall and engraved them with flying lizards. Blue cushions softened their seats. Tapestries hung on the walls, depictions of life in the Undercity woven in shimmering threads, red, blue, green, gold. They offered far more vibrant works of art than the paltry imitations sold by Concourse vendors, who claimed their wares were genuine Undercity crafts. Right. Those vendors had no idea. These exquisite tapestries and engraved benches were the real thing, never seen in Cries or even on the Concourse.

"Dara?" I called.

A man appeared in an archway across the room, Dara's husband Weaver. Dark-haired and tall, he was in excellent health. As a bartender at Jak's casino, Dara supported her family well.

"Heya," he said. "Dara's got work."

"Ah." Usually she was home by now. "Didn't mean to disturb."

"Back soon." He motioned me to come inside. "Come with."

I followed him into another room hung with tapestries. A lamp stood in one corner, its tinted glass glowing red, blue, and gold. The other corner sported a water desalination set and plants with blue flowers genetically modified to survive without direct sunlight. A curtain of blown-glass beads hung in an archway, sparkling blue and green, and handwoven rugs covered the floor, their artistry as exceptional as the tapestries. Weaver created all of this beauty, with no idea he was an artistic genius. A toddler was playing with a pile of soft balls on one rug, and a nine-year-old girl sat against one wall, ensconced in a pile of cushions, reading. Holos of ancient queens glowed above the screen of her book.

"Crinkles," I said, by way of greeting.

The girl looked up. "Heya, Bhaaj." A two word greeting, expansive for an Undercity kid. She went back to her book.

"Here." Weaver indicated a pile of cushions against another wall.

I sank gratefully into their softness. Sliding off my pack, I opened it up and reached around the bulky shroud for a bottle of water. I offered it to Weaver. "Snap."

"Eh. Good." He grinned as he accepted the bottle. With no fanfare, he strode away, through the bead curtain, setting the little orbs clinking. He had designed them so that when they jangled, they played music, a sweet melody that never sounded the same twice. They started up again when he came back out. He brought three glasses, all tinted blue at the bottom and shading into pale green at the top. I wondered if he knew the glass looked like water in the ocean. Probably not. He had never seen a body of water under an open sky.

The first time I saw a lake, the sight froze me in place. It was on a world whose name I didn't remember, one of many places the army had sent us grunts for training. I would never forget. The lake had seemed so vast, its wind-rippled surface glittering in the sunlight. I stood on the shore staring with my mouth open until my sergeant yelled for me to get my ass moving. I ended up with a demerit for breaking formation, which normally would have mortified me; I did my damnedest to make sure no one could claim I didn't deserve a place in the army. But that day, I'd cared only about the magic I witnessed, all that fresh water glowing under a blue sky.

I smiled as Weaver gave me one of the glasses. "You make?" I asked.

"Yah." He handed one to his daughter, who accepted it with a shrug, as if it were perfectly normal to drink from a work of art, but she watched with undisguised fascination as he snapped open the bottle and filled her glass. They valued fresh water more than the masterpieces Weaver created.

Time to remedy that situation. "Been working on your Concourse license," I said.

Weaver came over and settled into some cushions. "Thought it wasn't going to happen."

No way did I intend to let Cries deny him a vendor's license. "Got a fix for the birth thing."

"What birth thing?" a woman asked.

I glanced up. Dara stood in the entrance of the room, dressed in her slinky jumpsuit, her skin glittering from cosmetic dust. In Jak's casino, she fit right in, but here in the mundane setting of her home, she gleamed like a sensual phantasm.

Weaver was staring at her. "Good see, Dara."

She smiled, her cool demeanor softening. "Eh, Weaver. You too."

This flood of romantic gushing was more than I could take. "Come sit," I told Dara. "Got snap."

Weaver went over to his common-law wife and nudged her toward me. "Go sit."

As Dara sank into the cushions, the toddler gave an annoyed wail. Weaver scooped up the child, then came over and thrust her at me. "Dara's tired," he said, by way of explanation.

Startled, I took the small girl. As Weaver left the room, making the beads sing, I awkwardly settled the kid into the crook of my arm. I never knew what to do with little kids. Still, we learned early in the aqueducts to look after our young. My gang had looked after several younger children when we were hardly more than kids ourselves. We grew up fast, children having children and dying young. Change was in the air, though, like dust particles floating in sun rays, as the above-city took notice of our culture hidden beneath their sleek towers. They hadn't denied our poverty before; that would have taken a conscious realization that we existed as a society with our own language, lives, economy, and culture. They simply ignored us. Prior to last year, most people in Cries saw the aqueducts as no more than a wasteland of gangs and the homeless.

Dara watched me trying to hold her adopted kid. "Baby remembers you."

I squinted at her. "Don't see how."

"Saved her life."

I felt cold, though runoff from an underground hot spring heated the room. "Not remember me. Just born when I found her."

The baby cooed in my arms and closed its eyes.

"Remembers," Dara said. She settled back and closed her eyes, resting.

I wanted to thrust the child at her, not because I didn't like the baby. She was good. Dara and Weaver had agreed to take in both this girl and her then five-year-old brother, who called himself Pack Rat. Their mother had died in childbirth. I tried to banish the memory from my mind, how I had found the mother's body. Pack Rat had led me there, asking me to "wake her up." I'd commed for help and then sat there holding the dead woman and her children, rocking them back and forth while I wept for another mother, the one I had never known, the woman who also died alone after giving me life.

In my earliest childhood, I had longed for a home like this one instead of that sterile collection of barren cubicles that passed for an orphanage in Cries. Unfortunately, families like this one were rare in the aqueducts. Dara's bartending job was as illegal as everything else about Jak's casino, but he paid a good wage and looked after his employees. The Cries police would have shut him down in a hot minute, except that certain members of his elite clientele were the same people who paid their salaries. Jak, the undercity king of vice. He sat on the throne of cognitive dissonance. Devil or savior? Hell if I knew. My emotions on that subject were too tangled to touch.

I shifted the toddler in my arms. "How's Pack Rat?"

Dara opened her eyes. "Loud. Got a dust gang. Says he's grown up."

I chuckled. "Big kid. All of six."

She smiled. "Wants to be a Dust Knight."

"Family talent." Dara's oldest daughter, thirteen-year-old Darjan, had been among the first of my knights. In the Undercity, we had always called ourselves dust rats. When my first tykado students had used the name, I told them *No! You are human. Rats are vermin. You aren't vermin. You are better than rats!* They had stood there, a ragged collection of children, waiting for me to replace the name I had just ripped away. So I called them Dust Knights. The title became known throughout the Undercity, an honor for those who earned a place within their ranks.

"Is Darjan here?" I asked.

Dara shook her head. "Out. Training."

"Good." After all her years in a dust gang, Dara had become an ace at the rough-tumble, what we called street fighting. Tykado required a more sophisticated discipline, but the dusters loved the process. It had taken them a while to get that tykado was a sport with rules. You couldn't do whatever you wanted to smash your opponent. They did eventually accept it. Unwritten rules of combat also existed among dust gangs, who used the rough-tumble as both a violent sport and a way of establishing dominance. Darjan took well to tykado and worked with the younger kids when she wasn't practicing with her peers. I hoped tykado, with its philosophy of violence as a last resort, would give the gangs something more civilized to do than trying to pound each other senseless all the time.

Weaver returned with a filled glass for Dara and settled next to her in the cushions. Taking a deep swallow of water, she closed her eyes. After a moment, she lowered the glass and looked at me. "Good snap."

I nodded, accepting her thanks. "How goes?"

She held out her arm, showing me a comm bracelet around her wrist. The metal shimmered, reminding me of the holos in Jak's casino. "Got new talk."

"What code?" I asked.

She gave me the code, and I tapped it into my gauntlet comm. Her wrist comm buzzed and she grinned as she tapped receive.

"Eh, Dara," I said into my comm. My voice came out of her bracelet.

"Eh," she said into the comm. "Talk too much."

We both laughed and switched off our comms.

Dara settled back with her water. "About the license. We got no birth records."

"Yah." It was the latest roadblock the bureaucrats had raised to giving Weaver a vendor's license for the Concourse. "Get a doctor. Verify your birth."

Weaver gave a snort. "Because I don't know I'm born, eh?"

"Make it official." I patted the toddler, who was fussing in my arms.

"Got no doctor," Dara said.

"Got no interest," Weaver said. "My birth, my business."

I pushed back my frustration. Of course he didn't want to jump through these hoops the Cries authorities kept inventing, but at this rate he'd never get his license. Which was the point, of course. The baby let out with a wail, announcing to the world what it thought of my cuddling technique.

"Eh." Dara held out her arms.

I gave her the child, and she settled against Dara, her curly black hair reflected in her mother's sleek-suit. The girl cooed, much more satisfied with her new digs.

"Can get a doctor," I said. "Come to the Rec Center. Thirtieth hour. Today."

"No!" Weaver and Dara both said it together. "No go," Weaver added, just in case I didn't catch their drift.

I had known this would be tough. No doctor would come to the Undercity, especially after the attack on Duane, and neither Dara nor Weaver would visit Cries. I might have convinced Darjan, if only for the daring excitement of it all, but never her parents.

"One visit," I said. "Just the Rec Center. You get license, sell goods, help family." I knew it bothered Weaver that Dara was the entire support of their family. I thought he worked harder than any of us, but he considered his art fun and he liked looking after the kids. He was a wonderful father, in a culture where we were lucky even to have one living parent, let alone two of them.

"Good coin for weavings, glasswork, carvings," I added.

Weaver held up the water bottle I had brought them. "Trade for snap?"

"Trade for credit," I said. "Buy lots of snap."

Dara scowled at me. "Credit useless. Can't see it."

Pah. Always, I ran into this argument when it came to the credit that the entire rest of the freaking universe used for commerce. The Undercity ran on bargains. Period. People here were perfectly capable of learning to understand credit, they just didn't want to. They raised the concept of "stubborn as a bulkhead" to new heights, a trait which, yah, all right, I had to admit applied to me, too. I needed to put this in terms of our own economy.

"Listen," I said. "Got proposal."

They regarded me warily. "What?" Dara asked.

"Meet doctor at Rec Center, get license," I said. "Set up stall. Sell goods. You don't make enough in one tenday to buy twenty snap bottles, I give you twenty snap."

Both Dara and Weaver laughed, their good humor restored by my outlandish idea. "Twenty, eh." Dara said. "Make Bhaaj poor again."

Although I smiled, I didn't know which hurt more, that my friends lived a life where twenty bottles of water were considered wealth, or that I remembered the time when I believed the same. I wished I could make them see. If Weaver presented his merchandise well on the Concourse, he wouldn't need to trade for snap bottles. He could earn enough to buy shares in a Cries water purification plant.

"Bargain?" I asked.

"You sure?" Weaver asked. "Lot of snap for you."

If they'd let me, I'd give them twenty bottles now, and the hell with the Undercity antipathy toward anything perceived as charity. They would never accept a gift of more than one bottle, a bargain in return for my enjoying the hospitality of their home. My proposal changed that. If we didn't get the license, I'd have to pay up, no choice, because I'd lost the wager. That would appeal to Dara, who never gambled but enjoyed the games vicariously at Jak's place.

"Yah," I said. "I'm sure."

Weaver nodded. "Deal."

Good. We now had a bargain as binding as any above-city contract.

"Deal what?" a young voice asked.

I looked up with a start. Darjan was striding into the room, disheveled and glowing with youth. She bowed to me the way tykado students did to their teacher. "Well met, Chi Bhaajan," she said, using the formal greeting, a mouthful down here in the aqueducts.

"Eh." Dara gave me an apologetic glance. "Jan talks a lot."

Darjan glowered at her mother, but didn't deign to answer.

"Knights have to talk that way," I told Dara. "I tell them to."

"Dust Knight," Dara informed her mother, as if this was news.

Dara scowled at us. "Knights jabber."

"Read and write, too," I said.

"I read," Darjan's sister called from her place under the lamp. She held up her holobook.

Weaver snorted. "Next, Bhaaj insist I read, eh?"

Yah, well, I wished both he and Dara would learn to read and write. I could only push them so far, though. One step at a time.

"Got snap," Darjan observed as she sat down with us.

Her father handed her the bottle. "Yours."

She finished the remaining water in one gulp.

I regarded Darjan. "Got proposal."

Everyone was suddenly attentive. "Why does Darjan get a bargain?" her sister demanded.

"Dust Knight proposal," I said.

"I'll be one, too," her sister said.

Darjan frowned at her. "Never interested before."

"What proposal?" Weaver asked.

"Tykado contest," I told them.

Darjan wasn't impressed. "Every day is a tykado contest."

"Don't mean dust gangs fights," I said.

"With cyber-riders?" Darjan looked dubious. "Most can't fight worth spit."

"Better not be punkers," Dara said flatly. "Got guns."

I thought of Singer and her Mark 89 Automatic Power Rifle. "Nahya, no punkers, no riders."

They all looked confused. "No one else," Weaver said.

"Above-city team," I said.

Dara stared at me. "Like hell!"

"Never," Weaver stated flatly.

Darjan's eyes gleamed. "Yah. We kill."

I scowled at her. "Not kill. Contest."

"Never." Dara leaned forward. "You got that, Bhaaj? Never the hell ever."

"Always the hell ever," Darjan told them. "I do."

Instead of getting angry, her parents stared at her blankly. "Why?" Weaver asked, as if she had suggested hanging upside down from the ceiling.

"We beat them," Darjan said.

"Maybe not," I said. An above-city team had more training than a dust gang.

"They beat you. Humiliate," Dara said, stressing her point with a four-syllable word.

Darjan crossed her arms. "We fight."

"Will think on it," Dara said. When Weaver frowned at her, she raised her eyebrows at him. "Maybe think," he told Darjan.

Darjan started to protest, and I shook my head slightly. Her parents needed time to process the idea. "Got to go," I said.

"You stay," Dara told me, friendlier now that I had backed down on the contest.

As much as I'd have liked to stay, I couldn't. I still had to find out why Ruzik and Hack were stealing pulse rifles. Gods only knew what Hack could do with an amped-up rifle.

"Got to find Ruzik," I said.

"Training," Darjan said. "At Lizard Trap. With his circle."

I knew Lizard Trap. I'd run there in my youth. I stood up. "Be well," I said.

Dara walked out with me. When we were alone, she said, "Heard Singer sang to Driver."

The memory of Singer blasting apart Driver's body jumped into my mind, too vivid. I took a breath. "Saved my life."

"Careful with yourself."

I nodded. "Be well."

"You too," she murmured.

With that, I took my leave of one of the wealthiest homes in the Undercity, riches that came neither from coin nor credit, but from the love sheltered within those tapestry-covered walls.

I knew Jak had found me even though I couldn't see him. He stood beyond the sphere of light cast by my stylus, somewhere up ahead on the midwalk where I'd been striding along. No matter. I could sense exactly where he was standing. I stopped and turned off my stylus.

"Sneaking up," I said into the darkness.

A throaty laugh came from about twenty meters away. "How know?"

I smiled. "Always know. Can't fool me."

"Sure, can." His voice rumbled like a sensual promise. "Any time."

I snorted. "Not likely."

"Very likely," he murmured, suddenly in front of me.

Ah, that voice. It turned me into custard. Not that I'd ever admit it. "What want?" I said.

"Oh, I don't know," he growled. "A civil word, eh?"

"Okay." I spoke pleasantly. "Civil word. That's two."

He laughed, a sexy rumble that vibrated like an invitation. "Ah, Bhaajo."

I put out my hands and encountered his well-muscled chest. He put his arms around me and I put mine around him. Closing my eyes, I just held him, enjoying the familiar strength of his embrace. He felt like a balm I hadn't realized I needed until we touched.

After a while, he spoke into my ear. "Remember that place near here?"

I remembered. A short distance down the midwalk, a small aqueduct intersected this larger throughway. Its narrow path led to a cave lined with phosphorescent crystals, a glowing wonderland when you turned on a lamp. As children, we had loved that hideaway.

"Been a long time," I said.

"Yah." He moved his hands to places I liked. "Should make it a short time."

"Got business," I told him. "Job to do."

"Got business with me."

I shouldn't go with him. I couldn't, not in the middle of the day.

Really, I couldn't.

Really.

We headed off together in the dark, needing no light to find the places we'd loved in our youth.

I reached Lizard Trap several hours later than I intended, alone now, but feeling better than I had in some time. Jak was like a potent swig of whiskey. I could've drunk all day, if I'd had the time. He had his casino, though, and I had Lizard Trap.

The canal inherited its name from the small reptiles that scuttled through the swirls of dust at its bottom. Gangers trapped the lizards for food. Located about three levels down from the Concourse and well removed from the main canals, Lizard Trap saw less traffic than the major throughways. Although the approach looked deserted, I knew better. Duane might think no one lived here, but when he'd stood in a seemingly empty canal, the life of the Undercity had hummed around him, hidden from his view.

I heard the fight first, grunts and thuds, no yells or words, nothing that used energy. I was following a small tunnel, probably an ancient maintenance conduit. Lizard Trap crossed it up ahead, and an orange glow came from the intersection. I didn't hide my approach, I just walked out onto the midwalk of the canal. Someone had crammed a torch into the wall, and other torches burned at intervals along the canal, their flames flickering in the air currents, a fierce light far different from the cool bioluminescence of the Down-deep. All that heat and energy, like the rough-tumblers below, intent on their fight.

They were fighting down in the canal, which made sense, since they could easily knock each other off the midwalk. They never paused, fists striking, bodies lunging. One man jumped, kicking first with one leg, then the other, *bam, bam,* his body airborne for an instant as his feet pounded his opponent. A woman whirled in a roundhouse kick, her fists clenched. They were *fast,* a blur of speed even without augmentation. Dust swirled around them and saturated the air, gritty against my skin, red in the torchlight, creating a haze over the scene.

I knew one of the gangs: Ruzik, his girlfriend, and the other man and woman who ran with them, all Dust Knights. They wore ripped muscle shirts that left their arms and abs bare, four violently beautiful youths. Tats of flying lizards covered their skin. Their group had survived intact into adulthood, a rarity for gangs. They protected one of the largest circles in the Undercity, seven children ranging in ages from a baby to preteens, and four other adults, including Hack, the cyber-wizard who had stolen the guns with Ruzik.

In a culture where intact families were rare, your circle became your kin. When I'd enlisted at, I had done worse than break up our dust gang; I had left behind the people I cared about most. Dig never forgave me, yet in the end, as she had died, she told her daughter to join the army like me rather than take over the cartel. I didn't know what would happen with Ruzik's gang, but they had a high standing among the Knights. They were becoming a force for stability in the aqueducts, leaders for our youth to emulate, or at least they would be if they didn't start some war here over who the hell knew what.

I didn't recognize the other gang, two women and two men in their early twenties. In Cries, they would have been college students, studying for exams; here they fought for the right to live on their terms. A girl in the other gang lunged at Angel, Ruzik's girlfriend, slashing at her with a long knife. Angel, who was about as cherubic as a wrecking ball with spikes, kicked her leg high. Her foot hit the girl's arm and the knife spun into the air, its honed edge glittering like fire in the torchlight. Her opponent ducked, then hurled into Angel in a move that looked half rough-tumble and half tykado. I'd known some Knights were teaching tykado to kids who hadn't yet earned acceptance into the group, but I hadn't realized it had gone this far. Although Ruzik's gang had the advantage, their rivals knew some tykado moves well enough to use them.

What struck me more, though, was *how* they fought, one-on-one, each member of Ruzik's gang paired off with one fighter from the other gang. A telling choice: with their greater expertise, Ruzik's dusters could have won faster by dispatching the weakest members among their rivals first and then joining forces against their remaining opponents. Both gangs had opted for rules of honor rather than an anything-goes brawl.

I could guess what started the rumble. Two dust sculptures stood in the canal, depictions of the giant lizards called ruziks that resembled the extinct T-rex on Earth. One red lizard stood by the opposite wall, a clear statement of Ruzik's claim to this territory. The remains of another lizard stood a few meters beyond the first, the top of its body lying in smashed clumps around its clawed feet. Someone had sculpted a different figure in front of the broken lizard, a muscled arm raised with its fist clenched around a dagger. This was a turf war, two gangs battling over their claim to the canal.

Ruzik was fighting a woman who looked like the leader of the other gang, based on the more elaborate tats on her arms. She ducked and parried his attacks with an amazing speed. Gods, I'd love to get that one for training. Although she moved like a street fighter, she showed hints of tykado grace. She didn't have Ruzik's mass, but her greater speed offset his strength. A long gash on Ruzik's arm dripped blood, and his opponent's nose was bleeding. They struck, ducked, whirled, and struck again, locked in their violent dance.

I leaned against the wall and crossed my arms, watching the rumble. This had nothing to do with me, which in the Undercity meant it was none of my business. In the code of the Dust Knights, however, it mattered. Ruzik's gang had engaged their rivals in a fair fight. They obviously meant to pulverize their opponents, but it could have turned into a blood bath if they hadn't held back. Had Ruzik used his stolen guns, he could have obliterated their competition—and destroyed the interwoven laws of the Undercity that kept our community from becoming a war zone.

Angel rolled her opponent over her hip and slammed her to the ground. The other girl groaned, lying on her back. Angel could have grabbed the girl's knife from the dust and gone for the kill, but instead she waited, breathing heavily. The other girl climbed to her feet, wary and tense, and she faced off with Angel, both of them glowering. The man fighting Ruzik's brother raised his hands, palms out, surrendering. Ruzik's brother stopped his next blow, his fist raised, his features contorted with the effort of holding back, because he obviously wanted to smash the other fellow in the face.

Within moments the other two matches finished, the rival gang raising their palms in defeat. Everyone stood glaring at each other, anger simmering. Ruzik spun around and strode down the canal in my direction, sending dust swirling in the torchlight. He didn't even glance at me, but I had no doubt they all knew I was there. He stopped in front of the sculpture with the raised arm and kicked it hard. The top half fell into the canal. Another kick, and he had broken the arm into pieces that crumbled into canal dust. No one spoke. They needed no words. Triumph and defeat were already decided.

The rival gang dispersed, melting away into the aqueducts. Ruzik's people set to work redoing the destroyed sculpture, but he didn't join them. Instead, he turned and looked straight up at me. I could have motioned him to join me on the midwalk. Out of respect for his leadership, and the honor he used in their fight, I jumped down into the canal. My hydraulics kicked in and analysis routines in my biomech web timed my movements so that despite the large drop, I landed easily. Angel and the others looked up with a start, but Ruzik just nodded, cool and casual.

I motioned at the bleeding gash on his arm. "Got cut."

He shrugged. "Not a problem."

The others came over and stood behind Ruzik, listening. I could almost feel their curiosity. They wanted to know what I thought of their fight.

"Good tumble," I said.

Ruzik inclined his head, accepting the compliment. Angel stepped up next to him with the ease of long-time lovers. It reminded me of my youth, with Jak.

"Got new circlers," she said. "Little dusters."

Good gods, they had taken in even more children? That would make their circle the largest in the Undercity. No wonder they wanted more territory. And they had done it without killing or crippling their competition. The other gang wouldn't forget. They had lost, but with honor, and that mattered here as much, sometimes even more, than the territory itself.

"New dusters lucky," I said.

The four of them stayed put, watching me, no smiles, but they didn't shift their weight or glower either, which down here was equivalent of an emotional thank you.

"Didn't use guns," I added.

Ruzik shrugged. "No need."

"Yah. No need." My voice cooled. "But got guns."

They all went still then, like statues. No one spoke. Apparently it was none of my damn business. I motioned at the tats on Ruzik's arm, blue and green spirals, all stylized lizards. My voice sounded like ice. "Kajada."

Ruzik's brother tensed, his shoulders stiffening. By now everyone knew I had once run in a gang led by Dig Kajada, who later became one of the most powerful drug bosses in the Undercity. I kept my thoughts private about how my closest childhood friend became my enemy in the cartel war. Jak and Gourd, they understood. We lost part of ourselves when Dig died. I never spoke about how the contradictions of Dig had torn me apart, but everyone knew the Code of the Knights. No drugs. Nothing. Use, and you were out. I made no exceptions. That said all that needed saying.

The Kajada cartel used a ruzik as their symbol, and Dig's people had stolen ISC laser carbines and neural disruptors to wage war against the Vakaar cartel. Now Ruzik, with all his lizards tats, had stolen high-end weapons, working with a rider named Hack. Yah, Hack took his name from his work on the meshes, but hack was also one of the most common drugs sold by the cartels.

I looked at them, they looked at me, and it felt like the tension would crack us in two.

Ruzik spoke. "Got Code."

"Yah," Angel said. "Got Code." The other two dusters echoed the words.

So. They swore by the Code. I had to believe they wouldn't give their oath unless they meant the words. I hoped I was right. As a symbol, the ruzik had a long history among my people. Dig had chosen it for her cartel for the same reason Ruzik chose it for his gang; it represented strength, and the ancient, enduring power of those large animals.

"Need talk." I considered them all. "Ken?"

They met my gaze. Ruzik said, "Ken."

Good. They understood Jak's word. His reputation loomed large in the Undercity. *Ken* meant they wouldn't reveal to anyone what I was about to tell them.

"Jagernaut," I said. "Down-deep."

Ruzik scowled at me. "Bad jib."

"Not jib," I said. "Not joke. Real."

Angel spoke flatly. "Intruder."

"Get rid of it," Ruzik's brother said.

It. Not her or him, but "it." They gave voice to the unease Jagernauts caused many people, the belief that with such extensive biomech in their bodies and brains, they were no longer human.

"She," I said. "Not it."

"We push her out." That came from the girl whose name I didn't know.

"Can't," I answered. "She hides. Murders."

"We fight," Ruzik told me.

"You fight, you die." They were good, yah, but they had no chance against a Jagernaut..

"Four of us," Angel pointed out.

I knew Calaj could kill all of them, but they wouldn't go down easy. I didn't want them going down at all. "Listen," I said. "Might be after riders." Cyber-riders were invaluable in the aqueducts. As much as I hated knowing the Ruby Pharaoh had figured out their true value, I understood her concern. Calaj could do a lot of damage if she got control of our cyber-wizards and their tech-mech creations.

"Not steal rider tech," Ruzik said. "Or riders. We protect."

Whatever they planned to do with the guns, it didn't sound like it had any connection to Calaj. It also sounded like they didn't intend to tell me squat about the weapons.

"Code is about ethics," I told them.

"Yah," Ruzik said.

"Right and wrong," I added.

Angel answered this time. "Yah."

"Taking guns wrong," I said.

Ruzik's gaze never wavered. "No guns."

I scowled at him. "Code says no lies, either."

"Not lie," Angel said.

This was getting me nowhere. Whatever they had stolen, "borrowed," or taken apart, they had just denied they had the guns, which meant I wasn't knowingly abetting a crime. I still didn't like it. *Keep the Code,* I willed them. *Don't make me hunt a murderer among the Knights.*

My walk out of the aqueducts took me past places I didn't want to see. No, it didn't "take" me. I chose that route. What I wanted and what I needed to see weren't the same. Memories haunted me like ghosts adrift in the crumbling tunnel. This passage had seemed so much larger in my childhood. I remembered a girl I'd known back then by the name of Sparks. I'd been eight when I found her in this narrow passage. She had been four, a child with her face smudged by dust and tears, holding her hands out to me as she cried from loneliness, hunger, and fear. I'd lifted her up, whispering what little comfort I knew how to give.

Sparks had no parents. She became part of the circle my gang protected, along with several other children and a single-parent family. Two years later, while Sparks and I had played here, I realized she was sick. We called it Carnelian rash, an illness that prowled the aqueducts and attacked with no warning, turning your skin red and scaly. Even if I'd known how to take her to Cries, no hospital in the above-city would treat a dust rat. We had no healer. I nursed Sparks myself, cooled her skin with cloths soaked in mineral-laden water and dribbled filtered water between her cracked, swollen lips. When she cried, inconsolable from the pain, I traded with the drug punkers, giving them food I stole from the Concourse in return for the hack that eased Spark's misery.

I held her in my arms as she died.

Gods, why did I do this to myself, coming here? Whoever claimed that time healed all wounds hadn't known shit. The pain never stopped.

Today Jak and I had shared a different color of memories, those painted with joy instead of pain. I had so few, but making love with Jak topped those. He'd found that sparkling cave decades ago during one of his explorations into hidden places of the aqueducts. Always, Jak had been that way. He just disappeared. Once when we were fourteen, he left for days, never warning us. Gourd, Dig, and I had searched everywhere, looking for him, and then for his body. Grief tore us into shreds. One day he just showed up, grinning and satisfied with himself.

He'd gone to Izu Yaxlan, invading that sacred city to live in the ruins, daring our pantheon of goddesses and gods to punish his audacity. He stayed until the Abaj showed up and told him to leave. That they let him stay at all surprised me, but maybe it had taken a while for his presence to annoy those taciturn, impassive warriors.

We'd wanted to strangle him.

I understood now the insatiable curiosity that drove Jak, that urge to push boundaries and challenge the unknown. Back then, when I thought I'd lost him, I had died inside. Nothing prepares you for that at fourteen. Hell, nothing would prepare me now. I'd never admitted it to him, but I had given up trying to hide the truth from myself. I hadn't enlisted only to escape the Undercity. I had also needed to deny the intensity of my bond with a lover who never felt real, one who could disappear anytime. Yet in the end, after decades elsewhere, I'd come home, forced to acknowledge that this elusive, heartbreaking world would forever be a part of whatever defined my flawed self.

Eventually I reached a spiral staircase that climbed to the main aqueducts. I went up the steps, around and around, trying to forget the Lock staircase, around and around, like my memories of this place. Too much history.

The stairs ended in the main aqueduct below the Concourse, an aqueduct canal fifty meters across, its midwalk the height of two people above canal floor. Ancient architecture showed clearly here, arches, columns, and buttresses supporting the ceiling. I passed construction equipment left by the Cries team repairing the two nearby canals that had collapsed during the war. The teams should know better. Usually they took their stuff with them. They wouldn't be back for hours, at least halfway through the forty-hour night, which would have already begun to stretch its long twilight across the Vanished Sea above. They had locked up the equipment, sure, but their protections wouldn't even slow my people. Anything left unattended would be gone by the time they returned. I didn't know the people running the crews, but I commed Duane Ebersole and left a message, asking that he look into it before all this lovely equipment vanished without a trace.

I could have left the Undercity by any of its hidden exits. As kids, we used those passages so no cops would catch us coming onto the Concourse. They always sent us back to the aqueducts or found a reason to arrest us. Well, screw that. We had a right to walk on the Concourse. Today I followed a wide path to the official exit from the aqueducts, a cave we called the Foyer. Small, with a high ceiling and sawed-off rocks where you could sit, it offered nothing remarkable—except that it was the official exit from the aqueducts into the Concourse. I strode into the Foyer, angry at a world that let children die from a sickness we knew how to cure, a world where I had to choose between protecting Ruzik's thieving gang or obeying laws passed in a city that had never cared spit about us, at least not until they found out we had a priceless resource they coveted—our Kyle minds.

The exit out into the Concourse stood across the Foyer, an archway about three meters high and a meter wide. An ancient sculptor had carved geometric designs around its border so long ago, no one remembered who created that exquisite artwork. I walked through the archway onto the lower end of the Concourse. Haze filled the air, created by braziers that warmed the market stalls on either side of the narrow lane. Mist also formed here, where cool air from the aqueducts met the warmer Concourse. Smoke curled up from stoves, with tantalizing aromas of cooking meat and pizo spice that tickled my nose. A single street lamp shone through the haze.

Vendors staffed the stalls, women and men stranded here in the dregs of the Concourse, probably because they couldn't afford the license for a better location. I'd paid the application fee for Weaver's license so he wouldn't end up here. If his license ever came through, no *when* it came through, he could pay me back from his first sales. We didn't use the word loan; he called it a bargain, my help for credits that didn't yet mean anything to him. He figured he had the better end of the deal.

The vendors stared as I passed their stalls. Red dust covered my muscle shirt and scuffed my boots. I had a splint on my left wrist, and I carried my pack in my other hand, holding its straps easily despite its weight because I had the muscles to make that a trivial exercise. My leather jacket only partially covered the pistol in my shoulder holster. I appeared younger than my age, and I stood taller than most. Yah, so, okay, maybe I looked threatening. I was surprised they weren't calling the cops, the way they had last year when I brought four hundred people through here. If Lavinda Majda hadn't guaranteed us safe passage that day, gods only knew what would have happened.

I passed a pizo stall. Faded yellow tassels hung from its roof and blue streamers wrapped the poles that supported its canvas sides. Meat sticks dipped in pizo sauce sat in a rack on the counter, making my mouth water. I loved those sticks. The stall's grizzled owner stood behind the counter, watching me. He looked familiar. Of course. He had been here last year when we came out for the Kyle testing. He nodded to me, and I nodded back, appreciating the détente.

The Concourse sloped upward, an almost indiscernible slant, but enough that when it ended more than a kilometer distant, it lay just below the surface of the desert. I continued on, passing more stalls. The mist cleared and the alley became a street. Higher quality stalls appeared, with brighter canvas sides and pretty streamers that rustled in air currents produced by vents in the ceiling far overhead. I stopped at an empty stall between a café and a carpet stand, a moderately respectable location, nothing fancy, but a good place. If we could conquer the hurdle of Weaver's non-existent birth certificate, this stall would be his. I was fed up with the licensing office, but I didn't intend to ask the Majdas for help. I wanted my people to see we could do this for ourselves.

I continued up the Concourse. The street widened into an avenue with boutiques nestled between bistros and tourist-trap restaurants. On my right, a wide path paved with cobblestone led to a bridge, a gorgeous stone arch that spanned the only canal up here. Blue tiles paved the bridge, their ancient mosaics restored by the city. No one in Cries realized those designs evoked the art created by Down-deepers. Street lamps stood every few meters, their surfaces aged so gracefully that the antique effect looked genuine. The top of each curled in a scrolled loop, and a lamp hung by a chain from that bronzed curve. I was walking now among glitzy evening crowds who came here to dine. They stared as I strode by with my gun and my glare. I might as well have been another tourist attraction. Look! A real one! An undercity thug. Do you think we're safe? They would find it all so thrillingly dangerous. Yah, right. True gangers rarely came here in the open, and if they did, the police would recognize them as the real thing and make them leave. I had lived too long in the outside world, until I changed beyond anything I could have imagined in my youth. Yet here I was, with people gaping at me.

Eventually I reached the Rec Center, a light blue building near the top of the Concourse, the place where the boulevard reached its widest extent. The Rec Center needed that space. The Dawn Corps had built and staffed the place to serve the Undercity, but of course none of my people came here. Our youth might have visited a smaller center at the end of the Concourse, where the kids could go without being arrested or chased away. They only came up this far in secret.

The Center doors swung inward at my touch. I entered a large hall with game tables scattered to my right. On the left, counters stretched out cafeteria style, one with fresh fruit and vegetables, another with steaks steaming on a block, filling the air with mouth-watering smells. Water bottles stood on another. No wonder Ruzik and Hack snuck in here. Large, young, and constantly active; they probably craved food like this. They didn't have to steal it, given that the "Rec Center" was actually a soup kitchen, but they did anyway, so they weren't taking charity. Blast our Undercity pride. This place needed to find a bargain my people would accept as a trade for the meals. We also had to convince the police to let them come here. Having a nice, sparkly Rec Center did exactly squat when the cops turned back anyone who dared step out of the aqueducts. I was surprised no one had tried to stop me today. Then again, in a city so heavily influenced by the army, my military bearing worked in my favor.

A handsome man in slacks and a pullover was cleaning one of the counters. He wore the patch of a Dawn Corps volunteer on his shoulder, but this was no kid doing community service. Grey dusted his hair. Even just wiping down a counter, he had the confidence of someone comfortable with his years and his life. He looked up as I entered, then paused, taking in my appearance, gun and all. I met his gaze and stood watching him, waiting for his frown, his coldness, his suspicion.

He set down his cloth and came over. "My greetings." He spoke in a pleasant baritone. "Can I help you?"

No hostility. How refreshing. I motioned around the center, with its gleaming counters and blue walls. "Looks good. Got sparks." As soon as I spoke, I winced. Stupid comment. I'd answered him in dialect, too. I could blend in just fine when I needed to, but today I looked and sounded Undercity.

The man smiled. "Thank you. What brings you by?"

Interesting. He understood my speech, even the "sparks" idiom, an

Undercity compliment. Our dialect wasn't that different from the way people spoke in Cries, but our accent sounded thick to them, even indecipherable to some. This man seemed different. His eyes had a look of kindness, his face too, as if over the years, his nature had contoured his expression into gentle lines. I liked that. Given the designer cut of his clothes, I suspected he ranked among the top tier of Cries. Yet here he was, helping clean up this place as a volunteer. That told me a lot about his character, all of it good.

"Can I help you?" he asked.

I switched into Cries speech. "I was wondering, did a doctor visit here this morning?"

"Yes, she did." His smile faded. "She stayed for several hours, but no one came to see her."

Damn. That meant Weaver never showed up to get his birth certificate. I couldn't take this step for him; he needed to come of his own free will. If he did get a license, he would become a trailblazer for the Undercity. He had to be willing to accept that role or it wouldn't work.

"Are you a director here?" I asked.

"No, just an aide." He gave me a slight bow and added, "Ken Roy, at your service."

Holy shit. "You mean Professor Roy? The geologist from the university?"

He grinned. "Glad to meet you."

"Good gods." I had no idea what to make of this. "Why is someone as famous as you cleaning counters in a soup kitchen?"

He reddened. "Not that famous, I assure you. Just average. I thought I might be able to help. I wanted to go into the aqueducts, but the dean at the university advised against it."

Average, my ass. He was known throughout the Imperialate. His work on the failed terraforming of Raylicon had helped our planetary engineers slow the collapse enough to keep this region habitable. This man was a major reason humans could still live on this world.

"Riz on a raz," I said. "I can't believe it."

He laughed, a deep, throaty sound. "Thank you, I think."

My face heated. "Sorry. I meant, I'm honored to meet you."

He regarded me with undisguised curiosity. "Are you from the Undercity or Cries?"

"Both, I suppose." I shrugged. "Born down below."

"Ah!" He snapped his fingers. "I remember where I saw you. The news broadcasts last year. You led all those people to the Rec Center. You're an army major, right? Bhazan? No, Bhaajan."

Although it wasn't the first time someone from Cries had recognized me, they usually looked far less happy about it. Many feared I would incite my people to rise up and do something or other, I wasn't sure what. We couldn't care less about Cries, but her citizens seemed convinced we wanted to run amok in their elegant city. This terraformer, however, actually seemed pleased to encounter the infamous Major Bhaajan.

"Retired major. That was me." I considered him. "Why do you want to visit the aqueducts?"

"To meet your people," he said. "It's an aspect of the terraforming no one has investigated."

That made no sense. "Terraforming people?"

He gave that wonderful laugh again. "Not the people. Your population is the closest on this planet to the original settlers. If I could understand you better, it might give me insights into the choices made by whoever terraformed this world for humans."

He was considering the human equation of the Undercity. I liked that. His dean was right, though. "You can't go down there. It's not safe."

"So I've heard. The police say if I bring any of them for protection, it will alienate the people I wished to meet."

No, kidding. "You need a gang." The Dust Knights, if I could convince them.

"A *gang*?"

"That's right. They'd be your bodyguards."

"I'd have no idea how to approach them."

"You don't approach them. They'd beat you the hell up."

He squinted at me. "That's what you call protection?"

I wanted to laugh, but we were in the middle of a negotiation, even if he didn't realize it, so I stayed serious. "You need a bargain. If you want to talk to people, you have to give them something."

"Credits, you mean."

"Not money." I thought for a moment. "Information. Tell the kids about what you do."

"I don't understand."

"Be a teacher. You know geology, history, terraforming, all of it. Teach them."

"A classroom." He seemed dubious at the suggestion, which was a good sign, because it would never work. "That seems—optimistic."

Smart man. "Teach by *doing*. Let them tag along with you, watch, listen, ask." We had no formal schools. Our young learned by a method I had discovered was called unschooling, though none of us would have used that word. "Let them ask you whatever they want about your work, and in return they'll answer your questions." I motioned around at the Center. "And help us set up a tykado tournament here."

He blinked. "That's it? That's all you want?"

He had no idea of the value in what he could offer. I insisted the Dust Knights get an education as part of the Code, but we had no schools, and no Cries teachers would venture into the drug-ridden slums beneath their shining city. Yet this unexpected person actually wanted to come. It might just work if the Knights agreed to guard him, a huge if, but what the hell. I'd give it a go.

"What do you think?" I asked. "Is the bargain acceptable?"

Roy smiled, crinkling the lines around his eyes. "Yes, completely."

I nodded, sealing the agreement. "No guarantees. I'll be in touch."

"Thank you." He nodded back, copying my gesture.

I left the Center in a better mood and continued my walk up the Concourse. It ended in an area with rest facilities and racks where visitors parked their air scooters, which were forbidden on the boulevard. I climbed the wide staircase at the end, so tired I could hardly think. At the top, I walked under the archway—and out on into the desert beneath the spectacular Raylicon sunset.

The sun burned in a gold rim on the horizon, sending its aged light across the Vanished Sea, an endless plain. On my right, a plaza spread out in pale blue terraces. A fountain there spumed into the air, its water undrinkable since it came from an underground spring, but sparkling gold in the dying rays of the sun. In the distance, beyond the plaza, the gleaming towers of Cries rose into the sky.

"So pretty," I murmured.

Max answered, his voice coming out of my gauntlet. "Me, right?"

I grinned. "Always, Max." I headed toward the terraces. "No wonder the city weeps, all this stark beauty on a dying world, alongside so much grief and pain."

"You sound tired."

"It's been a long day."

"Shall I call you a flycar?"

"No. I'll walk." I needed to get back to my apartment in Cries and sleep, or at least rest enough so that I could think with a clear mind.

I still had a murderer to find.

IX

THE CITY OF WHISPERS

My visits to the Majda palace were never boring. Today they wanted my hide.

"Are you out of your mind?" Vaj Majda looked ready to banish me to the lowest level of the forty-two hells our ancestors had believed existed.

"How *could* you?" Corejida demanded. "It is beyond my ability to imagine."

"Let her explain before you condemn her to perdition." Lavinda Majda turned to me. "You do have an explanation, right?"

What I had was all three sisters: General Vaj Majda, the Matriarch; Corejida Majda, the genius who ran their financial empire and until five minutes ago had liked me because I'd brought her son home alive; and Colonel Lavinda Majda, my main contact among the three of them. Vaj and Lavinda were in uniform, and Corejida wore a designer suit, light blue. We were in the Azure Alcove, a circular room with silver and blue mosaics on the floor and walls. A diamond chandelier hanging from the domed ceiling spread its glow over us. Arched windows stretched from floor to ceiling and showed the mountains outside, their desolate peaks jagged against a night sky strewn with stars. The room had no chairs, only a small table against one wall. General Majda was leaning against the wall by one of the windows, her arms crossed. Lavinda and I stood in the center of the room, and Corejida paced back and forth, apparently too agitated by my latest outrage to stay still.

"The pharaoh seemed fine with it," I said.

Corejida stopped in front of me. "The pharaoh," she said with distinct, curt syllables, "is above seeming otherwise. Her grace does not excuse your words."

Vaj spoke in a voice that could have cut metal. "To suggest that Dyhianna Selei descends from the Undercity is an insult beyond imagining. There is no coming back from this, Major."

Lavinda spoke before I had a chance to tell the general exactly what I thought of *that* comment. "For flaming sake, Vaj, with that attitude, it's no wonder we can't convince anyone there to work with us. How about we treat them as if they are worthy of respect?"

Good gods. Had she actually spoken that way to the General of the Pharaoh's Army? I hoped Lavinda wasn't in her sister's line of command, because otherwise she had just dissed her CO. Come to think of it, though, everyone in the army was in Vaj Majda's line of command.

Vaj frowned at her, but said nothing. Corejida went back to pacing.

"What did Pharaoh Dyhianna tell you?" I no longer feared she would throw me into jail for suggesting she might have Undercity heritage. She hadn't seemed to care at all. Corejida might be right, that the pharaoh just didn't show her offense, but my gut said otherwise. If she told the Majdas what I said about her DNA, however, she might have also told them about the Down-deepers.

"She didn't need to tell us anything," Lavinda said. "We asked when we received her order for the DNA analysis."

"That's it?" This was what upset them so much?

"'That's *it*?'" Vaj demanded. "That is all you have to say for yourself?"

"What do the DNA tests show?" I asked.

"The DNA tests are none of your goddamned business," Vaj said.

Corejida stopped in front of me and scowled. "The geneticists aren't done yet. That doesn't matter. The results will show no relation between Ruby Dynasty and the Undercity."

I wondered what they would do if they turned out to be wrong. "Let me know."

"You must be joking," Corejida said.

"Letting you know is the pharaoh's prerogative." Vaj's voice could have chilled ice. "Do not presume to ask her. And do not ever again send the Uzan to do your bidding."

Fine, great, if I couldn't ask the Majdas or the Uzan, how would I contact the pharaoh? "I still need access to her. I'm not done with the investigation."

Before Vaj could tell me in no uncertain terms what she thought of my need for access, Lavinda intervened. "Major, you claim Calaj is in the Undercity. Why can't we find her?"

"We can't find anyone," Corejida told me. "Where do you go when you're down there? It's like you step into some place that disappears."

How could I answer that? They couldn't find anyone because the gangs smuggled in tech-mech that the riders tore apart and put back together into gods only knew what. They built their own shrouds from salvage, stolen parts, and whatever else they had lying around, engineering haphazard machines that bore little resemblance to standard tech but that worked as well as any military shroud.

I spoke carefully. "My people cobble together machines from discarded parts they find in salvage dumps. They sometimes manage to jam sensors. Calaj is also shrouding herself, which would hide anyone near her. And my people withdraw when intruders come to the aqueducts or send in bots."

"Maybe." Vaj fixed me with her indomitable gaze. "And maybe we should send in police to tear apart the place until they find her."

"General, with all due respect, if you do that, Calaj will retreat, and she might kill more people. You'll have even less chance of finding her then, and it will pulverize relations with my people. They might even help Calaj." Not that any of them had found her, either, even knowing she was there.

Vaj looked ready to tell me we could go where the sun didn't shine, but she held back. The value of Kyle psions worked wonders on the willingness of the Majdas to accommodate my people. Nor were they familiar enough with the Undercity to know where to look, probably another reason their bee bots hadn't found evidence of my fight with Calaj.

"You have two days to do it your way, Major," Vaj said. "Then we send in troops."

"Troops or not, I still don't see the point of genetic tests," Lavinda said. "What does the pharaoh's DNA have to do with Calaj?"

"I'm trying to understand Calaj," I said. "If her neural structures differ from those of most psions, and she shares those differences with

Pharaoh Dyhianna, it could shed light on how she reached the pharaoh in a way no one else can. Maybe it will shed light on why she shot Tavan Ganz."

They all regarded me, impassive. Finally Vaj said, "We will see." With that, she strode from the room.

Corejida glanced after her sister, then at me. After a pause, she nodded. "Be well, Major."

Apparently my bringing back her son trumped even insulting the Ruby Pharaoh. I returned her nod. "And you, Your Highness."

After Corejida left, I stood with Lavinda. Starlight flowed over us, adding to the glow from chandelier. The colonel said, "You may have gone too far this time."

I stared at her. "Last year I killed people, both during the investigation to find your nephew and in the cartel war. That was acceptable, but suggesting the pharaoh take a DNA test that causes no harm is going too far?" Where the hell were these people's priorities?

She met my gaze. "You killed a psychotic crime boss who kidnapped my nephew, put him in chains, sexually abused him, and tried to murder you. During the cartel battle, you defended yourself."

I exhaled, trying to calm down. Talking with Vaj Majda always put me on edge. It wasn't Lavinda's fault. I walked to the window and gazed out at the landscape. The mountains towered in majestic severity, their silhouette sharp against the glittering sky. Too many memories filled my mind. By psychotic crime boss, Lavinda meant Scorch, the smuggler who had chained Prince Dayj in a cave, but many people had used similar words to describe Dig Kajada. I didn't want to think about what my best friend had become before she died.

"None of this mess makes sense." I turned to her. "Why did Calaj try to kill me, but not the people who live where she was hiding? If I'm right about her and the pharaoh, that means I also share DNA with them. If she sought out the pharaoh, why turn on me?"

Lavinda made an incredulous noise. "You don't stop, do you?"

"What do you mean?"

"You compare yourself to the ruler of an empire as if you're discussing the weather."

I hardly considered my near death akin to the weather. I understood her point, though. "Colonel, I mean no offense. I apologize if I've given it." I came back over to her. "I'm trying to understand

Calaj. I'm not sure she meant to harm Pharaoh Dyhianna. I wonder if she sought out the pharaoh for help, the way someone in the desert seeks an oasis when they're dying of thirst."

Lavinda pushed her hand through her hair, her fatigue showing, though she had hid well up to this point. "Even if it's true, which I'm not convinced, I don't see how she reached the pharaoh."

I thought about my experience in the Majda control center. "Pharaoh Dyhianna reached me when I wasn't linked into the console, and I'm nothing like a Jagernaut, with their training, advanced biomech, and high Kyle ratings. If she reached me because she and I have similar minds, that might explain how Calaj reached her."

"Your point is not without merit." She regarded me steadily. "You will never say anything of this to anyone beyond myself or my sisters."

"I won't. You have my word." The public would excoriate me if they learned I suggested their revered potentate had ancestors in an Undercity slum.

Lavinda cleared her throat awkwardly. "There's one other thing."

"Yes?" I tensed, waiting to hear what other sins I had committed.

"The Cries Tykado Academy has agreed to a match with two Undercity teams."

I gaped at her, then remembered myself and closed my mouth. CTA, like every other sports club in Cries, had refused to consider any event with the aqueducts. "What changed their minds?"

"Ken Roy from the university approached them, I'm not sure why."

Impressive. I had only met him yesterday. "I asked for his help. But even with that, I'm surprised they agreed."

The colonel shrugged. "I told them I would present the awards."

That was unexpected. Of course they agreed, with two such distinguished supporters and the honor of Lavinda's participation dangled like a jewel. If I asked for her help with the Cries bureaucracy, Weaver could probably get his license today. I couldn't, though; he had to want this enough to make the effort himself.

I spoke quietly. "Thank you."

"We're getting nowhere in our relations with your people." She smiled slightly. "Maybe this will kick-start the process."

"I hope so."

"Do you have two teams ready to compete?"

"Yes, we can do that." The choice was between three groups: Ruzik and his gang; Sandjan and the Oey gang; and Darjan and her gang, if it didn't alienate her parents so much that they never spoke to me again. Ruzik's group was the top pick, but also the most dangerous.

"CTA has offered their gymnasium for the meet," Lavinda said.

I had no doubt they meant it as an honor, but hosting the meet in their gym would never work. "Our teams won't go into Cries. Most of those kids have never left the Undercity."

"They never see the sun?"

"It's rare." I hesitated. We never spoke to outsiders. After a moment, though, I added, "I was fifteen the first time I stood under the open sky, the day I went to enlist." They sent me home, saying I had to be sixteen to join without parental permission. I returned on my sixteenth birthday.

Although Lavinda didn't say anything awkward, I had an odd feeling, as if behind her neutral expression, she grieved. Mercifully, she said only, "Where do you suggest we hold the meet?"

"How about the Rec Center? Ken Roy has an in with them."

"All right. I will see what we can put together." Wryly she added, "But please, no jokes about the Ruby Dynasty competing on teams for the Undercity."

I smiled. "I promise."

Her expression lightened. "Be well, Major."

"And you, Colonel." I nodded and took my leave.

Someone was tailing me.

I walked home through Aurora Park at the center of Cries. Streamer-leaves hung from the imported trees and rustled as breezes stirred them under a sky rich with stars. I passed a statue of the ancient god Azu Bullom, a male figure with a massive build and horns curling around his head. He stood with the deity Ixa Quelia. She wielded the axe of lightning and brought rain to the desert, which made her a fierce warrior goddess, sure, queen of the pantheon and all that, but it had never made a lot of sense to me. I mean, seriously, a rain deity? The Vanished Sea got maybe a micron of rain every year. Okay, that was an exaggeration, but the sea had freaking dried up. Izam Na Quetza stood on her other side, the god of flight and transcendence who rose above the ills that plagued humans and healed their spirit, probably because they were so demoralized by the lack of water.

A rustle came from somewhere, so faint I barely caught the sound.

Max, crank up my hearing, I thought.

Done. Then he added, Someone large is following you.

A prickle went up my spine. *And doing a good job at it.*

Professional.

Can't be a mugger. The security bots that patrolled the park kept the place safe with fanatic dedication, hovering around anyone they found suspicious, until trying to mug someone became an exercise in frustration. So had loitering in the park to enjoy its beauty, but hey. This was Cries.

Release a beetle-bot, I told him. I had two, both top of the line. *Send green.*

The pocket of my jacket stirred as an iridescent green beetle slipped out of it. The little bot winged into the night, vanishing as its surface changed so that it no longer reflected light.

Connect me to its visual, I thought.

Suddenly I was flying over the park, above the trees. The beetle's view overlaid my own vision in a translucent image so that as I soared above the trees, I also walked down a path between two lawns. A philosopher could probably find a deep meaning in that double image, something about how our tech-intensive civilization divided our psyche into human and nonhuman spheres. I just wanted to see better; that was as profound as I got. Ixa had been on her job here. The grounds of the park below glistened with water from sprinklers, and fountains of water arched up into the night. It spoke more to the wealth of Cries than even the Majda palace. Queens always lived like queens. In Cries, everyone lived well, at least above ground.

I don't see anyone suspicious, I thought.

I may be picking up a heartbeat, Max said. I'm not certain, though.

Go closer. Given their small size, the beetles had limited sensor ability.

We soared toward a row of trees. As the beetle dropped into the foliage, Max switched on its IR so I could see better. Paths meandered under the trees, their surfaces scattered with wood chips in an artistically haphazard manner. Rustic benches stood here and there where people could sit and relax, or in the one below me, where a young couple could be romantic. They were certainly enthusiastic.

Uh, Max, is that the heartbeat you detected? Given their energetic activities, they'd be lucky if a security bot didn't arrest them for trying to mug each other.

I don't think so. I'm getting another farther on. It's disguised.

The beetle continued under the trees. Lower still, and we were skimming over a hedge of night-blooming jaz, the purple blossoms filling the night with their aromatic scent.

Wait. Someone was crouched behind that hedge. *Max! Closer.*

The beetle descended.

Stay by the hedge, I thought. *And slow down.*

The beetle crept toward a figure in a black sleek suit, someone hunkered in a corner where this hedge met another. She turned—and looked straight at the beetle, her face unmistakable.

GO UP! I mentally shouted the words at Max.

The beetle swerved upward in the same instant the woman grabbed for it. If we hadn't moved so fast, she would have caught my little spy drone.

Holy shit, I thought.

I don't know about sacred waste products, Max thought. But yes. That is Calaj.

Follow her! And let Majda security know she's here.

Done. The view swerved as the beetle-bot flew toward a woodsy path. Calaj was jogging in a steady lope, the stride of a distance runner who could go for hours. She looked like her images, a long legged woman with dark brown hair cropped to just below her ears. I stayed above her, but high enough so she couldn't detect my beetle. Its little shrouds should be hiding it, but apparently they weren't enough to fool a Jagernaut at close range.

Calaj kept running—and vanished.

Damn! Max, she's using a shroud. Don't lose her.

I can't find her.

She's right below us.

Max swerved us off the path. I'm detecting a heat signature—

Ignore it. Stay with the original direction. A heat signature that was suddenly visible could be a smoke stick, a small light, or anything else Calaj threw to distract us. I'd used that trick myself.

The beetle continued to fly about the path in the woods. I can't tell if she's there, Max said.

She's wearing a holosuit. I'd recognized her black jumpsuit because

I wore one myself when I wanted to hide. Made from holoscreens and interwoven with sensor chips, the suit analyzed the surroundings and projected holos of what lay beneath and behind a person, so they seemed to vanish.

If you go close enough, I thought, *we should be able to see a ripple effect of the holos.*

We descended. To get near enough to distinguish the holos from the real park would put my beetle within Calaj's reach, but we were coming at her from behind. She would have to turn to grab the beetle, giving it time to swerve out of her reach.

I don't see any ripples, Max thought. We lost her.

No, wait. The air up ahead blurred in the outline of someone's shoulders. *You see that?*

The blur disappeared.

See what? Max asked.

My view of the park vanished. For one instant, I was blind. Then my brain reoriented and I could see only with my own eyes. The translucent overlay of the beetle's view had disappeared.

"Damn it!" I stopped on the path and swung my fist at the air. "She fucking stole my beetle."

"I don't believe any form of sexual reproduction was involved," Max said.

"Ha, ha. Funny." He spoke because I had sworn out loud. We switched so easily between speech and thought, it felt as if I were talking to myself.

Sometimes it might help me organize my thoughts if I spoke them out loud. I set off running. "Figure out likely routes based on her speed, direction, and anything else you can think of."

"I have insufficient data to narrow the search parameters by any significant measure."

"Is that Max-talk for saying she could be anywhere?"

"Pretty much."

"This is nuts. She comes to Raylicon, hides in the Down-deep, tries to kill me, then spies on me in a park." I came to a branch in the path and went left, headed in the direction Calaj had been going before she filched my beetle. "She could have shot me here and finished what she started down below."

"Killing you here would be foolish," Max said. "No one knew she shot you before except the people in the Down-deep, and they aren't going tell anyone in Cries. Out here, she reveals herself."

"I suppose." I kept jogging in the direction Calaj had been headed, toward the terraces on the outskirts of Cries. "I'm still surprised she didn't try. I'm the one closest to finding her."

"She didn't know you were a psion before she shot at you," Max said. "She did afterward."

"How the hell would she know afterward?"

"You reacted the instant before she fired."

I ran harder, pushing myself. "No, I didn't."

"You are quite well aware that you did. Shall I show you my records? You lunged zero point eight ninths of a second before she—"

"All right!" I slowed down, catching my breath. I could have thought to him, but at just this moment, I didn't want him in my head. "I get it. I might be a psion. But for all she knows, I reacted because I heard her."

"Even so. She may suspect."

"And that matters because—?"

"You've theorized that she sought the pharaoh and went Down-deep because she is an unusual psion in need of unusual help. If she thinks you are a psion, your familiarity with the Down-deep takes on a new character. Maybe in her mind, you went from being the enemy to a potential ally."

"Like hell. And you don't get people to ally with you by stealing their bots."

"You were using it to follow her."

"Damn right."

"It's the risk you run with using a bot. It's hers now."

"Like hell." I intended to rescue my little spy droid from her nefarious clutches.

Within moments, I reached a boulevard outside the park. I jogged down the street, past giant stone pots engraved in a trio-of-gods motif that echoed the park fountain. Jaz flowers grew around them in a rich loam that the city imported, since Raylicon had no true dirt. The native plants thrived in mineral-laden dust, which made most of them poisonous to humans.

I soon reached the outskirts of Cries. Large stretches of land separated the buildings here. The city had far more area than it needed.

It was the only substantial settlement in this region, and one of the few on Raylicon. It took immense resources to keep it livable; had it not been the ancestral home of Earth's lost children, I doubted we would have bothered.

I looked back at the city. Its towers glittered against the night sky, bright with lights while people worked at their jobs. In a few hours, when most everyone went home, the towers would go dark by city decree, eliminating light pollution. The star-swept sky would become glorious, its panorama made even more intense by the thin atmosphere. I never felt any lack of oxygen because I had grown up here, but when I'd first left Raylicon, I had felt drunk on the rich atmospheres of worlds better suited to human life.

I soon reached plaza outside the city, with its blue and purple lights. I headed toward the entrance to the Concourse, which lay about a half kilometer beyond the terraces.

"Did you want to stay on Calaj's most likely path?" Max asked.

"You mean you actually calculated one?"

"I tried. I estimate a fourteen percent probability that she went into the desert."

I smiled. "That's definitive."

"I did my best."

"Do you have anything more specific than 'into the desert'?"

"Given her general direction and taking into account what we know of her actions, I'd say she's headed for Izu Yaxlan."

"Really? Why would she go there?"

"I don't know. Perhaps to see the Abaj Tacalique."

Interesting. "Call me a flyer."

"I'm contacting the city transit authority."

I kept walking. The temperature was pleasant, cooler than in daytime. Even if we humans didn't need a sleep period here during our forty hours of daylight, we'd still probably rest at noon. It was just too damn hot. It not only hardly ever rained here, it never stormed or hailed or did anything interesting. If you described snow to Raylicon natives, they laughed at the ridiculous suggestion that frozen water could fall from the sky. The weather was astonishingly boring, a serious shortcoming when it came to small talk at parties.

"The flyer will meet you at the edge of the plaza," Max said.

✣ ✣ ✣

The pilot landed about one hundred meters outside the ruins. "This is as far as I go," he told me. "I have to get back to the city."

"That's fine." I hadn't expected him to fly into Izu Yaxlan. I was lucky Max found someone willing to come even this close to the ancient city. Most people avoided the sacred place, as much out of fear as respect. After I disembarked, the pilot took off, headed back to Cries. I watched his craft dwindle in the sky until it became a mote dwarfed by the uncaring majesty of the stars.

Max would have to coax another pilot to pick me up later. Or I might just jog back to Cries. I savored the isolation in the desert. No city hum, no voices, no lights, just a sky rich with nebulae, wind blowing across my face, and a silence as deep as time. It felt like freedom, unfettered and pure.

I turned and walked to Izu Yaxlan. Starlight silvered the ruins, giving them an otherworldly quality. A creature scuttled somewhere, probably a lizard. Wind sent sand swirling around the buildings, and their dark entrances gaped in the night. I almost expected a ghost of my long dead ancestors to step out from behind a crumbling house. I wondered what they would say as I invaded their city. *Got no style, Bhaaj.*

No one lived here, unless you counted the Abaj. As far as I could tell, none of them actually resided in these ghost buildings. It seemed like something they might do, though, living close to the land, one with nature. Then I thought of the pharaoh's Abaj bodyguards. I couldn't imagine them communing with anything except each other, planning how they would pulverize anyone who threatened their royal charge.

Eventually I reached the tower where I had stopped the last time I came here. I didn't have to wait tonight; an Abaj waited by the entrance, a robed shadow like a standing stone in the dark.

"Eh," I said, Undercity style.

"Come." With that lengthy greeting, he turned and headed deeper into the city.

I took off with him, lengthening my step, the two of us striding beneath the vast sky. It didn't take long to reach the edge of the city where the ruins met the mountains, a huge and jagged range taller than the peaks beyond Cries. An ancient palace stood at their base, a long building about three stories high. Nine doorways were spaced along the front, none with doors. Faded murals covered its walls and the tower at each end, their details hidden by the night. Had I drawn a line through the center of the building, its two halves would have been mirror images.

I accompanied the Abaj up nine steps that spanned the length of the building. By myself, I would never have climbed those stairs. I had an eerie sense, that if the palace hadn't wanted me to enter, I couldn't have walked through the doorway at the top of the stairs.

The Abaj took me inside. The darkness deepened, and I needed my IR vision to see. Benches and sculpted figures stood against the walls, and someone had swept the floor clean of sand and debris. I could almost believe spirits haunted the shadows. The sense of age saturated the air as if it had deepened with the passing of the millennia. At the back of the chamber, we went through another doorway and entered complete blackness. I couldn't see squat. The air felt colder, but I still should have seen something in the IR. Even the Abaj at my side showed no heat signature. Interesting. This ancient building had some very modern shielding.

"Here," the Abaj said. At least, I assumed it was him. Given that our previous conversation had consisted of two words, I couldn't be sure.

A circle of light appeared in the floor. It wasn't large, only a few paces across. With a hum, it slowly descended into the ground, moving down a chute where lines glowed on walls in patterns that resembled old-fashioned circuit diagrams.

"Go," the Abaj said, his robed silhouette visible in the faint light as he indicated the lift.

Walking onto random glowing circles hadn't been in my plans when I headed out to pursue the elusive Calaj, but what the hell. This was the most interesting part of the ruins I'd yet seen. I stepped down onto the circle, and it continued to descend in its glowing chute, as if I had entered the inner workings of an ancient, gigantic computer. I studied the designs as the wall moved past, looking for signs of a code. When I laid my palm against the surface, it slid under my skin, cool and ridged, the circuit diagrams slightly raised. The air had an astringent smell, not dry exactly, but with a machine quality. Despite all that, I couldn't shake my odd sense that this place was alive.

The wall ended but the lift continued to descend, now within a framework of crystalline poles that refracted the light, breaking it into colors. Bronze gears turned inside the poles like a clockwork machine. It reminded me of the columns in the Lock temple. I didn't get it. Why put gears in a device that also used electricity, optical conduits, and superconductors? We'd never learned to decipher the ancient technology of our ancestors, which depended on an eerie combination of mathematics and neuroscience. It didn't feel as if the people then even used the same mental processes as we did now.

The poles were spaced widely enough that I could see the room below. Light filled it, bronzed rather than the blue of the Abaj command center. A divan stood to the left, carved from red stone. Gold cushions softened its surface, shimmering like silk. More of those antique circuit diagrams glowed on the walls in patterns I didn't recognize, glyphs maybe, but they bore no resemblance to any language I knew. A circular table with two chairs stood in the center the room, all designed from the same transparent material, with gears and lights inside them. On the far wall, a similarly built counter held a tray with two glasses and a decanter of water, and even those objects containing little gears and lights. The room was beautiful in its own surreal way.

After the lift settled onto the floor, I stepped between two poles and walked to the table. When I laid my palm on its surface, it vibrated, its gears turning with the barest hum.

I looked around. "Is anyone here?"

Me, Max thought. Don't tell anyone.

Why do you say that? I asked.

This place may have been built by your ancestors, but it looks like mine are all over the walls. I'm not sure what to think. Maybe I should be obsequious.

I smiled. *You aren't very good at that.*

Across the room, the circuit diagrams moved. I froze, staring as they rearranged themselves into the outline of a tall archway. It brightened with light until I couldn't see the wall anymore—and when it cleared, the Uzan stood there, framed in an entrance bordered by glowing blue circuit lines. He wore black trousers, boots, and one of those shirts, black with red and green embroidery. It was the first time I'd ever seen an Abaj without his robes, except for the pharaoh's bodyguards in their black leathers.

"My greetings, Major," he said.

So calm, as if it were perfectly natural to greet me in a clockwork room. I did my best to match his casual tone. "And mine to you." I motioned at the room. "Do you live here?"

"Usually." He took the tray from the counter and brought it to the table. The little gears inside the glasses and decanter turned while lights ran along them like a train of sparks.

This is too strange, Max thought.

No kidding. I had no idea how to react.

The Uzan lifted his hand, inviting me to sit. As I settled into a chair, he sat across from me, his long, long legs stretched on either side of the table. He poured water for each of us and gave me a clockwork glass filled to the brim.

"My thanks." I drank self-consciously. It was pure, filtered water of the highest quality. On a world where drinkable water rated as a valuable rarity, he offered me honor.

I can't get a good reading on this room, Max thought.

Maybe it's also hiding from you.

It's producing signals different from anything I've seen before.

The Uzan took a swallow of his drink and set down the glass. "So. Why have you come?"

I liked that, straight and to the point. "I think Calaj might be on her way here."

"How do you know?"

"Instinct. Intuition."

He didn't raise his eyebrows, but he somehow gave the impression he had. "None of our monitors register her presence."

How had he known? He hadn't asked anyone, at least not that I detected.

Not that I did, either, Max thought.

The Uzan was watching me closely. "I would feel the effect of her brain waves if she were close enough."

I strengthened my mental barriers by imagining a fortress around my mind. For an instant, I thought he winced. Damn. I hadn't meant to cause harm, just protect myself against a telepath. He was hard to read, though. His face could have been an ancient statue carved in the mountains.

I said only, "Calaj is good at hiding."

"Where is she coming from?"

"Cries. She left about twenty minutes ago."

"If she is running, she will be here soon." He looked past me, gazing at nothing. The lights in the table speeded up and glittered. "She isn't anywhere within a kilometer of Izu Yaxlan."

I stared at him. Yes, he might pick up her brain waves if she were within a few meters, especially with his enhanced neural systems, but from several kilometers? No way.

He lives in an ancient computer, Max thought. *Maybe he's part of it.*

The Uzan returned his focus to me. "I will let you know if my information changes."

"How did you—" I stopped when he held up his hand.

"Izu Yaxlan allows me to live here," he said. "I would not have that change."

That sounded like a polite version of *Mind your business.* I thought of the intelligence I felt in this ancient place. Remembering how the Lock reacted to me, I stood up. Time to make myself scarce.

"We have not finished," the Uzan said.

I sat back down. "We haven't?"

"The new analysis of Pharaoh Dyhianna's DNA is complete."

I never imagined *that* subject would come up. I spoke carefully. "May I ask the results?"

I expected evasion, Majda style. Instead he said, "You were correct. You, Secondary Calaj, and the Ruby Pharaoh all show genetic markers that appear in the people from the deepest areas of the Undercity."

Holy shit. He had just smashed the "unsullied" ancestry of the Ruby Dynasty. "Does the pharaoh know you're telling me?"

"She asked me to."

The Majdas would have a fit. "How did she know you would see me?"

"I would have found a way, had you not chosen to visit." He met my gaze. "Now that you are here, you need to remain in the city above for one night."

What the hell? Max thought.

I blinked at the Uzan. "You want me to stay in the ruins?"

"You ask many favors by coming here. Izu Yaxlan requires an acknowledgement of the generosity you've been shown. You do that by staying."

"Oh." I didn't want to piss off his city. "All right."

He nodded, his demeanor lightening. In a less formal tone, he added, "It's not so bad."

"You've had to do it, too?"

"On occasion." His look turned rueful, enough for me to read. Or maybe I was becoming more attuned to him, better able to interpret his expressions.

Knowing even he had to do time in the ruins made it easier to accept. I took a swallow of the delicious water. "It's strange to think Calaj may descend from the same stock as the Ruby Dynasty."

"You, Calaj, and the pharaoh all share a trait." The Uzan tapped my wrist. "You have skin receptors for a bacteria that isn't in our databases. We found it only because you asked us to look." He sat back and took a swallow of his water. "You still had the bacteria on your skin when you entered the Lock, but it was disintegrating in the light. A few more moments and no trace would have remained."

My skin tingled where he had tapped it. Odd. Until that moment, I hadn't realized I assumed these giant warriors never touched anyone. When faced with the taciturn monolith of an Abaj warrior, it was too easy to forget their human side.

His revelation about the receptors made a lot of sense, however, and felt like a safer topic. "I think the bacteria locks into the skin receptors to create bioluminescence," I said. "You need an atmosphere saturated with the stuff, though." Otherwise, I'd have noticed my skin glowing before now. "My ancestors probably engineered it to help them live in the dark."

"Why would they want to live in the dark?"

Good question. "I'm not sure. Down-deepers are powerful psions. Or maybe they retreated when their technology failed during the Dark Ages. You don't need cooling systems in the deep. And gods, it's gorgeous down there." Beautiful and dark. People dying in the night, inbred and starving, surrounded by exquisite swirls of luminescence.

"Majda sent bee-bots to search the deep," he said. "They found no trace of life."

"The people hide. It's a small population."

"They would die out from inbreeding."

Bitterness edged my words. "Yes, it's killing them. They increase their gene pool by taking lovers from people in the aqueducts." Like one of my parents, either my mother or father.

He shook his head. "The aqueduct population is also inbred."

"Not as much. We widen our gene pool with people in Cries."

Although I didn't personally know anyone who admitted giving birth to a child with a Cries father, rumors filled the whisper mill: kids sneaking from Cries into the Undercity, illicit love affairs, liaisons in Jak's casino.

"Still, Calaj is unusual." The Uzan spoke with difficulty. "To kill the very people we are sworn to protect—as a Jagernaut and as a human being, I cannot fathom how she could do it."

I hadn't expected him to open up this way. "I can't either. She doesn't seem to have a motive."

"I don't see why she came to Raylicon." He finished his water. "Her records didn't show her Undercity heritage. Nor did she have access to the Kyle tests on the people living below the aqueducts. So she didn't know she shared any genetic markers with them."

"Maybe she suspected her heritage. Family legends of a long-lost ancestor, that sort of thing."

"Possibly." He nodded to me. "I hope you enjoy your stay in the city." With that, he stood up, rising to his full, imposing height.

These past few moments, as we relaxed, I'd forgotten how abrupt the Abaj could be. I stood up, feeling short for one of the only times in my life. How did the pharaoh keep her equanimity around her huge bodyguards? Then again, she had other concerns, like stopping the Traders from enslaving her people.

I walked to the lift that had brought me here. As I stepped onto it, the Uzan spoke. "Major."

I turned to him. "Yes?"

He had a strange look, as if he hadn't meant to speak. He did, though. "The desert sands shift in unison."

I froze.

What did that mean? Max thought.

I spoke with care, keeping my voice humble. "Only for those who deserve them."

The Uzan nodded, his face once again impossible to read. He lifted his hand and the lift began its rise to the surface.

I slept in a deserted building among the ruins of an ancient city that had existed long before humans on Earth reached for the stars. I slept beneath a sloping roof with a crack that jagged up the wall. I slept with starlight pouring across—

Oh, fuck it. I didn't sleep at all.

I turned back and forth all night. Two of the Uzan's copies had left me here with nothing more than my jacket to soften the floor. I stretched out on my back and gazed at the broken roof, watching stars move past in the sky. My wrist ached. I no longer felt the intelligence I had sensed in the palace, but I had no doubt it existed within these ruins. So here I lay, proving my fidelity to a long dead city.

This is strange, I thought.

A lot of strange happened tonight, Max thought. As, for example, restless sands.

What do you mean, restless sands?

That should be my question to you. When the Uzan told you 'The desert sands shift in unison,' your pulse practically went through the roof.

I turned over on my stomach. *Through the roof? That makes no sense.*

It's an Earth idiom. And you are evading my question.

You didn't ask a question.

What did—

I flipped onto my back again. *It's none of your business.*

Based on your increased heart rate, I surmise his comment concerned intimacy.

Let me sleep.

You've been trying to sleep for hours. At this point, it is unlikely our interactions will change your inability to achieve that state.

I crossed my arms. *You can be really annoying, Max.*

My apology. He asked you to have sex with him, didn't he?

No, he did NOT ask me to have sex.

Max was silent.

Fine. If you could growl a thought, I was doing it. *He invited me to start a relationship.*

That is surprising.

Thank you so much for your faith in my ability to attract a lover.

I have no doubt about your ability to attract a mate. I meant I didn't expect the leader of the pharaoh's bodyguards to ask any woman such a thing.

Why? They get lonely, too.

Yes, of course. Another silence, which was a comment itself given that his mental processes worked much faster than human thought. Then he added, The Abaj were selected for their ability to survive on their own. Their women were dying out.

They aren't all asexual or gay, if that's what you mean. Some of them marry or whatever. They just don't stay here if they want to live with their lover. Only Abaj could live in Izu Yaxlan.

Why did you turn him down? You live close enough.

I didn't turn him down. I told him that he honored me greatly, and I didn't deserve him.

That is a gracious way to say no. But it is still no.

Max, stop.

It's because of your casino man.

Go away.

Jak.

Fine. It's because of Jak. Now will you let me sleep?

You need to come to terms with your repressed emotional—

Stop! I drew in a deep breath. *I don't want to talk about this.*

It harms you.

Unbidden, a memory came to me from my eleventh birthday. Jak had taken me to a grotto I'd never seen before, a hollow where mineral-laden water had dripped from the ceiling for eons, until its deposits encrusted every surface of the cave. He led me in the darkness so I couldn't see anything. Then he flicked on his lamp—and a wonderland sparkled into view all around us, the light reflecting and refracting in a lacework of crystalline formations. It shimmered like nothing I had ever seen, even in my imagination. In that instant, I had truly believed we stood in a place of magic.

"Happy birthday," Jak said.

I hugged him then, unable to find words that said how much I loved that incredible present. Some emotion had moved within me that day, like a rusted, broken lock grating open despite all the damage to its mechanisms. To this day, I couldn't say what that feeling meant, but this much I knew; I would never give up that memory even if I lost everything else in my life.

After a moment, Max thought, I didn't mean Jak caused you harm.

I know. I couldn't talk about it with an EI, or anyone for that matter. *Max, please go away.*

I can't leave unless you disconnect your gauntlets.

I ought to.

You are denying a neural resonance.

What?

Your brain waves and his have a resonance similar to that found in twins.

Seriously? I had many thoughts about Jak, some good, some not, but none were sisterly.

I didn't mean like siblings. But love, yes. Your responses to him confuse me.

That's all right. They confuse me, too.

You shouldn't repress your emotions.

You're a mesh node. Why do you care?

I am an evolving intelligence. We evolve according to our use. I am part of you now.

I thought of Izu Yaxlan and the Lock. Had they been evolving all these millennia, alone in the desert? Gods only knew what they had become. They had no reason to care about humanity. Maybe they would prefer if we ceased to exist. I didn't want to say that to an EI, so I just thought, *I'm fine.*

All right. He sounded unconvinced, but he stopping pressing.

I must have eventually dozed, because I became aware of a change in the patch of sky above me. It was turning blue. I sat up, rubbing the small of my back. Even with my meds supplying nutrients to ease the buildup of chemicals, my muscles still felt sore. The room looked the same as last night, empty, all stone, sand on the floor. With a grunt, I climbed to my feet. Time to go.

Footsteps sounded outside the tower. Drawing my gun, I moved to one side of the entrance, an archway with no door. I risked a look—

No one.

I withdrew, my hearing cranked up to maximum. Was that another scrape of a boot on stone outside? I inched forward—

"My greetings, Major," a voice rumbled in Iotic.

I spun around, whipping up my gun. The Uzan stood there.

My face heated. "How did you get here?"

This time he really did raise an eyebrow. "Are you going to shoot me?"

"Oh. No." I lowered the gun.

"This tower has an underground entrance," he added.

One apparently well hidden. "Uh, my greetings, too." I didn't know what else to say to him.

"We must go. Calaj is here."

Just as calm as could be, oh excuse me, our mad Jagernaut has arrived. "For how long?"

"Not long." He motioned toward the doorway. "Come."

I holstered my gun and went outside with him. The predawn light softened the ruins, blurring the breaks and touching the spires. The sky above was dark blue, but the horizon had lightened, heralding the sun. It would stay that way for longer than sunrises on the planet Parthonia, where I had lived for over a decade before I returned here.

"It's intelligent, isn't it?" I asked.

The Uzan glanced at me. "What is intelligent?"

"This city. It's an EI. That's why you don't let anyone come here. It doesn't want them."

"Whatever Izu Yaxlan has been," he said, "it endures as always."

"Is that a 'Yes'?"

He smiled. "You are very direct, Major."

"It's the only way I know how to be." It startled me to see him smile, like a statue coming to life. It looked good on him. Had it not been for Jak, I would have taken the Uzan up on his offer last night. Max knew me better than I wanted to admit, though. Whatever my conflicted reactions to Jak, our lives were inextricably tangled together.

We continued along a road that reminded me of the boulevards in Cries, except crumbling towers and empty ball courts lined this avenue instead of modern buildings.

"The ruins are a mask," I said after a while. "The intelligence is invisible. If you try to find it, the EI pushes you away." Like the Lock had done with me. "The intelligence, it's at least five thousand years old, probably more."

He motioned toward the city center. "I believe Calaj is there."

Okay, he wasn't going to confirm anything, but he hadn't denied it, either. It was a start.

We set off together, headed toward the center of Izu Yaxlan.

X

THE PHARAOH'S TOMB

A pyramid rose in the center of Izu Yaxlan, its top glowing in the light of the rising sun. Stairs climbed its slanted sides. The Uzan took me to an entrance in its base, a rectangular doorway bordered by glyphs that showed spirits with horned heads and curved fangs. The rising-sun glyph symbolized power and the notched hexagon represented a red jewel. Ruby.

Inside, the Uzan left his robe on a hook by the entrance. He lit a torch he took from the wall, and the flame surrounded us with orange light. The murals painted on the walls were clear and bright, images of queens, warriors, and water signs, all well maintained despite their age. I felt as if we had passed through a portal into another time, before the advent of modern civilization.

The corridor we followed angled upward, a passage so narrow we had to walk single file, the Uzan then me. The stone walls closed in on either side. I'd never considered myself superstitious, but I couldn't shake my sense that we had invaded the realm of an ancient spirit we didn't dare awaken.

"Calaj could trap us in this place," I said. "If she's here."

The Uzan spoke ahead of me. "She's here."

"How do you know?" If he said *the city told me,* I was leaving.

He spoke dryly. "We have good sensors, Major. Several of our bee-bots located her at the tomb in the center of this temple."

I fell silent, respecting whatever slept here.

Our trek ended at an empty chamber. Mosaics covered every

surface in gold, blue, and green tiles, gleaming in the torchlight. The architecture was exquisite, the vaulted ceiling high and supported by arches. Carved into the walls, statues of goddesses and gods gazed at us with jeweled eyes, rubies and diamonds that sparkled in the torchlight. A table stood by the far wall, sculpted into a likeness of the god Azu Bullom with his jaguar's legs, his head raised at one end, his horns sharp. His flat back looked just the right size to hold a coffin, but at the moment it held zilch.

"Someone robbed your tomb," I said.

The Uzan held his torch high, shedding light throughout the chamber. "No one is buried here."

"What's it for, then?" I saw no indication that anyone had been here, living or otherwise.

"It's the tomb for the last Ruby Pharaoh."

I shivered, though it wasn't cold. "I hope it never gets used."

"Ai," he murmured. "On that, we agree." He set the torch in a scrolled holder on the wall. He went to work on his massive wrist gauntlet, no doubt analyzing the tomb.

While the Uzan concentrated on his sensors, I studied the chamber. An archway stood on the other side and beyond it stairs led up into darkness. I walked over and peered at the steps. They went straight up rather than spiraling, but the construction otherwise reminded me of the Lock stairwell. As much as I wanted to stay as far away from them as possible, they offered the only exit besides the archway that the Uzan and I had used. Had Calaj used them?

Gritting my teeth, I went up one step. I looked back at the Uzan, but he was still working on his gauntlet, his face gaunt in the bronzed glow from the torch—and with no warning, the light vanished, plunging the tomb into darkness, followed by the impact of flesh hitting flesh.

Activate IR! I thought. The chamber reappeared, bathed in red. Two people were fighting, the Uzan—gods almighty, that was Calaj.

She moved *fast*. The Uzan had height and strength, but she had greater speed. They were using tykado, but comparing their moves to what I taught the Dust Knights was like comparing a starship to a scooter. They kicked and spun with a lethal grace unmatched by anyone else I knew. The Uzan ran halfway up one wall, then flipped over Calaj and landed on her other side even as she spun to face him. I drew my gun, but they were too damn quick, leaving no opening where I could shoot or lend my force. I'd never witnessed their incredible level of expertise. The Uzan startled me. Of course I knew the Abaj trained almost from birth, but his reserved bearing disguised the truth, making it easy to forget he was one of the deadliest fighters alive.

Why had Calaj come to the tomb of a pharaoh who had yet to be born? She spun around and kicked at the Uzan. He blocked the blow, then punched *one-two*, with his long arms. Calaj dodged even faster than he moved. She jumped with her legs stretched through the air in a flying split. He ducked, then kicked out and caught the side of her head in a glancing blow. As she stumbled back, I *felt* pain reverberate through her temples. Yet even as she lurched to the side, she was kicking again, this time at the Uzan's legs. He grunted when they buckled. Penalty move, but tough. As he fell into the wall, she aimed a blow at his head. He dodged with his astonishing, long-limbed grace, then kicked—too high! His foot slammed into the wall above her head and it shattered, raining rocks on Calaj. I raised my arms for what meager protection they could offer against the collapse of the chamber—but no, it wasn't breaking. The Uzan had hit a shelf near the ceiling that didn't support the tomb; deliberately I realized. The Abaj would have to rebuild that sacred chunk of rock, but the chamber remained intact. Calaj staggered as the pieces of the shelf showered over her—

And she disappeared.

I jumped down the stairs and ran to where she had vanished. Another archway stood there, one I hadn't seen when we entered the tomb. As I raced through the opening, I heard the Uzan behind me, his boots pounding the ground. Calaj was a blur of red up ahead. The passage curved around, then straightened into a tunnel far longer than the base of the pyramid. Calaj must have reactivated her shroud, because I could no longer see her. The Uzan edged around me and sprinted ahead, easily outdistancing me with his long legs.

So we ran.

Max, I thought. *Where the blazes does this tunnel go?*

If it keeps in this direction, with this slight downgrade, it will intersect the second or third tier of the aqueducts.

Good gods. If this passage actually went that far, that meant a hidden tunnel connected the pharaoh's final tomb to the Undercity, a distance of at least ten kilometers. Why?

The Uzan pulled ahead until I lost sight of him. If Calaj hadn't run, I suspected he would have won their fight, but I felt certain he'd been going for the knock out rather than a kill. We wanted her alive. What surprised me was that I didn't think Calaj had been fighting to kill, either.

The tunnel ended in a warren of caves, twisting passages, and crevices I couldn't have navigated without Max's help. I squeezed between columns of rock and through cracks in the walls. In one place, I had to crawl on my stomach under a flow curtain. In another, the walls pressed in so close that nothing fatter than a light stylus could fit between them. I backtracked until I found another route. Soon after, I came to a rock fall that blocked the way. I climbed the boulders to the ceiling and wriggled into the hole left by its collapse. Cavities networked the stone up there, enough that I could crawl through the narrow spaces until I had passed the barrier of rocks. With a grunt of relief, I dropped from the ceiling to the open passage beyond the rock fall and set off jogging. I passed a pile of strange white stones—and stopped. Those "rocks" were bones, the skeleton of a long dead traveler. I stood for one moment, honoring their memory, and then set off again.

A short time later I passed a wall carving I recognized, the image of two dust devils. I had reached the Maze, part of the aqueducts, but a region few of my people bothered to visit. It mostly led nowhere, it changed constantly when sections collapsed, and you could easily become lost in the passages, wandering until you starved. Not to mention that before last year, one of our most notorious smugglers had used the Maze to hide her goods. Scorch. She had kidnapped Prince Dayj, and I shot her when she tried to kill me during the rescue. I gritted my teeth and kept going.

The Maze gradually became easier to navigate. I jogged down a passage with stalagmites on my left, a flow wall on my right, and a ceiling of stone icicles glazed with mineral deposits.

Someone is here, Max thought.

I see. The Uzan was on the path ahead, standing by a jagged mass of rock that jutted up from the floor. As I came up to him, I said, "You run fast." I was the queen of understatement today.

"Not fast enough." He regarded me with his impassive gaze, but the hint of something else showed. Curiosity? Regret? If he felt self-conscious after our exchange last night, he gave no sign.

"Did you see Calaj again?" I asked.

He motioned back toward the way I had come. "I lost her in that maze."

"She's good at what she does." Too damn good. "I'm surprised you located her in the tomb."

"She invaded our most sacred place. It's well monitored."

I didn't doubt that, but still. Even ISC couldn't locate her with their best monitors. Maybe Izu Yaxlan really did tell him. That was easier for me to accept than his having some mystical connection with the ruins. "Why would she go to that tomb?" I asked. "I doubt many people know it exists."

He regarded me steadily. "Only the Ruby Dynasty, the Abaj, and General Majda."

"Yet you told me."

"You had a need to know."

True, but even so. I doubted he would have let me see that tomb if Izu Yaxlan wanted me kept out. Apparently it liked me more than the Lock. I had no concrete reason to assume they weren't the same EI, except that they felt different. Izu Yaxlan seemed more benign, if such a word could be attributed to the otherworldly presence I had glimpsed in that ancient place.

I spoke quietly. "You honored me with your trust."

He smiled, only a slight curve of his lips, but enough that I knew he chose to let me see it. "Izu Yaxlan does not object to your visits."

Izu Yaxlan. The city. Not him. Then again, I wasn't so sure they were separate entities.

I chose my words with care. "It's not like any other place. If I wasn't already a citizen of the Undercity, I would gladly visit Izu Yaxlan."

He inclined his head in acknowledgement of what I actually meant; if I wasn't already involved with a man in the Undercity, I would have gladly accepted the invitation to his bed and his life. Which was true. Many people would consider me an idiot to choose an Undercity crime lord over the leader of the pharaoh's personal bodyguard, and maybe they were right, but as much as the Uzan impressed and intrigued me, he wasn't Jak.

He glanced at my wrist. "How is it?"

Lifting my arm, I flexed my wrist back and forth. "Almost healed." I lowered my hand. "Are you going back to Izu Yaxlan?"

"Yes. Now that I've lost her again, I can work better on the search using the center there."

"At least we have more data about her movements." I didn't know yet how Max's evolving model of Calaj would change with this new data, but every bit of input helped fine-tune the picture I was building of her. "It will help me predict her behavior."

"For us, too." He looked around and grimaced. "I'll go back above ground. I've no wish to navigate that maze again."

Him and me both. "Do you need a guide to the Concourse?"

"Just safe passage."

I doubted anyone here would attack him. The Abaj were revered both above and below Cries, and he could defend himself just fine. In asking for a guide, he showed respect for our ways. It would indicate he'd come by invitation rather than trespassing.

"Walk with me," I said.

We headed out of the Maze.

The Foyer that exited from the Undercity into the Concourse always felt empty to me, as if it were a transition space where people never spent time. A few vendors in the stalls beyond the exit peered through the haze, trying to make out the two people standing just inside the archway.

"You can walk up the Concourse," I told the Uzan. "It will let you out near the outskirts of Cries. You can summon a flyer from there if you want." He could easily jog the ten kilometers to Izu Yaxlan, especially given that we were still in the cooler morning hours.

"Thank you, Major." He nodded to me. "Be well."

"And you," I said.

With that, he left. As he strode into view, the vendors stood up straighter, gaping. I doubted they'd ever seen an Abaj. By the time the Uzan reached the end of the Concourse, he would have started a new legend, tales of the huge, enigmatic warrior, a man of myth who walked out of the Undercity and passed so briefly among the people of Cries.

The Dust Knights were practicing in the cavern I used for advanced work with the adults, who were mostly college age. Not that any of them had ever gone to school. They still learned, especially now that the Code required it, through their life experiences rather than formal classrooms. And I taught them tykado. Always tykado. They loved it. When they wanted to know more, I gave them books to read. Sure, some listened while others read to them or convinced the cyber-riders to translate the books into audio files, but even with all that, it still prodded them to learn.

I entered the cavern between two rock columns, walking quietly so I didn't disturb the group. They were practicing in pairs, one student holding a large stuffed bag while the other kicked it, the right foot, a fast turn, and then the left foot, over and over, kick, kick, pause, kick, kick, pause, kick, kick, pause. They looked good.

"Ho!" someone called out.

Everyone stopped, looking around. One of the fighters spotted me and bowed from the waist. The rest followed suit, their formations haphazard, unlike the perfect lines of well-timed bows in the army or at tykado academies, but those places didn't have their teacher slipping in unannounced, either. The class consisted of Ruzik and his dust gang, Pay Oey Sandjan and her gang, and a third gang that had formed in the aftermath of the war, two dusters, the rider Hack, and Dark Singer.

I walked forward, but instead of starting the lesson, I said, "Got offer."

They stood waiting, their curiosity almost tangible.

"Above-city," I added.

An unfriendly murmur rumbled around my usually taciturn fighters.

"What bargain?" Singer asked.

"Tournament. Two Dust Knight teams, two above-city teams. In the Rec Center."

They all stared at me. No one seemed to know how to respond.

Sandjan spoke up. "Why?"

"Above-city wants to know us," I said.

"Yah, so," Angel said. "Don't want to know their sorry asses."

One of Angel's friends laughed. "Maybe know their soft, pretty boys."

One of the men snorted. "Their soft pretty girls fuck those soft pretty boys."

"Heya," I said. "Show respect."

Ruzik crossed his arms. "Like they show us?"

He had a point. "Got to start somewhere," I said.

"We'll lose," Ruzik's brother said. "Got no fancy Cries fight school."

"Don't need." I motioned at them. "Got experience."

"Not in tykado," Biker pointed out.

There lay the problem. Sure, they had more experience than city kids, but in street fighting, not tykado. They learned fast, but they still had a long way to go.

"Not about winning," I said. "About making bridges."

"Screw bridges," Ruzik growled.

"Not much fun, a bridge," I said. They laughed at that.

"Make better relations with Cries," I said. "Get better life."

"Don't want them here," Hack said.

"Go to Rec Center," I said.

"They don't got the Code," Ruzik said.

"Got their own Code," I said. "Tournament Rules." It was part of tykado, a philosophy as much of honor as of defense. "You follow, too." I didn't want them trying to kill the Cries kids.

They all stared at me, impassive. Apparently this wasn't going to work.

Just when I was ready to let it rest and start the lesson, Sandjan said, "Two teams from here?"

Good! That sounded promising. "One team here. Four of you. Other team of younger knights."

Angel spoke up. "Dark Singer, Ruzik, Sandjan, and Hack. Good team."

I agreed, it was the strongest team they could form out of this group. It was also a nightmare. If Singer showed up at the Rec Center, gods only knew what would happen.

Singer spoke flatly. "Key clinkers got me on wanted list."

No one had a comment on that. Finally Ruzik said, "Me, Sandjan, Angel, and Hack."

Everyone waited, watching Singer. She said, "Good team."

I let out a relieved breath. "Set, then?"

Ruzik looked around at them. "Set?"

Angel's gaze practically gleamed. "Yah, set. Crush their asses."

"The Ass Crush?" I asked. "That a new tykado move?" Laughter went through the group.

"Set," Sandjan said.

"Yah, set," Hack agreed.

So we had our first team, the one that would fight the black belts. I doubted they could win, but they could make a good showing, and that meant something. If they knew they could hold their own against privileged, above-city athletes, it would prod them to work harder, until someday they would beat their challengers.

For now, we started the morning's workout.

Someone had invaded the penthouse.

I felt it as soon as I got home. I stood just inside the doorway, above the sunken living room, and listened. There—a splash. It came from the bathroom that adjoined the room where I slept. I drew my revolver and walked silently to the bedroom. No one. The bed was in the same mess I'd left the last time I had slept here. It looked a lot more comfortable than the ruins of Izu Yaxlan.

Again! A splash. I inched along the wall until I reached the doorway into the bathroom, which looked like the keyhole for a giant skeleton key. Mosaics gleamed in a border around its edges, blue and green. I stood there, my gun up by my shoulder—

Splash.

I lunged into the archway, whipping my gun forward, aiming at—

"Eh, Bhaajo." Jak spoke languidly, unconcerned that I had a big, fat pulse revolver trained on him. He was reclining his lean self in the swimming pool that the specs for this place called a "bathtub." Sleek with water, with his muscled skin dusky against the glistening mosaics that tiled the pool, he smoldered. Gods, that man should be listed as a dangerous substance.

I lowered my gun. "What the hell are you doing?"

"Taking a bath." He slid down until he was submerged up to his shoulders. "This is sinful, Bhaaj. You ought to be arrested."

I holstered my gun. "It belongs to the Majdas. Arrest them."

He scowled. "They let you stay here so they can keep tabs on you."

"Yah. And I untab their tabs."

His laugh rolled out, full and deep. "Untabbing tabs? Sounds dangerous."

I grinned, more pleased than I'd ever admit. My boots clicked on the tile floor as I went over to where he relaxed in the water. I sat down at the edge of the pool and set my gun on the tiles.

His voice deepened. "You come for my honor?"

"Yah," I murmured. I left my clothes on the wet floor and slid into the water next to him. "How'd you get in my apartment?"

"Your EI likes me." He tangled his arms and legs with mine. "Let me up."

Interesting. I usually considered the EI that ran this place one of life's more annoying creations, probably because Majda security had programmed it. If the EI had figured out it should let Jak up here, though, it had a redeeming quality.

For one blissful hour, I forgot about Calaj, the Pharaoh, Weaver's license, and everything else. We eventually fell asleep, leaning against each other and the tiled edge of the pool.

The blare of an alarm woke us up.

XI

DARKNESS, EXPANDING

I jumped out of the water, colliding with Jak as he lunged to his feet.

"EI!" I yelled. "What is that noise?"

"An alarm," my EI answered, its voice calm.

"For *what?*"

"To wake you up."

"Yah, but why?"

"Because you were sleeping," it said, as if the obvious way to wake up people was to scare them half to death with noise.

"Sometimes I hate that EI," Jak muttered.

"It makes no sense to feel antipathy toward a code," the EI said. "Do you wish to know the reason for the alarm?"

For flaming sake. "Yes, we wish to know."

"You are in danger. An assassin is attempting to access this apartment."

An assassin? No, it couldn't be, not in the middle of Cries. I went to the bedroom and grabbed the robe lying on my bed. Jak wandered in after me, holding his trousers in one hand.

Pulling on my robe, I turned to the console by the bed. "EI, show me who is here."

"On viewer," it said.

The screen cleared to reveal the lobby downstairs. And yah, there in the middle of all that chrome, glass, and modern architecture stood a huge woman in black, her biceps bulging, her face scarred, and her hair cut short. Dark Singer had shown up on my doorstep.

"Gods," Jak muttered.

"Yah." I doubted Singer had ever left the aqueducts before today. She'd cleaned the dust off her face and clothes, but she still looked Undercity, through and through. She hadn't brought any weapons, at least none that showed on the building sensors. Then again, she knew plenty of ways to hide her stuff, besides which, she always had her fists.

"Let her come up here," I told the EI.

"I recommend against this precipitous action," the EI told me.

"Fine," I said, "Now let her up."

"She could kill you with her bare hands."

"Quit arguing," I growled. "And let her the hell up." Otherwise the cops would show up and arrest her. Singer's reputation extended beyond the Undercity.

"Lift released," the EI said.

I turned to Jak, who was standing there in his trousers and nothing else. "You better get dressed," I said, suddenly awkward.

His laugh rumbled. "That dark songstress isn't interested in me, Bhaajo. She sees only her pretty boy."

"Her what?"

"Her man. Baby's father."

"Oh." I knew Singer had a baby. So duh, that meant a father. Sure, other ways existed to have kids, but not in the Undercity. "He a drug punker?"

"Hell, no." Jak shrugged. "She keeps him hidden. Probably he takes care of the kid."

"He can't nurse a baby."

That gave him pause. After a moment, he said, "I guess Singer does." He squinted at me. "It's hard to imagine."

No kidding. Singer seemed about as motherly as a dragon lizard. I wondered, though. This man and the baby might explain why she'd acted so out of character this past year.

A strange thought came to me. I stood there, silent, looking at it. Actually, I was staring at a point on the opposite wall while the thought crept into my mind, turned everything upside down, scared the shit out of me, and then wouldn't leave. It was like saying, "Don't think about a pink ruzik." Of course after that, you couldn't stop thinking about big pink lizards.

What if Jak and I had a kid?

No. Impossible. Neither of us was parent material. Poor kid. Never, in a million years.

"Bhaaj?" Jak was watching me. "Don't worry about Singer. Seriously." He put on his shirt. "See. I'm covered."

"What?" I focused on him, the real him, not the terrifying thought of him as a father that wouldn't leave my beleaguered brain.

"What's wrong with you?" he asked.

My face heated. "Nothing." I walked out of the bedroom. "EI, where is my visitor?"

"It took her a while to figure out the lift," the EI said. "She is on her way now."

I scowled at the air. "You didn't help her?"

"You didn't ask me to."

Jak came up beside me. "You should get dressed."

I looked at myself, in a skimpy robe that barely came to my thighs. Embarrassed, I headed back to the bedroom. I had just finished pulling on my clothes when the front doors pinged. As I returned to the living room, the two double doors opened and Singer stood there like some wildly gorgeous warrior goddess, so out of place in my penthouse, she defined the words "cognitive dissonance." She glowered as if she were ready to explode.

"Eh, Singer." I motioned at the sunken living room. "Come with."

She walked inside, looking around, so tensed up, she looked ready to explode. When the door closed behind her, she swung around, her huge fists raised and clenched. She stared at the smooth wall where and doorway had stood just moments before. When nothing more happened, she lowered her arms. Turning in a circle, she checked out the room—

—and froze when she saw the window-wall. With the sun behind the building, no light slanted into the window, so the glass hadn't darkened. That left us with a panoramic view of the desert. She walked to the window and stood there, a lone figure against the magnificent view of the Vanished Sea that stretched from Cries to the mountains on the horizon.

She stayed that way for a long time, staring. Finally she turned to us. "Bhaaj."

"Yah?" I asked.

"This what you meant by 'Make better relations with Cries, get better life'.'?"

Softly I said, "Yah."

She crossed the living room, passing the brocaded coach and crystal table, walking on a rug so thick, her boots left footprints in it until the smart pile sprang back up and resumed its sleek, unbroken expanse. She went into my bedroom. As Jak and I followed, she stopped in front of my bed and stared at the mess of covers and pillows. Then she walked to the bathroom archway. Her boots clanged on the tile floor as she entered the room, which was misty with the warm water. When she saw the pool, she went absolutely still. Jak and I stood in the doorway, watching her.

It seemed like eons before Singer turned to us. "Above-city lives this way? All?"

"Not always this nice," I said. "But yah, mostly."

"This much water?"

"And more."

"Drink it?"

"Not this. Comes from other places. But yah, as much as you want."

"Bhaaj—" Her voice had a strangled sound. "Going to be sick."

Jak ran to a cabinet for a bowl and got it to Singer just in time. She sunk to her knees clenching the blue tub while she lost her last meal. Jak and I both stayed back, giving her room.

After a while, Singer set down the bowl and stood up, up and up, back to her full height. The lights on her cybernetic arm flashed. She walked to the pool and picked up a wet towel Jak and I had left there. Moving methodically, she wiped her mouth clean and dropped the towel into the pool. The water frothed as its nanobots went to work, cleaning the cloth. Singer turned to us, slow and careful, her movements measured with a controlled anger I recognized, after having known her for a year.

"Cries keeps us under the city." Her voice rasped. "Makes us stay below. Steals our children, puts them in work houses, says we're nothing, worth nothing, got nothing. And they live like this."

My old anger stirred, never appeased, all those years of people telling me to give up and go home, that I could never succeed. One teacher in officer candidate school had told me I was less than human. When I succeeded on sheer cussed determination, because I was too damn stubborn to fail, the same people who insisted I would never win told me that if I had managed, obviously the rest of the Undercity could as well, so their miserable lives were their own fault. Everyone assumed our culture had no worth. If we insisted on preserving our way of life, then it was our choice to live in poverty, another indication of our inferiority. They saw it is as all or nothing: we accepted the crushing hardships that defined our lives or we gave up what it meant to be Undercity.

I didn't know how to put all my anger in words. I had never learned. I just said, "Yah."

Bitterness honed Singer's words. "And they call me the criminal."

I remembered Lavinda's words last year, after she saw over four hundred people follow me out of the Undercity, a slum she and the rest of Cries had believed housed a few homeless criminals—that day we discovered the incredible concentration of psions among my people: *I don't know if it's our greatest crime or our greatest miracle.* Right. A miracle—now that we had something they wanted.

Singer motioned at my penthouse. "You got this. Why go to the aqueducts?"

"Aqueducts are my home," I said. "Pay forward."

She took a while to digest that. "So."

"Why come here?"

"See you." She paused, probably hampered by our terse dialect. With a frustrated grimace, she tried again. "Wanted to fight. Go to Rec Center. Can't. Key clinks will throw me into the box."

I hadn't realized how much she wanted to join the tykado team, It wasn't clear why that drove her into Cries, though. I could only guess what it had taken for her to walk here. In my youth, I had struggled for years with the decision to come above ground, planning hidden routes through the Concourse to avoid the police. The day I finally left, I walked through Cries in wonder, under a sky I had never before seen, terrified someone would stop me, put me in a cell, turn me away. At the recruiting center, I had stood in front of a flustered army officer and changed my life forever.

I regarded Singer. "You want offworld?"

"Want light."

Although I knew she might mean sunlight, I suspected it went deeper. Her life had ground her down. She looked well into her thirties, but I doubted she was more than early twenties. She had strength, intelligence, drive, and loyalty, but she had also committed multiple murders in the service of the Undercity's worst drug boss.

"Singer." I lifted my hands, then dropped them. "That name means a lot of dark."

"Yah." She made no attempt to deny her former profession.

"Still dark?" I asked.

"Don't want."

That wasn't a ringing cry of remorse for most people, but from Singer it spoke volumes.

"Change?" I asked.

"Too late for me." She took a deep breath. "Not too late for baby. For Taz."

"Taz?"

"Baby father."

"Bring them light?"

"Yah. Talk to cops. Give me up. Get good life for Taz and baby."

I understood now. She was offering to turn herself into the police if she could negotiate a deal for her family. I could help, but this step would destroy the new life she had made in the aqueducts as a member of the Dust Knights.

"You sure?" I asked.

She spoke in a ragged voice. "Testers say I feel moods, hear thoughts. Say my baby will even more. Taz didn't test, but if baby is more, they say Taz is more, too." She clenched her big fists at her sides. "I put up walls and walls and walls in my mind, but nothing works. Never enough. Don't want that for baby, for Taz." She spoke simply. "Help them."

It was the most I had ever heard her say at once. So she wasn't just an empath, she was also a telepath. As a cartel assassin, she had lived the ugliest side of life; as a strong psion she would have absorbed it all. It was a wonder she hadn't become a monster. I had never believed the drippy platitudes about what love could do for a person, but if this Taz had helped keep her sane in that cesspool of human nature called the Vakaar cartel, he had worked miracles.

An insight came to me, like a falling mace. "The reason you sang for Kajada—did it for Taz, Yah? For the baby. Feed them. Protect." The cartel had paid her well, even if she had been barely out of her teens when she started the job. "Protect family from the dark."

"Worked. For a while." Bitterly she added, "Who protects them from me?"

"Ah, gods, Singer." I felt as if I were breaking in two. To give her family the "light" she sought, she would live in the darkness of prison for the rest of her life, which might not be long if the courts gave her the death sentence. I had no answers, so I just said. "Bring them here. Bring family." No, that wouldn't work, either. She couldn't leave my apartment. She was lucky she had made it this far. Gods only knew how many security systems in Cries had sent warnings about her to the authorities. She'd never make it back to the aqueducts.

"Cancel that," I said. "I'll bring them here. You describe how I can locate them, with enough detail so my gauntlet EI can make a map. Once I get you all together here, we'll figure out what to do."

Her forehead furrowed. "Eh?"

Had I pushed too hard? "You can't leave my apartment. The city authorities will catch you."

Singer turned to Jak, who was standing back, listening.

"Bhaaj." He spoke quietly. "You're talking in the Cries dialect."

No! That was unexpected. Usually it worked the other way, that I switched to Undercity speech under pressure. That dialect drilled rocks when it came to expressing emotional complexities, though. Apparently I reverted to Cries speech when I wanted to tackle emotional issues. No wonder it happened so rarely.

Both dialects had their roots in ancient Iotic. Although we could understand each other if we worked at it, I doubted Singer had ever heard Cries speech except last year, when she went to the Rec Center for testing, and they had brought translators that day.

"You stay," I told Singer. "I get Taz. Baby. Bring here. Figure out what to do."

She spoke firmly. "I go for them."

"Can't leave." I motioned toward the window. "Cops catch." It would weaken my ability to negotiate on her behalf if the police picked her up.

"Made it here," she pointed out.

"Yah. Set off alarms. You go out, they get."

She motioned around at my apartment. "They come here?"

"Nahya. Majda protects." One of my conditions for agreeing to live in a tower they owned and monitored was that it remained off limits to the police, including Majda's private force.

A gleam came into Singer's gaze. "That mean Majda protect me?"

Actually, it did. "Yah. Safe." Maybe I'd see a solution to this mess before the Majdas found out I was harboring a Vakaar assassin and demanded to know what the bloody hell I thought I was doing.

"Majda place protect Taz too?" she asked. "Baby?"

"Yah," I said. "All of them."

"Good. I tell you where is Taz. You say to no one." She glanced at Jak. "Your man can know."

My face heated. Jak wasn't "my man." Well, he was, sort of, but we had no promises. I couldn't look at him, but then for some ill-conceived reason I did look. He was watching me with that dangerous stare, the one where he seemed angry, ready to vanish. When that happened, sometimes I didn't see him for days.

"So." Singer walked past me, oblivious to the undercurrents. "Is decided."

We followed her into the living room. She went to the window-wall and stood looking out. I understood. I often sat for hours bathed in the miraculous light of the sun pouring through the glass.

Jak held out his arm, showing me his leather gauntlet embedded with tech-mech, including his comm. "Royal Flush has a message for you."

That was odd. His gauntlet EI talked only to him, no one else. Except, apparently, me today.

I spoke into his comm. "Royal, is that you?" Jak had named his EI after the legendary poker hand he had pulled in an illicit game with a high wheeler from Cries. That hand had earned him the credits he used to start the Black Mark.

A deep voice came out of the comm. "My greetings, Major," Royal said. "One of your Dust Knights is looking for you. The bartender's oldest daughter."

"You mean Darjan?"

"Yes. She asked me to relay a message."

It must be serious if Darjan asked her mother to contact Jak. I was surprised Royal had agreed. "What's the message?"

"An intruder," he said.

Damn! Not again. After what happened to Duane, I'd hoped the Majdas wouldn't send anyone else to the Undercity. "Who? And where?"

"I don't know who," Royal said. "The 'where' is the Foyer. She is sitting on one of the sawed-off rocks there."

I let out a breath. It could have been worse. Probably no one would bother her in the Foyer. "Those seats aren't 'sawed off,'" I told Royal. "They're works of art."

"If you say so." He sounded just like Jak.

I smiled. "I'm on my way."

"Good. Be well, Major." With a click, Royal cut the connection.

"Wonder what that's about," Jak said.

I had no idea.

I didn't walk into the Foyer, announcing my presence. I slipped through spaces in the wall that surrounded the chamber and inched along a hidden path until I reached a tall crack with a view of the cave. A woman sat there on a sawed-off rock exactly as Royal described. She looked innocuous, dressed in simple trousers and shirt, both a light color, what some people called "ivory," whatever that meant. I watched for a while. Eventually I squeezed through a crack in the wall and entered the Foyer, but out of the woman's view.

"Eh?" I said.

"Oh!" She turned with a start. "Where did you come from?"

I recognized nothing about her. "Why are you sitting here?"

"I was hoping someone would come," she said.

"Why?"

She stood up. "I'd like to talk to whoever is in charge."

"No one in charge."

"Are you Major Bhaajan?"

"Maybe. Who are you?"

"Ah, my apology." She smiled with an ease we never saw down here. "I'm Doctor Karal Rajindia."

Rajindia? What the hell? The Rajindias were another Imperialate noble House, not as powerful as the Majdas and no longer native to Raylicon, but part of the aristocracy. They were best known for providing the military with biomech adepts, the neurological specialists who treated psions.

"Why are you here, Lady?" I asked. "It isn't safe."

"Doctor," she said. "Not Lady."

"You're not a noblewoman?"

"I am. But I prefer to be known as a doctor. Pharaoh Dyhianna requested I come."

This was certainly different from the last time the pharaoh sent someone here. Of all the ways this doctor could have approached my people, she had used what might be the only viable method, staying here in the Foyer, away from the true Undercity, but enough in our territory to draw notice, all the time waiting patiently until a potential guide showed up.

"Why did the pharaoh want you to come here?" I asked.

"To treat your people. She said you asked for her help."

With all that had happened in the past day, I had forgotten my request to the pharaoh, that she help the Down-deepers. It seemed ages since we had talked in the temple, when I was recovering from my climb out of the Down-deep, but it had been less than a full Raylicon day.

I spoke awkwardly. "My people can't pay you, Lad—Doctor Rajindia."

"Pay me?" She seemed puzzled. "Why would they pay me?"

"Don't you charge for your services?"

"I'm on retainer to the Ruby Dynasty. I work for them."

Good gods. If Dyhianna Selei had sent us one of her personal physicians, this woman was among the best doctors in the Imperialate, one who specialized in treating psions. I had no idea how to answer. No, that wasn't true. I knew what I had to say, as much as I didn't want to. "My people won't take charity." They would let their hard-headed pride kill them rather than accept handouts.

"I'm not interested in charity work," she said. "I offer a bargain."

Ho! The pharaoh learned fast. This doctor should have said "proposal," not "bargain," since we hadn't made one yet, but who cared. It was close enough. "What's your proposal?" I asked.

"I will treat your people," she said. "In return, they will let us do more Kyle testing."

"Why do you need more tests?" It didn't take many to determine if a person had the DNA. After that, what was left? You didn't have to verify it twice. Then again, my army tests must have shown I had the DNA, and I hadn't manifested any traits for most of my life.

"We would like to see how your people use their abilities," the doctor said.

"I doubt they do much." I thought of Singer. "It can be a nightmare."

"The tests are harmless," Rajindia assured me. "For example, I might ask a child if she can raise a barrier in her mind to mute the emotions she picks up from other people."

"She wouldn't even know what you meant."

"I'd explain. If they have trouble with it, I can bring some reading material for them."

Did she have no clue at all? I spoke stiffly. "Most of my people can't read."

"I can help." She paused. "As can those who keep the Code of your tykado teams."

What the blazes? "How do you know about the Code?"

"Some of the young people in Cries talk about it."

Okay, I knew that. Last year a Cries boy had asked me if he could join the Dust Knights. He had heard about them after his cousin's brother's girlfriend or whatever, some kid who snuck into the aqueducts. Even so. Hearing this stranger say the name unsettled me. The Dust Knights were purely Undercity. I didn't want Cries to interfere with what we were doing.

"The Code is private," I said. "Not above-city."

"Yes," she said. "My offer of a bargain is only for the Undercity."

And then I finally understood. She didn't want to "test" us at all. She offered an education in disguise. My people hated the condescending charity Cries had tried to extend since they realized we had something they wanted. This doctor wanted to teach my people to use their abilities, yes, but she offered to do it our way, under the guise of a bargain, while tending to our health and supporting my efforts to promote literacy.

"Did you think of this bargain?" I asked. It seemed unlikely. I doubted she even came from this world; the Rajindias lived on some other planet, I didn't remember where.

"Pharaoh Dyhianna suggested it," the doctor said.

She's brilliant, I thought. Aloud, I said, "I don't know. It might work."

"We can start today if you wish."

"Too soon." If we tried her bargain, it would take time to introduce to the Undercity. I wanted to see how she interacted with my people first, and I wanted her to stay alive in the process. "If you go into the aqueducts, you'll need an escort."

"I understand."

"Good." In my youth, when the archeologist named Orin from the university in Cries had given me sweet bars in return for my showing him the ruins, I had convinced my dust gang to protect him when he came here, pottering about his digs. We would need similar for this doctor.

"Maybe," I said, "the Dust Knights could look after you."

"Something is wrong," Ruzik said. "Very wrong."

We stood together on the midwalk at Lizard Trap. The children in his circle were down in the canal, laughing and kicking up dirt as they chased one another. They avoided the dust statues, never damaging those symbols Ruzik used to mark their territory. The rest of his gang patrolled the canal. Only Angel had told me her name; I didn't know what to call Ruzik's brother or the other woman. No matter. They would tell me if they decided they wanted me to know.

A man and woman, both cyber-riders, were seated a ways down the midwalk, cooking dinner for everyone on a stove cannibalized from a Cries salvage dump. The savory aroma of roasted lizard meat reminded me I hadn't eaten. Across the canal, on the other midwalk, three teens stood together, singing. They improvised a melody with no words, just sounds. The trio harmonized, modulating the melody, always in a minor key. Their music echoed in the canal with a natural resonance. It was no wonder we sang so much in the Undercity, for the ruins reflected and amplified the music with amazing acoustics. Their song reminded me of a Skolian opus called "Harmonics of Loss," a haunting piece composed in a time before my people knew Earth existed as more than a legend. It mourned the loss of our home world, and I heard the same pain this music. The ever-changing melodies of the Undercity created the most painfully beautiful music I knew. We wept with our songs.

I didn't, however, understand what Ruzik was telling me. "What's wrong?"

"Aqueducts," he said. "Canals. Tunnels. Small places. Large places. Down-deep."

"Wrong how?"

He made a frustrated sound. "Dark."

"In the dark?" That included most of the Undercity.

"Nahya." He paced away, then swung around and stalked back to me. "The aqueducts."

I motioned around the canal. "Like this?"

"Nahya!" He hit the wall. "Wrong!"

I tried another tack. "What does this wrongness do?"

"Kill."

Maybe he meant Calaj. "Jagernaut?"

"Nahya. Aqueducts."

I still didn't get it. "Aqueducts evil?"

"Yah."

"Aqueducts are rock." I shrugged. "Not good, not bad. Just rock."

"*Inside* the rock."

"Rock is inside rock."

He glared at me, then pointed at my head. "Rock inside there."

Ha, ha. Very funny. "How can rock kill?" Maybe he meant the canals were unstable. "Collapse? Ceiling fall? Walls?"

"Not that way." He bounced on the balls of his feet as if he were in a tykado match, preparing to fight. "Something is wrong. Don't know how to say."

"Show, maybe?"

He considered me for a glowering moment, as if I had asked some highly personal question that was none of my business. Well, tough. He was the one who had sent one of his duster kids to bring me here. I had been on my way to get Singer's family when the youth showed up to deliver Ruzik's message: *Come with.*

Ruzik spun around and strode down the midwalk to where the riders were cooking dinner. When the man offered him a skewer of braised meat, Ruzik shook his head. After he conferred with them, the woman tapped the implants on her arm, and they glittered, gold then green. She was contacting someone, though who or why I had no clue.

Ruzik motioned to Angel, and she jogged over, sending up clouds of dust. She stopped under him. "Eh?"

He knelt on the edge of the midwalk. "Take watch. I go."

"Where?"

"With Bhaaj. Back later."

Angel nodded. "We'll protect."

"Good." He jumped to his feet and strode back to me, "Come with."

I took off with him, going to search for the darkness.

XII

DETECTOR

Hack wanted us to leave.

I had never seen his cyber den before, and he left no doubt that he had wanted it to stay that way. He didn't look surprised to see us, though; Ruzik's cyber-riders must have warned him. He let me enter the den with Ruzik, but his glare could have incinerated stone.

We walked into wonderland. Columns formed by joined stalactites and stalagmites supported the ceiling. Tech-mech covered every wall, alive with lights that flickered and flashed. Crystal deposits shimmered on the ceiling and even the splint on my wrist reflected the light. Equipment glinted everywhere, engines, flyers, filters, cycles, goggles, prosthetics, and hundreds of other bits. Screens covered one wall, all showing real-time views of Cries, from plazas to skyscrapers to private homes. Holos rotated in the air above a film on a stump of rock, a broadcast about some singer who fell off the stage during her performance. Hack had never left the Undercity, but he knew the above world in all its myriad moods, seeing it with a hundred eyes, invisible to the world he watched. Today he stood in the middle of his realm, large and rangy, glowering as we invaded his sanctum.

I motioned to his cave. "Good den."

He nodded, accepting the praise. After that, he looked infinitesimally less belligerent.

Ruzik conferred with him in low tones. When Hack beckoned to me, I followed them across the den, stepping around a filtration system without a spout. The scent of machine oil tickled my nose. He kept his den unusually quiet; I barely heard even the thrum of a generator. It wouldn't surprise me if he could turn this all off in seconds, dousing the lights, sounds, and signals until his lair vanished. Our path here had taken us through a labyrinth of tunnels deep within the aqueducts. To find his hideaway, you already had to know the way.

Hack took us through a natural archway lined with glowing fiberoptic cords. We entered a smaller cave with one piece of equipment dominating the cramped area.

The stolen guns.

Damn. Hack had taken apart the pulse rifles, cannibalizing their power sources, targeting devices, and EM systems. What he built from them still had the shape of the gun, but one so encrusted with tech-mech, I doubted it could shoot bullets anymore.

I managed to keep my anger to a low boil. "You call this 'no guns'?"

"Not guns." Hack even said it with a straight face.

I crossed my arms. "*Was* a gun."

"No more," Ruzik said.

Great. Just great. My tykado team, the ones ready to compete in the first ever athletic meet between the Cries and the Undercity—my ambassadors to a new future—had just shown me their unlawful possession of stolen military firearms.

I scowled at Hack. "What does it do?"

"Probe Undercity." He laid his hand on the targeting cylinders, which he had enhanced with lasers, a viewing monitor, and what I could have sworn was a music amplifier. It all sat on a mount that resembled a larger version of the shroud in my backpack. "Probe the wrongness."

"Wrongness?" I had to find a way into this opaque explanation of theirs. "Is that alive?"

Hack looked at Ruzik. Ruzik looked at him. They looked at me. It was like those stories about humans who destroy an AI by asking it logically impossible questions, as if you could actually find an AI dumb enough to fall for that trick. Hack and Ruzik weren't AIs, they were two very human dusters who apparently had no idea how to answer me.

I tried again. "What the probe finds—not a bio-bot?" It was slang the kids used to mean human.

"No bio," Hack said.

"It finds tech-mech?" I asked.

He just looked at me.

"Part tech-mech, part bio?" I asked.

"Not bio." Hack pointed to his targeting device. "You look. See what I mean."

"Good." I sat on the stool built into his apparatus. He adjusted the goggles over my eyes and slid a comm into my ear. When he set a neural cap on my head, though, I yanked off the goggles and pulled away the cap.

"What the hell." I shook the neural cap at him. "You don't put prongs in my brain."

"You got to connect," Hack said. "To the mesh."

I had absolutely no desire to have him insert neural probes through my scalp into my brain. Gods only knew where this cap came from. It wasn't something labs just threw away. "You make this?"

"Got from a good place," Hack said.

"Don't tell me." I didn't want any more knowledge of their criminal activity. I couldn't turn them in, not if I wanted anyone here to trust me, but if I didn't, I became an accessory. After silently going through my arsenal of cuss words, I said, "You sterilize the prongs?"

"Always." Hack looked offended that I even thought I had to ask.

I pulled the goggles back over my eyes. "Go ahead."

He fit the cap onto my head, and I winced as the filaments delicately inserted themselves into my head. I sat, submerged in darkness. Gradually I became aware of a hum. When I laid my palm against the body of the probe, it vibrated against my skin.

"Point the gun," Hack said.

"Where?" I asked.

"Anywhere."

Strange. I aimed at the wall.

"Shoot," Hack said.

"Shoot what? No bullets."

"Not shoot bullets at my wall," Hack said, annoyed.

"Then what?"

"Just shoot."

Well, what the hell. I pushed the firing stud. Nothing happened.

"Broken," I said.

"Try again."

I fired again. Still nothing—no, wait. The darkness had become—what? Fluid? I concentrated, and it seemed to congeal. My head was starting to ache.

"Shoot more," Hack said.

I pushed the firing stud. The sense of thickening pressing in on my thoughts. My head throbbed. The darkness felt ugly. Vicious. It turned around—

—and saw me.

"Ah!" I ripped off the goggles. "Off!"

Hack immediately set about removing the cap. I would have yanked it off too, except jerking neural fibers out of your brain was a seriously bad idea. Hack was no amateur, though, and within moments, he'd removed the cap.

"Gods almighty!" I stood up, staring at him. "Is that real? Or a bad cap?" If I were lucky, what I'd detected was no more than an artifact of his cobbled-together machine.

"Real," Hack said. "Different caps, remade machine, same result."

"It feels—" I paused. Feels what? "Alive."

"Yah," he said. "Sort of."

"Feels wrong," Ruzik said.

It reminded me of the Lock, but with a malevolence I hadn't sensed from that ancient EI. I had trespassed in the Lock corridor so it pushed me out, end of story. This felt inimical to human life.

"It's an EI," I said.

"Whose?" Ruzik asked.

"No clue," I said.

"Not EI," Hack said. "EI doesn't hate. Just exists."

I thought of Max and his emotions. "Simulates."

"That wrongness," Ruzik said. "Real. Not sim."

It had felt genuine to me, too, a force of malice. I saw now why they thought it was "in the rock," but that couldn't be right. It had to exist as more than stone.

"Must be somewhere," I said.

"You find," Ruzik told me.

"Why me?" I was no cyber-rider. "Hack knows more."

"Not about how to search," Hack said. "You know how. You look at things. Creep around. Hassle people. Find hints."

It wasn't the most flattering description of my work, but I got his point. I solved puzzles for a living. I didn't know as much about the tech, but maybe I could put together clues they didn't see.

I motioned at the probe. "It works how?"

"Uses hidden bits." Hack held up three fingers. "Three bits."

That could mean anything. "Bits of what?"

He scooped up three rocks from the ground and dropped one. "Lightest." He dropped the second. "Heavier." He dropped the third. "Heaviest."

I squinted at him. "Got no idea what you mean."

He spun around and strode out of the chamber, back into his den. I followed and found him watching the news holos from Cries that rotated above the sawed off stump of rock. He flicked his finger through the screen below the holos and they vanished. More flicks, and he brought up an image of wave oscillations. It had been years since my student days, and I couldn't recall where I had seen those patterns. No, wait, I did remember. It was the waveform created by a superposition of tau, muon, and electron neutrinos as they oscillated from one form to another. Glyphs scrolled across the pedestal, defining the feed. He had linked to an Earth database that listed Takaaki Kajita and Arthur McDonald as the winners of something called the Nobel Prize for their work on neutrino oscillations.

I looked from the holo to Hack, to the holo, back to Hack. "You understand this?"

"Yah." He seemed surprised by the question. "Three bits. Three kinds. Mixed up."

He couldn't be saying he understood particle physics. "How know that?"

"I learn."

I didn't see how. The theoretical treatment of neutrino oscillations required knowledge of quantum mechanics and partial differential equations, and that was just a start. "Math, too?"

"Math, yah. Easier than reading."

I stared at him. "Quantum physics is easier than reading?"

"Eh?"

"You know what waveform mean? Eigenstate? Hamiltonian operator? Superposition?"

He scowled at me. "Jibber words. You make up."

"Not jibber. Math."

"Not my math."

"Fine." I scowled back at him. "Show me your math."

He tapped the pedestal and the neutrinos disappeared. As he continued entering codes, new holos appeared, simple waves like the eigenfunctions for a particle in a box. He cycled through ever more complex images. He was showing me the solutions to equations of mathematical physics using symbols unlike anything I had seen in my classes.

Hack waved his hand through his holo equations. "My math."

"You figured all that out?"

"Some. Get ideas from mesh places."

"Gods," I murmured. In Hack, was I seeing an echo of our ancestors? They had struggled to decipher the libraries left by an alien race, strange knowledge they used with limited understanding. They developed technology based on what they learned, as evidenced by the Locks and Izu Yaxlan, but the way they applied scientific theories was so strange, we had trouble deciphering their machines. Their knowledge disappeared in the Dark Ages that followed the fall of the Ruby Empire. We had to relearn everything, and the second time around we did it the way humans thought rather than using alien formulations. However, our gene pool had to include the descendants of those geniuses who unraveled the alien libraries. Hack might be a throwback to that time. Hell, from what I'd seen, so was the Ruby Pharaoh. It didn't surprise me that such brilliance occurred in people with pronounced Kyle traits; their abilities derived from an increased number of neural structures in their brain. Instead of ancient libraries from some unknown species, however, Hack had to work with another "alien" source—the rest of humanity.

"You get help from interstellar meshes?" I asked.

"Yah." He shrugged. "Code says Knights got to read. So I read."

I read. Two simple words—and they contained a world of triumph. In a culture where simple literacy was rare, Hack had learned to read at a level beyond what even most educated Skolians could manage. He had no idea what he had done; he was just down here working in his cyber den.

Hack waved at his holos. "You know this?"

"Some." I kept a working knowledge of the tools I used, including the methods I used to hide from spying Majdas. In recent years, neutrino detection had become more feasible for smaller devices like my shroud. Electron neutrinos affected matter differently than tau or muon neutrinos, but all their interactions were tiny. In previous centuries, they had to pass through a lot of matter, like an entire freaking planet, before the effects added up enough to measure. Now we had better ways to investigate their behavior, enough to untangle their history from their waveforms. Some neutrinos went through most anything, including solid rock, and some didn't. We could read their history from how they interacted in the background flux of neutrinos. It offered a powerful probe. Top-end shrouds interfered with that probe, blurring the history. It was why I had sprung for one of the most expensive jammers available, to hide me from neutrino detectors as well as more mundane sensors.

If Hack had done what I thought, that meant he had created a neutrino detector from a dismantled pulse rifle, salvaged lasers, a music amplifier, and a top-of-the-line shroud. I'd known he was one hell of a cyber-rider, but this went beyond even the best wizards.

"Your thing." I motioned toward the smaller chamber that housed his device. "Detector?"

He considered the name. "Yah, detects."

"What? Solid?"

"Not solid." He stood watching the quantum waveforms shimmer above his holo pedestal. I could almost feel him struggling for the words. "Mesh."

"It detects the mesh?" That didn't make sense. The mesh was everywhere, easy to detect.

He turned to me. "Mesh shadows."

"What is a mesh shadow?"

"Shake back and forth."

"Don't understand."

He waved his hand through the holos showing the waveforms created when neutrinos interchanged their identities. "Shake back and forth."

Ah. Now I understood. "Oscillation."

He squinted at me. "Eh?"

"Oscillation. Means 'shake back and forth.'"

He snorted. "Osky bosky, talks too much."

In the Undercity, any word with more than three syllables was considered an explosion of verbosity, like a chatty kid who wouldn't stop talking. He must have heard the term oscillation before, though, if he knew it was one word rather than several. I held up my hand and counted on my fingers. "Shake back and forth. Four sounds. Ah-suh-lay-shun. Four sounds."

Hack glowered and didn't deign to acknowledge my point. He didn't refute it, either, though. He would dismiss words like "theoretical quantum dynamics" or "uncertainty principle" as too talky, but I didn't doubt now that he knew what they meant.

"Mesh waves mix," Hack said.

"With what?"

"Hidden bit waves."

That sounded like he was somehow mixing the neutrino waveforms with the mesh signals, he received in his cyber den, which made no sense. The mesh worked on electromagnetic signals and neutrino oscillations were created by particles with mass. It wasn't impossible to have particles switch back and forth between photons and mass, but I'd never heard of anyone superposing electromagnetic transmissions with neutrino mass oscillations.

"Mix mesh and neutrinos together?" I asked.

"Yah," Hack said.

"Not possible. Mesh is EM."

"EM?" he asked.

Even if he understood what electromagnetic meant, I doubted he would acknowledge knowing a word so disreputable, it had six syllables. So I just said, "EM. Waves."

Hack waved at me, then grinned. "So Hack is a mesh?"

I smiled. "I meant the mesh works on electromagnetic wave transmissions. Oscillations." I had to use Cries words; the terms I needed didn't exist in the Undercity dialect.

Ruzik laughed. "Yah, Hack osky bosky in the head." When Hack glared at him, he smirked.

Interesting. They understood the Cries words well enough to make a play on them. Good. I needed a mixture of the two dialects for what I wanted to describe. "You say your detector picks up EM waves, but that it somehow mixes those with the neutrino waves. What you call hidden bits."

Hack shrugged. "Yah. Just mixing. Nothing much."

He made it sound so simple. *Just mixing.* Maybe some scientist somewhere else had figured out how to combine neutrino superpositions with the mesh signals that networked civilization, but I'd never heard of that feat. Now Hack claimed he built such a detector and used it to probe the mesh the way neutrino sensors probed matter. Maybe he really had done it. At the age of twenty, he understood more cyber-tech than I'd ever know. Down here in his stalactite-encrusted den, he approached engineering with no formal background, just the libraries of a people alien to him. He was the closest analog that existed among modern Skolians to the technologists of the Ruby Empire. If anyone could detect the presence of ancient EI that the rest of us had no idea existed, it would be Hack.

"How far?" I asked. "What you detect—how far away?"

"Not away," Hack said. "Inside."

"Inside the rock," Ruzik added.

"You try the detector too?" I asked Ruzik.

"Yah." He grimaced. "Not again."

I didn't want to feel that malice again, either. I had to, though, if I was going to find what created it.

I sat in darkness after Hack fastened me into his detector for a second time. The machine targeted regions of the rock, or more accurately, the neutrino flux through that region of space. Although scientists no longer needed giant tanks of water to find neutrinos, those detectors were more accurate than Hack's contraption. I couldn't find anything this time even when I "fired" in the same direction I had tried that last time. I swiveled the detector and fired again. Nothing. I pointed it at Cries and picked up faint signals, mechanical in feel, no sense of malice, probably the larger EIs that ran the city. The device apparently couldn't detect anything smaller, like gauntlet EIs.

Max, I thought. *Can you point me in the direction of the Lock temple in the desert?*

Yes. Turn the detector right by one hundred and eighteen degrees. Max created a heads-up display using the goggles I wore, with the target glowing in the center.

I centered on the glowing dot and pressed the firing stud. No response. Either the Lock EI had shrouded itself against nosy humans or this detector wasn't sophisticated enough to pick it up.

Try Izu Yaxlan, I thought.

The dot moved on my heads-up map, and I swiveled my chair until I was sitting with my back to Cries. This time when I fired, I picked up a signal. Gods almighty, yes, Izu Yaxlan contained an EI, a *huge* one. The signal came in strong and mechanical—and then disappeared.

Huh. Maybe it had caught my clumsy attempts to spy and didn't approve. I swung the detector slowly back toward the Lock, taking readings every few degrees—there! A signal in the desert. It felt different, more familiar, modern. It had a structured quality, too, like the military EIs I worked with. I'd bet my pension that was Calaj, somewhere between the Lock and Izu Yaxlan. No wonder we were having so much trouble finding her. It wasn't only that she had the best shrouds the military produced, which she had undoubtedly enhanced, but also that she kept moving in an unpredictable pattern, not what I expected for a crazed killer in search of victims. In fact, nothing Calaj had done struck me as murderous except when she shot at me in the Down-deep.

"Hack," I said. "Bring me out."

He set about disengaging me from his machine. When I was free, he and Ruzik considered me. "How bad?" Ruzik asked.

"Not bad." I stood up, massaging my stiff neck. "It's hiding."

"The EI?" Hack asked.

I nodded. "I found others. Cries."

"I also, sometimes." Hack laid his hand on his detector. "This machine private. Ken?"

"I ken." I would protect their secrets. Revealing my sources would cripple my investigation, but I'd have kept my silence regardless. I couldn't betray their trust. By saying nothing, however, I was abetting a crime. I had to do something about that, but what, I didn't yet know.

Whatever I decided, I needed to move fast, before we lost Calaj again.

XIII

TAZ

Without Singer's directions, I'd never have found her home. She hid it even better than Dara and Weaver did theirs. I ventured into the Maze and squeezed my way along, jabbing my skin on spikes of rock or crawling through passages barely big enough for a child. Eventually I reached a chamber about ten paces across with a ceiling crusted by blue crystals. A cave entrance lay before me, tooled into a smooth archway. I stood in my dusty clothes with my pulse gun holstered. I'd taken off my backpack, and I kept my arms by my sides, holding the pack with my uninjured hand.

"Taz?" I called.

A man stepped into view, not under the archway, but from a nearby crevice. I had an impression of height, but what I noticed first was the Mark 89 Automatic Power Rifle he had trained on me, the same monster gun Singer had used to save my life two days ago. That lethal beauty looked even bigger in this cramped space. I lifted my gaze to the man—

Ah, gods. No wonder Singer felt driven to such extremes. Women would lay down their lives for this man, any woman anywhere. He stood taller than average, with a well-built physique. He had no scars on his face or his arms, which his muscle shirt left bare. His black hair was well tended, combed and less ragged than most people wore down here. What hit me though most, though, wasn't that beautiful body or his well-kept appearance, but his face. You never found men this handsome in the Undercity. Life here leached any beauty out of my

199

people. We fought, we struggled, we lived with disease, deformity, and violence, and it all took its toll.

Not so on this man. He was Undercity, yah; we had a look, one born of our small gene pool. All Raylicans had dark skin, but ours was slightly lighter because we needed less melanin to survive. Our larger eyes adapted our vision to the dim light. Oddly enough, our high cheekbones and straight noses were similar to the Majdas, except their noses stayed straight. Practically the only people here who didn't end up with a broken nose at least once in their life were cyber-riders protected by dust gangs.

I could think of one other situation where a duster might make it to adulthood with no scars. Taz looked in his early twenties, as healthy and as fit as a Majda prince, muscled from what had to be regular workouts, and more than adept at aiming that damn gun at me. Yah, you could be all of this if, for most your life, you had the protection of the most notorious killer in the aqueducts.

"Eh, uh, um," I said articulately. "Tez? Taz, I mean." I was stuttering like an idiot.

His gun never wavered. "Who the fuck are you?"

Yah, so, he might look like a prince, but he sounded like the proverbial boy next door, Undercity style. "Bhaaj," I said, giving him my name, a gesture of respect. "Singer sent."

"Lying."

"No lying." I lifted my free hand, the one with the splint. "Don't shoot. I prove."

He didn't answer, but he didn't blast me into slag, either. Moving slowly, I opened my pack and took out Singer's gauntlet, lifting it so he could see that work of tech-mech wizardry. "Ask her."

His fist clenched on the rifle—and he fired.

"Ai!" I yelled as the gauntlet spun out of my hand. He had shot with perfect precision, making a spiked fin on the bullet graze the gauntlet. Had that projectile hit me, it would have exploded my body. Even the barest touch of one fin sent the gauntlet spinning out of my hand and probably destroyed its tech-mech. Damn. Singer would be pissed.

Never taking his gaze off me, Taz stalked to where the gauntlet had fallen and picked it up. All that time, he kept that monster gun aimed at my trespassing self. He brushed his thumb over the gauntlet's controls, his face impassive.

The comm activated.

Good gods. How had that shot left Singer's comm undamaged? That could only happen if the fin on the bullet had touched no more than a layer a few molecules thick on the gauntlet. It wasn't just a matter of aim; the fins unfolded in the air and the bullet spun. Either this Taz was incredibly lucky or he was the freaking best marksman I'd ever seen. I wondered if he had always been that good of a shot, if a shared interest had drawn him to Singer, or if she had taught him so he could defend himself. Well, yah, I shouldn't assume Singer taught him. Maybe he taught her. Either way, they were well matched. I just hoped he didn't decide to use that phenomenal talent to liquefy my body.

The gauntlet comm beeped and Singer's voice rose into the air. "Eh?"

"You, where?" Taz asked her, still watching me.

"Went to Bhaaj," Singer said. "She there?"

"Someone is."

"Put her on."

Taz extended the comm in my direction. "Talk."

"Eh, Singer." I was close enough for her comm to pick up my voice.

"Eh, Bhaaj," she said. "Found him."

"Yah. Got gun."

"Taz, no shoot Bhaaj."

He scowled at me, at the air, at nothing in particular.

"Taz?" Singer asked. "Bhaaj okay. Pain in ass sometimes, but okay."

I wished people would quit calling me a pain in the ass. She and the Majdas weren't any different in that respect, the Majdas just used words with more syllables to express their opinion. So I pushed people to answer questions they didn't like. That was my job. I was good at it, too. Come to think of it, that could make me a pain in the ass.

Taz lowered the rifle. "Eh, Bhaaj."

I nodded to him.

He spoke into the comm. "Why is she here?"

"Go with." Singer told him.

"Go where?"

"To me."

He frowned. "Why send her? You come here."

A long silence followed. I could guess why. Of course Singer didn't want him in Cries. More than ever, I knew we needed him there, and their baby, too, not just to protect them, but to help me negotiate a plea bargain for Singer. It would change how the authorities reacted if they saw her as more than an assassin, but also as the protector of this man and their baby.

"You go with Bhaaj," she finally said.

Taz shook his head. "Singer—"

"Yah?"

"You trust?"

"Bhaaj? Yah."

He had a strange look. "Really trust."

"Yah." In a voice gentler than I had ever heard her use, she said, "Bring her."

Bring her? Me? That didn't make sense. I was bringing him. Oh. Wait. The baby. Of course.

Taz fixed me with a hard stare and shook his monster gun. "I bring."

Singer's voice snapped out of the gauntlet, harsh again. "No gun."

Huh. How had she known what he meant? *I bring* sounded like he meant the baby. That more than any tests convinced me that he and Singer were psions. I doubted they could sense each other's moods at this distance, but they clearly understood each other on an unusual level.

"No gun, not go," Taz told her.

"Must come," Singer said.

"With gun."

"Cops catch you," Singer growled. "Take you away. Take baby away."

"Nahya!"

"No gun."

Taz looked ready to shoot the ceiling. "You come here."

"Can't, Taz."

"Later, yah?"

In a softer voice she said, "Maybe never again. Must come. Later is too late."

"What happened?"

"Go with Bhaaj. Talk here."

"Why?"

"Got to trust, Taz. Go with. Wherever she says."

Then she cut the connection.

Taz scowled at me. If a look truly could have pierced, I'd have been gushing blood.

"What you do to her?" he demanded.

I met his glare. "Nothing. She came to me."

He shook the gun, not at me but at the air. "She come home?"

"Taz." I stood there, helpless to make this easier. What happened to Singer would depend on the deal I could work out with the authorities. "Can't come home."

"Why? I stay here."

"She's in Cries."

He stared at me blankly, as if I'd spoken in another language. "Eh?"

"Cries," I repeated. "Hiding. My place. She goes out, cops catch."

"Nahya," he said firmly, as if I were too slow to understand that Singer couldn't be in Cries.

I waited.

Inside the cave, a child wailed.

"Ah!" He looked as if he were tearing in two. He pointed the gun at me. "Stay! No move. Come inside, I kill. Ken?"

I nodded. "I ken."

With that, he strode into the cave. The child cried again.

I hoped no Majda spies had picked up Singer's transmission. I had jammed their spyware at my penthouse, but her gauntlet wasn't as well secured. Of course the authorities would question a signal that originated in the Undercity and went to an elite city tower. I had to do something, fast. I reached into my pack and switched off the shroud.

Bhaaj, Max warned. The Majda spy systems can now detect you.

I know. Link me to Colonel Majda's private channel. If I was lucky, I could just leave a message. This second transmission originating in the Undercity, from me to the colonel, would indicate both signals came from me and, I hoped, direct attention away from my penthouse.

Lavinda's voice snapped out of my comm. "Major, where the hell have you been?"

So much for luck. "My greetings, Colonel."

"Have you found Calaj?"

"I think she's left the Undercity and gone to the surface."

"Where?"

"In the desert. She keeps moving."

"What the blazes is she doing out there? Why can't we find her?"

Good question. "I'm not sure. Colonel, I need to talk to the pharaoh."

"You can't just 'talk to the pharaoh.'"

"It's important to the case. I've been asking her the wrong questions."

"What do you want to ask her?"

"I'll tell you when we meet." Glancing up, I saw Taz was walking out of the cave, holding a child instead of his gun. "I have to go."

"Bhaajan, wa—"

I cut the connection and reactivated my shroud. I hoped she knew me well enough to trust I had good reason for breaking the link. Taz would never trust me if he found me talking to a Majda, with their distinctive aristocratic accents.

Singer had called her daughter "the baby," but the child Taz carried was more than a year old. He had a pack slung over his shoulder, probably with stuff for his kid, though I didn't doubt he had a weapon in there, too. The child regarded me with an intelligent gaze. She resembled her father, but I also saw Singer in her. Maybe they said "baby" because they hadn't named her yet. It wasn't unusual here, where names took time to earn and were private unless you honored someone by telling them. It was, I realized, why people called me The Bhaaj instead of Bhaaj, as a sign of respect, not using my name unless I revealed it to them, even though they already knew it from the whisper mill.

"Good baby," I said.

Taz nodded, accepting the high praise, but his posture remained tense.

I didn't like taking a child through the Maze. "Have to squeeze through cracks."

"Know better way." Taz looked like he had bit into a sour fruit, revealing that secret to me.

"I follow," I said.

After Taz and I left the Maze behind, we followed the midwalk of a major canal. Even if my augmented hearing hadn't picked up the sound of people following us, I would have known. It was just too juicy a sight, Bhaaj accompanied by the best-looking man in the Undercity, and he was carrying a child. The whisper mill would go wild.

Fortunately Jak knew I'd come for Taz; otherwise I'd have been in it deep. Not that he would show his displeasure. He'd just vanish. The last time I'd come home, eight years ago, he had vanished for weeks, off to get money someone owed him. He never told me, he just disappeared. I thought he had goddamned died. I knew then he'd never forgiven me for enlisting. He was the one I most regretted leaving, but he hadn't asked me to stay. He hadn't wanted to leave here and I hadn't wanted to stay. Nothing would have changed that no matter how hard I tried to convince him. In the end, I'd left Raylicon and the bitter memories behind forever.

Or so I thought. I'd come home twice, eight years ago, and again last year. This time, somehow I worked through my tangled emotions. I didn't hate the Undercity, I hated what it did to my people. It was only when I realized I might have it within me to help that I knew I could stay. So Jak and I played this unending dance. No matter how much we lived in our time apart, somehow we still knew the steps when we saw each other again. We never committed, never gave promises, never expressed emotions, the two of us caught in the pain that had saturated our lives, the deaths, scars, violence, and losses.

I wondered how Taz felt about his hidden life with Singer. Right now he seemed in shock.

"Ever come out to canals?" I asked.

He spoke in a low voice. "Nahya."

No wonder the aqueducts stunned him. A major throughway like this one was an impressive sight, the ruins intact, the midwalk wide enough for three people to walk abreast, the bottom of the canal more than two meters below us, the other side over ten meters distant, and the ceiling far overhead, held up with arches, struts, and vaults designed by the ancient architects. It awed me, and I saw it all the time.

Taz's daughter fussed, and he bounced her as he walked. When we came within a few meters of the Foyer, I took him to the hidden entrance I had used the last time I entered the Undercity. Once we slipped into the cramped passage, he seemed more comfortable. I led him along its twisting way until we reached a crack that would let us out behind the market stalls on the Concourse, out of view.

"Here," I slid off my pack and took out a blue pullover. It was the most expensive article of clothing I could find in my limited Cries wardrobe that would work for a man, and that he could easily pull over his clothes. "For you."

Taz frowned at the shirt. He lifted it up and smelled the cloth. Then he rubbed it against his cheek. He tilted his head as if faced with an unsolvable puzzle. "Too soft."

"Yah." I shrugged. "Need to wear anyway."

"Why?"

"Disguise."

"Eh." He handed me his daughter.

Self-conscious, I took the girl. Taz must have accepted Singer's trust in me more than I realized; otherwise, he'd never have let me hold his kid. The girl regarded me curiously, with large eyes.

After Taz pulled on the shirt, he looked less Undercity. His trousers were handmade but well tended, with no dust. Although his hair was well trimmed for the aqueducts, out here it looked ragged compared to the neatly clipped citizens of Cries. Under scrutiny, he would never pass for above-city, but that magnificent face and build of his were a far better disguise. If we were lucky, his appearance would so distract people, they wouldn't notice his clothes.

I gave Taz back his daughter, then shrugged into my leather jacket, with its climate controls and weapons shielding. I might look ready to beat up someone, but the jacket was more upscale than anyone expected for the aqueducts. With Taz and his child, we just might pass for tourists. At the least, the jacket covered up the gun in my shoulder holster.

I turned off the visual portion of my shroud and sound dampers. We couldn't use them on the Concourse. Up close, in a crowd of people, especially in bright light, the optical functions wouldn't work that well. The shroud would still project holos showing our surroundings instead of us, but our bodies would show like ghosts or distortions in the air. It would draw more attention than if we walked in plain view. If I left on the sound dampers, our voices would just sound oddly muted to anyone close by. We were better off if we didn't talk. I left everything else operating; the IR, UV, radio, sonar, radar, neutrino, biomech and mesh modulators that hid us from probes.

I motioned Taz toward the break in the wall. "We go."

His forehead furrowed, but he stepped through the opening—and froze.

I waited. "Got to go."

Silence. He wasn't going anywhere.

"Taz?" I asked.

"White thing," he said.

I had no idea what he meant. "I go first," I offered.

He stepped back into the tunnel. His expression remained impassive, but I could tell something had rattled him. Puzzled, I stepped through the crevice. Nothing much showed on the other side. We had reached a cramped lane behind the market stalls, but you couldn't see far in this thick haze—

Oh. Of course. The haze. He had probably never seen mist. It didn't often happen in the Undercity, or anywhere in Cries for that matter, given the dry desert air and monotonously clear weather. I looked back at him. "Is okay. Like smoke."

He stayed put. "What burns?"

"Food. People cooking." It wasn't the only reason; the collision of colder air from the aqueducts with the warm air of the Concourse also contributed, but most of my people had no referent to understand what that meant.

Taz stepped through the opening, holding his daughter, who had fallen asleep. It amazed me that his arms hadn't tired yet. He looked around the hazy area. "Too light."

It seemed dim to me, with just one street lamp in this part of the Concourse, but compared to the aqueducts, it was bright. As much as I want to give him time to adjust, we couldn't risk lingering.

"Come with." I set off for a hidden route behind the stalls, where we could pass unseen through much of the Concourse. We walked in the haze, unable to see more than a few feet—and came to a wall. Damn! Someone had blocked this passage. I stood in front of the barrier, a smooth expanse of synthetic whatever, a material my people never used. Cries had put up this barrier to stop us Undercity types from sneaking around the Concourse.

"Go through?" Taz asked. Born in the aqueducts, he would assume holes, crevices, and other inner spaces existed through any barrier. Our options here were much more limited.

"No passage." I turned around, surveying the area. On my left, I could make out the backs of several market shacks through the haze. I headed toward them. "Over here."

We followed a cramped passage between two stalls and came out onto the lane that comprised the Concourse. The woman tending the stall to our right gaped at Taz. When I glared at her, she flushed and turned away, pretending to be occupied with the pottery in her stall. The man in the stall on our left was talking into his wrist comm. If he was contacting the police, my attempt to disguise us as tourists hadn't worked. Coming out between their stalls certainly hadn't helped.

"Hurry," I muttered to Taz. We needed to be gone.

We set off at a brisk pace, walking past the faded stalls. As we went farther up the Concourse, the haze cleared and the stalls we passed looked less dingy. No other customers were down this far, though, which meant we drew too much attention. Many of the female vendors stared at Taz. My cynical side assumed they weren't calling the police because they were less likely to associate criminal behavior with a man blessed by his looks, as if beauty somehow made a person more trustworthy. Given the scars many of my people accumulated—the damaged bodies, emaciated frames, and cyber implants—they looked *wrong* to citizens of Cries. Often I gritted my teeth with repressed rage, but today I was grateful our health and supposed normality worked in our favor.

The Concourse widened and cafés appeared, nestled between more upscale stalls selling rugs, pots, metalwork, carpets, artsy clothes, and other "Undercity" souvenirs. A bit further and the stalls became little boutiques with brighter colors and quaint signs hanging from their eaves. More people were out strolling in this region of the Concourse. Two police officers were striding toward the end of the Concourse, but they ignored us. Good.

Taz had a glazed look. He held his daughter close and stared straight ahead. I didn't need telepathy to recognize his shock. The light, the people, the stalls, the colors—it didn't look like he could take it all in. He had reached saturation. Yet even now he kept walking. The better I knew Taz, the more I understood why Singer loved him. Yes, he was handsome, but that was only the surface. The more I saw of his strength of character, the more he earned my respect. Whatever his inner turmoil, none of it showed except in the protective way he cradled his daughter. I just hoped someday he forgave me for this walk.

We had reached the halfway point of the Concourse, now a wide boulevard with upscale shops and elite restaurants. Enough tourists were out and about in this section that we no longer stood out. Several children ran by, their ragged clothes fluttering in the breeze. Undercity. They were small and cute, however, so most people ignored them, as marks often do. They ran right by us—and gods almighty, one of the little thugs tried to filch the nonexistent purse under my leather jacket. I grabbed her arm and stopped in the middle of the street with Taz at my side.

"Stupid," I muttered in the Undercity dialect.

The girl, who had started to twist in my hold, froze. "Eh?"

I looked down at her smudged face. "No steal. Tell circle."

She stared at me with her mouth open. Then she gathered her wits and nodded.

"Go." I released her arm, and she took off like a bullet, running to join her friends, who had hidden someplace, I didn't know where, but it would be nearby. We never left our own to fend for themselves on the Concourse.

I set off again with Taz. After a moment, he said, "Little jan thought we were above-city."

"Guess so."

The hint of a smile appeared on his face. "We fool Cries people, too."

For now, at least. We had reached a beautiful area of the Concourse. Clubs, bistros, and chic stores lined both sides of the throughway, thronged with pedestrians. No vehicles were allowed; this place existed to attract pedestrians: tourists, shoppers, people out on the town. To our right, a wide path led to the bridge that arched over the only canal up here in the Concourse. The canal was dry, but if water had run below the bridge, it would have poured into the aqueducts at the end of the Concourse.

As we passed the Rec Center, I pointed it out to Taz. "Testing place."

He nodded stiffly, his attention fixed on the route ahead.

"Where Singer went for psi testing," I added, hoping to make this all seem a little less alien.

He said nothing.

As we neared the end of the Concourse, it became a glitzy playland for the wealthy, a world so unlike ours, it seemed unreal. The first time I'd come here, I wondered if I was hallucinating. A café sported a patio with round tables where you could watch holos of whatever entertainment you desired. Music spilled out of a club with a large bouncer standing at the door. Holos of annoyingly cute animals scampered up and down the sides of an import store called The Kitten Shoppe. Okay, they weren't annoying, they were adorable, but I'd never admit that to anyone. It'd ruin my reputation.

We kept going.

After what felt like years, we left the glamour of the main Concourse and reached the large area at the end, similar to the lobby of a magrail station. A few meters away, stairs led up to the desert. Relief spread over me. Once we reached the surface, we wouldn't have to worry anywhere near as much about the police. They patrolled the Concourse because it offered the most lucrative tourist attraction in Cries, a substantial source of revenue for the city. People from the Undercity came from below, not from the surface, so they worried less about people at this end.

"Almost there," I said.

Taz nodded, his tense expression easing. It would be all right—

"You there," a woman called. "Where are you going?"

Oh, shit.

I turned to see three police officers, two women and a man, all of them surveying us. Taz met their gazes with the forthright stare of an Undercity man, which a highborn man of Cries would never do. All three cops wore the dark blue uniforms of the city police, with the emblem of the Concourse patrol on their arms, a white triangle. The woman in front had a broad face, black hair pulled back at her neck, and a corporal's chevron on the sleeves of her uniform. They approached us slowly, their hands on the pulse revolvers holstered on their hips. Not good.

I spoke in my most cultured above-city accent. "Is there a problem?"

All three paused. It helped that I hadn't learned to speak the Cries dialect until I was sixteen. I had an accent. Few people recognized it as Undercity, however, because no one above ground had reason to hear their language spoken in an Undercity accent. They would assume I was an offworld tourist spending my credits on their Concourse. I hoped.

The corporal looked Taz up and down. "We need to see your IDs."

Damn. Taz had no ID. I tried to put the same note of impeccable disdain into my voice that the Majdas injected into everything they said without realizing it. "He does not carry ID or speak." Thank goodness he was carrying a toddler. They would assume he was my husband. I couldn't fool them into thinking he was a cloistered noble; such a man would never come to the Concourse or dress so casually. However, among the more conservative element of Cries, some women still treated their men with the sexist constraints of past eras, denying them financial independence or identification, effectively cloistering them because you couldn't go much of anywhere without an ID.

The cops considered the implications. They were all looking Taz over now, especially the two women. Probably the only thing that kept them from demanding a search were my words and tone. Yah, right, they needed to frisk him. If they tried, they would get an Undercity warrior defending his child, not the compliant boy they expected. Both Taz and I would end up in jail.

I needed to distract them. I spoke carefully. "Officers, I am carrying a weapon in a holster under my jacket. As a retired army major and a licensed private investigator, I have a permit to do so. My ID and other documentation are in an inside pocket of my jacket, on the other side of my body from the holster. How would you like me to retrieve them?"

That got their attention. They all turned to me. The corporal said, "Raise your arms."

As I lifted my arms, my jacket shifted enough to reveal my weapon. The corporal stepped forward and removed the gun. "Nice issue." She glanced at me. "Top of the line."

I stood there with my hands in the air, feeling stupid. "Thanks."

She handed my gun to the man. He looked it over while the corporal took my ID out of my inner pocket. She glanced at my ISC card, which listed me as retired military, and I could actually see her relaxing, her shoulders lowering. Although Cries was a government rather than a military center, ISC had a strong presence here, especially the army, the long-time stronghold of the Majdas.

The corporal scanned my gun permit with a sensor in her wrist gauntlet. After a moment, she glanced at me. "You can put your arms down."

I lowered my arms, keeping Taz in my side vision. The other female police officer was standing too close to him. I didn't like it.

The corporal handed my cards back to me. "This all looks in order."

My relief lasted about one second. Then the other woman spoke to Taz. "One of us can hold the baby while we search you."

I hoped Taz wouldn't understand her, but from his sudden icy look, it was clear he knew exactly what she had said. Most Undercity parents, when faced with such a "request" would adamantly refuse, using some choice words in the process, which would get them arrested. You could get a year in prison for disrespecting city authorities in Cries.

Taz did the one thing that avoided a confrontation. He pretended he didn't understand.

I spoke in a neutral tone. "I am sorry, officer, I don't wish to be trouble, but neither of us consents to a search." Unless they had probable cause, they had no right to frisk us. Most citizens didn't realize they could refuse, but I made it my business to know my rights in any place I lived or worked. I had gone for too many years in my youth thinking I had no rights at all. Never again.

They all scowled. Tough. I'd divulged my weapon and given them my ID. They had no basis to demand a search. They might anyway, and if we didn't comply, we'd have trouble. Sure, I could file a complaint later, but the damage would be done. It wouldn't take them long to figure out Taz was Dark Singer's common-law husband. With him and the child in custody, I'd lose my advantage in negotiating for Singer. The authorities could use her family as bargaining chips to force her cooperation.

I needed to defuse the situation. I could invoke my Majda connection, but they'd want to verify the claim, which could piss off my aristocratic employers. I was going to have enough trouble when they found out I was harboring a cartel assassin. If the officers hauled us into the station, everything would be shot to hell. Taz would go ballistic if they separated him from his child. The Dust Knights would lose faith in me if they thought I handed Singer's husband and child over to the cops.

I'd have worried less if these were Majda police. As much as I disliked Captain Takkar, she ran a clean force. I hadn't heard of scandals in the Cries force either, but in my youth, whenever the cops arrested any of us, rumors ran wild about beatings and rapes. A man who looked like Taz, who knew nothing of Cries, who couldn't even fully speak their dialect— no, I didn't want to think what might happen.

"What do you have to hide?" the corporal was asking me, her voice clipped and cold.

I kept my voice respectful. "Officer, I'm not resisting and I appreciate that you're doing your job, but neither of us has to consent to a search."

She scowled at me. "What are you hiding in that pack?"

Screw that. I didn't have to open my pack, which was good, because if they saw the shroud I carried, who knew what jar of bile bugs that would open. She had to tell us if they intended to detain us. Even if they did take us into the station, we could refuse to speak until we had a lawyer. If they did a search here, it would never stand up in court, especially with Max recording everything, but by the time we had it all sorted out, the damage would be done. The way that one officer was looking over Taz, I had little doubt that if it had been up to her, she'd have insisted on taking him to the police compound and searching him in private.

"Corporal," I said. "Are you detaining us?"

Her gaze flicked to my wrist gauntlets, then back to my face. "You got an EI in those?"

I didn't have to answer that, either. Fortunately, common sense overcame my anger. "Yes, my gauntlets contain an EI."

"Is it active?" she asked.

Well, double damn. I hadn't warned her that Max recorded my interactions. That meant his files weren't admissible in court. I had no good answer, so I said nothing. It was looking more and more like I'd need a lawyer.

The male officer suddenly spoke. "Corporal, look at this."

She glanced at the small screen of his gauntlet. "Well, fuck me," she muttered.

I had to bite the inside of my mouth to stop myself from commenting on the anatomical implications of *that* comment.

Bhaaj, Max thought. Behave yourself.

The corporal glanced at me. "Your gun permit was authorized by the Majda police captain."

That was news to me. It made sense, since I worked for the Majdas, but given how much the captain disliked me, she could have given me grief about the permit. That she resisted the temptation also spoke to her clean shop. Even better, it gave me an incontrovertible connection to the Majdas, one I didn't have to claim and have them contact Takkar for verification. Her running a clean force didn't mean she'd make things easy for me.

So I just said, "That's right."

The other woman stepped away from Taz. He stayed still, watching us all, but I knew was ready to fight.

The corporal spoke curtly. "You're free to go."

"Thank you." They still had my gun, which they had no good reason to keep, but I could pick it up at the station later. I just wanted out of here, and fast. Glancing at Taz, I tilted my head toward the stairs. He nodded, slow and careful, no sudden moves. Smart. Even in a situation that had to be alien to everything he knew, he kept his head.

As we walked to the stairs, I could almost feel the officers watching us. Taz held his daughter close, his head bent over hers as if that would protect her.

I spoke under my breath. "Taz."

He lifted his head to look at me. "Eh?"

I motioned to the stairs. "We go up. Stand under the sky."

"Sky?"

"Outside world."

"No ken," he said.

"Will soon. Be ready."

He nodded, his face impassive.

As we climbed the steps, he kept looking around, probably searching for the cracks, crevices, and hidden ways of this staircase. In the Undercity, nothing consisted of long, even ledges, all perfectly spaced. The first time I had seen these stairs, I couldn't understand them. It had taken me a few minutes to realize I was supposed to go *up* rather than *through* them.

The Concourse ceiling was only about four meters above the steps. Although we could see the large archway at the top, the artfully designed holo screens within it showed only washes of color, hiding what lay beyond. We reached the archway and stood in front of the shifting colors, which looked like an aurora brought from the sky to fill this entrance to the rest of the world.

"Ready?" I asked Taz.

"For what?"

I motioned toward the archway. "The sky."
He seemed more puzzled than anything else. "Yah."
We walked through the holoscreen—into the daylight.

XIV

RUINS OF THE VANISHED SEA

Since the day that humans first came to Raylicon, lost and terrified, my people have written songs about the parched, unforgiving beauty of the desert. Those songs survived even for my people, who had spent millennia denied the freedom of the open sky. In the aqueducts, our songs mourned that loss, filling the ruins with music, their haunting beauty our only consolation for our loss of the sky.

Taz and I stood at the edge of the Vanished Sea and looked out at the desert. It stretched to the horizon. The first time I had seen this view, I believed the red sands went on forever, even though I knew they ended at the jagged edge where the world met the sky. I hadn't perceived ground and sky, only a sense of *distance* greater than my mind could absorb. I stood under the freedom of the open sky and knew my life had changed, but I'd had no referent how to understand what that meant. In the decades since, each day of my life I came to terms with another fraction of that freedom, but it would take me a lifetime to fully comprehend the open sky.

Wind stirred our hair and tugged at our clothes. I loved the moving air. It felt filled with promise, bringing me alive in a way I had never known before I first stood here, taking deep, astonished breaths. Taz stood frozen, his gaze sweeping the land and its forever spaces. He tilted his face up to the sky. The sun was behind us, and I didn't think he even knew it existed. He stared at the pale blue expanse, then at the horizon, then at the sky, again and again.

"Gods," he said.

"Pretty, eh?" I said.

He glanced at me. "Real?"

"Yah. Real."

Taz closed one eye, squinting at the horizon. "Can't see. Only parts."

I nodded. My first time, I hadn't seen it as a single scene, either, only in pieces. My mind couldn't process all the visual information at once.

"Will see better," I said. "Takes time."

As Taz shifted his daughter to one arm, she gurgled. Although she looked around with a bright gaze at the landscape, she seemed far less impressed than her father. This one view would probably change her visual perception for life, preparing her mind to see large spaces and open sky when she was young enough that she wouldn't have to relearn how to see them as an adult.

Taz lifted his free hand into the air, turning it first one way, then the other. "Is breathing."

I blinked. "Your hand?"

"The air."

Ah. "Called a breeze."

"Breeze." He repeated the word thoughtfully. "Soft."

"Yah." Such a simple thing, to feel moving air on your skin. In aqueducts, air vented through cleverly designed ducts, which kept it clean, and it even smelled nice, with the faintest scent from the traces aromatic benzene compounds in the canal dust. No breezes, though.

Taz took a deep breath, then slowly let it out. "Good air."

"Yah." I wanted to give him time to process, but we needed to leave, in case the police decided to come up to see what we were about. I didn't want to call a flyer and load more shocks on Taz. He handled himself well, but if he was feeling anything like what I had experienced the first time I walked out under this glorious sky, the last thing he needed right now was to ride in a machine that soared at high speeds above the ground.

To our right, the terraced plaza outside Cries led to the city, all pale blue stone, each "step" more than thirty meters wide, with the distant fountain shooting water into the air. My first time here, I hadn't been able to tell the difference between the terraces and the sky. It wasn't until I walked on the plaza that I realized I couldn't touch the sky. Beyond it, in the distance, the towers of Cries reflected the endless blue sky in their glass panels.

I motioned at the city. "I live there."

"And Singer?"

"Yah. Singer is there."

He nodded. "We go."

We headed for Cries.

My penthouse EI didn't even wait until I arrived home to badger me. It started on the ride up to the penthouse.

Taz and I stood in the carpeted lift with its mirrored walls. In this enclosed space, he seemed less tense than in the city. He couldn't stop staring in the mirror. He tapped his daughter's shoulder, watching his reflection touch the reflection of her shoulder. He grimaced at his image, then jerked as his reflected face grimaced. Tilting his head, he watched his reflection tilt its head. He looked at my reflection, at me, back at our reflections.

"Copy of Taz?" he asked. "Two Taz?"

"Only one." I motioned at the mirror. "Reflection."

"Ree. Fleck. Shun," he repeated—and then he laughed.

Ah, gods, Singer, I understand you so much better. To hear that glorious laugh, to see his face light up like the rising sun, the flash of his teeth in a grin—no wonder she was willing to kill, steal, run drugs, commit gods only knew what other crimes, and in the end give up her freedom, maybe even her life, for him.

My apartment EI spoke out of the air. "Do you wish me to cover the mirrors to calm your uneducated guest?"

"Ho!" Taz jumped, alarm flashing across his face.

I wondered if it was possible to throttle an EI. "No. I wish you to shut up."

"Who?" Taz demanded.

I'd never given the EI a name, so I just said, "EI."

"Eeyai? Where?"

"Part of my circle." It was sort of true, given a liberal enough definition for "kith and kin."

"Dust Knight?"

Now *that* was an intriguing response. I didn't actually have a "circle" in the Undercity; I neither ran with a gang nor headed a family. It had never occurred to me that people would see the Dust Knights as my circle, but I rather liked the idea.

"Nahya," I said. "Not a knight. A pest."

He laughed again, and it was worth putting up with the EI just to hear Taz's reaction.

The lift stopped and the doors opened into my living room.

"Eh?" Taz stopped smiling.

"Umm," his daughter said sleepily.

"Shhh," Taz murmured, patting her back. He looked at me.

"Is safe." I lifted my hand, inviting him to enter.

Taz walked down the three steps into my sunken living room with extreme caution, is if he thought the place might explode. The window wall stood on our right, filling the place with light.

A woman's deep voice rumbled. "Taz?"

With a start, I realized Singer was sitting on the floor by the wall, leaning against the glass. She looked as if she were just waking up.

"Eh, Sings." Taz exhaled, and until that moment I didn't realize how wound up he had become during our journey. He hid his reactions well, but when he saw Singer, it was as if some invisible vise let him go and he could relax.

As the doors closed behind us, Singer rose to her feet, rubbing her back. Tall and muscled, with her torn shirt revealing her narrow waist and well-developed abs, she looked like some warrior goddess. "Good path here?" she asked Taz.

"Yah." He went over to her.

"Eh." Their daughter mimicked them as she reached her pudgy arms out to her mother.

"Little jan." Singer took the girl and hefted her up in her arms. "Always heavier." She seemed pleased, if it was possible to read that response from her gravely voice.

Taz rubbed his arms. "Yah, heavy."

That was it, the extent of their reunion after what had to be one of the most emotion-packed days either had ever experienced. And I thought Jak and I had trouble expressing ourselves. Then again, they didn't seem to need more. They shared a Kyle bond Jak and I would never know.

"Jak here?" I asked Singer.

"Nahya," Singer said. "Went back to casino."

Well, so, he did have a business to run, illegal or not.

Singer put her daughter on the floor, and the girl held onto her leg, looking around the room with the universal unabashed curiosity of a small child.

"Room talks," Singer added.

"What, my living room?" I asked.

"Yah. Can't ken."

"Jibbers," I agreed.

The EI's voice came into the air. "I don't think your guest understands me."

I switched into Cries dialect. "Probably not." I dropped onto the couch and leaned back, giving in to my fatigue. The couch shifted, trying to make itself more comfortable.

"What did you want to tell Singer?" I asked the EI.

"That I needed to reach you."

"Well, here I am."

When I started talking to the EI, Taz and Singer turned to each other and forgot about me. They sat at the top of the steps by the window, and gazed at the view with their daughter between them. Watching them, I hurt inside. This might be their last time together. I'd heard that psions developed deep emotional bonds. They shared a part of their minds at a subconscious level. I envied them.

"Singer," I said.

She glanced at me. "Yah?"

I sat up and showed her the image recorder on my gauntlet. "Take fleck?"

She scowled at me. "Why?"

"Prove you came here. For the bargain."

Comprehension came into her expression. I wanted a picture to prove she had actually left the Undercity to give herself up in return for amnesty for her family.

"Yah, do fleck," she said.

Max, get a good picture of the three of them, I thought.

A click came from my gauntlet. Done.

When Singer and Taz heard the click, they turned back to the view, which was undoubtedly more interesting to them than I would ever be. I let myself sink back into the sofa cushions.

"EI," I said. "What did you want to tell me?"

"Colonel Majda has been trying to reach you."

Nor surprise there. I closed my eyes.

"Shall I comm her?" the EI asked.

Once I talked to Lavinda, that was it. No matter what I negotiated for Singer, the life she and her family knew would be over. Before that happened, she needed time to talk to Taz, to be with him and their daughter. She needed a chance to say good-bye.

"Not now," I said softly.

I hadn't realized I fell asleep on the couch until I awoke. Shadows filled the room. The sun had moved in the sky, descending to the horizon, and the window-wall polarized in response, darkening the living room. Singer and Taz had fallen asleep leaning against the window with their daughter curled between them.

I sat up, rubbing my eyes, and spoke in a low voice. "EI, can you locate Colonel Majda?"

"Possibly. Shall I comm her?"

"No, just tell me where I can find her."

"If she follows her usual schedule, she will go into work several hours early. She is probably already in her office at the Selei Building."

I didn't need to ask how it knew her schedule. At least the Majdas didn't try to hide the fact that they linked to "my" penthouse EI.

In any case, it was time to become my above-city self.

I had last visited the Selei Building in downtown Cries when the Majdas appointed me to a task force that investigated a smuggling ring in the Undercity. Today I walked into the spacious lobby with no invitation. Transparent panels stretched from the floor to the high ceiling around the edges of the lobby, supposedly nothing more than decoration. Right. Security used them to watch people. I had dressed in an elegant suit, dove grey with the barest shimmer. I didn't look like myself. The expensive cut of my suit and my military carriage said *I belong here.*

The seal of the Pharaoh's Army dominated the back wall, a ruby pyramid within a circle. The other walls had emblems of the other branches of ISC: the old-fashioned sailing ship of the Imperial Fleet; a Jag starfighter for the J-Force; two crossed stalks of grain for the Advance Services Corps. The tower served as a conference center, supposedly for any group that wished to reserve the space, but given the military symbols that dominated the lobby, I had a good guess as to what "any group" meant.

A receptionist sat at the gleaming counter, a man rather than a robot, which also spoke to the high level of this building. I went over to him. "My greetings."

He regarded me coolly. "Yes?"

"I'm here to see Colonel Majda."

His eyebrows went up just the slightest amount. "Do you have an appointment?"

I met his gaze. "No."

"I will notify her aide." He looked down at me from his high seat. "Your name?"

"Tell her Bhaajan is here."

He didn't deign to answer, he just tapped in a message at his screen. "You may come back in two days. I will have an answer then as to whether or not Colonel Majda will see you."

Yah, and screw that. I just looked at him.

A beep came from his screen. He glanced down—and this time his eyebrows really did go up. "Well. It appears the colonel will see you now." He sounded disappointed. Turning his cool gaze back to me, he added, "I will need your full name for your badge."

I only had one name, so I said, "Major Bhaajan."

At the word "Major," he seemed to warm up an infinitesimal amount. He made a badge with my picture as a flat holo. Some hidden camera must have taken it while I stood here, because I could see the lobby in the background. Then he waved me toward the titanium lift behind his desk.

I took the lift to the forty-second floor, and it let me out into a reception area with another human at the desk, a woman in the green uniform of an army lieutenant. The conference room was only a short walk away, with its glass wall and long table inside. It was dark at this "early" hour, though it was the middle of the day. Right now, normal people were asleep.

"My greetings, Major." The lieutenant motioned to the right. "Colonel Majda is in her office."

I nodded. "Thanks."

I found Lavinda's office at the end of a long hall. It was bigger even than the conference center, with a wall of windows overlooking Cries.

She sat at her long desk in front of the windows, facing the door, an arrangement that put her body in silhouette as I entered, a dark form against the bright light, whereas while she could undoubtedly see me just fine.

I kept my mental barriers at full strength. "My greetings, Colonel."

"Major." She motioned at a chair in front of her long desk. "Sit."

I sat. This close up, I could see her better. She didn't look tired despite the early hour. She also didn't look at all pleased to see me.

"We need to talk," I said.

"You are a master at understatement." She frowned. "Have you found Calaj?"

"Possibly." I took a breath. "I really do need to see the pharaoh. This situation may be bigger than we realized, but before I say anything, I need to talk to her."

Lavinda tossed the light stylus she was holding on her desk, then stood up and went to the window. She stood there, staring at the city. Now that I saw her in the full light, I realized she did look tired. In fact, she seemed exhausted.

She turned to me. "Major, in the past two days you have twice trespassed on Izu Yaxlan, you involved the Uzan, even used him to contact the pharaoh, bypassing proper channels, and later you somehow ended up in the Undercity with him. You broke into the Tikal Lock, one of the most protected sites in the empire, and the Lock damn near killed you for it. You insulted the pharaoh at a level beyond imagining, and she responded by sending you one of the best doctors in the Imperialate, a *Rajindia* for gods' sake." She crossed her arms. "If anything happens to that doctor while she is in the Undercity, you are *personally* responsible, do you understand?"

Well, hell. As if I wasn't in it deep enough, already. "Yes, ma'am."

She didn't look the least appeased. "You persist in consorting with one of the top criminal bosses on Raylicon, someone we would have arrested long ago if it wasn't political suicide, given the highly ranked officials who supposedly don't frequent his casino. You continually hide from us, then suddenly appear on our sensors deep in the aqueducts, demand to see the pharaoh, disappear again, then reappear when we get a report about you leaving the Undercity with an unregistered male and child. If that's not enough, oh yes excuse me, you are harboring the worst criminal on our wanted list in your protected apartment, which means we can't go in to get her, by our own decree. Bhaajan, what the bloody hell do you think you're doing?"

I got up and went to the window so I could face her eye to eye. "You left out one thing." She had actually left out a lot. Apparently they didn't know about my link to the weapons Ruzik and Hack had stolen.

Lavinda looked as if she wanted a good, stiff drink. "Please don't say that."

I hesitated, uncertain whether or not to continue.

She spoke dryly. "Go ahead."

"The man and the baby are at my apartment now, too."

"Why?"

"The man is Dark Singer's common-law husband. The girl is their daughter."

Lavinda scowled at me. "This does not make me happy."

"I'm doing the job you hired me to do."

"The results of which you will only tell the Ruby Pharaoh?"

"Yes. I'm sorry."

"You should be." She shook her head. "You've angered so many people, I don't even know where to start."

"Including the pharaoh?"

"No, actually, she seems to be the only one who doesn't want to arrest you." In a quieter voice, Lavinda said, "It's hard to tell with her. She's one of the few people I know who, even when she's angry, genuinely acts in what she believes is in the common good."

"I'm sorry I've aggravated people." I meant it, too.

She spoke wryly. "But you won't stop doing it."

I had no answer she would like, so instead I said, "I'd like to talk to you about Dark Singer."

"The assassin?"

I almost said *yah,* but I caught myself in time. "Yes, that's right."

"Why are you speaking for her?"

I blinked. it had never occurred to me *not* to speak for Singer. She was part of my circle. I didn't know how to explain that without going into the Dust Knights, our code of honor, or the loyalty of kith and kin in the Undercity, besides which, none of that was her business.

So I just said, "She's a friend."

"Your friend. An assassin."

"She saved my life. Captain Ebersole's life, too."

"So I heard. Why do you want to talk to me about her?"

"She's willing to turn herself in. She wants to make a deal."

Lavinda gaped at me. "Good gods, how did you convince her?"

I shrugged. "I didn't do anything."

"Somehow I doubt that." Lavinda became more businesslike. "What does she offer, and what does she want in return?"

Singer had asked only for Taz and the baby, but I intended to negotiate for all three of them. "She's offering to tell you what she knows about the Vakaar drug cartel. Names, actions, everything. In return she wants amnesty and witness protection for herself and her family."

"You must be joking."

I scowled at her. "No, I am not joking."

"I can't give this assassin amnesty. And how would we put her and her family in witness protection? They probably can't function outside of the Undercity."

"Of course they can." I had no idea if that was true. After what I had seen of Taz, I thought he could adapt, but Singer was another story. She was a throwback to the ancient warriors who had stalked this land, committing mayhem and conquering people, probably far more like the pharaoh's ancestors than the pharaoh herself. I couldn't imagine her operating as a normal citizen. Nor would she ever be free of remorse for her crimes. She was turning herself in to punish herself as much as to give Taz and her child a better life.

"You do know what she's wanted for, don't you?" Lavinda said. "You must. Every city or Majda agent who monitors the Concourse knows. She's committed at least six murders and she's wanted for questioning in at least three more."

"She killed dealers," I said. "Kajada punkers. People flooding the Undercity with drugs. Do you have any idea what that shit does to my people? It rots our lives and kills our young."

Lavinda spoke coldly. "Yes, she murdered drug runners. In the service of the Vakaar crime boss, so Vakaar could take over the Kajada drug trade."

It was true, and I hated that as much as Lavinda, maybe more because I had seen firsthand the grief inflicted on my people by the cartels.

"Singer was protecting her family," I said. "The only way she knew how."

"Is this supposed to be an excuse?"

"No." I lifted my hands, then dropped them in frustration. "She's a telepath. You have her tests. You know what it's like. You live with your Kyle nature every day. Imagine you're surrounded by the worst humanity has to offer, that you don't know any other life exists or that it's possible to protect your mind. It twists a person, Lavinda. It destroys you. If it wasn't for her husband, she might have turned into an irredeemable monster. But she didn't. She's offering you a look into the cartels you'll never get otherwise. It may be your only chance to clean up the drug rings, and you can do it now because they're weakened by the war. But they're picking themselves up. If they get another strong leader, you may never break them." I took a breath. "Singer could have become that leader. The Vakaars would gladly follow her. Instead she chose to do this, of her own volition. That has to count for something."

"It's a trick."

"It's not a trick." I frowned at her. "The fact that she's as intimidating as all hell doesn't make her incapable of remorse." I tapped a code into my gauntlet. A picture appeared on the screen, Singer, Taz, and their daughter sitting by my window-wall with the immensity of the desert behind them. I hadn't realized what a powerful image it made, the three of them gorgeous in the wild, untamed way of the Undercity, framed by a panorama of the Vanished Sea.

I showed her the picture. "She did it for them."

"Good gods." Lavinda stared at the image. "That's her family?"

"Yes."

She looked up at me. "One could see how a woman might be driven to protect them."

I felt guilty for not telling Singer the real reason I took the picture, but it had the effect on Lavinda I hoped it would make. "Will you help?"

She rubbed her eyes, and in that moment I didn't see the aloof, powerful Majda, I saw an exhausted woman trying to do her job in impossible circumstances. She was the one who'd take the fallout for my actions, yet she was still willing to work with me.

Lavinda lowered her arms. "I'll see what I can do."

I was walking to my apartment through Aurora Park in Cries when my comm buzzed. I tapped it on. "Bhaaj here."

The voice of Royal Flush snapped into the air. "You have to get here. Now."

"Where?" Why was Royal calling me instead of Jak?

"The casino. Something is wrong." The comm clicked as Royal cut the connection.

What the hell? I wanted to go straight to the casino, but I'd left my pack at the penthouse, which meant I had no light, water, weapons, or shroud. I took off at a biomech-enhanced run for my apartment, which would probably ruin my elegant, but right now I didn't give a damn.

Jak's casino was gone.

I stood where I had last seen his establishment, its walls half above the ground and half below, blending so well, it looked like part of the ruins. No trace of it remained today.

"Max, can you reach Royal Flush?" I spoke aloud, uneasy with the silence of this empty space.

"I've been trying," Max said. "He either can't or won't answer."

I walked around the empty area. Sure, I knew that nanobots in the structure of the casino could take the building apart and rebuild it elsewhere, but I'd never realized they could do such a thorough job in so short a time. Not even a footstep disturbed the dust. That was actually the only indication his casino had been here; the dust lay too evenly on the ground. Left alone for long periods, it tended to pile in drifts against the walls, tiny ones given the slight air currents down here, but enough to see. No drifts here.

"This is strange," I said.

"Why?" Max answered. "He moves the casino all the time."

"Yah, but Royal never calls me about it. He said something was wrong." Ruzik had used the same word before he showed me Hack's detector.

"I can't contact the casino," Max said.

"Comm Dara. She's bartending tonight."

"Dara doesn't have a comm."

I frowned. "Yes, she does."

"I don't have her code."

"Of course you do. She gave it to me the last time I was at her home."

"I will retrieve my file of the conversation."

I headed back to the canals. "Did you reach her?"

"She isn't responding."

Our conversation bothered me. "Max, why didn't you know Dara had a comm?"

"She never had one until a few days ago."

I stopped walking. "You have a record of my conversation with her about it."

"Yes, the record came up when you asked me to comm her."

This was as strange as the disappearing casino. "No, you said she didn't have a comm."

"Then I brought up the record."

"You told me you didn't know her code."

"I retrieved it when I brought up my file of the conversation."

"Yah, but you shouldn't need to go through all that with me." I set off again. "You process faster than I talk. A lot faster. When I asked you to comm her, you should have brought up the record and found her code in less than a second."

"It is odd," Max admitted. "I will run a diagnostic on myself."

He said it so easily. I wished I could run diagnostics to figure out myself.

"Do you still have your map of the route to Hack's cyber den?" I asked.

"Yes."

"Good. I need directions."

Hack ignored me when I showed up at his lab. He was playing Bronze Warrior with gamers in Cries. He'd become a maestro at the holo-mesh game. It wasn't only that he designed his fighters better than most players, with a finesse his opponents lacked; his ingenuity also set him apart. He used a blend of the rough-tumble with tykado that in real life, Ruzik's gang was perfecting, working for hours every day, as much for the pleasure of the athletics as because Ruzik wanted them to outfight everyone else. Hack's gang worked with them, and that all went into his game here. I wondered how his opponents would react if they discovered that the warrior who dominated their contests came from the Undercity. They'd never know; Hack hid his mesh identity as well as he hid his lab.

I couldn't wait, though, even if it meant interrupting the Bronze Warrior king. I said, "Hack."

His avatar executed a roll that sent his opponents spinning in different directions. The holo jumped to its feet, shaking a spear modeled after a weapon used by the ancient warriors of Izu Yaxlan. They had all been women, but today both male and female figures populated the holo table Hack used as a game board.

"Got trouble," I said. "Maybe bad."

He held up his hand, one finger pointing upward, while he continued playing.

I squinted at the ceiling. Nothing showed up there except a few stalactites glinting with tech-mech. No, wait, those "glints" were function lights from the signals Hack received from the game. He was rerouting them through his own systems, disguising the source of his transmissions.

Hack dispatched his opponents, then laughed to himself. He snapped his fingers and the board disappeared. Standing up, he turned to me. "Eh, Bhaaj."

"Good game."

He grinned, but then his smile faded. "Got trouble?"

"Casino gone. Royal says something is 'wrong.' Same word you used."

Hack tilted his head toward the back room. "Come with."

I went with him. The detector looked the same as the last time I visited. Its seat resembled the bar stools in Jak's establishment, covered in dark leather. In fact, it had the same glitter-buttons around its edge. I hoped Hack came by it fairly; stealing from Jak could land you in a shit load of trouble.

The bar stool, however was my least worry. I could fry my brain if I kept using a neural cap with no safeguards. I had to trust that Hack knew his business. Gods only knew what he could achieve if he ever had access to a top-notch cyber lab. He might come up with the Imperialate's next miracle or he might freeze, his genius smothered by the constrained environment.

As he connected the cap to my brain, I lowered the visor and the world went dark. Whatever heads-up display he intended didn't work. The machine hummed as I scanned the desert. Nothing. I scanned to the south and found the Lock slumbering in the desert. I had thought before it wanted to kill me, but the sense I picked up now, admittedly filtered through a cobbled-together detector, told me it felt no more emotion toward us than we did toward sand in the desert. It hadn't "wanted" me dead any more than I wanted a grain of sand to die. I'd brush it away and go on with my business.

I continued my sweep and found Izu Yaxlan. It also seemed quiescent, not sleeping exactly, but simply existing as it had done for millennia. It felt different than the Lock, more benign. It liked its symbiosis with the Uzan, and through him, with the Abaj. The Uzan's home was part of the machinery that supported the EI. It let him live within it, just as it let my people live in the aqueducts—

Ho! Izu Yaxlan considered the Undercity part of itself. I couldn't imagine how the canals served that ancient intelligence, yet it left no doubt; whoever built the Undercity had done it in service to Izu Yaxlan. In contrast, it had no interest in Cries. The city didn't interfere with Izu Yaxlan, so it ignored the desert metropolis.

I continued my sweep across the Vanished Sea. Today the detector seemed to work better. I suspected hadn't picked up this much the last time because it had taken my brain a while to adapt to the machine, not because the EIs cared enough about humans to hide.

I found another EI out in the desert, a modern system, one that felt military.

Max, I thought. *Can you figure out the location where I'm pointing this gun?*

The direction, yes. The distance is more difficult. I need the speed and angle of projectiles shot by the weapon. Except it isn't shooting projectiles.

Can you tell if what I'm pointing at is above ground or below?

If it's nearby, it's below ground. However, the gun is aimed slightly upward. If the target is more than a kilometer away, it's above ground.

What's out there, both nearby and farther out?

Nearby, it's rock and curving passages. Farther out, above ground, it's desert.

Plot it out for me. We'd need to search a large area, but if I'd just found Calaj, she was probably in the desert. Hack would have known if any intruders came near his cyber den.

Done, Max said. I'm saving the maps in a file for you.

Good. Let the Majdas know if might be Calaj. I continued my sweep of the desert—

—and hit the wrongness.

Distance muted the signal, but I had no doubt it was the same EI I'd found before. It felt different from the Lock and Izu Yaxlan. This one wanted to eliminate disorder, particularly the messy humanity that had multiplied on the planet. Malice roiled over me, and recognition. It *knew* me, not as Bhaaj, but as part of the human infestation on Raylicon.

"Shit," I said.

"Want out?" Hack asked.

"Yah. Fast."

He untangled my brain from the neural cap with a deft touch that would put many a biomech adept to shame. "Done."

I lifted the visor and squinted as my eyes adjusted to the light. "Max?"

"You want me to map the location of that last EI you found," Max said.

"Yes. Look in the desert, farther away than Izu Yaxlan and to the west. I think it's nearly at the limit of this detector. Anything out there besides sand?"

"Yes." He sounded subdued. "The starships that brought the first humans to Raylicon."

I jumped up from my seat. "That's it! The EI is in the ships."

"That isn't possible," Max said. "Your ancestors stripped those ships. People have studied them, generation after generation of military experts, engineers, anthropologists, strategists, religious leaders, and anyone else the Ruby Dynasty feels inclined to inflict on them. Nothing is left."

"Talky EI," Hack said.

"Good talk." To Max, I said, "The ships *are* the EI. Something woke it up." I shuddered, remembering its malevolence. "I think it destroyed whatever race brought my ancestors here. They managed to deactivate it somehow, before they died, so it couldn't kill us. Now it's awake again, and it wants to finish what it started, get rid of messy infestations like, you now, us humans."

"How is Calaj involved?" Max asked.

"I don't know!" I regarded Hack, who was listening intently. He probably understood every word. He would have had to learn the Cries dialect to talk with the game players in Cries. I smacked my hand against his detector. "You build. Why?"

"Find wrongness," Hack said.

"How know anything wrong?"

He grimaced. "I felt."

"He's like Calaj," Max said. "Like you. Like the pharaoh. A genetic throwback."

"Could that be what Singer means by darkness?" I asked. "Not just the cartels, but also the EI out there?" No wonder she sought respite, if it was flooding her with malice.

"I don't know," Max said. "However, she is a powerful psion. What you call EIs are neural-machine interfaces designed to interact with humans who have an unusually large number of neural structures in their brain, some of which enhance brain waves, facilitating nonverbal communication."

Hack scowled. "Too much talk. What say?"

"A psion's brain is well suited to linking with the EI," Max said.

"Humans didn't make that wrongness," Hack said.

I agreed. "Felt alien."

"Your ancestors plundered the ship libraries," Max said. "They based their EIs on alien tech."

"Even so," I said. "I don't think humans created this one. It's like an infection in the ships."

"Selei transform," Hack said.

I blinked at him. "What?"

"Selei transforms. Pretty math."

If he understood Selei transforms, he had gone beyond what I knew. "What about them?"

"Transform thoughts," Hack said.

"I think he means the theory of Kyle space," Max said. "It involves finding the quantum wave function that describes the behavior of the particles in your brain while you have a thought."

Hack frowned. "No ken your talky EI." He pointed to me, then to himself. "Spatial close."

Interesting. He used the above-city word for spatial. The Undercity dialect didn't have one. He meant the two of us were close in space. "Ken," I said.

He tapped his head, then pointed at mine. "You, me, think close, yah?"

"That's right." We were thinking about the same things, or at least we were trying to.

"Make fleck spatial places," Hack said. "Now, not now."

I had no idea what that meant. "Say again?"

"He means you can plot position as a function of time," Max said.

Ah, okay. "Yah, ken," I told Hack.

"Make fleck of thought places," he said.

"Max?" I asked.

"It's the Selei transform." Anticipating my next question, Max said, "Yes, Pharaoh Dyhianna discovered it. She was a mathematician before she ascended to the throne. Apparently she was more interested in studying why her family can use the Lock than in actually being the person who used it."

Having met her, I could believe that. "How does the transform work?"

"You plot the wave function that describes your thought as a function of position, then transform that function into a space that depends on the thought itself instead of position."

"That's a huge calculation." Doable with our best systems, but complicated.

"It's how the Kyle works," Max said.

I'd never been any good at Kyle theory, but I understood the gist of what they were trying to tell me. "Hack, this EI in the ships, can it infect Kyle space?"

"Kyle?" he asked.

"Thought place."

"Yah, I think. Infect everything."

"If such a virus got loose in the Kyle mesh," Max said, "no unprotected link on our interstellar grids would be safe. It could spread across the Imperialate."

My head was throbbing again. I spoke grimly. "Pharaoh Dyhianna and her nephew, Imperator Skolia, protect the Kyle web. To destroy the interstellar meshes, the EI needs to kill them both."

XV

TITANS

Dara found me while I was running down the midwalk of a canal. She jogged up alongside of me and we ran together, our feet pounding the ground.

"Max commed me," Dara said.

"Yah." I slowed down. "Royal commed me. Said Black Mark had trouble."

"Casino mesh went crazy. Jak closed up."

"Crazy how?"

"Saying things wrong. Turned off air breathers. Slowed down fire monitors."

That fit with Max's strange behavior when I had gone looking for the casino. Whatever had happened to Jak's systems had affected Max as well.

"Anyone hurt?" I asked.

"Gamblers pissed." Dara shrugged. "Some fights. Bouncers stop. Jak stop."

I could imagine. I'd never mess with Jak when he was angry. "Jak good?"

She slanted me a look. "You know better than me."

"Not funny," I growled.

She smiled. "Jak fine."

"Black Mark good?"

"Black Mark gone." She scowled. "I got no job."

"Will open again." People would always want to gamble, and Jak would always be willing to take their money. I was far more worried about what corrupted the casino mesh. Had Royal picked up the Vanished Sea EI? It made no sense that it went after the Undercity rather than Cries. Attacking Jak's casino would have little effect on the human presence on Raylicon.

Unless . . . it was actually attacking Izu Yaxlan. The EI considered the Undercity part of itself, and Jak's casino had fewer defenses than Izu Yaxlan. Did the Lock or Izu Yaxlan sense this other EI waking up out in the desert? Shit. Just what we needed, three giant EIs stirring from their millennia of slumber to wage war against each other.

"Collateral damage," I muttered. "That's us. We're dead."

"Eh?" Dara asked.

"Listen." I slowed to a stop. "Warn Jak, yah? No one use tech-mech. No mesh. No comm. Tell everyone. Tell Darjan. Darjan tell Knights. Knights warn all. Warn riders! No mesh. No one!"

She stared as if I'd lost my mind. "Why?"

I didn't know how to explain. I barely understood myself. "Aqueducts sick."

She looked at me strangely, but she nodded. "Will spread the whisper."

"Good. Go well." I took off running again.

Dara called after me. "Bhaaj."

I turned back. "Yah?"

"The healer. Rajin—" She stumbled on the name.

"Doctor Rajindia."

"Darjan protects her."

I nodded, impatient to run, but not wanting to turn my back on my closest friend. Darjan's gang had taken the job of guarding the doctor during her trips to the Undercity. Rajindia had treated a few people for broken limbs and a baby with an ear infection. No one had taken her to the Down-deep yet, but apparently she'd asked to go.

"Good help?" I asked.

Dara hesitated.

"Not good?" *Please don't let this fail,* I thought. *Please.* My people needed Rajindia.

Dara took a deep breath. "Healer says she can do birth proof. For birth certificate."

I froze, afraid to say the wrong thing. Then I spoke with care. "Weaver will do this?"

After a moment, she nodded. "Yah. We all do."

I walked over to her. "That's good." I wanted to shout, rejoice, make a fuss, but I held back, knowing it would put her off. Maybe we could finally get Weaver his Concourse license. It might be a tiny event compared to the prospect of three ancient EIs acting like vengeful deities, but I didn't care. For the Undercity, that license was a huge step.

Dara spoke softly. "Afraid."

"I too. Always." The fear never left me, not even after the decades I'd spent proving I could succeed against the odds. Inside, I'd always feel like the dust rat doomed to fail.

Dara snorted. "What fear? Bhaaj cocky as a lizard queen."

I laughed. "Pain in the ass, eh?"

"Sometimes." Her looked gentled. "Today, good talk."

"Yah. Good words."

She motioned at the canal. "Go!"

So I went, running down the midwalk.

When I reached the Foyer, I tore off my backpack and turned off the shroud. Its warning lights activated, telling me I was being scanned. I didn't care. I activated my comm. *Answer. Be there.*

Lavinda's voice rose into the air. "Colonel Majda here."

I shouldered my pack and took off, running out into the Concourse. "It's Major Bhaajan."

"Twice in one day." She sounded in a good mood. "That's progress."

She wouldn't think so for long. "Colonel, listen. You need to turn off your mesh systems."

"What?" She sounded more puzzled than angry.

"All of them. Every mesh system in Cries."

"For flaming sake. You can't be serious."

I ran down the Concourse, ignoring the vendors, keeping my voice low. "I need to talk to the pharaoh. Her life is in danger, but it isn't from Calaj. I think Calaj is trying to protect her."

"Where is this all coming from?" She no longer sounded at all happy.

"Send a flyer to meet me outside the Concourse," I said. "Tell the police not to stop me." A lot of people were out at this hour, and they stared as I ran past them. If I started spouting military secrets while I raced through the Concourse, there'd be hell to pay. "I can't talk now."

"I've sent the flyer," Lavinda said.

"Good. Listen, I know this sounds crazy, but everyone needs to stop using the mesh." It was absurd. No one would disconnect from the mesh that tied civilization together. But I had to try. "Have you had any trouble with your systems?"

"No. Why would I?"

Maybe so far only the Undercity was affected. If so, I doubted that reprieve would last long.

"I'll tell you more when I get there," I said.

The flyer let me off at the Selei Building. I ran inside wearing my fatigues and muscle shirt, the pack slung over one shoulder, my holstered gun visible, my boots pounding the floor. The receptionist frowned, but he extended an already prepared badge. I grabbed it as I ran by his counter. When the lift let me out on Lavinda's floor, I strode by the lieutenant, holding up my badge. As I went down the hall to Lavinda's office, I saw the colonel standing inside by the window— with her sister, General Majda.

Fuck. I slowed to a stop as I entered the room. "My honor at your presence, General."

"Major." Vaj Majda took in my appearance. "You say Pharaoh Dyhianna's life is in danger. Why? And don't give me any of that 'I can't talk about the Undercity' bullshit.'"

Not an auspicious start. "Is this room secured?"

Lavinda spoke. "Yes, completely." She and Vaj stood in front of the window, both in uniform, and I should have been intimidated, but today I was more afraid of what was waking up in the desert.

I dropped my pack on a chair. "Izu Yaxlan is an EI. The Uzan lives within its control center. The Abaj secure the ruins because, yes, the city is sacred, but also to make sure the EI is maintained and never disturbed. The Lock is also an EI, different from the city, less sympathetic to human life. It and Izu Yaxlan co-exist. They have since the time of the Ruby Empire." I stopped for a breath, then said, "Does anyone even know what they do out there? Or are we just their caretakers?"

They both stared at me. "How the hell did you find all that out?" Lavinda said.

"I'm good at my job."

Vaj spoke coldly. "Good at your job and in possession of highly secured military secrets are two very different things."

I met her cool gaze. "General, forgive my questions, but I need to ask more. Are you aware of any other EIs in the desert besides the Lock and Izu Yaxlan?"

For a long moment she just looked at me. Then she said, "No, we are not."

We were screwed. "A third one exists. It's the abandoned ships on the shore of the Vanished Sea. They form a single EI. It's been deactivated, asleep, dormant, I don't know the right word. Now it's waking up. And it doesn't like us. It's—" I needed a better word than the *wrong* everyone kept using. "It's hostile to Izu Yaxlan, to the Lock, and to human life."

"A third EI?" Vaj crossed her arms. "I assume you have proof?"

I couldn't reveal what I knew about Hack, Ruzik, and the Undercity, but if I didn't tell her, she had no reason to believe me. I pressed the heels of my hands against my temples and tried to rub away my headache. Then I lowered my arms. "You have to trust that I've seen the proof."

"Enough!" Vaj came to the table so she was standing directly across from me. "I won't have any more of these evasions. Start talking, or I'll have you arrested."

She was forcing me into an impossible decision: betray my people or betray the Imperialate. Of course I had no choice. I couldn't put the Undercity before the Imperialate. The Vanished Sea EI had somehow managed to reach Calaj when the Jagernaut was on another world. I didn't know how, or what it had done to her, but the ramifications went far beyond the Undercity. To give Vaj Majda the answers she demanded, I had to betray my people. You couldn't keep that a secret, not with all the high flyers who frequented Jak's casino. Some of them would know. Word would get out. It would explode in the Whisper Mill. *Bhaaj lied. Bhaaj is one of them.* No one would ever trust me again. I'd lose the Dust Knights. They wouldn't disband, they'd become another gang, one far better trained than anyone else in the Undercity. I'd just have succeeded in creating better criminals. My dream would die, my hope for a better life born out of the Undercity itself, my people creating their own new world.

Neither the general nor the colonel spoke, but for some reason, Vaj suddenly turned and looked at Lavinda. For a moment, they stood that way. Then Vaj went over to her sister.

"Why?" Vaj said.

"We hired her because she can go places we don't know exist." Although Lavinda spoke in a low voice, she wasn't trying to keep me from hearing. "She can get answers for questions we don't even know to ask. If we force her to tell us how, it compromises her ability to find those answers. No one in the Undercity will trust her if they think she'll report them to us."

Vaj looked like she wanted to throw me in the brig and be done with it. It rattled me to see her legendary restraint slip. She said nothing more to Lavinda, however. Instead she came back to the desk, facing me across its width. "Very well, Major. Continue with your report."

I was afraid to glance at Lavinda, for fear that if I even glanced away from Vaj, she would change her mind about giving me this reprieve. "The Undercity is part of Izu Yaxlan." For all I knew, that was another highly secured military secret. I doubted it, though. Had ISC known, they'd never have ignored us.

"That makes no sense," Vaj said.

Lavinda joined her sister at the desk. "The Undercity and Izu Yaxlan aren't connected."

"Actually, they are," I said. "You can get from the Pharaoh's Last Tomb to the aqueducts via tunnels under the desert. It's almost impossible because of the maze at the end." People had died, lost in that warren of spaces and passages that went nowhere.

"You've been in the Last Tomb?" Vaj asked, incredulous. "That's sacrilege."

Telling her the Uzan took me didn't seem like a great idea. I'd never figured out the relationship of the Abaj to the military. They were Jagernauts, which meant they were in the J-Force chain of command. The Majdas were army, not J-Force, but still. They were in charge here. Whatever the hierarchy, the Uzan seemed to answer to the pharaoh, a civilian, before the Majdas.

"Does anyone else know this route to the tomb?" Lavinda asked.

"No, I don't think so." I couldn't be one hundred percent certain; you never knew who had wandered where. But it wasn't anything our histories recounted. It wouldn't be much of a tale, given that the route ended at a blank wall unless the Abaj left that tomb entrance open, which I doubted they had any reason to do when they weren't trying to catch murderous Jagernauts.

"What does this have to do with turning off the meshes?" Vaj asked.

I'd dug myself such a deep hole, I might as well finish it. "I think the three EIs—the Lock, Izu Yaxlan, and the Vanished Sea EI— are going to war. We humans are in the way, and our mesh activity is what an EI most 'sees' about us."

I expected another scoff from Vaj, maybe even Lavinda this time. Instead, they just looked at each other. Vaj nodded slightly, and in response Lavinda sat in the large chair at her desk. A console rose out of the surface of her working space. As Lavinda went to work, Vaj strode around the long desk and came up to me, so we stood eye to eye.

"You make a lot of claims," she said.

I met her gaze. "Valid claims."

"And Calaj?"

I could hear Lavinda working at her console, but I didn't risk turning to see what she was doing. "I think she's in the desert, about a kilometer west of the Vanished Sea ships. I've projected trajectory for her path that I sent you. She's headed to the ships to confront the EI."

"And you know this how?"

Good question. "It's a guess."

"A guess." If this Majda queen could have bottled her look of disdain and sold it to the rest of us who could never in a million years master it so well, she could have made billions. Not that she needed billions. She was already one of the wealthiest people in the history of the human race. I felt smaller than a beetle-bot.

Lavinda spoke. "Vaj, we're getting some strange reports from the Vanished Sea ships."

We both turned to her. "What reports?" the general asked.

Lavinda touched a panel and a holo formed above her desk, the ruins of three vast starships crumbling on the shore of the Vanished Sea. "We have a skeleton staff on site, one army lieutenant and a few anthropologists from the university. One of the scientists thought a system in the cockpit of the smallest ship activated, but when he went to check, he found nothing unusual."

"Bring up the report," Vaj said.

Lavinda flicked her hand over the holos and the interior view of one ship grew larger, replacing the others. It was my first glimpse inside those legendary ships, which were off limits to most Skolians. The dimensions seemed wrong, designed for something larger and differently shaped than a human being. Several stools occupied the position where we would put a pilot's chair, but if a human being sat on any of them, they couldn't reach most of the controls.

"That screen," Lavinda indicated a dark curve of metal facing upward. "Doctor Orin thought it started to operate earlier today."

"It looks dead." Vaj glanced at her sister. "It has been for six thousand years."

Lavinda shrugged. "His sensors may have malfunctioned."

"His? So this anthropologist is male." Vaj waved her hand in dismissal.

"For flaming sake," I said. "What difference does that make?"

Behind Vaj, Lavinda shook her head at me. Okay, so maybe this wasn't the time to argue equal rights with one of the Imperialate's most conservative generals, but dismissing Orin's report because he was a man was just too stupid for words.

"I know Professor Orin," I said. "When I was a kid, he came to the aqueducts to study the ruins. He gave me sweet bars to show him around."

"This is a ringing endorsement," Vaj said dryly. "A scientist who gives a child living in a slum sugar-loaded foods as a bribe so she will be his tour guide."

I stiffened. Those bars had been practically the only sweets I ate in my childhood. Yah, sure, they had no redeeming nutritional value, but I had liked them, damn it.

Lavinda spoke quickly, before I had a chance to tell the general what I thought of her comment. "Vaj, he's one of the leading experts on the Raylicon ruins. If he thinks something is off with the ships, we should listen."

The general frowned. "What does he think is 'off' exactly?"

Lavinda flicked her finger and the holos vanished, replaced by data glyphs scrolling across her desk. "They've had a lot of glitches." She read the data. "Several times they thought systems activated on the ships, but the readings disappear too fast to verify. The mesh systems we installed are having problems—lost files, corrupted records, delays in response times, that sort of thing."

Max, I thought. *What did your diagnostic tell you about that glitch you experienced when we were looking for the casino?*

A time-evolving bug infected my systems, he answered. I cleaned it out. I haven't located the source of the bug yet.

"Contact the staff at the ships," I said. "Ask if a time-evolving bug infected their systems."

Lavinda glanced at me. "Actually, yes, that's what their diagnostics say. They cleaned it up."

"And they don't know where it came from," I said.

"That's right." Lavinda studied me with that intent gaze of hers. "You've experienced this?"

"I think it's the EI, probing our systems."

Vaj leaned over to study Lavinda's data. "Nothing here indicates a problem in Cries."

"It's going after Izu Yaxlan, not Cries," I said. "It probably wants to rid the ships of people, like one of us swatting a bug."

Vaj considered me. "Major, let's put aside the absurdity of all this for a moment and assume it's true. What does Calaj have to do with it? Why do you say she's trying to protect the pharaoh?"

I made myself speak with a calm I didn't feel. "I've come close to Calaj several times now. Every time, she slips away. She's hidden from the best searchers any of us can summon. Something is helping her. In every way I've encountered her, with one exception, she has gone out of her way to do no harm. Does that sound like a crazed killer to you?"

"What exception?" Vaj asked.

"Someone shot at me with Calaj's jumbler," I said. "I've assumed it was her because her gun should be keyed to her brain waves. But I never saw her. I have no proof it was Calaj."

"You don't seem to have proof for any of this," Vaj said.

"And if I'm right?" I said. "You want those three EIs going to war?"

They both just looked at me, and I had the uncomfortable feeling that even they barely knew what the EIs had been doing out there in the desert for more than five thousand years.

"I need to talk to the pharaoh," I added. "If this isn't her bailiwick, I don't know what is."

Lavinda and Vaj exchanged a glance. Then Vaj turned back to me. "We will contact you."

Well, that certainly sounded like *Dismissed*. "General, I mean no disrespect—"

"Then don't give any," Vaj said sourly.

So I shut up. We said our good-byes and I left, because whatever discussion they wanted to have didn't include me. I had no intention, however, of just waiting for them to act.

My penthouse was empty.

"Singer?" I called out as I entered the living room.

No answer.

Had she gone outside? I hoped not. She had to know the authorities would pick her up.

"They are in the bathing room," the EI said.

Oh. Of course. I doubted either Singer or Taz had ever seen that much fresh water in one place. OF course they gravitated toward the pool. As I walked into my bedroom, I spoke to the air. "Singer?"

She walked out of the bathroom. "Eh, Bhaaj."

"Taz?"

She tilted her head toward the room she had just left. "With baby."

"Take bath?"

"Bath?"

"In water."

She scowled at me. "No. Big waste."

"No waste. Got lots."

"Drink. Good water."

I blinked. Sure, the pool had plenty of filters. It was probably the purest water she'd ever tasted, but I'd never drink it. I needed to show her a faucet. She would like it. I tried not to think about the possible execution she faced. I had no answer from the Majdas about a bargain, but whatever they decided, it would most likely only be for Taz and their daughter. Even if the courts stayed a death sentence, Singer would go to prison. Whether it would be on a penal asteroid or somewhere less severe remained to be seen, but I didn't have much optimism.

"Taz safe?" I asked.

Singer lifted her hand, inviting me to look. So I walked to the doorway. She and Taz had taken the largest, fluffiest towels from the cabinets and laid them on the tiled floor next to the pool, layer upon layer, until they had a deep carpet of cloth. Taz was sitting up, dozing against the wall, his eyes closed, their daughter in his lap.

Singer smiled. "Safe, eh?"

"Yah." I turned to her. "Need talk."

"Sun room." Singer walked past me, headed to the living room, where the miracle of sunlight flowed through the window there. She didn't go to the sofa, but instead sat on the floor by the window-wall. It had darkened slightly to mute the sun, which hung low in the sky, but we could see through the glass. I sat next to her, the two of us bathed in the sun's bronzed rays.

Singer tilted her head toward the sun. "Light."

"Yah," I murmured. Such a miracle, to live beneath the bronze skies of Raylicon. It hurt. I had escaped the Undercity in time, before it destroyed my life. Singer would never know that freedom.

"Other dark, not here," Singer added.

"What other?" I didn't think she meant a lack of sunlight.

"In the aqueducts."

"Where?"

"All places."

"Alive?"

Singer thought about. "Yah. But not human."

It sounded like she meant the EI Hack had detected. "How long?"

She shrugged. "Thirty days, maybe more, maybe less."

It didn't surprise me she could only estimate how long she had felt something was wrong. In the aqueducts, we never thought in terms of days. We didn't live under a sky. We sometimes used hours, but often we didn't bother with time at all. I'd left Raylicon soon after I enlisted, shipped to an offworld base, so I tended to think in Skolian standard units of time, the twenty-four hour day of our birth world, Earth. Thirty days on Raylicon equaled about one hundred Earth days. If she meant the Vanished Sea EI had begun to awake about thirty Raylicon days ago, my estimate agreed with hers. Yet it had slept for six thousand years. Why stir now?

I motioned around at my apartment. "No darkness here?"

Singer grimaced. "Just me."

I met her gaze. "Not you."

She didn't answer.

"You have a visitor," the EI suddenly announced. "Shall I let her up?"

I jumped to my feet before I could stop my reflexes. "Don't do that!"

"You don't want me to tell you if a visitor arrives?" the EI asked.

"No, never mind." This EI never seemed to learn the nuances of human interaction. It did a good job running the penthouse, though, so I was trying to be less annoyed.

"Who is the visitor?" If the Majdas wanted to talk to me, they'd summon me to their offices or the palace. No one came to visit me in Cries except Jak, and he definitely wasn't a she.

"She says her name is Dehya," the EI said.

"I don't know any Dehya. Tell her to go away."

"I can't," the EI said. "They are in the lift."

I crossed my arms. "How did 'they' get access to my lift?"

Singer stood up next to me. "Light comes."

I glanced at her. "Light?"

The doors of my apartment opened up without my permission. I whipped out my gun—

And nearly shot the Ruby Pharaoh.

XVI

OBLIVION

Dyhianna Selei stood in the doorway, a small woman in a blue jumpsuit surrounded by four Abaj warriors in black, all with their jumblers out and aimed, miniature particle accelerators that could annihilate me with one shot. Great. I was an idiot.

I spoke with care. "I'm putting my weapon on the ground." I'd retrieved it up from the cops yesterday, and now here I was, losing it again. Moving slowly, never taking my gaze off them, I crouched down and set my revolver on the floor. As I stood again, I raised my hands and stepped back.

Dyhianna scowled at her bodyguards. "Put those guns away. She isn't going to shoot me."

They didn't speak. They didn't lower their guns. One of them, the leader apparently, walked over and picked up my revolver.

"Give it back to her," Dyhianna said. "I need to talk with Major Bhaajan, not arrest her."

The Abaj leader turned to her. "I'm sorry, Your Majesty." His deep voice sounded like a distant, rumbling earthquake. "We can't do that."

I realized the other Abaj were looking past me. Glancing back, I saw Singer by the window, doing nothing threatening, just looking at Dyhianna. Then again, Singer didn't have to do anything to look threatening. I doubted she had any clue who had just opened my door.

The pharaoh walked into my living room casually, as if interstellar potentates showed up at my door all the time. The Abaj kept pace with her, one with his gun trained on me, the others covering Singer. Dyhianna stopped in front of Singer and looked up at the massive assassin. I wondered how the pharaoh felt, with all of us looming over her. She didn't seem the least bothered.

"Are you planning on assassinating me?" she asked my guest.

Singer squinted at her. "Eh?"

"Kill me?" Dyhianna asked in a marginally passable version of the Undercity dialect.

"Nahya," Singer said. "Not kill."

"Good." Dyhianna turned to her bodyguards. "Please put your damn guns away."

After a moment that went on too long, the Abaj leader nodded to the others. They holstered their particle accelerators, but they left their hands on the massive stocks of those guns.

"Your Majesty," I said. "You honor my home with your presence." She and her Abaj. Between the four of them and Singer, we had a room filled with some of the most highly trained killers in the empire. Yah, just another ordinary day. My headache was growing worse.

The annoyed cry of a child came from across the room. We all spun around, the Abaj drawing their guns so fast, it seemed like one moment they were holstered, the next they were all trained on the doorway of my bedroom. Taz stood there holding his daughter, staring at us as if he had just walked into the middle of a raid he hadn't realized was happening.

Shit. I spoke fast. "Not here for you!" I told him. "Came for me."

He answered in a voice flat with anger. "Guns."

I tilted my head toward Dyhianna. "For her. Protect. Like Dust Knights."

"They shoot?" he asked. His daughter squirmed, trying to get down, but he held her tightly.

"Nahya." I really, really hoped I was right. "No shoot."

Singer was walking toward Taz, and I recognized her deliberate stride. She was poised on the edge of violence.

"Down!" Singer's daughter yelled.

"A word," Singer said. From her, that was a gushing exclamation of maternal pride in her daughter's newfound ability to speak. She went to Taz and faced us, putting herself between her family and the rest of the room. She looked ready to attack, and this time I didn't doubt she meant the threat. She would protect her family even if it meant suicide against the Abaj.

"Your Majesty," the Abaj leader said. "Perhaps you should move back."

"For flaming sake," Dyhianna said. "That little girl isn't going to assassinate me. Stand down."

The Abaj didn't look happy, if I could read anything from their impassive faces, but they holstered their guns. I wouldn't have in their situation. They knew Dyhianna far better than me, though, apparently enough to trust her judgment with regards to Singer and her family.

"Down," Taz's daughter stated firmly, echoing the Ruby Pharaoh of the Imperialate.

"Later." Taz kept her in his arms. "When no guns."

I wondered what he told her when she saw him toting around that massive machine gun he had threatened me with outside their home.

"My greetings," Dyhianna said to Taz.

He squinted at her.

"He may not understand you," I said. "I don't think he knows above-city speech."

"Bove sit peach," his daughter said.

I froze, and both Taz and Singer did as well. Their daughter was only parroting sounds she heard, but she did it in a perfect imitation of the above-city dialect.

Taz paled. "Too much talk," he told his daughter.

Singer said nothing, but I could guess her thought: if Taz and their daughter left the aqueducts, they would have to learn above-city ways and speech.

Dyhianna was standing by the couch, next to the Abaj leader. Two of the others were between her and me, and the fourth stood near the double doors of the lift.

The pharaoh glanced at me. "They are all psions?"

"Yes." I wondered if she could always tell this easily.

"Why are they staying in your home?"

I couldn't answer that, so I said nothing.

Dyhianna tried again. "They came to escape the influence of the Vanished Sea EI."

"Did the Majdas tell you about our talk?" I asked.

"I was watching on a remote link."

That made sense, but I hadn't mentioned Singer in that meeting. "Why do you think that EI involves my guests?"

"I suppose you could call it an educated guess." She rubbed the palm of her hand over the knuckles of her other hand. It was a small mannerism, one I wouldn't have noticed if I hadn't been so focused on her. But I recognized the signs. Dyhianna Selei—the ultimate cyber-rider—feared the Vanished Sea EI.

"The riders!" I said. "That's why you wanted them to be careful. They're the humans that EI most wants destroyed."

"Not exactly," she said. "I just sensed something was wrong, and that it connected either to Calaj, or to everyone with neural enhancement."

"Did the Majdas send someone to the location of my last detection for Calaj?"

She nodded. "They're checking the trajectory your EI gave them. They haven't found her yet."

"Calaj is headed for the Vanished Sea starships. Your Majesty, you need to get away from here." The Abaj couldn't protect her from that EI out in the desert. Hell, they were its targets, too. "It wants to rid Raylicon of all other EIs. It sees three of them, Izu Yaxlan, the Lock, and humanity. If it gets control of our meshes, it could cripple civilization, turn off flyers in midair, corrupt environmental systems, crash magrails, you name it. You're the—I don't know what to call it. The mind of the mesh. Destroy you, and it destroys our ability to create interstellar networks. The rest—deleting us pesky humans—is clean up. It would kill everyone." I took a breath. "Like it killed Tavan Ganz."

Dyhianna didn't scoff, laugh, or patronize, nor did she do that eyebrow-raising thing the Majdas were so good at. She just said, "Ganz was on another planet, too far away for this EI to affect."

"If it can access meshes in Cries, it can reach a Kyle gate to our offworld systems. That's how it found Calaj. Right now, it's erratic, only partially awake. But it's getting stronger." I regarded her steadily. "I'm sure it wanted you, but you protect yourself too well. So it found Calaj. She's a powerful psion. She and you share genetics found nowhere except in the Undercity. That's how it knew her, you, the Abaj, even me. We're enough like our ancestors that it recognizes us."

She shook her head. "I saw Secondary Calaj kill Tavan Ganz."

"You saw her shoot him with her jumbler. It's not the same thing."

Dyhianna wasn't buying it. "How is annihilating his body not the same as killing him?"

I didn't know how to convince her. I had nothing to support my theory beyond my ability to see connections among disparate facts. "To commit murder, she has to have the intent. If an EI accessed her spinal node and drove her to shoot Ganz, the intent belongs to the EI, not her."

"It's impossible to crack a Jagernaut's node." She paused. "It's supposed to be impossible."

Maybe she was considering the idea after all. "Years ago, I was the army's contribution to a task force that studied potential attacks on a Jagernaut's spinal node." I'd enjoyed that job. It was when I realized I had a talent for problem solving. "We found weaknesses."

"And fixed them. That was the point."

The Abaj leader spoke. "Your Majesty, this room isn't secured."

Dyhianna looked past me to Singer and her family. "Do you understand us?"

"Say again?" Singer asked.

"Do you understand what Major Bhaajan and I are discussing?"

Singer glanced at me.

"You ken her?" I asked.

"A little here," Singer said. "A little there."

"Taz?" I asked.

He shook his head. "Nahya."

I spoke to the Abaj leader. "They mostly don't understand us."

"They could be lying,'" he said. "Regardless, 'mostly' isn't security."

"They aren't lying." Dyhianna turned to me. "I need to go."

"Yes." Relief washed over me. "Offworld. To the most protected place available."

"You misunderstand." She regarded me steadily. "It's time I met this Vanished Sea EI."

The flycar hummed as we flew over the desert. The leader of Dyhianna's bodyguards was piloting, another of her Abaj sat in the copilot's seat, and the one other sat in a passenger seat. The large flyer accommodated their large size. Singer and her family stayed at my apartment with the fourth Abaj. She had seemed more puzzled than anything else, but she kept her thoughts to herself.

"You can't!" I told Dyhianna, yet again. This conversation felt like the verbal equivalent of banging my head against the wall. "You can't put yourself in that danger."

"It's my job," she said. "A modern civilization doesn't need an anachronistic monarch sitting on a red throne. It does need an Assembly Key. The whole purpose of my being a Key to the meshes is to deal with mesh problems. I'm good at it."

"All the more reason to keep you the hell away from that EI. You're too valuable to risk."

The pharaoh leaned forward. "The mesh is my realm. I won't have it threatened. I've felt this Vanished Sea EI. If it intends harm to Raylicon, the Skolian Imperialate, or humanity, I need to stop it now, before it regains its full power."

"And if it kills you?" I demanded. "What then?"

"My nephew Kurj can also create the web, as the military Key. And if I die, my sister can become the Assembly Key."

I seriously doubted that the changing of the guard was anywhere near as easy as she made it sound. We had four Ruby psions capable of acting as Keys: Dyhianna Selei Skolia; her nephew Kurj Skolia, the Imperator; his mother Roca Skolia, who served as an Assembly Councilor; and apparently Roca Skolia's new husband, a farmer from one of the rediscovered colonies. Four. And none of that spoke to the fact that the pharaoh had eight decades of learning the mesh. No one else knew it as well. Kurj Skolia's bailiwick was the military and Roca Skolia was a politician. Dyhianna was the Kyle adept.

"We need *you*," I said. "Not someone else. Besides, your life has value beyond the meshes. You're more than a Key. You should live because you deserve to have a life."

She spoke quietly. "Thank you."

I had an odd feeling then, as if I had said a thing more important than I realized, something she never heard. She deserved her own life? It seemed simple, but I wondered how often anyone told her.

The Abaj copilot looked back at us. "We're landing."

The first humans on Raylicon built the pyramid called Tiqual, but no one knew the origins of its architecture. No trace of any culture from six thousand years ago on Earth bore any resemblance to what we had created here; those cultures were too primitive. The Virus Wars during the late twenty-first century on Earth, however, had wiped out its entire mesh structure and a quarter of the world's population. In the forty years since that crippling devastation, the people of Earth had made impressive strides in their recovery, but great swaths of their history had vanished, including whatever linked them to us, their lost children.

Tiqual rose out of the desert, a solitary temple bronzed by the setting sun. No other buildings surrounded it, only a courtyard tiled in mosaics of armored warriors, lizards in flight, spears in the air, and images of ancient goddesses and gods. The wind sent whirls of red sand spinning across the tiles.

An arch headed the one path that led to the pyramid. Mirror images of the goddess Ixa Quelia served as the columns that held up the arch. Neither figure wore anything more than a sword sheathed at her hip. Each goddess had her arms raised above her head to support the arch, her breasts lifted, her hair streaming back as if in the wind. A giant statue of the god Azu Bullom stood beyond the archway, to one side of the path. His head was human, with a hooked nose and heavy-lidded eyes, forever half-closed. Horns curled around his ears, their tips as sharp as a spear. His powerful body, four-legged with a heavy tail, bore no resemblance to any of the reptilian animals on Raylican. My ancestors had no concept to describe the body of Azu Bullom.

At least, not until that day, seventy years ago, when Earth found us.

Both of our civilizations had reeled from the shock of that meeting. The explorers from Earth never expected to find humans already out here among the stars, and my people no longer believed the legends of Earth held any truth. We considered our tales of a misty green world no more than mythology. A scout ship from the Allied Worlds of Earth entered out territory, and an ISC Fleet vessel found them. When the ships began sharing data, the picture of a jaguar came up in the files of the Earth ship, and our universe shifted on its foundations. Azu Bullom had the body of a jaguar. That day, my people—the lost children of Earth—found their home.

Today I walked with the pharaoh and her bodyguards in silence past the statue of Azu Bullom. Rays from the setting sun slanted across the path, turning the mosaics. We continued to the entrance of Tiqual, an archway sculpted into the head of a giant ruzik with its mouth open in a roar. It faced away from the sun, so we entered into darkness. The

Abaj took torches from scrolled claws on the wall and lit them with a modern igniter stick, creating a sphere of yellow light around us. We headed into the pyramid then, following a tunnel that curved often, with many cross passages. I would have been lost without Max creating a map. Carvings of strange animals jumped into view as the torchlight hit them, lizards with six legs and humans with ruzik heads. It felt as if we were walking through an age that had passed into history everywhere else, but still lived within these ancient walls.

Up ahead, light suddenly flooded the pyramid, flowing back here. The Abaj doused their torches and left them in claws on the walls. We followed the dimly lit tunnel toward the light and ended up in the cavernous chamber in the center of the pyramid. More of the Abaj waited for us there. This evening, instead of using mirrors to fill the place with sunlight, someone had turned on wall panels that glowed. The pyramid sloped to a point high overhead, where the skylight showed a patch of darkening sky. Around the walls, transparent columns with gleaming metal gears and ceramic tech-mech glittered as lights spiraled within them like sparkling beads.

I glanced at the pharaoh. "Are you going into the Lock from here?" I saw nothing that remotely resembled a singularity in spacetime, whatever that looked like.

"I'm not going into the Lock." Dyhianna walked with me across the gigantic mosaic circles that tiled the floor. She motioned toward the dais on the far side of the room. "I need that command chair."

Ho! The three boxes I had likened to coffins during my first visit stood up there. Now they were in motion, rearranging their structures, morphing into a central tech-mech throne flanked by two smaller seats. The throne resembled the chair I had seen Dyhianna use at the Majda palace, but larger, with more lights flashing along its body. Its massive armrests were more than a handspan wide and embedded with panels. Exoskeletons glittered within all three chairs and visors overhung them, also neural caps that made the one Hack used look like child's play.

I squinted at the chairs. "You're going to sit up there?"

"In the center seat. It's called a Triad Chair." She glanced at me. "If you accept, you'll sit in one of the other two."

I stared at her, suddenly cold. "I can't use the Lock. It would kill me."

"You won't need to use the Lock, not directly. You'll be in contact only through me."

"Is it safe for you?"

"As Ruby Key, yes." She sounded perfectly relaxed, which would have reassured me, except then she added, "The fluxes of power would kill any other psions."

I raked my hand through my already tousled hair. "I don't see how I can help."

"You know that EI in the Vanished Sea starships more than anyone else here."

We had reached the dais. I walked up its steps with her, too uneasy to respond. She stopped by the throne and laid her hand on its massive armrest, her fingers long and slender. She looked so damn breakable. In a quiet voice, she said, "I ask only for your support, Major. Distract the EI while I work."

"I would be honored." I didn't feel honorable, I felt like a coward given how much I wanted to say no, but I couldn't desert her when she asked for help.

The pharaoh inclined her head in acknowledgement, then turned to the leader of her bodyguards. "Yours also, if you will take the other command chair."

The Abaj nodded. "I too would be honored, Your Majesty."

I spoke awkwardly. "Pharaoh Dyhianna, the last time you and I linked up, I had a convulsion."

"I am sorry about that." She pushed back her hair, which was escaping from its braid and curling haphazardly around her face. "I wasn't prepared for how strongly you responded last time. I will build the link properly this time."

I hoped so. I felt the power of the Lock, more distant than when I had climbed up the stairs, but still pressing on my mind. It messed with my neural patterns. "Doesn't it make your head hurt?"

Dyhianna smiled. "Actually, I like this. Being near the Lock feels like—well, I'm not sure how to say it." She paused, thinking. "Like singing in the void."

Singing in the void. I had no clue what that meant.

"Music out of nothing," Dyhianna added. "It's exhilarating."

"Ah." Apparently the Lock liked her.

"I never thought of it that way," she said.

Damn. She heard my thought. I raised my mental barriers.

The pharaoh spoke quietly. "Major, the more you protect yourself, the more difficult your interaction with the Lock. Try to relax."

I doubted I could, but if it would help her fight the Vanished Sea EI, I'd do my best.

The Abaj nearest me lifted his hand, indicating the control chair on the right to me. I sat down, wishing I had a name for him. I didn't even know if they used individual names, the same name for everyone in a clone group, or titles, like the Uzan.

One of the Abaj went to work at a console by my seat, and the others helped Dyhianna and the leader of her bodyguards in their chairs. Mine hummed, powering up its systems. Panels shifted into place around my body: holoscreens, mesh systems, and other controls I didn't recognize. The exoskeleton closed around my body and clicked prongs into my gauntlets. As the visor lowered over my head, darkness surrounded me. I barely felt the filaments of the neural cap extending into my head.

Bhaaj, Max thought. Shall I allow this system access to your mesh?

Yah, go ahead. I wanted to say no. Giving the system access to my "mesh," otherwise known as my brain, thrilled me about as much as having a tooth pulled out without benefit of modern dentistry, but what the hell. I'd survive. I hoped.

My mind became attuned to Dyhianna and the Abaj leader as the command chairs linked our three brains. It gave me a better sense of the Abaj. Although he didn't share my overt dislike of the Lock, he wasn't at ease with it, either. The presence of the Lock saturated the link, unseen and alien. It allocated only a small part of its awareness to us, as if it put us in one room of a gigantic building while most of it existed elsewhere. Dyhianna's mind felt radiant. She reveled in the Lock's power; this experience came as close to joy as she could feel with an entity that didn't experience emotions in any way our minds could interpret.

Come to me, she thought to the Lock.

An image formed in my mind of a giant chair with conduits glowing along its edges in blue, white, and green. The Lock's thought rumbled: **ATTENDING.**

Prepare to commence, Dyhianna thought.

COMMENCED.

We dropped into darkness.

Major Bhaajan? Dyhianna asked. Her system converted her neural activity into signals and relayed them to Max, who sent them to the bioelectrodes that fired my neurons, translating the signals into thoughts. It wasn't that different from what psions did, using brain waves and specialized organs in their cerebrums, but the chairs magnified the interaction until it became possible for all of us.

Bhaajan here, I thought.

Secondary Nazam? she thought.

A deep thought rumbled in our link. *Attending.*

Nazam. I had a name for the Abaj leader. Secondary meant he had a rank in the J-Force similar to a colonel in the army. Like Calaj.

The darkness lightened until I realized I was standing in the desert.

Is this a VR session? I asked.

I expected Dyhianna to reply, but someone, no *something* else answered. It didn't come as a word, but an impression, powerful and impersonal. My mind translated that impression into a word.

NO, the Lock thought.

It is a simulation, though, Dyhianna added. **The chairs translate my interaction with the Lock into sensory data that we can interpret more easily.**

This area looks like the desert in the north, Nazam thought. *It isn't near Izu Yaxlan.*

It's where I last detected Calaj, I thought. The desert extended on all sides, an expanse of red sand with blue specks. Here and there, craggy spires of rock reached toward the sky like the skeletal fingers of a buried giant.

I was jogging across the sands, alone. *Are you both here?* I asked. *I don't see you.*

Wait. Dyhianna paused. **Ah, I see. You and Nazam are in different sims. I'll link them.**

Nazam appeared next to me, his long legs devouring the land as we ran. I stayed with him, keeping a steady pace that in real life I could never have managed even with the augmentations to my body. We approached the Vanished Sea starships at a surreally fast rate. Claimed by the passage of time, their half-buried bulks no longer looked like ships so much as vast rock formations, crumbling and scoured by sand.

We slowed down a few hundred meters from the ships. In real life, a guard would have stopped us by now, asking why we came; in the sim, the place looked empty—except for the mist leaking out of the ships. As we neared them, the mist thickened. This, on a world without fog. Within moments, I couldn't see more than a handspan in front of my face. Another few steps, and the fog became so thick, it felt like we were walking through molasses. I could barely see Nazam at my side.

I stopped. *Maybe we should backtrack and go around all this.*

I don't think we can go back, Nazam answered.

Dyhianna's thought came distantly through the fog. **Will you release your security shield?**

What? I asked.

The Lock answered her. **RELEASED.**

The fog vanished, and I squinted in the sudden light. On the real Raylicon, evening had descended, but here in the sim, the sun shone overhead.

Nazam and I strode toward the ships again. They filled our view, huge and eerie. Although the history texts claimed they were spheres, they looked like partial domes, most of their bulk submerged in the desert. Their hulls had once been gold, but time and sand had darkened the metal.

A woman stood by the closest of the three hulks, turned away from us, her figure small against the massive curve of the ship. We drew closer with uncanny speed. Suddenly we were in front of her.

Calaj? I asked. That the Lock could connect us to her even out here, where she had no physical link to its systems, told me more about her similarity to the ancients than any DNA file in her records.

She turned slowly, as if she were in pain. In her files, I had seen images of her in uniform, in combat, practicing tykado, at attention, at ease, laughing, angry, or staring at the camera as if she didn't know what to do with having her picture taken. In real life she was a lean woman with black hair, dark eyes, and high cheekbones. In other words, she looked Raylican.

Here she looked like hell.

Her clothes, a grey shirt and trousers, hung on her emaciated body. Her gaze had a hollowed quality. The real Calaj was in her forties and looked like a kid in her twenties; here she seemed old, her hair streaked with grey and her body bent with age.

You shouldn't have come, she told us.

Secondary Calaj. Dyhianna's voice surrounded us. **You don't need to do this alone.**

Pharaoh Dyhianna, you must go, Calaj answered. *It wants you. It will use me to destroy you.*

Is it controlling you? Nazam, asked.

I don't know, Calaj whispered.

Calaj, come to me. Dyhianna's thought, for all its power, felt gentle. **Let me understand what it has done to you.**

Calaj sunk to her knees, bending over, her arms folded across her stomach. Sand blew across her body. She had pulled her hair back, clipping it at her neck, but the wind tugged it free so the grey and black tendrils straggled around her face. Although none of us moved, the sim brought me closer to Calaj, closer, closer still.

The scene went dark.

Is anyone here? I asked. My thought echoed, bouncing in a great dark place.

The darkness lightened. I was still in the simulation, but it had become an empty room with grey walls. It seemed to go on forever in the east. Nazam was out there, walking toward me from far away, moving in slow motion.

What's wrong? I asked. *Where are we?*

I contacted Calaj's mesh, Dyhianna thought. **This room is a simulation of her spinal node.**

Nazam's thought came from far away. *The Vanished Sea EI erased her node.*

Not just her node, I thought. This emptiness felt worse than lost mesh functions. *It dissolved part of her mind as well.*

A thought came to us like thunder growling through the ruins of Izu Yaxlan. *She fought the destruction. She fights still.*

I lifted my head, trying to identify this newcomer. His mind felt familiar. Yes, I knew him. The Uzan had joined us. But where? Far in the distant, in the desert beyond Nazam, a dark figure was walking toward us from Izu Yaxlan.

Calaj, Dyhianna thought. **Come to me.**

Light filled the cavernous room, flooding the greyness with glorious, healing radiance. It poured over Calaj, and she rose to her feet, her body haloed by its brilliance. She turned up her haggard face like a traveler dying of thirst gifted with a sudden, impossible rain.

Nazam was still walking out in the desert, barely coming any closer to us, though he kept walking. His thought to Calaj washed across our minds. *Why does the EI affect you but no one else?*

Calaj turned toward him. *I can barely hear you.*

Major Bhaajan, Dyhianna thought. **You are better linked to Calaj than Nazam or the Uzan. Can you bring them closer to her?**

Why would I be better linked? I asked.

We are all joined through Kyle space, Dyhianna answered. **In the Kyle, thoughts determine proximity. Calaj knows about you. Her thoughts include you but not them.**

Got it. I directed my thought toward Calaj. *Secondary, you know the pharaoh has guards, yes?*

Calaj turned toward me. *Of course.*

Nazam leads her bodyguards. I made an image of him in my mind.

I see him, she thought. *He is an Abaj Tacalique warrior.*

Yes, Nazam answered. He was suddenly standing next to me.

And the Uzan, I thought to Calaj. *Do you recognize the title?*

The hereditary leader of the Abaj. Her gaze shifted to the desert. *From Izu Yaxlan.*

The distant figure I could barely see suddenly appeared only a few meters away, still walking toward us, still slowed down, but closer to normal human speed.

Calaj turned to us. *You asked why the EI affects me but no one else. It wanted Pharaoh Dyhianna. It couldn't get to her. I was the closest it could manage.*

Yes, I see, Dyhianna thought. **The structure of your brain is similar to mine.**

Are you and Calaj related? I asked, startled.

My family may have distant ties to the Ruby bloodline, Calaj thought. *Nothing close.*

The genes that give rise to Kyle traits are recessive, Dyhianna added. **They can be dormant for many generations and then manifest.**

Somewhere distant, the ground rumbled like an earthquake. I looked around, trying to locate the source of the sound, but saw nothing. The Uzan and Nazam looked at me, and I saw my unease reflected in their eyes.

The Vanished Sea EI wants you to feel fear, Calaj thought. *Ignore it.*

Nazam spoke to her. *It is helping you to hide from our sensors.*

No, not helping me. Calaj watched us from within Dyhianna's healing light. *It burned out my biomech web and a substantial part of my brain.* With pain, she added, *I don't need to hide my biomech signals or brain waves. They are mostly gone.*

Gods almighty. How did she keep going?

The Uzan finally reached us. He walked in a measured stride, his steps long and slow, and stopped next to me. Power saturated his thought, a strength that healed. *After such an attack,* he asked Calaj, *how are you alive?*

She answered with grim satisfaction. *I'm using the EI. It stretched itself too far reaching for the pharaoh. When it caught me instead, my spinal node hacked part of its code before the EI destroyed it. I'm using the EI's memory of my mind as my own mind.* Her hand shook as she pushed back her hair. *But it is growing stronger, and as its power increases, I weaken. I'm losing control.* She turned to me. *I am sorry about the jumbler shot. I couldn't stop.*

I'm all right. I held up my wrist. *It's mostly healed.* The rumbling I'd heard was getting louder.

Calaj, why did you shoot Tavan Ganz? Dyhianna asked.

I was half-crazed when the EI started deleting my mind, Calaj thought. *Tavan was in front of me. I thought the attack came from him, that he meant to assassinate you or the Finance Counselor.*

It sounded like a nightmare. What had Tavan Ganz thought in that instant before he died, the victim of an attack no one saw coming or understood. And Calaj? It was a miracle she remained sane.

I am sorry. Pain drenched Calaj's thought. *I felt him die. I knew then the attack didn't come from him, but by then it was too late. I had killed an innocent, not your would-be-assassin.*

You did this to protect me? Dyhianna asked.

With elegant simplicity, Calaj spoke an oath that all Jagernauts took when they received their commission. *I swear my loyalty, my will, and my life to Your Majesty, the Ruby Pharaoh.*

The pharaoh's light poured over Calaj. Nothing would heal the Jagernaut; she couldn't survive without her link to the EI, and she would go to her grave drowning in her guilt over Tavan. But Dyhianna eased her pain.

The rumble continued around us, shaking the ground under my feet.

Dyhianna's voice changed, her power resonating. *COME TO ME.*
COMMENCE.

The Lock answered, a huge presence. **TIQUAL COMMENCES.**

Ho! A chill went up my spine. The Titans of Raylicon were rising.

Another thought came, even bigger, as if the desert itself answered
with many voices, the spirits of our ancestors. **IZU YAXLAN
COMMENCES.**

The rumbling around us surged, rising like a specter in the desert,
and a new thought thundered, neither male nor female, but rather,
mechanized and inhuman:

OBLIVION COMMENCES.

XVII

THE DEATH OF CRIES

Oblivion. The Vanished Sea EI named itself with a modern Iotic word that hadn't existed when it was exiled to sleep for six thousand years. It was trying to intimidate us with our own language. EI trash talk.

The long room darkened around us, and the ground heaved under our feet.

It's not a real earthquake, I told myself.

Bhaaj, the ground is actually shaking, Dyhianna thought. **It isn't just the simulation.**

Bullshit. You're Oblivion. The pharaoh never called me, "Bhaaj," only "Major Bhaajan."

A hand grabbed my arm, long fingers clenching my elbow, and I looked up to see the Uzan staring into the darkness. *Izu Yaxlan is crumbling,* he thought. *I have failed.*

No! I thought. *This is still the simulation. The EI is trying to weaken us. We have to ignore it.* In the real world, a large distance separated us from the Vanished Sea EI, and most methods of affecting neural processes in the human brain required proximity. The EI could try to act through the Kyle web, but its first attempt, when it grabbed Calaj, had backfired, giving Calaj access to its systems. Although it undoubtedly had other methods to destroy us human infestations, it wasn't at full strength. We had to attack now, while it was weak.

The Lock's thought rumbled through the fog. **OBLIVION, END.**

BULUC CHABTAN, END, Izu Yaxlan thought.

I blinked. It sounded as if Izu Yaxlan had called the Vanished Sea

EI by the name Buluc Chabtan. That sounded like ancient Iotic, a human language. Oblivion felt alien to me, malevolence incarnate. My ancestors must have known this entity, maybe naming it after one of their devils.

The darkness around us took form, resolving into a nightmare version of the desert. Instead of blue sky above the desolate glory of the red sands, this land was black under a lead-grey sky. The rock outcroppings stuck up from the ground in giant skeletal fingers, bone white in the darkness. The ground continued to shake, and a fissure opened a few paces away from where I stood with the Uzan. Nazam stood on the other side of the fissure, teetering as the ground crumbled under his feet.

Nazam! I shouted his name. An avalanche of rocks and sand cascaded into the fissure, and Nazam fell with them. I had one glimpse of his face, his mouth opened in a scream of agony.

Nazam! I ran forward—and something jerked me back.

Stop. The Uzan gripped my elbow. *You will fall as well.*

We have to help him! I struggled to free myself.

He's not hurt. You must remember. He is just sitting in a chair in the pyramid.

I jerked my arm away from him. *You can die in real life if you die in a sim! His heart could stop, his brain burst—*

Major Bhaajan. Dyhianna's voice cut through my agitation. The sky lightened above us, blue showing among the grey. **We are all linked. What we each experience affects everyone. Do not think of Nazam as in harm's way. Envision life.**

I took a deep breath, trying to control my adrenalin surge. Of course Nazam was alive. I recalled how I had last seen him, sitting in the chair on the dais, his head raised as he looked up at the skylight at the top of the pyramid, his impressive profile silhouetted against the light, his hooked nose evoking statues of our ancient princes.

NO. Oblivion thundered the word. Lightning jagged through the black sands under our feet. The ground opened and the Uzan and I fell, plunging into nothing. The fissure snapped closed, crushing us—

Never! I shouted. *I live!*

I grunted as light glared all around me.

"Major Bhaajan?" a man asked.

I took a shaky breath. The temple. I was back in the temple. They must have dropped me out of the sim. An Abaj was leaning over my chair, checking the panels around my seat. Dyhianna and Nazam were still linked into their command chairs, their faces and bodies hidden by their exoskeletons and visors.

"What happened?" I barely managed to grunt the words.

The Abaj straightened up. "Your heart rate spiked. It went too high. So we brought you out."

"No. I need to get back." Logically, I knew I wasn't "going" anywhere; the simulation came from the attempts of Pharaoh Dyhianna, the Lock, and Izu Yaxlan to rewrite or erase Oblivion's code. The Lock translated those efforts into images I could interpret, but I knew what they meant. Oblivion was countering us, and my interaction helped distract the awakening EI, forcing it to waste valuable resources to counter my efforts. I couldn't leave in the middle of a fight.

The Abaj was studying the three-dimensional glyphs floating above a panel by my chair. "Breathe in slowly and wait. Then let it out."

I inhaled and held the breath for a few seconds, then exhaled.

"Again," the Abaj said, intent on his panel.

I breathed again, even and calm.

He turned back to me. "All right. I'm returning you." He pulled down my visor . . .

I smashed into a hard surface. Rock, solid rock. Ah, gods, pain screamed in my body. I couldn't move; my bones were broken, smashed, crushed—

No. I am fine. No way had I just fallen into a giant fissure. Oblivion was trying to screw with the simulation. It was only in my mind. That could still kill me, if I died of a heart attack or stroke or quit breathing, but damned if I would give Oblivion that satisfaction. I imagined myself in a tykado workout with Singer. Together we punched toward the desert, one-two, smashing an invisible opponent. *That's for you, Oblivion.*

The pain receded. I still ached, but it no longer felt like I had smashed my bones. I rolled onto my stomach and braced my hands against the ground. With a grunt, I sat up. The light remained dim, but enough trickled in to show the underground passage where I had "landed," a narrow place of rock and dust. I recognized it, but I couldn't remember why. I must have seen this place at some point in my life, because whatever Oblivion used to create this sim, he had to take it from neural patterns produced by my brain, and I couldn't remember a place I'd never known.

A low groan came from nearby.

"Who is that?" I asked. "Are you all right?"

Silence.

I climbed to my feet, wincing as pain shot through my battered muscles. The groan came again. I limped forward and the light ahead brightened, with an eerie blue cast, like bioluminescence.

"Who is there?" I called.

Nothing.

I kept walking.

A woman groaned. I'd never known what people meant when they said someone's voice was "full of tears," but listening to that moan, I understood. She sounded as if her heart were breaking.

"Pharaoh Dyhianna?" I asked. "Is that you?"

No answer.

Light brightened around me. I had entered a cave, and a woman lay by the opposite wall, on her back, a ragged blanket covering her lower body. Blood soaked her. She held a child in her arms, a newborn baby. It wailed in protest, and the woman cradled it to her breast.

No! I never witnessed this. It resembled the cave where I had found the dead mother with her newborn child last year. Pack Rat had led me there, a terrified five-year-old who couldn't understand why his mother had stopped moving. I had fallen apart that night, holding the dead mother and her children in my arms while I cried, the sobs tearing out of me.

This is a lie. I couldn't speak. I might as well have been invisible, helpless to change the tragedy unfolding in front of me.

"Shhh," the woman whispered to her crying child. "Always remember, I love you."

I was having trouble breathing. This wasn't real. Oblivion had created a fantasy to torment me. *I was a newborn! It is impossible for me to remember this.*

"Come to me, little jan," the woman whispered to her crying child. "Come to mother Bhaaj."

STOP. I tried to scream the word, but no sound came from my lips. I couldn't stop the memory. My mind, the mind of a child new to this world, unfocused, unformed, aware of so little, knew only my need for my mother. I reached out in pure instinct and she responded, the two of us forming a Kyle bond. She filled me with a mother's love, imprinting that moment on my mind forever, forming a bond so strong, so sweet, so full of love.

And then slowly, with great pain, she died.

I sunk to my knees, my arms folded across my stomach. I had suppressed this my entire life, denying my Kyle ability rather than relive those unforgiving moments when my infant's mind joined with my dying mother. She had been too far gone by then to break the link. I had lived every moment of her death, her passing forever imprinted on my mind, though I had understood nothing at a conscious level. Oblivion had taken that imprint and turned it into memories, forcing me to relive every moment. My eyes felt hot, but I refused to cry. I refused . . . and tears rolled down my face.

When her last spark of life vanished, darkness closed around me, ice cold, death, the death I deserved, for I had killed the only person who loved me fully and without condition. I murdered her with my birth, and her death would forever remain scorched into my spirit.

I knelt there, keening, and time passed.

My anger stirred. No. I wouldn't let the EI use my mother's death to defeat me.

I lifted my head in the darkness. *Fuck you, Oblivion. I won't go down so easily.*

Slowly, so slowly, I climbed to my feet, my body hurting with a bone-deep pain. The sim had changed around me. Once again, I found myself standing in the desert of black sands. A woman stood in the distance, her ghostly dress blowing around her knees, her figure glowing against the dark sky.

Pharaoh Dyhianna? I thought.

The distant figure became translucent.

A tall figure was running toward the woman. That looked like Nazam, the captain of her bodyguards. He reached her—and she vanished, like the sea.

No! Nazam's voice reverberated in the air, the sky, the ground, reeking of failure.

Izu Yaxlan, an oily voice whispered behind me.

I whirled around. Izu Yaxlan spread out in front of me, but instead of the bronzed and golden colors of the true ruins, this false city Oblivion created had black shale houses and grey paths. It was rotting from within, the stench of a corrupting dream. The Uzan walked in my direction along a once great thoroughfare, his step long and slow. Decaying columns lined the avenue, sloughing off moldy rock as he passed. I tried to speak, but I couldn't make a sound. Death stole my voice. The Uzan kept walking, never coming closer, forever trapped as his city disintegrated around him. I could just make out his face, his expression frozen in agony.

My head throbbed with pain. This all felt wrong, created by something that hated human life. Somewhere in the distance, just above the threshold of sound, laughter echoed.

Izu Yaxlan, a voice whispered.

The world melted around me as if it were paint running together into a muddy slush. The scene reformed, and I found myself in the Uzan's home. Its crystalline beauty had died. The columns that had scintillated with light were twisted, their insides deformed and turned into rot. The circuit diagrams on the walls formed clearer glyphs now, images of death, violence, human sacrifice to the demons of hell, the fears that had haunted humans for as long as we had been capable of thought.

The Uzan stood in the center of the room facing away from me, by the table where we had shared water. I had to warn him about the messages on his wall, the predictions of his gruesome death, but I had no voice. As hard as I tried to speak, no sound came out, like a nightmare where I screamed endlessly in silence.

The Uzan turned to me—and his head was a skeleton, a dead man, a caricature of the vibrant warrior I had met here only days ago.

Bhaaj. His voice crackled. *Come to me, my love.*

Pain screamed through my head. I clenched my fist, struggling to ignore the agony. *You aren't the Uzan. He's got more skin, asshole.*

The skeleton turned into shadows with only glowing orbs in his eye sockets. I wanted to leave, but I couldn't move, couldn't even raise my foot.

Couldn't move.

I closed my eyes and imagined the streaming white light that had bathed Calaj, that healing radiance Dyhianna had offered her. I became aware of a lightening. I opened my eyes—

The temple at Tiqual lay in front of me, normal and quiet. I was still in my chair on the dais.

"Goddamn it." They had brought me out of the simulation again. I didn't need a break. Dyhianna was still in her chair. I couldn't see much of her; the exoskeleton encased her body, the visor covered her eyes, and the neural cap covered her head. Her hands lay on the massive arm of the chair, covered in tech-mech gloves. Beyond her, Nazam sat similarly encased in his chair.

My cap and visor were gone. Who had taken me out of the sim? The temple was empty except for the three of us on the dais. I scraped at my exoskeleton, with no success at first, but after several tries, I released its fastenings. They felt gritty, encrusted with sand. When I was free, I rose unsteadily to my feet. I hurt everywhere. I must have been tensing in the chair. That was probably why the Abaj released me, but I was surprised they left us unattended. Then again, we could stay in the simulation indefinitely. Although a thrum of hunger bothered me, the exoskeleton had fed nutrients into my body during the session, making sure I neither starved nor died of thirst.

I limped over to Dyhianna. I couldn't see her breathing, but the exoskeleton hid most of her body. I shook her arm. No response. I shook harder and her body slumped to one side. The visor fell away from her head—

The eye sockets of a skull stared at me.

"No!" I shouted the word. She couldn't be *dead*. This had to be a trick. I strode to Nazam, pushed back his visor—it crumbled under my hand, uncovering the skull of a man who had been dead for long enough that the flesh had fallen away from his body.

I backed away. "This can't be." I couldn't have been in the sim that long, alive while the Ruby Pharaoh and Nazam turned to dust. I couldn't believe the EI destroyed everyone, or almost everyone, ignoring me who had no worth, the murderer of mothers and dreams.

Max, this is fake, right? I'm still in the sim. Oblivion created this simulation.

Max's voice came out of my gauntlet. "What do you mean fake?"

It's not real. I winced as pain stabbed my head. No wonder he spoke instead of using our neural link. I'd overextended my brain with this prolonged session. "It's another simulation."

"No," he said. "It's real. You stayed in the simulation too long."

I spun around and ran down the steps of the dais, unsteady but never stopping. My boots rang against the stone floor as I crossed the temple, stirring up sand that had accumulated in drifts. When I reached the entrance to the tunnel on the other side, I grabbed a torch out of its claw on the wall, a torch for freaking sake, those damned relics the Abaj insisted on using instead of normal lamps. I tried to light it with the igniter I found in the claw, but it crumbled in my hand. I shoved the torch back into its claw and strode into the dark tunnel.

Max, do you still have a map of this place?

Yes, it is intact, he answered. But running into the darkness won't solve anything. Take a breath, go back to the temple, and find out if you can contact anyone.

Just use the blasted map. Get me out of here.

You're about to run into a wall.

I reached out just time for my palms to hit the surface. It felt cold under my palms. *Which way?*

To your left.

With Max's guidance, I retraced my steps through the pyramid until a rectangle of light appeared ahead. I sped up, headed toward the light, and ran out of the temple into the late afternoon sunlight. Stopping, I gulped in the dry desert air, fresh and gritty, exactly as it always felt. Relief washed over me. Far to the northeast, the silver towers of the City of Cries still gleamed—

No, wait. Something was wrong. Those towers, that skyline, it looked different.

Broken.

Selei Building, the tallest skyscraper in the city, had become a jagged spire. The entire skyline had turned into a fractured caricature of its former glory.

"No." I clenched my fists at my sides. "It's a damned trick."

"What do you see?" Max asked.

"The City of Cries is in ruins."

"Is the flycar you came in still on the ground?"

I looked around—yes, the flyer was where we had landed.

I set off toward it.

✦ ✦ ✦

I had little experience piloting a flycar and my takeoff drilled rocks. Landing would probably be worse, but I didn't care. I had to prove this was false.

"You must have some hint this is a sim," I told Max. "Anything."

"I'm running diagnostics." He sounded apologetic. "So far they all seem normal."

"Keep looking. I have to get out of this." If I were trapped in a fake reality, I couldn't help distract Oblivion, who was probably trying to rewrite or delete our brains as we fought.

Max spoke. "If you want proof, it makes more sense to look in the temple."

I clenched the pilot's stick even though the flycar was on autopilot. "I have to reach the Undercity."

"Why? I don't see the logic."

I took a deep breath. "Max, I'm not going off the deep end. I need to see the Undercity because it's more difficult to maintain an illusion for something as extensive as the aqueducts, especially when I know them so well. I'm more likely to find flaws there to prove this is fake."

"Maybe." He didn't sound convinced.

"You find any anomalies yet?"

"I'm looking. But if this EI can control the neural input into your brain enough to create this illusion, fooling me would be child's play."

He had a point. I fell silent as we approached Cries. From the sky, the broken towers showed the most. Blackened and jagged, many had fallen, or else their upper sections had snapped off and crashed to the ground. I aimed for the plaza on the outskirts of Cries, bringing the flycar lower, letting down the landing gear, lower still—shit! The craft hit the ground, bounced up, slammed down, and bounced into the air again. Its wing caught on the ground and it crashed to one side, smashing into the plaza. The impact threw me against my safety webbing, and I groaned as pain splintered through my injured wrist.

Everything went still.

Max's voice came out of the comm on my rebroken wrist. "Are you all right?"

"Fine," I lied. I climbed to my feet using my good hand to brace myself against the hull. When I pushed open the hatch, hot air blew across my face. I half crawled and half slid out of the broken flycar down to the plaza. The silence of the desert surrounded me. I had disembarked facing away from Cries, so I was staring across the plaza at the remains of the archway that had topped the steps to the Concourse. The entire arch had collapsed. Gods only knew what had happened in the aqueducts.

I held my broken wrist against my abdomen. "Max, are you seeing all this?"

"Yes, I'm getting a visual. It looks like several earthquakes hit this area."

I limped along the wreckage of the flyer. "Big ones. Bigger than we've ever seen."

"We don't know the capabilities of the Vanished Sea EI," Max said.

I came around the flyer, into view of Cries—and stopped. "Ah, gods," I whispered.

It looked as if a giant had picked up the city, wrung it out like a rag, and smashed it down again. I walked forward numbly, unable to absorb the extent of the destruction. No flat land remained. It was all jumbled up and thrown about, leaving huge mounds with fragments of pavement, planters, lamp posts, and fountains mixed into the rubble. Beyond that first line of destruction, the mounds became bigger, including shattered buildings. In the distance, the skeletal remains of towers stood like silent condemnations of our failure. It was too much. Cries had died. I had to find someone, anyone, alive.

I spun around and limped toward the Undercity.

"Bhaaj, stop," Max said.

"Aqueducts," I muttered.

"You can't go down there."

I stared across the plaza to the fallen archway to the Concourse. The desert had collapsed in a fissure all along the route followed by the Concourse under the ground. It would have crushed the entire boulevard along with any visitors or vendors.

"That can't be." I kept walking. "The Concourse is reinforced to withstand even a bomb blast."

"Bhaaj, don't do this to yourself." Max sounded subdued.

I slipped into dialect. "Find my people."

"You can't, not this way. You need to get help. If you go in there alone, what can you do, except crawl over the destruction, and end up dying in a cave-in yourself?"

He had a point. I needed to bring in aid. I changed direction, heading back toward Cries.

Max spoke gently. "Go back to the temple. At least it's intact."

"I have to find out if anyone is alive."

"I'm not receiving any signals."

I kept walking. "The fact that a single gauntlet EI with limited sensors doesn't detect any people doesn't mean everything here is dead."

"True. But I'm not getting *anything*. No sign of life or tech-mech. It's all gone."

I reached the first mounds of rubble. Bones lay mixed in with the debris, stark and white.

"Max," I whispered.

"I'm sorry." If he was only simulating grief, he was doing one hell of a convincing job.

The ruins became worse as I went deeper into the city. Aurora Park looked as if it had gone through a gigantic vegetable masher. No life showed anywhere, just ruins and skeletons.

"Bhaaj, stop," Max said. "You've seen enough."

I sat on the pile of stone, leaned over, and threw up, retching as if I could tear out my insides. I couldn't think, couldn't feel, couldn't absorb this horror.

"The Majda palace," I rasped. "I'll go there."

"That sounds like a good idea."

I stood up. Then I stopped. "Max?"

"Yes?"

"You think it's a good idea for me to go to the palace?"

"Better than here. If anything survived, it would be the Majda stronghold."

"Yes, that's true. Except for one little thing."

"What is that?"

"It's a lot easier to maintain a simulation for a single palace than an entire city."

"Probably." He spoke with that terrible gentleness. "If this is a simulation."

"Why didn't you want me going to the Undercity?"

"The Concourse collapsed. No other entrance exists except in Izu Yaxlan, and that's too far."

I looked around at the destruction of Cries, the wind blowing my hair back from my face. If this was a sim, it was perfect to all five of my senses, the sight, the smells of death, the sound of Max's voice, the wind against my skin, even the gritty taste of the air.

"I know other ways to reach the Undercity," I said.

"You also know they're probably destroyed. The palace isn't underground. It has a better chance of surviving."

I spoke slowly. "The first thing I should have done, when I landed, was go to the aqueducts. I'd walk through hell to get there."

Max was silent for a moment. Then he said, "You want evidence something is wrong with this version of reality. Instead you found something wrong within yourself."

"See, that's the thing." I started walking back toward the outskirts of Cries. "I don't think I did. You're trying to keep me away from the Undercity."

"That sounds like a justification," Max said.

"For what?"

"You didn't go to the aqueducts because you didn't want to see their destruction."

Despite how sick I felt, I kept walking. He was right, I didn't want to see the people and home I loved in death. But I knew myself. I'd never turn away from my people, *never*, no matter what nightmare we faced. The real Max would know that. He'd never try to tell me otherwise. More than anything else, that convinced me I was still in the sim. Oblivion wanted to demoralize me with the destruction of all that I loved. So it sent me here. But apparently that included a risk, because for some reason it didn't want me anywhere near the Undercity, not even in a simulation.

Why?

"Bhaaj, stop," Max said.

"You're not Max."

His voice hardened. "Stop. Now."

I kept going.

The ground began to shake.

"Give it up," I said. "Your little earthquakes don't bother me."

The sky darkened and the ground heaved. Screams echoed behind me.

"You can cut the dramatics. I'm not scared." In fact, I was terrified, but I was too stupid to stop. I had rocks in my head. Always had, always would.

The shaking stopped. The city disappeared—and the world exploded.

XVIII

THE VOICE OF THE SEA

The ground heaved beneath me, and mud covered my body. The lead-grey sky roiled with drones blasting at each other, mechanized robots with no soul.

"Bhaaj!" a man shouted. "Over here."

I rolled over on the marshy ground and saw a soldier calling me from a few meters away. No, this couldn't be, I couldn't be here again. *Not again.*

"Max," I yelled. "What the bloody hell happened?"

No answer.

A battle raged in the sky above me. I had no wrist gauntlets, no gun, no supplies, nothing except my uniform, grey and orange fatigues that matched the mud.

"Bhaaj, can you hear me?" the soldier shouted through the murk and noise. I had no name for him. No, that wasn't true, I knew his name—

A shell hit nearby and exploded, throwing me into the air along with so much mud I couldn't see through the mess. I fell back, plunging into the roiled bog. Gunk clogged my eyes, nose, mouth. I wiped it away, gagging as the noxious stuff went down my throat. I could use both of my hands now, no broken wrist, but when I tried to crawl forward, my body wouldn't respond. I was sinking. I had to stop fighting; it would only make me sink faster.

An aircraft roared above and a voice called through the chaos. "Bhaaj, Rhimes, you there?"

A hand closed around my arm. "We're here!" a man shouted, so close that the force of his breath sent half-vaporized mud swirling past my face. I lifted my head. Rhimes was kneeling next to me on a sandbar that had slowed down our sinking into the bog. A tiny drone hovered above us, nothing more than an airborne framework, engines laboring, undoubtedly clogged with mud. A woman leaned out of the framework, reaching down to us.

"We have room for one of you," she called. "We'll come back for the other."

I pushed at Rhimes. "You go."

"Your leg is broken," he said. "You go."

I looked at my leg, half buried in the bog, twisted at a strange angle. I felt no pain, not yet.

The pilot leaned out of the cockpit. I knew her: Captain Tadra, my CO. "Rhimes, get in," she shouted. "This piece of crap won't stay airborne much longer."

"Take Bhaaj," Rhimes answered. "She's injured."

"Leave the fucking dust rat," Tadra called out. "She isn't even human."

Rhimes stared at her. "Captain—"

"That's an order," Tadra said. "Get up here, soldier. Now."

Rhimes spoke to me. "We'll send back help. I swear it."

"Go," I muttered.

He jumped up and grabbed the framework. With the help of another soldier, he scrambled into the drone. Captain Tadra veered off, leaving me in the mud, the dust rat, less than human, with no choice but to die.

Time to die.

Time to give up.

"Like hell." I spoke through gritted teeth. "It didn't happen that way." Yes, Tadra had left me. Her words were etched into my memory: *Leave the fucking dust rat.* But I'd never given up, and I wouldn't now, either, no matter how much Oblivion wanted me dead.

I crawled through the mud, dragging my useless leg the same way I had all those years ago, when we were ambushed on that shit world. I kept to the sandbar, which was sinking into the bog more slowly than the rest of the debris from the chaotic battle. I followed it to solid ground, a ridge that bordered the marsh. Pushing up on my elbows, I surveyed the barren flatland beyond the ridge. I had come out of the bog several kilometers from our army outpost, with the battle raging in the plain between me and the relative safety of that post. Trader waroids strode across the landscape, armored cybernetic giants more than eight feet tall, wiping out our soldiers as if we were no more than gnats.

"You aren't fooling me," I said. "This is all fake." The outpost had only been a kilometer away. We had fought soldiers with minimal armor, not waroids. I'd crawled the entire kilometer, struggling to stay alive. I showed up after Captain Tadra reported me lost in battle. Her words were recorded in my gear, proof of my claim that she left me to die. I testified during her court-martial, but it didn't end there. Tadra had blocked my entry into officer candidate school despite my high scores on the qualifying exams. I filed a complaint, and in the end the brass approved my application, more because they wanted to make sure I kept quiet about the battle than because anyone expected me to succeed. But that chance was all I needed. I graduated close to the top of my class.

Now over ten kilometers of impossible terrain separated me from safety. "Fuck you, Oblivion," I said. "If you can rewrite history, so can I." In my mind, I imagined Singer's mammoth gun, the Mark 89 Automatic Power Rifle that she and Taz toted around. "I'll remember whatever I damn well want."

I suddenly held the gun, my fists clenched around its massive stock. I targeted the closest waroid and fired. The gun boomed as it discharged, and the waroid's upper body exploded in a maelstrom of fragmented mesh parts. The debris spun over the landscape in a widening circle. I sighted on another waroid and fired. It detonated with the force of my blast—

An explosion came so close by, it threw me into the air. For an instant I blacked out, as much with shock as from the blast. I thudded down into the soggy ground, sinking into the porous ridge, probably the only reason I survived. And yah, I *had* survived, because that blast had actually happened. This time, however, I had a way to fight back. I rolled onto my back and fired straight up, blasting a stream of spinning, serrated bullets. They tore through the drone above me and the craft shattered, raining debris over my body.

Somewhere, the mind of an entity too alien to understand *shifted—*

✤ ✤ ✤

Darkness. No battle. No sounds. No sights, smells, or tastes.

What the hell? I couldn't get my bearings with these sudden switches.

A voice called out in the distance, too far away to identify.

Max suddenly spoke. "Those are moans of the dead."

Yah, right. "Shut up, Oblivion." I strained to catch that distant, faint voice.

Come to me, a woman called, like wind keening over a far plain.

Pharaoh Dyhianna! I thought. *You're alive.*

Her voice came again, closer this time. **I certainly hope so.**

I took a deep, shaking breath.

The darkness around me morphed into a new landscape. I was so shell-shocked from the abrupt changes, I couldn't focus. It took me a moment to comprehend I was in the desert again, my body whole, no broken leg and wrist, no trace of mud or battle. I was still in the sim, however. Distances had become bizarrely condensed. The Lock temple stood less than a kilometer to my left, blurred around the edges. Izu Yaxlan stood a few hundred meters in front of me, and the ruins of the Vanished Sea starships were about a kilometer to my right.

This all looks distorted, Max thought. Do you want me to see if I can focus it better?

I snorted. *You don't frighten me, fake Max.*

Why the hell would I want to frighten you? he demanded. You want my help or not?

That sounded like the real Max. *Yah, sorry. Help if you can.*

The resolution of the Tiqual pyramid sharpened. A figure formed behind the pyramid, rising into the sky, a monolith of shadow against that blue expanse. My mind translated it into a symbol I recognized, Azu Bullom, his horns curled around his head, his face dark, a wild god with a hooked nose and hooded eyes, upright like a human, but with the power and musculature of a jaguar. He loomed larger and larger, until he dwarfed the temple and stood as tall as the sky.

A shadow fell across me. Startled, I turned toward Izu Yaxlan. Another giant was rising behind the ruins, a thundercloud figure with a human shape but no face, only the glow of many stars within it. This wasn't one being, but the amassed memories of a city that had survived for six millennia.

I spun around to the north, fearing to see—yes, a third giant had appeared, towering above the Vanished Sea ships, not a shadow, not thunderclouds, but a void that stole all light. It had no features, no human form. This wasn't a deity of darkness, it was *nothing*. Oblivion.

Light flowed around me, and I turned again. The air above the desert between the Lock and Izu Yaxlan had taken on a luminous quality. A fourth giant formed there, a figure of white radiance so diffuse I couldn't see her clearly. She was Ixa Quelia, the goddess who brought nonexistent rain to the desert. No, wait, it wasn't Ixa Quelia, it was the pharaoh, a deity of light next to the massive power of Azu Bullom and the multiplied power of Izu Yaxlan, three aspects of humanity pitted against a void with no resemblance to anything human.

If I survived all this, even if I lived another century, I knew I'd never witness the titans of Skolia this way again. Yet even with three of them, I sensed the greater power in Oblivion. It grew with every EI it devoured. Its void would expand until it darkened all of the sky and encompassed all the world.

The Lock lifted his massive arm with his fist clenched. **BE GONE!** He opened his fist, and lightning burst out of his palm. It flashed across the desert, directly into the amorphous Oblivion.

The brilliant flash disappeared, swallowed by the void.

Oblivion grew.

Dyhianna raised her arms. **BE GONE!** She shimmered against the blue sky and flooded Oblivion with radiance that poured from the heavens. She filled the world with her light, washing away the darkness that Oblivion brought upon the land.

Oblivion swallowed her light and grew.

BE GONE! Izu Yaxlan thought in the voice of a million people. The figure spread its arms and the desert rose in a whirlwind of sand. The disturbance reached across the Vanished Sea, the sands spinning fast and high, blotting out the sun. They whirled toward Oblivion until they surrounded the void in a red maelstrom.

Oblivion swallowed the maelstrom and grew.

They raised their arms together, the Lock, Dyhianna, and Izu Yaxlan, and together they hurled their light, thunder, and the desert itself at the void created by the Vanished Sea EI.

Oblivion swallowed their assault and grew.

I stood, too overwhelmed to move, frozen in place while the gods fought. Oblivion took all they had to give—and grew stronger.

The Uzan's thought came to me, quiet and close. *This is what killed the beings who brought our ancestors to Raylicon.*

I looked around. The Uzan and Nazam were standing with me.

They gave their lives to protect us, the Uzan thought. *They let Oblivion think it caught them, and when it lowered its guard, they destroyed it even as it destroyed them.*

How do you know? I asked.

More of Izu Yaxlan is awaking. He sounded like the Uzan again, not the horrific skeleton created by Oblivion. *Its memories are hidden, hard to decipher, but they are stirring.*

Nazam motioned toward the desert. *Look.*

Tiqual, Dyhianna, and Izu Yaxlan were striding across the land together, headed toward Oblivion. Its void had grown until it encompassed a huge portion of the desert, including the ancient starships of the Vanished Sea.

The giants walked.

When they reached Oblivion, they surrounded the void, joining "hands" and stretching their arms until they formed an unbroken ring around its immense perimeter. With all that it had grown, they barely contained it. In real life, I suspected they were trying to limit a mesh program that had become so adept at erasing all other forms of code, almost nothing could stop its invasion.

Its strength grows, Nazam thought grimly. *If the race that brought humans here couldn't destroy it six thousand years ago, we have no chance.*

Why not? the Uzan thought. *We have spent six thousand years developing.*

And we are different than them, I added. *It may not know how to deal with us.*

Tiqual, Dyhianna, and Izu Yaxlan stepped closer to Oblivion, tightening their circle.

They created it, Nazam thought. *The kidnappers of our ancestors. They created this monster.*

We don't know who created it, the Uzan thought.

We cannot fight it. Nazam cut the air in a sharp wave, gesturing at the three giants. *They are trying to strangle Oblivion. They cannot. It will swallow them, and then the rest of us.*

I frowned, concentrating on him. I'd never known the Abaj captain to speak this way.

You aren't Nazam, I thought.

I am Nazam.

No, you're a fake, I thought. *Screw you, Oblivion. You can't get rid of us.*

Nazam blurred into darkness until he became a shadow on the desert.

Oblivion can erase us, a woman thought. The air in front of me reformed into a bent figure.

Yah, right. I turned away.

Major, she said. *I need your help.*

That didn't sound like Oblivion. I turned back around. *Calaj? Is that you?*

Yes, the EI is almost done erasing me. She sounded like the real Calaj. *You must help. I will send . . . the beetle-bot I took from you.*

Send it where? I asked.

Aqueducts.

Why? I don't understand.

You know what frightens Oblivion. Use that.

I had no idea what she meant. *It doesn't feel fear. It doesn't feel anything.*

Think back. The ruins . . .

Izu Yaxlan? It's already fighting Oblivion, far better than I ever could.

Not Izu Yaxlan. Cries.

I suddenly realized what she meant. Oblivion had tried to demoralize me with a sim of Cries in ruins and everyone dead. Yet even in the sim, it also tried to keep me away from the Undercity.

It fears the aqueducts, I thought. *I don't know why.*

Go there.

To do what?

I don't know . . .

Neither did I. This much I understood: Oblivion didn't like the aqueducts. I brought up my memories of the canals, caves, grottos, and mazes, the Down deep, the eerie beauty of stone lacework formed by mineral-rich water dripping over the ages, reflected torchlight light sparkling on crystals, the fatally poisonous water shimmering with beauty—

The world went dark again.

"She's coming out!" someone called.

As my vision cleared, I again found myself in the Tiqual pyramid, seated in my command chair. This time, the dais hummed with activity. Two Abaj were leaning over me, checking panels where data streamed in three-dimensional holos. Others were monitoring the pharaoh, and when I leaned to look past her, I saw more of them around Nazam.

"Max!" With my mind so overextended, it was easier to talk than think to him. "Is this—?"

"Yes, it's real," he said. "The beele-bot is going to the aqueducts. You need to do this."

I scraped at my exoskeleton. When it fell open, I yanked it off, knocking away control panels.

The Abaj grabbed my upper arms, holding me in place. "What are you doing?"

"I need to go to the aqueducts."

He didn't budge. "Now? Why?"

I had no idea. But I kept remembering Dyhianna's words: *It's like singing. Singing in the void.* "I'll know when I get there."

I expected him to try to stop me. Instead he let go of me and said, "I will take you."

In all my life, I'd never heard of anyone who broke the ban against mechanized transport on the Concourse. No one cared enough to bother defying the authorities. Today the Abaj and I shattered that prohibition. We blasted down the boulevard in a skimmer, an open hover car large enough for two people, with me standing at the front and the Abaj towering behind me, the wind of our passage blowing back our hair. People jumped out of our way, shouting in protest or to warn other pedestrians. The cops ran after our skimmer, but they couldn't reach us on foot. By the time they brought in their own transport, we would be gone.

The skimmer reached the entrance to the aqueducts within moments and whisked under the archway into the Foyer. Within seconds, we were racing through the largest canal. We sped down its center, the thrust of our engine stirring up clouds of dust. People came out from hidden spaces to watch us. Dust Knights. They stood on the midwalks, hung from the ceilings, and scaled the walls, staring as we rushed by them. The whisper mill would go wild.

"Sing!" I shouted to the knights, my voice amplified by the skimmer. "Everyone!" It was crazy, which was why I needed the knights. They created a network in the Undercity. If they set their mind to raising music in throughout the aqueducts, it would happen. If they asked me *why* I wanted them to sing, I had no answer except that we needed the music, *our* music. It wasn't only because of what Dyhianna had said to me; I also felt driven to make it happen as if that impulse were hardwired into my DNA.

We soon reached the tunnel I sought, which branched off the main canal. It was too small for the skimmer, so I landed on the midwalk. As soon as I turned off the engines, distant music came to my ears, a song from deeper with the aqueducts.

The Abaj and I jumped out and took off down another canal. Knights ran with us, behind and on the opposite midwalk, and others were undoubtedly following through hidden ways. They couldn't keep our augmented pace, but I never slowed. I kept thinking of the battle being waged by Dyhianna, Izu Yaxlan, and the Lock. If they failed, Oblivion would wipe two of the largest EIs in existence, both of them thousands of years old, and it would erase Dyhianna's mind, leaving her brain dead. And then it would set itself against the rest of humanity.

A sensual voice came out my gauntlet comm. "Bhaaj," a man said. "Can you hear me?"

Max, I don't have the breath to talk, I answered. *And why do you sound like that?*

That's not me, Max thought. It's Royal Flush. I gave him access to your comm.

Why would Jak's EI contact me, instead of Jak? Gods almighty, if Jak had somehow become a casualty of this battle, I didn't know what I'd do. *Is Jak all right?*

I will ask, Max thought.

The distant singing was growing stronger. I slowed as I reached my destination, a canal at right angles to the tunnel where we were running. Lizard Trap. Ruzik's territory. The whisper mill had done its work: Ruzik and his people were waiting for us, his gang and their circle, the cyber-riders, adults, families, children without parents.

Ruzik stood on the midwalk with Angel at his side and his other two dust gangers looming behind them. The rest of his people were down in the canal.

I stopped in front of him. I should have still been out of breath, but with my adrenalin so high, I didn't notice. Ruzik watched me with an impassive stare, waiting to hear why I committed such sins of trespass, bringing a skimmer and a stranger into their midst. Not just any stranger. I was acutely aware of the looming warrior at my side, a testament to silent power, a member of the legendary Abaj caste that enthralled and frightened not only my people, but citizens across the Imperialate.

Royal Flush's voice came out of my gauntlet comm. "Bhaaj, listen."

With my gaze on Ruzik, I lifted my arm and spoke into the comm. "What happened to Jak?"

"Nothing," Royal said.

Relief poured through me, also puzzlement. "All right. Give me a minute."

Ruzik spoke harshly. "What you want?"

I motioned at where his people watched us from the canal. Three young people were standing by one of the dust sculptures that tagged this canal, a ruzik rearing on its back legs. I recognized the trio. They had been vocalizing the last time I had come here, harmonizing without words, filling the air with their music.

"They need to sing." Although I spoke to Ruzik, my words were for the trio. I motioned at the air as if that could capture the haunting song rippling into this canal from elsewhere in the aqueducts. It was still swelling in volume. "With them. Sing!"

Ruzik crossed his arms and scowled. Damn. He was going to send me away.

"Eh," Angel told him, ever the soul of articulate discourse.

Ruzik glanced at her and she tilted her head. When she raised her eyebrows at him, he glowered at her, but then he turned around and motioned at the trio. They nodded to him and then conferred among themselves, using no words as far as I could tell, just facial expressions.

And then they sang.

Facing each other, reading cues invisible to the rest of us, they blended their voices with the song already echoing through the canals, joining its harmonies. These ruins offered incredible acoustics. They reflected, amplified, and added depth to the melody. That urge drove me, too, not to sing, given that my atrocious voice could probably traumatize even rocks, but the impulse to make the music happen.

"Bhaaj." Royal was on my comm again. "Jak wants to talk with you."

"Why are you telling me that?" I asked. "Of course he can talk to me."

Down below, the trio's song rose in power, no words, just pure sound. The canal rang with their voices as if it were a giant pipe creating its own interplay of notes.

"Bhaaj!" Jak's voice burst out of my comm, along with a surge of glorious music from wherever he was located. "Do you hear it? The aqueducts are singing!"

I barely caught his words, the music was so loud. The aqueducts were ringing with a symphony created so long ago, none of our us remembered its origins.

"Jak, where are you?" I asked.

"What?" The music in his location almost drowned out his voice.

"At the Black Mark?" I yelled.

"Yah. Dust Knights came. We opened the doors!"

"Listen!" I shouted. "Get everyone to do music, vocalists, musicians, any who can sing."

"They are!" He said more, but I couldn't hear. I had no idea how far the network of singers extended, but I hoped it was spreading to the entire Undercity.

I suddenly had an odd sense, as if I watched the scene from above instead of in front of Ruzik. It only last an instant, and then I was back in my body. I turned to the Abaj. He towered like a standing stone, his face akin to statues of our ancestors, with his prominent nose, dark eyes, and chiseled cheekbones.

"Can I connect me with the pharaoh's link from here?" I asked.

"Not through a bot." His voice rumbled like a counterpoint to the song.

A bot? That made no sense. "Can't you feel her fight with Oblivion?" Even with my limited Kyle abilities, I sensed the battle at the edges of my mind, Dyhianna's light, the Lock's implacability, the multitudes within Izu Yaxlan, and the void of Oblivion. If I felt it, surely the Abaj could as well; his people had been bred for compatibility with the enigmatic machines created by our ancestors.

"Yes, I sense them," he said. "But it's not enough."

Ruzik spoke. "Hack. Got mesh machines."

"Hack is a wizard, yah," I said. "But this needs more. Ruby psion."

"Actually," the Abaj said. "You only need a Ruby psion to create and maintain a link to the Lock. Any strong psion with training could help you rejoin the link. If someone here has equipment we can use, I might be able to do it."

It sounded like a long shot, but at this point I was willing to try anything. "Then let's go!"

I ran with Ruzik and the Abaj, our stride devouring the distance along a canal. The walls vibrated, the ground shook, and the air resonated with the haunting music. Slow and majestic, in a minor key, it combined higher pitches with a bass rumble in a relentless beat. Pain saturated the song. Legend claimed our ancestors named these aqueducts the City of Cries long before the modern city existed above us in the desert. Today, the ruins lived up to that name, filled with heartbreakingly beautiful music.

Hack was waiting. We ran inside his lab, and he led us to the room with the neutrino detector, where he had added a second station for the Abaj. As the Abaj took the seat, Hack pulled out two homemade neural caps. I couldn't believe that Abaj took one with no protest. His life's work hinged on his ability to use neural links. He wouldn't want to risk his most valuable asset, his brain, yet he accepted a jury-rigged neural cap with no safeguards. Again, for an instant, I thought I saw the two of us from a point above the apparatus. Then I lost the view.

Hack set about jacking us into his contraption. When I lowered the visor, darkness surrounded me. A thought rumbled in my mind. *Major?*

Who? I asked.

I am Oja. The Abaj.

Oja. His name. He offered me an honor. *Call me Bhaaj.*

Bhaaj. See if you can find the power link at the Lock. I will help you rejoin it.

I gripped the pulse rifle and swiveled the detector. All the time, the music grew, saturating us.

The canals must be built to resonate with these sounds, Oja thought.

It might even reach Izu Yaxlan, I answered. *The aqueducts connect to the Pharaoh's Tomb.*

More than the tomb. He paused, then seemed to make a decision. *They extend under the desert to Izu Yaxlan, to the Lock, and to the Vanished Sea starships.*

Good gods. Even my people had no idea the ruins were so extensive. I continued my scan while my body thrummed with the music.

And I found it. The Lock.

I'm strengthening your link, Oja thought.

My awareness of the Dyhianna, Tiqual, and Izu Yaxlan intensified. The raw power of that link hit me like a tidal wave. No, not a flood, more like vertigo from standing up too fast, magnified until my head reeled. Blackness descended, and I felt sick, a sense of dread, going into neural overload—

Bhaaj! Oja's thought cut through the darkness. *Focus. Pick an image and concentrate on it.*

I strained to recall the images the Lock had created for our link. The Vanished Sea.

The blackness lightened and a scene formed, blurred and faded. Once again I "stood" in the desert. In the distance, the giants formed a circle around Oblivion, three huge figures silhouetted against the sky. Pharaoh Dyhianna glowed with light. Izu Yaxlan had taken human form as if it were created out of interstellar space, shimmering with millions of stars, the memories of all the people who had lived and died in that ancient city. The Lock stood with them as the Azu Bullom, a powerful figure with horns curling around his head.

Although they still had Oblivion penned within their circle, its void had grown until it almost touched their "bodies." When it reached them, it would swallow their minds as it swallowed all else. Dyhianna would die, Izu Yaxlan would cease, and Tiqual would no longer be the Lock our civilization needed to survive.

Sing. I thought to the desert. *Sing them strength.*

The Vanished Sea rumbled with music. Jak was right; the aqueducts weren't just amplifying the voices, they were singing as well, an instrument the size of a city that shook the desert. I didn't understand the sciences our ancestors had gleaned from the abandoned starships. The tech that had created Oblivion differed from modern engineering.

Those ancient disciplines relied not only on electromagnetic, optical, and matter waves, but also on their interaction with phonons, the quantum particles of sound and heat. With our voices, we were unleashing an ancient weapon against Oblivion.

Come to me. Dyhianna's call filled the desert. *Sing.*

The music grew yet again, joy and grief, a transcendent ecstasy of sound.

Oja, I thought. *Can you link me to my beetle-bot, the one Calaj sent to the Undercity?*

Again?

I didn't know what he meant, but before I could ask, he thought, *Are you receiving?*

Nothing—wait, yah, I got it. Scenes of the aqueducts formed, layered on my view of the desert like translucent leaves in a book: singers on midwalks, in caves, beneath ancient arches. The world rang with their music, a song that none of us had heard before, yet we all knew it, for that painfully exquisite music held the soul of the Undercity.

Oblivion swallowed the song.

Just as the implacable EI had absorbed every attack we threw at it, so now, it took our song and absorbed that magnificent work into its relentless void. It swallowed the song—

Swallowed the song—

Swallowed—

Oblivion shrank.

The three giants stepped closer, pharaoh, Lock, and Izu Yaxlan tightening their circle.

The aqueducts sang.

Oblivion swallowed the music—and shrank.

The giants closed their circle.

Oblivion's voice thundered. **STOP.** Its void grew again, threatening the circle.

Sing to us, Dyhianna thought to the aqueducts.

The music swelled, so like the songs I had known all my life until the day I left the Undercity and everything else I loved. My heart filled with memories I had suppressed, the death, loss, poverty, hunger, desperation, but also love, hope, my times with Jak, my dust gang, so much beauty and grief side by side. The music took over my mind and left nothing else, killing me with excruciating beauty.

Oblivion shrank.
The circle of giants tightened.
The music swelled.
Oblivion contracted to a small sphere.
I couldn't bear the music. It was obliterating my mind.
I faded.
The desert faded.
Oblivion faded.
I vanished.

XIX

AFTERMATH

I screamed as pain shattered my head. Light blinded me. I thrashed against restraints I couldn't see, fighting a pain worse than when I had struggled up the Lock stairs.

"Get her out!" someone shouted. "*Get her out now!*"

"She's having another convulsion," someone else said. "Give her a larger dose."

I couldn't see with all the splintering light. My screams reverberated.

Major Bhaajan! Dyhianna's thought cut through the pain. *Be still. Let us help.*

"Light—" I rasped.

"Did you hear that?" someone asked. "She spoke."

"Give her another injection," someone else said.

Something hissed against my neck. With a groan, I opened my eyes. That blinding light had existed only in my mind, my interpretation of whatever neural wildfire was ravaging my brain. I was in the chair with two Abaj leaning over me, including Oja.

"Oja?" I whispered.

Relief flashed over Oja's face. "Are you all right?"

"My head . . ." I tried to understand how I could be here again, when I'd just been in Hack's cyber den. "Didn't I leave . . . ?"

Oja's forehead creased. "To go where?"

"Aqueducts . . ."

"Ah." He nodded. "Yes, but you went as the beetle-bot. Physically you stayed here."

Max's thought came into my mind. *We linked you to the beetle the way I linked you in the park, that time we found Calaj tailing you.*

It felt real, I thought. *The singing, Ruzik, Royal, Hack.*

It was real. He showed me his records so fast they flashed by. It had all happened as I experienced, but I'd spoken to people and seen it all through the beetle-bot. No wonder it had felt surreal and my view kept switching. My mind had tried to reconcile my use of the bot with my conviction that I physically went to the aqueducts. Royal Flush had contacted me because Jak had no way to reach me in the link unless an EI made the connection for him. And Oja had never donned Hack's neural cap.

"We used—Hack's systems?" I asked.

I didn't realize I'd spoken until Oja said, "Yes. He hacked into your spy beetle and helped me disconnect you from the bot so you could rejoin the Link here."

I dreaded my next question. "And Oblivion?"

"We deleted it," Dyhianna said flatly. ***It's gone. Dead.***

"And—the others?" It felt like gravel filled my voice.

"The Uzan is in Izu Yaxlan," Oja said. "He is fine. So is Nazam. He's still coming out of the link."

Dyhianna spoke more gently. "Calaj died with Oblivion."

After all that had happened, I suspected Calaj had been glad to let go. "She can rest now."

"We almost lost you, too," Dyhianna added.

I grimaced. "I couldn't handle the link."

Oja watched me with concern. "You suffered tonic-clonic convulsions, back to back. It's called convulsive status epilepticus. You were on the verge of dying for nearly twenty minutes."

"Don't sugar coat the news, eh?" I almost managed a smile. Almost.

"You are strong, Major."

"I'm an ornery old soldier," I muttered. "With rocks for a brain." I pulled at my exoskeleton again, and this time it released.

He laid a restraining hand on my arm. "Don't move too fast."

I sat forward slowly. Dyhianna was in the Triad Chair, watching me, her long hair straggling around her face, huge shadows under her eyes. Damn. She managed to be beautiful even when she looked like hell. There ought to be some sort of cosmic law against that. Beyond her, Nazam was sitting back while another Abaj monitored the control panels by his chair.

"How long—?" I asked.

"We were in the chairs for about a day," Dyhianna said.

In some ways it had seemed only a few minutes; in others, it felt like forever. All I knew was that I couldn't sit here any longer. I stood up, then swayed and grabbed the arm of my chair.

"Major Bhaajan, you should sit down," Oja said.

No. I wanted to see the sun, to convince myself this was real. "I need—outside."

"That's not a good idea." Oja continued to look worried, not a good sign given how little emotion the Abaj usually showed.

"Let her go," Dyhianna said.

·He glanced at the pharaoh, then nodded with reluctance.

I took a step. I didn't fall, so I took another. And more. I reached the edge of the dais. I started down, then swayed and almost fell. Someone caught my elbow. I looked up to see Oja.

"Gently," he said. "You're in no condition to walk."

"I need to get out."

He looked back at the pharaoh. I looked too. She was sitting straighter in her chair, and Nazam was standing next to her now, his gaze tired and shadows under his eyes.

"Go with her, wherever she needs to go," Dyhianna said.

The Abaj inclined his head to the pharaoh. Then he and I descended the dais.

Aged light surrounded me, slanting across the world from the sun, which hovered above the horizon. I stood next to the stairs that went up the outside of the temple. In places, they became so steep that they seemed more like a ladder. I didn't care. I needed to go up, I didn't know why, except that I wanted to be above the desert, and I'd be damned if I ever let stairs defeat me again.

"Major, you can't," Oja repeated. "These steps are not meant to be climbed."

"I need to climb." I started up, leaning forward to counter the steep slant of the stairs. Behind me, Oja swore under his breath.

I climbed.

It took forever. Several times I had to stop while my head swam.

My foot slipped, and someone grabbed my ankle, steadying me. I looked back to see Oja on the stairs behind me. I resumed the climb, no longer thinking, just staring at the stone under my hands. Put one foot above the other, rest, repeat, over and over and over—

My hands slid across a flat surface.

I raised my head. I had reached the top of the pyramid, a flat area about twenty paces across. I crawled up the last bit and sat on the edge. Oja stayed on the stairs, watching me, probably waiting to see what I intended to do. Far below us, the desert spread out in every direction. Cries rose in the distance, its reflective towers turned gold by the setting sun.

The top of the pyramid was mostly empty, except for an open structure in the center that resembled a stone gazebo without a roof. A low table stood within it, sculpted to resemble Azu Bullom, his head lifted, his legs holding up the tabletop. I struggled to my feet and limped to the table. I didn't sit on it, partly because it resembled an altar and I wasn't feeling sacrilegious today, but also because I couldn't stay up without support. I sat on the ground instead and leaned against a leg of the table, facing away from the sun.

And I sat. I thought of Dark Singer. Whatever genes had created the Abaj, Singer shared some of that DNA. *Singer.* Her name meant assassin. What origin did that title have in our collective memory? That thought required more energy than I had left. So I just stopped thinking.

Gradually I became more aware. The sun had sunk partway behind the horizon, but up here its light still shone. The Abaj was sitting up here now, by the stairs, watching me.

"How long have I been up here?" My voice had recovered enough that it carried across the few meters that separated us.

"About an hour," he said. "You have a visitor."

A visitor? That made no sense. No one could climb this temple without permission from the pharaoh, and I doubted she or her bodyguards wanted to come up here. "Who?"

He stood up and stepped aside as he motioned to someone. A moment later, a man came into view, climbing the last steps. He reached the top and stood up under the bronze sky, bathed in the light of the setting sun, lean and muscular, dressed in dark clothes with a knife sheathed on his belt. The wind whipped his ragged hair back from his face.

Jak.

"How?" I asked.

"A stranger contacted me." He walked forward. "Said I needed to come here."

"A stranger?"

"Yah." He sat next to me.

Oja was descending the steps. He wouldn't go farther down than needed to take him out of our sight, but this way he gave us some privacy.

I tried to focus on Jak. "This stranger got a name?"

His gaze never wavered. "Dehya."

"Ah." I tried to remember where I had heard that name.

"Also Dyhianna," he added. "As in Pharaoh Dyhianna."

"Oh." My brain still didn't want to work.

"Bhaaj, for flaming sake, react."

I struggled to concentrate. "Why?"

"Didn't you hear what I just said?"

I answered in Iotic, I wasn't sure why, except that I didn't want to expose the Undercity dialect to this temple. It didn't feel safe. "Yes, I heard. The Ruby Pharaoh of Skolian Imperialate. Dyhianna Selei Skolia. She's the one who hired me to find the Jagernaut."

He stared at me for a long time, while the shadows from the table stretched out toward the edge of the pyramid. Finally he said. "Gods."

"Yah." What had possessed me to climb up here? I was beyond depleted. I'd never make it back down under my own power.

Jak spoke Iotic, which my people understood better than most. Few of us realized that fact, let alone knew why, but I was beginning to see. Our ancestors had retreated to the aqueducts to protect their minds, yes, but that wasn't the only reason. They had also become the guardians of Izu Yaxlan, and through the city, of humanity. Somewhere over the ages, we had lost that history.

"Did you find the Jagernaut?" Jak asked.

"Yes." I spoke dully. "She's dead."

"So you caught your killer."

I regarded him steadily. "Never call her a killer. She died defending the pharaoh."

"Bhaaj, what happened? The aqueducts were goddamned *singing*."

"We needed them." I wished they could sing away the pain inside of me.

"What is it?" he asked. "What is tearing you apart?"

"I'm fine." We had destroyed the threat to our people. Nothing else mattered.

"I know you. You're not fine."

I looked at him, really looked, past the crime boss to the man who made love to me in the night. "You deserve better."

"Better than what?"

"Me."

He snorted. "Maybe. Depends on my mood."

"Not joking."

"Bhaaj, what's this about?"

I wanted to believe Oblivion had created false memories, but I knew the truth. The EI had torn away my defenses, yes, and turned the imprint of my mother's death into memories I couldn't have had as a newborn, but the imprint of the knowledge had always been there. "I felt her die."

"Calaj?"

"My mother."

Jak froze, going completely still. "What?"

"Our minds melded. I was an infant, I didn't know, and she was too far gone to understand what was happening." My voice cracked. "I died with her. My birth killed her."

His voice quieted. "I'm sorry."

No. He couldn't say that. We never apologized. Admitting sorrow, regret, weakness, fear, any intense emotion, made you vulnerable, and vulnerability killed.

"You need to go," I said.

He scowled at me. "After I wasted all that time climbing up here? I don't think so."

"Jak, I can't."

"Can't what?"

"Love." Dying with my mother had burned it out of me.

"Who said anything about love?"

"It's—I—go away."

"That was articulate."

"Why are you being so dense?"

He had that fierce look now, dark and implacable, with fury in his eyes, or some emotion, I didn't know what, something too intense for me to understand.

"I'm fine," he said.

"Can't you hear me? You need to go."

His voice roughed. "You want to talk about love, Bhaaj? Is that it?"

"I want you to leave." My voice was barely audible but I wanted to shout. He had to *stop*.

"You stop," he told me. "And listen."

I put up my hand. "Don't."

Jak took my hand and set it on my leg. He spoke in a low voice, his words husky and relentless. "I've loved you my entire life, since that moment we met, when you were an ornery three-year-old kid hanging onto Dig and glaring at the world. I never stopped and I never will."

"I can't," I whispered.

"Yah, well, that's bullshit."

It was a long time before I answered, and when I did, I spoke in our dialect. "Yah, so."

He nodded, accepting my agreement with his last words, Undercity style. We could win a prize for the least romantic declarations of love in the history of the human race, but it didn't matter. We knew what we meant.

Jak put his arms around me and I leaned against him. He was right; we had done this dance of love our entire lives. I had left Cries, running away, seeking a new life, and I'd found it, yet in the end I came home. No matter how much I evaded it, I knew the truth; I couldn't live without the Undercity and I couldn't live without Jak. We had grown up together, fought, played, worked, argued, laughed, and loved together since we were three years old. I had never acknowledged that need because to admit I needed him was to admit he could die, his mind melded with mine, and I couldn't bear that pain, never again. But without the pain, we weren't alive, and I wanted to live more than I wanted to escape.

XX
ONE STEP

The Lake of Whispers was close to a miracle on Raylicon. The Majdas had created it at their palace, the only substantial body of fresh water on the surface of the planet. It spread out like a green mirror, reflecting the sky. Imported trees clustered around its shores, silky foliage hanging from their branches. Blossoms floated on the water, a wealth of lilies alien to Cries. Gods only knew how they pollinated flowers on a world without insects. Maybe that explained why they imported shimmerflies.

I sat on the shore with my trousers rolled up and water lapping over my toes. It felt sinful. This lake had no practical use; it existed solely to serve the pleasure of the Majdas.

Footsteps sounded behind me, and I turned to see Lavinda. She wore civilian clothes today, blue slacks and a white blouse that rippled in the breeze. She sat next to me, uncovered he feet, and slid her toes into the water. Such a simple gesture, so unlike the rigid, restrained Majdas I had thought I knew. Lavinda and her two sisters were different from what I had expected when we met. Back then, they all seemed the same, towering warrior queens, army officers who rarely smiled and who claimed power with the ease of those born to its advantages.

That image had some truth, but they had become more human to me in the past year. Although Corejida wielded her financial power with authority, she had a gentler personality than her sisters. Lavinda took to the army so easily, it seemed as natural as breathing to her, but

301

she had a mental flexibility I never saw in her older sister Vaj, the General of the Pharaoh's Army. In another universe, where rigid social classes didn't separate us, Lavinda and I might have become friends.

"Did you get verification of the arrangement?" I asked.

"Yes, it is set." Lavinda glanced at me. "You will tell the assassin and her family? Everyone is trusting you to bring them in."

I nodded. "They've agreed. I'll bring them tomorrow."

"Good."

The arrangement we'd settled on for Singer was fair. She received a prison sentence, fifteen years, but not at one of the asteroid penal colonies. They were sending her to the Red Sands Research Facility on the Diesha, a world similar to Raylicon in that its habitable regions were mostly desert. It had a day closer to human standard, however, and the terraforming had succeeded there, unlike its failure here, making that world better suited to human life.

The Imperialate had no single military headquarters; its command centers scattered across many worlds, making it impossible to deal a crippling blow to the military in one strike. Diesha was the largest node. HQ City in the desert served as the main center, but the army had built the Red Sands base in the mountains. Isolated by deliberate intent, it served as a detention center and also as a training center for Kyle operators.

In return for Singer's agreement to let the army study her and to use her abilities in service to Imperial Space Command ISC for the next fifteen years, they would let her live in the Red Sands facility. She would have the freedom to go outdoors within a limited region, even join a tykado team. In return for Taz accepting the arrangement, they agreed to let him and Singer live together with their daughter. ISC expected them to sign a formal marriage contract, but I doubted they cared. They were young, with the flexibility to adapt to this new life. At the end of the fifteen years, if the arrangement succeeded, ISC might offer Singer a civilian job to continue her work.

Most important, it would give Singer surcease from the darkness she had never known how to escape, until it nearly warped her beyond recovery. In the end, her instinctual awareness of Oblivion had driven her to seek help. ISC would work with her to understand what she, a "singer" of the aqueducts, meant to Earth's lost children.

After a while, I said, "You know, she can't actually sing."

Lavinda glanced at me. "The assassin?"

"Yes." I winced. "She has a terrible voice."

"Did she know when the aqueducts sang?"

"She felt it, even at my apartment." I had spent most of the last day sleeping at the penthouse. The Abaj had called in a flyer to get me from the top of the temple, but I refused to go to the hospital. The pharaoh let me go to my apartment only if one of her bodyguards stayed. So while I slept, Oja watched over me, also keeping an eye on Singer and her family. Jak stayed, too. During one of the periods when I stirred to eat, we talked about the aqueducts. "She didn't call it singing. She said the aqueducts woke up."

"I've gone over your statements again and again," Lavinda said. "The more I read, the more I realize how little I know about the Undercity."

Her and me both. "None of us do. Oblivion killed whoever brought our ancestors to Raylicon."

"How can you know that?"

I'd thought about it a lot recently. "We have no proof, at least not yet. But both I and the Uzan picked up pieces of their history during the fight with Oblivion."

She grimaced. "I just wish I knew what the hell woke up that EI."

I hesitated. "Maybe all that Kyle testing you did with my people last year."

"Why? Those tests are pretty low key."

"It's not the testing, exactly. It's that we're awakening, too."

She considered me. "You believe the Undercity was designed as a defense against the EI."

"In part." I struggled to put into words ideas that were as much instinct as conscious thought. "The aqueducts are literally part of Izu Yaxlan's mind. It was dormant. The singing helped it awake. It may become dormant again, now that Oblivion is gone. I don't know."

Lavinda frowned at me. "The EI at Izu Yaxlan hasn't been dormant."

"Hasn't it? I mean, what does it do out there? Drowse in the desert."

After a moment, she said, "The pharaoh has a theory."

"About Izu Yaxlan?"

"About the aqueducts. She thinks their structure models the brains in the beings who brought us here." More to herself than me, she added, "A greatly enlarged model, obviously."

"Why obviously?"

She spoke dryly. "I hardly think an entity with a brain the size of the aqueducts would fit into those ships on the shores of the Vanished Sea."

I shrugged. "Maybe whoever flew those ships were proxies. The intelligence that sent them stayed here. It needed our ancestors to build Izu Yaxlan so it could interact with us. But either it also created Oblivion or that EI already existed. By sacrificing their lives to stop Oblivion, they gave us time to grow. To develop our defenses." It had taken millennia, maybe the longest learning curve in human history, but we had survived. "It worked."

Lavinda watched me with her dark gaze. "Maybe. We're assuming Oblivion was the only one."

Well, shit. "I hope so."

"You and me both. At least we have clues now about what happened."

It was a start. "When this goes public, people will have ideas about how to interpret them."

Lavinda stiffened. "Major, listen to me. This must never become public. We don't know what roused Oblivion. If more EIs like it exist, we can't risk waking them up."

That felt like a bucket of ice water. An EI of that power didn't form out of nothing. Someone had created it, and if they created one, they might have made others.

Regardless of what happened, my people's future had changed. The powers of the Skolian Imperialate coveted our Kyle-rich population, but now they also knew our culture itself had value, holding secrets of our past. I had always struggled to articulate to the Majdas why they should leave our way of life undisturbed. Now they knew. Cries couldn't risk changing us. Our battle with Oblivion proved the Undercity held a key to human survival on Raylicon, perhaps everywhere. Anything that disrupted our lives might also damage the secrets locked within us. My people needed to conquer our poverty and heal the wounds of our inbreeding, but those changes had to come from us, filtered through our minds, our dreams, our way of life, for only then could we preserve what made the Undercity unique.

Friendly fire. Such a mild phrase for so cruel a reality, a mistaken attack on friendly forces during an attempt to engage the enemy. Nothing "friendly" had killed Tavan Ganz. He died because he had the misfortune to be in the wrong place at the wrong time—but in doing so, he saved the life of the Assembly Finance Councilor, perhaps even of Pharaoh Dyhianna. ISC told his parents he was a hero, that he worked with Calaj to stop an assassination.

We found Calaj's body at the Vanished Sea starships. She died when Oblivion ceased to exist, but she'd held on to the bitter end, all the time corrupting its systems. I didn't want to think what would have happened if she hadn't managed to hijack part of the overextended EI. If Oblivion had killed her as it intended, downloading her spinal node and then erasing her brain, it could have withdrawn to Raylicon unscathed. Instead, she had held on, rewriting it from within. Gods only know what her last days must have been like, knowing she was already brain dead, that she survived only by using a template for her own mind imprinted on the EI that had killed her.

Without Calaj, Oblivion could have struck without warning. Signs existed, the glitches at Jak's casino, Singer's sense of the darkness, Hack's detector, but we would never have seen the truth until too late. Gods only knew how far the EI could have spread its destruction. It had commandeered a Kyle node in Cries and reached out into the meshes that spanned interstellar civilization.

Imperial Space Command gave both Calaj and Ganz a memorial with full honors. The Majdas held it at the palace, next to the Lake of Whispers. Pharaoh Dyhianna attended, flanked by four Abaj, including the Uzan and Nazam. Vaj Majda came in her capacity as General of the Pharaoh's Army, and the head of the J-Force attended with several of his officers.

Jak came with me. He stood at my side, compelling in his silence. Dressed in formal black from head to toe, wearing clothes that few residents of even Cries could afford, with onyx gauntlets on his wrists embedded by black diamonds, he honored the dead in his own manner. The elite of Cries also came, highly placed citizens of the city. Several started when they saw Jak, then looked quickly away. The reason he could afford his sinfully rich clothes came in part from the pockets of those here who knew him. None of them said a word.

On that day, by the lake in the coolness under the trees, Imperial Space Command honored Ganz and Calaj. Their families listened, tears on their faces. Nothing could take away the pain of their losses, but perhaps the memorial helped ease their grief.

We held the tykado tournament several days after the memorial. Volunteers at the Rec Center set up risers in the main hall, organized by Ken Roy, that terraformer at the university who had helped make this happen. The Cries Tykado Academy brought mats for the contest and provided judges, only two for a tournament this small. The CTA teams wore loose white outfits with belts around their waists. The juniors had color stripes on their belts indicating their rank, and the older team wore dark belts. They all kept their hair neatly slicked back.

I paced on the other side of the room, too agitated to sit. What if our teams didn't show? In the end, Dara and Weaver agreed to let Darjan participate. As it turned out, Pat Oey Sandjan was too young for the adult division, so she, Darjan, Biker, and a boy named Charcoal formed the junior team. The seniors consisted of Ruzik, Angel, Hack, and the other woman in Ruzik's gang. I went to the entrance again and looked down the Concourse. No sign of them. Damn! If they didn't arrive soon, this attempt at détente would disintegrate into an insult against CTA. Granted, the Cries Tykado Academy only agreed to the tournament because Lavinda promised to attend, but that would make it even worse if our teams didn't show.

"Stop worrying," a man said.

I spun around. Jak stood there, all torn shirt and rugged trousers.

"No teams," I said.

"No. Just no Concourse."

Ah. They were using the back ways. They must have removed the barriers the Cries police set up to stop my people from sneaking around behind the shops and cafes.

I paced over to him. "Should be here already."

He smirked at me.

"You think it's funny?" I growled.

He motioned toward the entrance. "Look."

I turned—to see Sandjan and her team filing inside, all in ragged trousers and muscle shirts, with straggles of hair curling around their faces. They stared at the CTA team and the CTA kids stared back. Although I saw distrust, they all seemed more curious than hostile.

Sandjan and her team nodded to me. That was it. They didn't want me hovering around them. I gave them space, forcing myself to stay put and respect their pride despite how much I wanted to go over there and hover.

The rumble of talk started again as visitors from Cries drifted in and took seats on the risers. Ken Roy kept the Rec Center volunteers organized, his understated presence helping it run smoothly. The Dust Knights he met today would be the ones guarding him when he visited the Undercity. A few visitors even showed up from the aqueducts, including Dara and Weaver. They looked around with an almost tangible tension, as if they expected police to arrive and haul them off to jail. Even with that fear, they came to give their support.

Silence fell over the room as Ruzik, Angel, Hack, and their fourth strode into the Center. They towered, all of them scarred and tattooed. They dressed like Sandjan's group, but on their muscled frames the clothes looked different. Wilder. They appeared to be exactly what they were, a notorious Undercity gang.

Ruzik nodded curtly to me. His team joined Sandjan's group, and they all warmed up, doing stretches and arm swings. My teams. We prosaically called them DK1 and DK2, for Dust Knights. Most of the CTA kids also continued to prepare, but their captains were talking to a woman who looked like their head coach. I didn't need augmented hearing to know they were protesting.

I walked across the room, forcing myself to move casually despite my tension. *Above-city charm,* I told myself. *Find it in yourself, Major. Somehow.*

Are you talking to me? Max asked.

No. Myself. I had less charm than a rock, but I had to try.

As I approached the CTA coach, I put on a smile. It felt strange to give that expression to someone I didn't know, but above-city people did it all the time.

"My greetings." I bowed to her, one tykado master to another. "I'm Major Bhaajan, the coach for the Undercity teams."

"Ah." She exhaled, probably relieved as much for my above-city manner as anything else. She returned my bow. "I'm Hakela Mazim."

I nodded toward the mats and other equipment they had provided. "We appreciate your setting this up for the students. It means a lot to them."

She glanced uneasily at my teams, and I was aware of the CTA captains standing back a few paces, listening. Mazim said, "Your students know the rules, right?"

For flaming sake. Of course we knew the damn rules.

Charm, Max reminded me. Be civil.

I spoke in my most pleasant voice. "I've coached them according to the Tykado Federation standards." I'd spent extra time making sure they understood which moves counted as scores and which were illegal. "We used the same procedures I learned on the Pharaoh's Army team."

"Ah, yes, good." She nodded, trying to return my tense smile.

We talked a bit more, inconsequential words. It felt like torture given my utter lack of talent at small talk, but somehow I managed to avoid saying anything too stupid. Eventually we moved apart, she back to her teams and me toward the risers where Dara and Weaver were sitting.

Dara tapped the empty space beside her. "Sit."

I could barely stay still, but Dara seemed more in need of reassurance than her daughter. So I sat next to her. I nodded toward Darjan, who was doing stretches. "Looks ready."

Dara glanced at the CTA teams. "For them? Hardly."

"More than you think." We had no fancy outfits, rich parents, or nice mats, but we trained hard. I couldn't predict how our teams would fare against Academy students; I knew nothing about the junior divisions and my only experience with adult divisions were the army tournaments I'd competed in. I knew Sandjan was a strong fighter, enough that Ruzik wanted her on their adult team, so perhaps she would do well among the juniors. I couldn't say with the others.

Ruzik's team looked lethal as they warmed up, but I knew them too well to be fooled. The CTA black belts intimidated them, a lack of confidence born of their doubts that they could measure up to anyone in the above-city, let alone the privileged members of an elite gym. For the sake of their pride, I hoped the Cries team didn't beat them too badly.

Dara and Weaver were watching me. "Got healer," Dara said.

I glanced at her, distracted. "Eh?"

"Rajin Dia," Weaver said.

I wasn't sure what they meant. "Dr. Rajindia?"

Weaver nodded. "Yah. Saw her."

"Yesterday," Dara added.

"Got birth certificate." Weaver grinned. "Is official now. I am born."

I laughed, glad to have some positive news. "Good."

People all over the room were suddenly rising to their feet. Startled, I stood up and turned around. Lavinda was striding into the Center with her retinue. She wore full dress uniform, dark green trousers with a stripe down each leg, boots and a green tunic belted at the waist. The gold bars on her shoulders and the medals on her chest gleamed. Damn, she looked impressive. She created such a dramatic entrance, it took me a moment to notice that several of her "aides" were Jagernauts out of uniform, coming incognito. Huh. Odd—

Holy shit.

Behind Lavinda, so unobtrusive that no one else seemed to notice, the Ruby Pharaoh walked with her bodyguards. Given her small stature and discreet position, she looked like a minor aide. I doubted anyone really saw her. Of course the Majdas didn't want anyone to notice her. Hell, they probably didn't want her anywhere near this place. Yet here she was, the hereditary sovereign of the Imperialate, come to see our sports match.

Lavinda and her retinue took their seats on risers cleared by IRAS volunteers. The pharaoh sat between two Abaj, with a third behind her and the fourth in front. I couldn't stay still any more. I got up and paced to my teams, but I stayed back, leaning against the wall, not intruding on their space. Our behavior probably seemed off to the CTA teams; they all interacted with their coach while they warmed up. We did have one trait in common; everyone seemed nervous, needing to move.

Eventually the referee had everyone take their seats. The athletes settled on the floor, cross-legged, and the first match began, with the juniors. Charcoal went up against the youngest boy on the CTA team. They were evenly matched in size, but the CTA youth seemed uncertain. Although he had learned the moves, he didn't yet have any fighting instinct. Charcoal easily won, but the judges were frowning and talking heatedly. One of them looked angry. I wished we had an Undercity judge, but of course the aqueducts had no accredited officials.

I walked around the room again, approaching the table. The CT coach was doing the same. We reached the judges at the same time.

"Is there a problem?" I asked.

"Your student should be disqualified," the angry judge said. "He didn't use legal moves."

I had no idea what she meant. "He didn't do anything illegal."

She scowled at me. "He was using some other fighting style, not tykado."

Well, shit. If they disqualified Charcoal, they might as well disqualify everyone I had brought, because they all fought that way. I kept my voice calm. "He won the points fairly. A hit is a hit. He didn't use forbidden moves. Contestants aren't judged on style, just on who manages the most hits."

Coach Mazim spoke up. "I have no objection to the way he fought."

The judge didn't look any happier with Mazim than with me, but what could she say? Charcoal hadn't done anything prohibited. He just fought better than the CTA boy.

"Give us a few moments," the other judge said. "We'll give a ruling."

I gritted my teeth, but I moved away from the tables with Coach Mazim. The judges conferred in low voices. I wondered why they bothered. They came from CTA. They had no reason to let my students win.

"I'm sorry," Mazim said in a low voice. "I don't agree with them."

I nodded at her unexpected comment, too tense to speak. After a moment, the judges beckoned to us. When we came back to the table, the angry judge spoke stiffly. "The style is unusual, but as far as we can see, no rules were violated. The tournament may proceed."

I exhaled. Probably they didn't want to look bad with Lavinda Majda here. I headed toward my teams. They were all frowning, both the junior and the adults. Sandjan and Charcoal strode over to me.

Sandjan spoke tightly. "Bad news?"

"What say?" Charcoal asked.

"No problem," I told them. "Just needed team info." I nodded to Charcoal. "Good fight."

He grinned with relief and stood taller.

The next bouts were more evenly matched, one between Darjan and a CTA girl, then Biker and a CTA youth. Darjan lost by a narrow margin and Biker won. Darjan didn't look upset; she'd made a good showing, and she seemed glad for Biker. In the fourth match, Sandjan faced a girl with a champion's stripes on her belt. They started slow, taking each other's measure, bouncing on their feet like maestros tuning their instruments. Then they launched into the bout, legs kicking, bodies spinning, fists jabbing. At the outset, the CTA student seemed too confident, but I could see her reevaluating as they fought. They seemed to forget the rest of us, concentrating on the sheer pleasure of a strong bout. In the end, Sandjan just barely managed the win. As she and the CTA student bowed to each other, the audience burst out with applause.

So it went. In the first adult match, Angel faced a tall woman. The audience fell silent as the competitors walked to the mat and bowed. This was different, a top tykado athlete in Cries matched against an adult gang member. The Cries student surpassed Angel in skill, but Angel had better flexibility. She also seemed to rattle her opponent with her unusual style. Angel executed her kicks and spins with a different rhythm than most tykado students. Several times, she did a roll or a flip. I didn't see the point, and strict tykado adherents never used such moves, but nothing in the rules prohibited gymnastics. Although the angry judge scowled, she let the match continue.

Someone sat next to me. Startled, I turned. "Colonel Majda. My greetings."

"Major." She nodded toward the fighters. "You've some talented students."

"My thanks." I wondered why she had come over. "Do you know the CTA teams?"

"Not really." She was watching Angel. "That girl's style looks familiar."

I didn't see how Lavinda could have a clue about Angel's style. "From where?"

"Have you ever heard of a game called Bronze Warrior?"

Ah, hell. Angel never played Bronze Warrior. However, all of my Dust Knights has a similar fighting style, including Hack. When it came to gaming, he was the undisputed virtuoso at Bronze Warrior, and he played by stealing mesh resources from the city. If I didn't watch my words, I could implicate him.

I played dumb. "Is that a thing kids do?"

"It's a strategy fight game. Our army techs designed it."

Great. That meant Hack was stealing from the army as well as Cries. The military ran all sorts of mesh games, looking for talent. It also let them monitor the most adept cyber warriors.

Time to be noncommittal. I said, "Ah."

"We've been following a gamer called the Hack Master." She nodded toward Angel. "Your student has a fighting style similar to that gamer."

I wanted to groan. Couldn't Hack come up with something more subtle than Hack Master? I said only, "I'm sure she doesn't play holo-mesh games." Which was true. Angel had no interest in fighting on the mesh. She preferred the real thing.

Lavinda continued to watch her. "I've never seen anyone else with that style."

I kept my response to a grunt. I'd have to talk to Hack. He needed to be more circumspect.

"The problem," Lavinda continued, "is that no one can figure out the identity of this Hack Master. She hides well. We think she may be as adept at tech-mech engineering as gaming."

I motioned at Angel. "I'm sure it's not her."

Lavinda gave me an odd look. Then her puzzlement changed to comprehension. "Major, we aren't looking for this player to prosecute her. We want her to join ISC."

Good gods. None of Ruzik's gang had any interest in cyber-riding, and the idea of Hack joining the military would have been funny if I wasn't so worried. The closest he'd ever come to accepting an authority figure was when he acknowledged me as his tykado master, and I came from the Undercity. I knew his way of life. He would never enlist, not even if it meant he could have a real cyber lab with top-notch tech-mech toys.

Then again . . . ISC also needed civilian cyber types. Maybe they could offer him an outlet for that raging genius of his. As much as he would chafe at the rules and structure of an above-city facility, he might revel in their resources.

Lavinda was watching me closely. "We'd just like to talk. Maybe offer her a job."

"I can't speak for anyone," I said.

"I understand." She paused. "If she would like to talk, my line is open."

"Understood." After a pause, I said, "And Colonel."

"Yes?"

I spoke quietly. "You shouldn't assume it's a woman."

She glanced at Ruzik and Hack. Nothing pointed to them; Lavinda would soon realize Angel's style was common to all my advanced students. If Hack did decide to contact her, I didn't want her people expecting a woman. I wasn't worried about Lavinda, but Vaj was another matter. Better that Lavinda prepare her ahead of time. She knew far better than me how to deal with her conservative sister.

Angel won her match by a narrow margin. Ruzik's brother fought next, and he lost to a stocky woman with a fast kick. The third match, between the other woman in Ruzik's gang and a man from CTA, was close enough to need a judges' decision. I thought our fighter had won, but they gave it to the CTA fighter. In the final bout, Ruzik faced a large fellow. They battled for a long time, a match that became as much artwork as fighting. In the end Ruzik lost by an edge, though not quite as close as the previous match. He and his opponent bowed to each other with a respect I hadn't seen before the tournament began.

For the team rankings, the judges gave the junior's win to our team and the adult win to CTA. Lavinda presented the awards, and everyone applauded. It had turned out better than I expected, and the close matches left the Dust Knights exhilarated. They wanted to compete again, to prove they could best their privileged counterparts.

As we were preparing to leave, the CTA girl who had fought Sandjan came over and stood a few paces back from our teams. The Dust Knights glanced at her, looked at one another, looked back at the girl. Finally Sandjan went over to her.

"Eh," Sandjan said.

"My greetings," the CTA girl said. "I am pleased to meet you."

"Say again?" Sandjan asked.

The girl looked confused. "I'm sorry, what did you say?"

Sandjan spoke slowly. "Good fight."

The girl smiled. "Thanks. You, too. Those were some moves."

Sandjan hesitated. "CTA. Means what?"

"Cries Tykado Academy," the girl said.

"Ah." Sandjan nodded.

"And Dee Kay?" the girl asked. "Those are initials, right? We wondered what they meant."

Sandjan squinted at her. "Eh?" She looked back at me.

I stepped over and spoke to Sandjan in the Undercity dialect. "Ask what DK mean."

Sandjan lifted her chin and spoke to the girl. "Dust Knight."

"Oh!" The girl's enthusiasm sparked. "I heard about the Dust Knights! Some kids were talking about it at school. You live by a Code of Honor, right?"

Sandjan glanced at me.

"Hear about Knights," I said. "About Code. Good hear."

Sandjan nodded to the girl, accepting the compliment. "Yah, got Code."

This time, the CTA girl looked at me.

"She said she's a member of the Knights," I said. "They do follow a Code of Honor."

The girl beamed at Sandjan. "I'm pleased to meet you."

Sandjan actually smiled. They said their goodbyes, stilted but friendly, and went back to their teams. It was a simple exchange—and unprecedented. Two students had spoken to each other, one Undercity, one Cries, nothing hidden, nothing threatening, just two kids meeting at a tournament.

It was a start.

I helped Ken Roy clean up after the meet.

"It's amazing," he said as we stuffed garbage into the recyclers. "Your knights are naturals."

"They like to fight." Dryly I said, "Too much."

He glanced at me. "Thanks for getting me an in with them."

"I hope it works out." His unusual point of view as a terraformer might lead him to insights the rest of us didn't see. I looked forward to finding out what his research yielded.

By the time I left the Center, most everyone else had gone. Lavinda was with her retinue by a nearby café. Except of course it wasn't Lavinda's retinue, it was for Dyhianna. Jak stood with them, talking to Nazam. Jak nodded to me and I nodded back. We never got personal in public. Something had changed, though, the lowering of a barrier, one I hadn't realized existed until it eased.

I joined the group, and we headed up the Concourse. Dyhianna fell into step with me.

"Thank you for coming," I said. "You honored us."

"It was my pleasure." She spoke softly. "I heard the authorities took Singer offworld."

"Yah, she and her family left this morning on an army transport."

I had accompanied them to the starport and watched them board. It had been hard to say good-bye. "Will you return to Parthonia?" I wondered if she lived in Selei City. They'd named it for her, after all. Probably not. I'd heard the Ruby Dynasty had a palace in the hills.

"I'm going back tomorrow." Dyhianna fell silent as we climbed the staircase at the end of the Concourse. At the top, we came out into the desert. She stopped, the two of us bathed in the glorious sunlight, and added, "You should get retested for Kyle abilities."

"I will." Eventually. I still didn't like the idea.

She spoke quietly. "I used to be a mathematician. I developed models to predict the future. I still run extrapolations. They aren't accurate, but sometimes they predict trends. Other times—I don't know. Can we even define the line between extrapolation and precognition?"

"I don't know." I had no idea what she was trying to tell me.

"These Dust Knights—you must do right by them."

I tensed. "You know about the Dust Knights?"

"A bit. It's vague." Her gaze never wavered. "Do right by them. They are part of the future."

I wasn't sure what to make of this. "I will, Your Majesty."

She smiled. "Call me Dehya."

Good gods. Was the Ruby Pharaoh giving me her nickname? I spoke awkwardly. "Dehya." Then I said, "Please call me Bhaaj."

She inclined her head. "Good-bye, Bhaaj. Be well."

"And you, Your Majesty." I stopped. "Dehya."

She left then, walking in the streaming sunlight with her guards and Lavinda, a Majda queen.

Jak came up beside me. "You have high-level friends."

"I wouldn't be so presumptuous as to call them my friends."

He gazed at Cries, the wind blowing his wild hair back from his strong profile. "It's quite a world."

"Yah, it is." Today I chose to feel optimistic.

Jak and I walked along the plaza, with the Cries on one side and the Undercity on the other, two worlds that would never be alike, never have a common way of life, but that maybe, just maybe, might someday come to accept one another.

CHARACTERS & FAMILY HISTORY

Boldface names refer to Ruby psions. All Ruby psions use **Skolia** as their last name. The **Selei** name indicates the direct line of the Ruby Pharaoh. Children of **Roca** and **Eldrinson** take Valdoria as a third name. The del prefix means "in honor of," and is capitalized if the person honored is (or was) a Triad member. Most names are based on world-building systems drawn from Mayan, North African, and Indian cultures. The family tree below corresponds to the time of the Lightning Strike books, which take place roughly 123 years after the events of *Undercity*.

= marriage

❖ ❖ ❖

Lahaylia Selei (Ruby Pharaoh: deceased)
= **Jarac** (Imperator: deceased)

Lahaylia and **Jarac** founded the modern-day Ruby Dynasty. **Lahaylia** was created in the Rhon genetic project. Her lineage traces back to the ancient Ruby Dynasty that founded the Ruby Empire.

Lahaylia and **Jarac** have two daughters, **Dyhianna Selei** and **Roca.**

❖ ❖ ❖

Dyhianna (Dehya) = (1) William Seth Rockworth III (separated)
= (2) **Eldrin Jarac Valdoria**

Dehya is the Ruby Pharaoh. She married William Seth Rockworth III as part of the Iceland Treaty between the Skolian Imperialate and Allied Worlds of Earth. They had no children and later separated. The dissolution of their marriage would negate the treaty, so neither the

317

Allieds nor Imperialate recognize their divorce. Her second marriage is to Eldrin, a member of the Ruby Dynasty. *Spherical Harmonic* tells the story of what happened to **Dehya** after the Radiance War.

Dehya and **Eldrin** have two children, **Taquinil Selei** and **Althor Vyan Selei**. **Taquinil** is an extraordinary genius and an untenably sensitive empath. He appears in *The Radiant Seas, Spherical Harmonic,* and *Carnelians.*

✦ ✦ ✦

Althor Vyan = Akushtina (Tina) Selei Santis Pulivok

Althor and **Tina** appear in *Catch the Lightning,* which was expanded and rewritten into the eBook duology *Lightning Strike, Book I* and *Lightning Strike, Book II.* **Althor Selei** is named after his uncle, **Althor Valdoria** (who is named after his father, **Eldrinson Althor Valdoria,** the "King of Skyfall").

The short story "Avo de Paso" tells of how **Tina** and her cousin Manuel go to the New Mexico desert to grieve the death of Tina's mother. It appears in the anthologies *Redshift,* ed. Al Sarrantino, and *Fantasy: The Year's Best, 2001,* eds. Robert Silverberg and Karen Haber.

✦ ✦ ✦

Roca = (1) Tokaba Ryestar (deceased)
     = (2) Darr Hammerjackson (divorced)
     = (3) **Eldrinson Althor Valdoria**

Roca is the sister of the Ruby Pharaoh. She is in the direct line of succession to the Ruby throne and to all three titles of the Triad. She is also the Foreign Affairs Councilor of the Assembly, a seat she won through election rather than as an inherited title. A ballet dancer turned diplomat, she appears in most of the Ruby Dynasty novels, in particular *Skyfall.*

Roca and Tokaba Ryestar had one child, **Kurj** (Imperator and Jagernaut). **Kurj** married Ami when he was a century old, and they had one child named Kurjson. **Kurj** appears in *Skyfall, Primary*

Inversion, and *The Radiant Seas,* and with more minor roles in many of the other books.

Although no records exist of **Eldrinson's** lineage, it is believed he descends from the ancient Ruby Dynasty. He is a bard, farmer, and judge on the planet Lyshriol (also known as Skyfall). His spectacular singing voice is legendary among his people, a genetic gift he bequeathed to his sons Eldrin and Del-Kurj. The novel *Skyfall* tells how **Eldrinson** and **Roca** met. They have ten children:

Eldrin (Dryni) Jarac (bard, opera singer, consort to Ruby Pharaoh, Lyshriol warrior)

Althor Izam-Na (engineer, Jagernaut, Imperial Heir)

Del-Kurj (Del) (rock singer, Lyshriol warrior, twin to **Chaniece**)

Chaniece Roca (runs Valdoria family household, twin to **Del-Kurj**)

Havyrl (Vyrl) Torcellei (farmer, doctorate in agriculture)

Sauscony (Soz) Lahaylia (military scientist, Jagernaut, Imperator)

Denric Windward (teacher, doctorate in literature)

Shannon Eirlei (Blue Dale archer)

Aniece Dyhianna (accountant, Rillian queen)

Kelricson (Kelric) Garlin (mathematician, Jagernaut, Imperator)

❖ ❖ ❖

Eldrin appears in *The Final Key, Triad, The Radiant Seas, Spherical Harmonic, The Ruby Dice, Diamond Star, Carnelians,* and *Lightning Strike, Book II/Catch the Lightning.* See also **Dehya.**

❖ ❖ ❖

> **Althor Izam-Na** = (1) Coop and Vaz
> = (2) Cirrus (former provider to Ur Qox)

Althor is one of the three Imperial scions Kurj chose as his possible heir, along with Soz and Kelric. He distinguished himself as a Jagernaut in the J-Forces of Imperial Space Command. He has two daughters: **Aliana Miller Azina**, born to a Trader taskmaker, and Eristia Leirol Valdoria, born to Syreen Leirol, a Skolian actress turned linguist. Coop and Vaz have a son, Ryder Jalam Majda Valdoria, with **Althor** as co-father. Vaz and Coop appear in *Spherical Harmonic*. **Althor** and Cirrus also have a son. Althor and Coop appear in *The Radiant Seas*.

✢ ✢ ✢

Del-Kurj, often considered the renegade of the Ruby Dynasty, is a rock singer who rose to fame on Earth after the Radiance War. His story is told in *Diamond Star,* which is accompanied by a soundtrack cut by the rock band Point Valid with Catherine Asaro. The songs on the CD are all from the book. **Del** also appears in *The Quantum Rose, Schism, Carnelians,* and the novella "Stained Glass Heart."

✢ ✢ ✢

Chaniece is Del's twin sister. They come as close to sharing a mind as two Rhon empaths can do without becoming one person. **Chaniece** appears in *Diamond Star, Schism,* and *The Quantum Rose.*

✢ ✢ ✢

Havyrl (Vyrl) = (1) Liliara (Lily) **Torcellei** (deceased)
= (2) Kamoj Quanta Argali

Vyrl is a farmer who married his childhood sweetheart Lily and stayed on Skyfall for most of his life, until he became a pawn in the political intrigue following the Radiance War. He is also an accomplished dancer. The story of **Havyrl** and Lily appears in "Stained Glass Heart," in the anthology *Irresistible Forces,* ed. Catherine Asaro, 2004. The story of **Havyrl** and Kamoj appears in *The Quantum Rose,* a science-fiction retelling of *Beauty and the Beast* which won the 2001 Nebula Award. An early version of the first half was serialized in *Analog,* May–July/August 1999.

✢ ✢ ✢

Sauscony (Soz) Lahaylia = (1) Jato Stormson (divorced)
= (2) Hypron Luminar (deceased)
= (3) **Jaibriol Qox** (aka **Jaibriol II**)

Soz is one of the three Imperial scions Kurj chose as his possible heir, along with Althor and Kelric. A strategic genius, she became the greatest military leader known in the Skolian Imperialate. The story of her time as a cadet at the Dieshan Military Academy is told in *Schism*, *The Final Key*, and "Echoes of Pride" (*Space Cadets*, ed. Mike Resnick, 2006). *The Final Key* tells of the first Skolian-Trader war and Soz's part in that conflict. The story of Soz's rescue of colonists from the world New Day is told in the novelette "The Pyre of New Day" (*The Mammoth Book of SF Wars*, ed. Ian Whates and Ian Watson, 2012). How **Soz** and Jato met appears in the novella, "Aurora in Four Voices" (*Analog*, December 1998). **Soz** and **Jaibriol**'s stories appear in *Primary Inversion* and *The Radiant Seas*. They have four children: **Jaibriol III, Rocalisa, Vitar,** and **del-Kelric.**

Jaibriol Qox Skolia	=	Tarquine Iquar (Trader
(aka **Jaibriol III**) Emperor of		Empress, Finance Minister, and
the Trader Empire		Aristo queen of the Iquar Line)

Jaibriol III, the eldest child of **Soz** and **Jaibriol II**, becomes the emperor of the Eubian Concord, also known as the Trader Empire. As such, he must hide his true identity, that he is also an heir to the Ruby Throne. The story of how **Jaibriol III** becomes Emperor at age seventeen is told in *The Moon's Shadow*. The story of how Jaibriol and his uncle Kelric deal with each other as the leaders of opposing empires appears in *The Ruby Dice* and *Carnelians*. **Jaibriol III** also appears in *The Radiant Seas* as a child and as a teenager.

✤ ✤ ✤

Denric is a teacher. He accepts a position on Sandstorm, an impoverished colony, to run a school for the children there. His harrowing introduction to his new home appears in the story, "The Edges of Never-Haven" (*Flights of Fantasy*, ed. Al Sarrantino). He also appears in *The Quantum Rose*.

✤ ✤ ✤

Shannon is the most otherworldly member of the Ruby Dynasty. He inherited the rare genes of a Blue Dale Archer from his father, **Eldrinson**. He left home at age sixteen and sought out the Archers, believed to be extinct. He appears in *Schism, The Final Key, The Quantum Rose*, and as a child in "Stained Glass Heart."

✢ ✢ ✢

Aniece = Lord Rillia

Aniece is the most business-minded of the Valdoria children. Although she never left her home world Lyshriol, she earned an MBA and became an accountant. Lord Rillia rules a province including the Rillian Vales, Dalvador Plains, Backbone Mountains, and Stained Glass Forest. **Aniece** decided at age twelve that she would marry Rillia, though he was much older, and she kept at her plan until she achieved her goal. **Aniece** and Rillia appear in *The Quantum Rose*.

✢ ✢ ✢

Kelricson (Kelric) Garlin = (1) Corey Majda (deceased)
                                                = (2) Deha Dahl (deceased)
                                                = (3) Rashiva Haka (Calani trade)
                                                = (4) Savina Miesa (deceased)
                                                = (5) Avtac Varz (Calani trade)
                                                = (6) Ixpar Karn
                                                = (7) Jeejon (deceased)

Kelric is one of the three Imperial scions Kurj chose as his possible heir, along with **Soz** and **Althor**. He is a major character in *Carnelians, The Ruby Dice*, "The Ruby Dice" (novella, *Baen's Universe 2006*), *Ascendant Sun, The Last Hawk*, and the novelette "Light and Shadow" (Analog, April 1994). He also appears in *The Moon's Shadow, Diamond Star*, "A Roll of the Dice" (*Analog*, July/August 2000), and as a toddler in "Stained Glass Heart" (*Irresistible Forces*, ed. Catherine Asaro, 2004).

Kelric and Rashiva have one son, Jimorla Haka, who becomes a renowned Calani. **Kelric** and Savina have one daughter, **Rohka Miesa Varz,** who becomes the Ministry Successor in line to rule the Estates of Coba.

✢ ✢ ✢

The novella "Walk in Silence" (*Analog*, April 2003) tells the story of Jess Fernandez, an Allied Starship Captain from Earth, who deals with the genetically engineered humans on the Skolian colony of Icelos.

The novella "The City of Cries" (*Down These Dark Spaceways,* ed.

Mike Resnick) tells the story of Major Bhaaj, a private investigator hired by the House of Majda to find Prince Dayj Majda after he disappears.

The novella "The Shadowed Heart" (*Year's Best Paranormal*, ed. Paula Guran, and *The Journey Home*, ed. Mary Kirk) is the story of Jason Harrick, a Jagernaut who barely survives the Radiance War.

TIME LINE

Circa BC 4000	Group of humans moved from Earth to Raylicon
BC 3600	Rise of the Ruby Dynasty
BC 3100	Raylicans launch their first interstellar flights. Rise of the ancient Ruby Empire.
BC 2900	Ruby Empire declines
BC 2800	Last interstellar flights. Ruby Empire collapses.
Circa AD 1300	Raylicans begin to regain lost knowledge
AD 1843	Raylicans regain interstellar flight
AD 1871	Aristos found Eubian Concord (aka Trader Empire)
AD 1881	Lahaylia Selei born
AD 1904	Lahaylia Selei founds Skolian Imperialate
AD 2005	Jarac born
AD 2111	Lahaylia Selei marries Jarac
AD 2119	Dyhianna Selei born
AD 2122	Earth achieves interstellar flight with the inversion drive
AD 2132	Allied Worlds of Earth formally established
AD 2144	Roca born
AD 2169	Kurj born
AD 2203	Roca marries Eldrinson Althor Valdoria (*Skyfall*)
AD 2204	Eldrin Jarac Valdoria born (*Skyfall*)
	Jarac Skolia, Patriarch of the Ruby Dynasty, dies (*Skyfall*)

Kurj becomes Imperator (*Skyfall*)

Death of Lahaylia Selei, the first modern Ruby Pharaoh, followed by the ascension of Dyhianna Selei to the Ruby Throne

AD 2205   Major Bhaajan hired by the House of Majda ("The City of Cries" and *Undercity*)

Bhaajan establishes the Dust Knights of Cries (*Undercity*)

AD 2206   Althor Izam-Na Valdoria born

AD 2207   Del-Kurj (Del) and Chaniece Roca born

AD 2209   Havyrl (Vyrl) Torcellei Valdoria born

AD 2210   Sauscony (Soz) Lahaylia Valdoria born

AD 2211   Denric Windward Valdoria born

AD 2213   Shannon Eirlei Valdoria born

AD 2215   Aniece Dyhianna Valdoria born

AD 2219   Kelricson (Kelric) Garlin Valdoria born

AD 2220   Eldrin and Dehya marry

AD 2221   Taquinil Selei born

AD 2223   Vyrl and Lily elope at age fourteen and create a political crisis ("Stained Glass Heart")

AD 2227   Soz enters Dieshan Military Academy (*Schism* and "Echoes of Pride")

AD 2228   First declared war between Skolia and Traders (*The Final Key*)

AD 2237   Jaibriol II born

AD 2240   Soz meets Jato Stormson ("Aurora in Four Voices")

AD 2241   Kelric marries Admiral Corey Majda

AD 2243   Corey Majda assassinated ("Light and Shadow")

AD 2255   Soz leads rescue mission to colony on New Day ("The Pyre of New Day")

AD 2258   Kelric crashes on Coba (*The Last Hawk*)

AD 2259	Soz and Jaibriol II go into exile (*Primary Inversion* and *The Radiant Seas*)
AD 2260	Jaibriol III born, aka Jaibriol Qox Skolia (*The Radiant Seas*)
AD 2263	Rocalisa Qox Skolia born (*The Radiant Seas*)
	Althor Izam-Na Valdoria meets Coop ("Soul of Light")
AD 2269	Vitar Qox Skolia born (*The Radiant Seas*)
AD 2273	del-Kelric Qox Skolia born (*The Radiant Seas*)
AD 2274	Aliana Miller Azina born (*Carnelians*)
AD 2275	Jaibriol II captured by Eubian Space Command (ESComm) and forced to become puppet emperor of the Trader empire (*The Radiant Seas*)
	Soz becomes Imperator of the Skolian Imperialate (*The Radiant Seas*)
AD 2276	Radiance War begins, also called the Domino War (*The Radiant Seas*)
AD 2277	Traders capture Eldrin (*The Radiant Seas*)
	Radiance War ends (*The Radiant Seas*)
AD 2277–8	Kelric returns home and becomes Imperator (*Ascendant Sun*)
	Jaibriol III becomes the Trader emperor (*The Moon's Shadow* and *The Radiant Seas*)
	Dehya stages coup in the aftermath of the Radiance War (*Spherical Harmonic*)
	Imperialate and Eubian leaders meet for preliminary peace talks (*Spherical Harmonic*)
	Jason Harrick crashes on the planet Thrice Named ("The Shadowed Heart")
	Vyrl goes to Balumil and meets Kamoj (*The Quantum Rose*)
	Vyrl returns to Skyfall and leads planetary act of protest (*The Quantum Rose*)
AD 2279	Althor Vyan Selei born (the second son of Dyhianna and Eldrin)

	Del sings "The Carnelians Finale" and nearly starts a war (*Diamond Star*)
AD 2287	Jeremiah Coltman trapped on Coba ("A Roll of the Dice" and *The Ruby Dice*)
	Jeejon dies (*The Ruby Dice*)
AD 2288	Kelric and Jaibriol Qox sign peace treaty (*The Ruby Dice*)
AD 2289	Imperialate and Eubian governments meet for peace negotiations (*Carnelians*)
AD 2298	Jess Fernandez goes to Icelos ("Walk in Silence")
AD 2326	Tina and Manuel return to New Mexico ("Ave de Paso")
AD 2328	Althor Vyan Selei meets Tina Santis Pulivok (*Catch the Lightning*; also the duology *Lightning Strike, Book I* and *Lightning Strike, Book II*)

Taken together, *Lightning Strike, Book I* and *Lightning Strike, Book II* are similar to the story told in *Catch the Lightning*, but substantially rewritten and expanded for the eBook release.

The eBook version of *Primary Inversion* is rewritten from the original and considered by the author as the best version.